PILGRIM
LOST

TIM MURGATROYD

Cloud Lodge Books
London

First published in the United Kingdom in 2020
by Cloud Lodge Books (CLB)

All right reserved. No part of the publication may be reproduced, stored in a database or retrieval system, or transmitted in any form or by any means without the permission in writing of the publisher, nor be otherwise circulated in any form or binding or cover other than that in which it is published and without a similar condition including this condition being imposed on the subsequent purchaser.

Copyright © Tim Murgatroyd 2020

The moral right of the author has been asserted.

A CIP catalogue record for this book is available from the British Library.

All characters and events in this publication, other than those clearly in the public domain, are fictitious and any resemblance to any real person, living or dead, is purely coincidental and not intended by the author.

ISBN 978-1-8380451-3-5

1 3 5 7 9 10 8 6 4 2

When Anacharsis was asked by someone what was humanity's enemy, he said "themselves".

— From *Gnomologium Vaticanum*, 18

Contents

PROLOGUE	1
ONE	9
TWO	21
THREE	33
FOUR	42
FIVE	51
SIX	61
SEVEN	68
EIGHT	77
NINE	87
TEN	95
ELEVEN	111
TWELVE	123
THIRTEEN	133
FOURTEEN	147
FIFTEEN	156
SIXTEEN	169
SEVENTEEN	183
EIGHTEEN	193
NINETEEN	204
TWENTY	216
TWENTY-ONE	228
TWENTY-TWO	241
TWENTY-THREE	252
TWENTY-FOUR	264

TWENTY-FIVE	275
TWENTY-SIX	287
TWENTY-SEVEN	296
TWENTY-EIGHT	308
TWENTY-NINE	321
THIRTY	335
THIRTY-ONE	350
EPILOGUE: BLEAK MIDWINTER	367
About the Author	374

PROLOGUE

That winter, a fire was visible from the Cumbrian hills, a lone flare rising from the old nuclear power station on the coast. Maister of Floggers Gil stared long and hard, night after night. Distant flames rose high then died to a sickly glow between shore and sea that finally went dark.

'I reckon there'll be plenty of changelings for boiling an' grinding,' he predicted.

The two Mistresses, Fat and Thin, agreed.

Even then, Seth Pilgrim knew which bonder would be driven into the briar-tangled woods not to return empty-handed. Who must risk the same sickness as bud and beast and bird's egg. It felt like his due.

* * *

The early spring was dank out west by the Irish Sea, far from Baytown.

Seth stood in the rain at the edge of woods from which poked chimneys, cooling towers, steel cranes draped with ivy, huge concrete rectangles, all that remained of the nuclear plant. Few in Cumbria came here by choice. The sickness — invisible as airborne plague spores — caused vomiting, cancers, deformed babies to expose on cold hillsides.

He glanced back at the knot of armed men watching from a nearby hill. Prominent among them was Maister Gil, scourge in his belt. They would camp up there until he returned and perhaps reward him with extra gruel and oat bread if he got lucky.

Seth waded into the shallow River Calder, running like a winding road through the many square miles of the overgrown site. Shackled ankles joined by an iron chain made him hobble. On his back, sacks to gather the harvest.

The water was icy, but Seth had grown accustomed to cold — what field-bonder was not? As he followed the gravel streambed, alder and willow cloaked him. Choruses of birdsong echoed in the woods. He glimpsed bluebells, purple-pink orchids, dog violets, and pink campion. An odd sensation stole up from his heart, one almost forgotten: freedom. Those bastards on the hill could not see him here and dared not follow. Even on the outskirts of Sellafield, the sickness lay strong.

But for now, he was free.

'Screw you!' His heart raced in a wild fantasy of power — cutting Maister Gil's throat like a squealing sheep's, oh yes, and turning on the Mistresses, Fat and Thin, like this. This.

* * *

They had given him a notched, rusty knife and hempen net to capture prey. Seth perched beneath a willow on the riverbank, reluctant to enter the pathless maze of thickets and buildings. For a while he sat, watching rain putter across the grey stream, sharpening the knife on a stone. He was hungry, as always. But only madmen foraged in Sellafield, except perhaps for fish swimming down from the high fells and lakes of the mountains. Clean soil up there. Clean water. Clean air.

Sighing, he wrapped grass around his ankle shackles so they wouldn't chafe or clank. Stealth was needed — and sharp eyes.

PROLOGUE

Half a mile from the river, Seth feared never finding a way out again. Birds chirruped excitedly as they squabbled and mated, but he saw none worthy of his net. Last summer's briars still bore thorns to snag his raggedy clothes. At last, he found a peculiar fungus sporting odd, noxious horns. Then, by a scummy pond, he came upon a frog with two heads. Into his sack they went.

It was warm in the wood, unnaturally so, for winter had not entirely relinquished its hold on the land. Again, he grew fearful and clutched the knife. What if the rumours of monsters dwelling around the power station were true? Of cursed survivors of the original plagues who could never die, forever famished for living flesh. Scarcely a soul among the folk he dwelt with doubted such stories. Dark, dark the forests and shadows and secret places. *Hell is hot*, taught the Mistresses, *Hell is hot*.

Seth sometimes remembered, even in his distress — like noticing a glowworm on a moonless night when black clouds choke the wan light of the stars — science lessons delivered by Father and Uncle Michael in the old library at Hob Hall. 'Humanity will never recover what it has lost through superstition,' Uncle Michael had taught his nephew and Seth's twin sister, Averil, and a dozen other kids bent over slates and chalk.

Slowly, his breath steadied as he pushed deeper into the woods towards the heat's source.

* * *

He stumbled upon a smoke-blackened cooling tower beside scorched walls and the remains of a collapsed roof. Whatever conflagration Maister Gil watched from the hills that winter had raged here. Something mysterious caused the blaze, but now it was cold, the soot and tar of its burning sticky with rain. Poison and sickness spread far and wide with the billowing smoke.

As Seth emerged from the trees, he encountered a hidden glen before the buildings, a car park sprouting grass. At his approach, a small knot of deer scattered, hooves clattering as they vanished among the trees. All except one.

A fawn — a few weeks old, still not weaned from its mother's teats — tried to follow its herd. Four legs it had, true, another two hanging limp and useless, like bizarre tails from its lumpy spine. An extra set of splayed teeth and moist gums protruded from its forehead.

Seth assessed the changeling hungrily. Deformities were common enough when the wind chose certain directions, and among humans too, but this was perfect. Precisely what the Mistresses rendered into magic salves stained bright with plant juice: good barter with credulous farmers all over Lake Country, even as far south as Lancaster.

He hobbled over, pushed it to the ground. On the grass-tussocked tarmac of the former car park, he slumped, the fawn beside him. Soft brown eyes stared up. It did not struggle.

Then Seth looked around. For all his weariness of soul, he noticed things.

First, the defiant green of the ivy, leaves, and stems, scaling up the burned cooling tower. No holding back life's climb towards the sun. The rain no longer irritated his face and hands. It cleansed him. Droplets gathered on the back of his branded right hand, lingered on his face that had forgotten how to smile.

He noticed a few early bees drifting between clumps of pale yellow primrose, flies buzzing over a pile of deer dung, red butterflies. He felt the raindrops on his cheek joined by something barely recalled: something salty, precious, his eyes' own creation. Something he dared never show before the Mistresses or their people because weakness invited bullying, taunting.

Memories flashed across Seth Pilgrim's mind, lost hopes and

dreams, before defeat and years of wretched slavery crushed them, one by one. A fantasy of himself in the fabulous City of Albion, beloved and feared by all, master of drones and legendary air cars.

Then it faded. Once more, Seth slumped on the rotting tarmac before a burned-out relic of mankind's lost dominions and powers. The rain quickened.

He positioned the panting fawn for the knife. Slitting its throat would be a mercy to them both. God knew it was ugly, crippled, weak.

Deep in a heart corrupted by cruelties — too gross to contemplate except in nightmares — he recalled another knife in his hand, another act of sacrifice, how he had... Oh, he could not bear.... Old Marley, the hapless tramp known since he was a small boy, the vagrant his Father fed and clothed out of charity each Christmas.

'No!'

His cry died amidst rain dripping from branches.

Shackles clanking, Seth rose and put the knife in his rope belt.

'Run along, ugly,' he said to the fawn with a boot up the backside. The changeling's extra limbs quivered as it stumbled away.

Seth Pilgrim's face resumed its customary absence of expression. He'd pay for this small mercy. No extra food for him, just Maister Gil's whip. Or worse.

* * *

The coven and its bonders occupied a hamlet of stone farm-buildings on a hillside eight miles inland from Sellafield. From this vantage, one could see the Isle of Man on a clear day. Turn east and the high peaks of Seatallan, Great Gable, Scafell Pike rose.

Maister Gil was out of love with the entire world. Since the Great Dyings reduced humanity to a scrape across the earth's surface, everyone might be called disappointed. Few vented their frustration quite like the bony little man. Five years earlier, he had led a band of floggers as their Maister, a petty king of sorts. Now floggers were outlawed after the defeat of Pharaoh Jacko at the Battle of Pickering — a slaughter Gil narrowly survived, exiled by the Commonwealth of the North to the wild Cumbrian hills.

On the way, he and a handful of loyal followers had captured other fugitives from Jacko's fall, Seth Pilgrim included, promptly branding them as bonders. Gil's destination had been old allies, the Mistresses of Fell Grange, where he joined their coven.

It was still raining when the horsemen led by Maister Gil plodded up the track to Fell Grange. Behind them shuffled an exhausted Seth Pilgrim.

Dragging the young man in chains across bog, rig, and beck could not appease Gil. Once dismounted, he loosened his robe and cowl, scratched his crotch, and took out a three-tailed scourge. This he tested playfully on the rump of his nag. It whinnied and snorted.

'You'll not make a monkey o' me again,' said the little man.

Seth cowered.

The first blow landed on his shoulders. The next bruised his back. He struggled to conceal layers of hatred behind his eyes. Then Gil found a rhythm, chanting the old flogger's hymn, sweat on his forehead:

> *Our City that art Heaven,*
> *Right feared be thy name.*
> *Thy kingdom's come and we obey.*
> *Punish any man that don't worship thee,*
> *Give 'em plague and daily woes,*
> *Make 'em starve that break thy laws*
> *And deliver us from drones.*

(In the mud, Seth balled as the whip rose and fell. Oh, he remembered another flogging by Gil, one given to his twin sister, poor Averil, at his own request. How clever he had thought himself then, how in control.)

> *For thou art the power and glory.*
> *Drink our blood forever and ever,*
> *Eat our flesh as thy daily bread.*

(Abruptly, unexpectedly, chains of submission that had kept his head bowed for five vile years broke. Even as he ached from buffets and cuts, Seth knew with utter certainty what debt must be paid for the treatment meted his way.)

> *Amen! And so say all of us!*

Gil leered at the young man curled at his feet. His panting slowed. Seth noticed a bulge in the coarse, woollen trousers of his tormentor. That, too, had been predicted.

* * *

Seth slept in a low stone byre and stable that was bolted on the outside each night. His companions in the gloom were shaggy hill ponies, cattle, and a brace of two-legged beasts less free than the other farm animals. Like Seth, the other bonders wore ankle shackles. Not that they could run far even without chains. Farmers in neighbouring vales feared spells and curses from the Mistresses of Fell Grange. Most of them would gladly help hunt down runaways in return for a blessing on their ewes or oats.

Maister Gil had never forgiven Seth's uncle, Michael Pilgrim, for outlawing the bands of floggers who once ranged from settlement to settlement with impunity.

'Them were grand days,' he reminisced in his cups one night when Seth was forced to serve supper to his betters. 'The City was friend to us wandering folk for many a year.' His eye fell on Seth, and his face darkened. 'I should have strangled that bastard Pilgrim in his sleep when I had the chance.'

Seth said nothing, his face blank. But he listened. As the two Mistresses were fond of saying, knowledge is power.

'Tinkers are telling,' Gil continued, 'the Deregulators are losing interest in the doings of us little folk.' His voice took on the whine of a complaint. 'I heard they even closed down their holy compounds in Hull and Scouseton. Places they've been deregulating for a hundred years! And some say they're taking their mighty drones back to the City, them that kept us rightly downtrodden.'

Maybe so. But drones could still be heard at night, jet engines roaring like dragons over Lake Country. There was even wild talk of magical City creatures out east, not so much changelings, as strangelings.

After his beating, Seth lay on his front in the byre while the animals shuffled and shat. New thoughts stirred. The fire in Sellafield might be a sign, like freeing the changeling fawn. The City was abandoning its Deregulators' compounds up and down the coast. Perhaps the all-powerful City was in trouble. Maybe it needed new servants — new men for a new time, who would be generously rewarded.

Slowly, as dawn bled light through the roof slates and his fellow bonders snored, Seth conceived of a future beyond Fell Grange. He recollected his store of carefully carved wooden wedges. He imagined flames, helpless, imploring cries, his own voice gloating, '*Hell is hot, you bitches! Hell is hot!*'

ONE

Helen Devereux left the museum perched on Baytown's cliffs to measure spring's progress. Soon must come the spring equinox, the exact midpoint between light and dark. Her route took paths familiar after five years' exile in the fishing village. The landscape was repopulating slowly under the guidance of its mayor, Michael Pilgrim, and the other councillors, among whom she numbered.

Despite a chilly wind from the east, signs of spring were everywhere: hedge birds trilling and fluttering, wildflowers of all textures and tints. Buds on trees poised to unfurl the bunting of green life, banishing winter for a spell.

Helen wandered far until twilight. Sometimes she needed to escape the confines of the museum where she lived and worked. Since the fall of Big Jacko, the Baytown School and Scholars' Library had flourished there under her direction, teaching the rudiments of literacy to child and adult alike.

The City, once a source of constant unease for Baytown folk, obtruded less and less. Stray spy drones flew over as they always had, but far less frequently. Hope rushed to fill the slightest void of Deregulation. Perhaps the plague-winnowed people of the earth would be allowed to revive.

'It's just a trick to sniff us out 'n' snuff us out,' speculated some.

'The City never changes. Never will.'

'Seize this new freedom with both hands,' urged others, a fever spreading across the entire Commonwealth of the North.

Night had gathered the tired corners of day when Helen returned to the museum for another evening alone. It was what she had chosen: to age then die in Baytown, beside the restless, ever-breathing sea.

* * *

Helen bolted the museum doors behind her. High-ceilinged halls and corridors waited in darkness. She lit a whale-blubber lamp, stepping around the old reception counter to reach her own quarters. Her nostrils caught an unfamiliar scent, and she paused.

A primordial sense warned she was not alone. Was that the sound of movement behind the door that led to her rooms?

But when Helen held up the lamp and peered into the dark hallway, nothing stirred. She edged over to the door and listened.

There seemed only one thing to do, or she would not sleep. Check that the exhibits and new schoolroom were secure, as any good curator should. Leaving the lamp burning on the reception counter, she took out a rechargeable torch from a drawer and switched it on.

Instantly she froze, her heart pounding. The beam had caught a flash of silent movement at the entrance to the gallery containing the Baytown Jewel.

'Who's there?' she cried, fumbling in the same drawer that held the torch. This time, she extracted a large double-barrelled pistol, a weapon forced on her by Michael Pilgrim. Cocking the weapon, Helen swept a feeble beam of torchlight around the room.

'My God,' she whispered.

The visitor floating towards her would take more than a pistol to bring down.

ONE

* * *

An aerial spy drone hovered before her, held aloft by two gently swishing propellers in a protective mesh. It resembled nothing so much as a gigantic wasp, two feet long and a foot in diameter. Where a wasp's legs would have trailed were arms with nimble mechanical fingers.

'Oh God,' she said, dropping the pistol. It clattered to the floor.

Never provoke a drone's defensive systems.

It had no need of lights to see, but whatever mind or programme determined its actions chose to cast a bright beam upon her shrinking figure. Someone was watching her through the drone. Deciding her fate.

'Who are you?' she cried. 'I have done nothing.'

The drone — or its controller — did not reply. Helen's breath came in gasps as she retreated, pressing back against the reception counter.

'Leave me in peace. I have left the City forever!'

The drone lunged forward, so swift she barely had time to react. Simultaneously, it fired a dart that struck her shoulder.

The world blurred. For a long moment, the machine loomed over Helen, the red lights of sensors flashing on its pointed snout. As one might watch a portion of cliff fold into the sea, her legs crumpled. Then she was on her back, blinking and struggling to breathe. The last thing her conscious mind took in was the machine hovering above her, a limb reaching down, a tiny pellet directed with hideous delicacy towards her skull. Amidst the fog, flashes and bangs. Then she faded out.

* * *

Rain slanted as Seth Pilgrim ploughed the lower slopes of the hill. He and a pony laboured up to their fetlocks in mud made pungent by liberal doses of manure. Fat Mistress loved her spuds, baking and smearing them with fresh-churned butter, pig-drippings, and salt. Mindful of this particular taste (she possessed others far less wholesome), Gil had ordered Seth out for a final cross-plough of the potato field. Wrong weather, the soil water-logged after the wet start to spring, but Seth knew better than to argue.

'Whoa there!' he called as the ploughshares snagged on rocks. 'Steady!'

Plumes of breath issued from the hot horse, its tail swishing flies drawn to its sweat. On the hill above, the dark silhouettes of the farm, smoke rising. Low, grey clouds obscured all points of the horizon.

Should I run now, wondered Seth, *on such a day as this? While night approaches to offer a little cover?*

Daily the urge tormented him. He could unshackle his ankles with the hammer and chisel he'd hidden, release the pony from the plough, and gallop, gallop until it was winded and broken. Run, run until he dropped. Surely that would be far enough away.

But Seth knew he needed patience. Nowhere could be far enough away. Nor had he a clue where to flee.

On a neighbouring track, he saw a party of folk approach. Most were prosperous by the look of their woollen clothes; even the servants wore shoes. A man with a breastplate fashioned from an oven door rode at the head, a pistol in his belt, three-pronged lance in his hand, leading two women on a farm cart that jolted and tilted over the stony way. The servants followed on foot, driving a fat ewe.

Seth bowed as they passed. He recognised the man as the Lord of Erringdale, a fanatical supporter of the Fell Grange Coven. On the cart, a bonny young girl sat alongside an older, hard-faced woman with a swollen stomach. Seth guessed the story, a pregnancy not going well. The woman's anxious old goat of a husband bringing her to the

Mistresses to set matters right.

In the rear of the cart, Seth noticed a large ale barrel as payment for the rites. His heart quickened. A mass followed by a barrel that size could end only one way. The thought of the carefully carved wedges concealed in the byre stirred a fantasy of revenge. Fire. Screams. Hell is hot!

* * *

Helen woke to find herself on a low couch in her living quarters.

A male figure was hunched at the table on the opposite side of the room. At first, Helen did not recognise him. When she did, she half-rose then fell back with a gasp. The tranquiliser fired by the spy drone was still in her system. She could only be grateful the dart had not carried poison.

For a long moment, they measured one another's outward changes. In Helen's case, fresh lines and wrinkles, frost in her hair; for the man in the chair, scarcely an hour might have passed since she last saw him. In one respect, however, he had changed thoroughly. Gone were the faux-medieval tights and doublet and feather-topped hat of former fashion. New modes were in force: sturdy plastic boots, trousers with loaded utility pockets, a duraplastic jacket she suspected would stop a cannonball.

'Blair Gover,' she said, 'another dramatic entrance.'

His youthful, unblemished face took on an ironic cast. 'I seem to remember more dramatic ones.'

A large, multi-function machine pistol lay on the table, beside a pile of rotten plastic from the Before Times.

'Was that awful spy drone your work?'

He shook his head. 'A long and sorry story, Helen. But you are safe now.'

Again they examined one another.

'Do you still call yourself Bertrand Du Guesclin?' she asked. 'Or has that conceit gone the way of its predecessors?'

'Bertrand has gone for good, I fear. The time for such frippery and games is over.'

She noticed something new about him: a deep tiredness, not so much of body, as of soul.

'For five years, I didn't hear from you,' she said.

'True.'

'Why have you come, Blair?'

He shrugged. 'I was flying north to a little hideaway in Greenland — such a delightfully savage setting, the geysers are spectacular. My aircar is parked near a wood at the rear of the museum.' He indicated the pile of plastic, and his voice grew less playful. 'I wished to harvest some of this stuff. That is why I believe the spy drone appeared here. They are watching me. Don't worry, your unwanted guest has been deactivated.' He patted the pistol on the table. 'And just in time. While I was in the wood my enemies tried to inject a monitoring device into your skull, so they could spy on our conversation. A bold move, to be sure. It raises many alarming questions.'

Helen shrank back on the couch.

'But, really, I came,' he continued, 'because of a new idea.'

'Well, you always have those.'

'This one might change the fate of mankind. An idea no one except I could conceive.'

He poked at the decaying plastic, the noxious stuff Baytown folk called *tilth*.

'I would welcome your help, Helen. Actually, I need it.'

* * *

While he spoke, Helen sipped camomile tea to calm herself.

'This is not a happy tale,' he said. 'Few apart from me come out of it well.'

He began at the beginning: how the founders of the Five Cities, not least himself, decided the Beautifuls' eternal existence should be serviced by drones to avoid dependency on human servants, who would inevitably rebel to gain access to cell renewal for themselves. 'And it has worked admirably, has it not?'

Helen chose not to answer.

'However, our wonderful founding vision is in danger. Incredible as it seems, my opponents refuse to see reason on such a basic question.'

'You mean those same opponents you destroyed with a fusion bomb,' she said bitterly. 'An episode that cost my sister's life. Don't think I've forgotten Mhairi so soon!'

He dismissed the loss with a flourish of latex-gloved fingers. Blair Gover had always been fastidious about infection when away from the sanitised City.

'As ever, you are charmingly naïve, my dear. Did you really think the laboratory you incinerated was the only one? Why, the same heresy has spread across all the Five Cities. My little display was intended as a warning — one my enemies failed to heed.'

Helen's eyes pricked with tears. Could he ignore her grief so casually?

'In fact,' he continued, 'I fear it brought forward their plans.'

Sudden suspicion gripped him. He rose and muttered into his screen, scanning the air. Helen heard a hum and clank in the lobby of the museum. Another drone! At the sound, he relaxed, sat again.

'Earlier, in a fit of sentimentality, I made the mistake of leaving my security with my aircarrier. Hence, the spydrone slipping through. But we are fully protected now. You see, I am forced to anticipate spies day and night.'

'How ghastly,' said Helen.

His eyes were unblinking. 'Since you wish to punish me for your sister's death, please have the honesty to admit that she played her part willingly. She understood the stakes. I begin to fear you do not.'

'Oh?'

'Like her enemies, *my* enemies are those who wish to continue their experiments to engineer entirely new life forms. They play with fire, risking the foundations of the Beautiful Life itself. Perhaps all human life.' His voice rose in pitch. 'Do you know what lies behind their insane tampering with aspects of nature we barely comprehend?'

Helen sighed. 'No.'

'It is this: boredom. The boredom of spoilt, ungrateful children who have been given everything. The Beautiful Life I created is not enough for them. They must have more, though it puts the Five Cities in jeopardy.' He laughed. 'But I have the perfect solution, Helen, one I am eager for you to hear. Who, after all, knows the primitives better than you?' Again he chuckled. 'Sometimes, I astonish myself.'

'Well, you are astonishing me.'

He spoke a code into his screen. 'You'll see.'

*   *   *

Night descends upon the Lake Country, a hundred miles to the west. Clouds tinted by a waxing moon blow over the mountains, over the old nuclear power plant, and out to sea. Parliaments of crows caw, settling to roost in young woodland — oak, beech, ash, beds of ferns — colonising abandoned farms. On the wind, the scent of leaves and manure, growth and decay.

Unmuted engines roar high overhead, an invisible surveillance drone. The City, scanning for forbidden technology: electric lights, broadcasts, machines powered by anything other than wind or water,

ONE

the slightest hint of progress. No need to fear that in Fell Grange. Nothing but humanity in retreat is ever found there.

Seth kneels in a corner of the barn with his fellow bonders. None wish to be noticed. He has positioned a pile of empty crates to slip behind when the dangerous moment arrives.

The stone barn is a granary of magical power. Its walls are stained black with tar gathered from old roads and melted in a pot, roof beams hung with countless skulls, both animal and human. Faint circles of smoky light glow, tallow candles of lamb's fat, their reek sickly sweet.

Upon the bare earthen floor stands a crude stone altar constructed of gravestones and slabs carted from the nearest churchyard. Stone steps lead up to it. Candles of pure beeswax, costly gifts to the nether world, gutter in iron holders gathered from former gift shops in abandoned towns.

Beside the altar, a foldable plastic picnic table, heirloom of days when the old gods slept, before plagues and seasons of dying awoke them. On the table rests a square, well-preserved plastic lunch box, decorated with the image of a plump, rearing pony. Hand-printed across the front in thick, indelible black marker pen:

> PRIVATE PROPERTY OF LAUREL ONLY
> KEEP OUT OR .. ? ! !

Within the box are treasures, the foundation of the Mistresses' power, revealed to them in an attic bedroom decades ago when they were but young scavengers.

Often Seth has longed to open the books in the box, learn what they contain. Only someone tired of life would risk it. The Mistresses preach a simple paradigm: *The Prince of Light rules the almighty City, and they are beloved of the Prince of Light.* Therefore, theirs is the power to protect or punish, kill or bless. To them alone have been granted the

Secrets.

Seth and the other bonders kneel in the temple. None wishes to be noticed. Tonight of all nights.

* * *

When the bowl of smoking hazel resin is brought in, acrid, heady, it begins.

Up strikes the flute, accompanied by a tapping drum. A discordant meandering tune without pattern or melody. Chanting voices grow louder as they approach the barn. Seth melts behind his flimsy barricade of crates.

The voices outside fall silent. A cold draught makes tallow candles shiver and dance. The big double doors creak open.

'*Agios ischyros Baphomet!*' cries a woman outside. Her voice firm, exultant.

No one moves. The foreheads of kneelers press the flinty earth.

'Agios ischyros Baphomet!' calls out a second woman, with a hint of petulance and vague threat.

Slowly, solemnly, the two Mistresses of Fell Grange — Fat and Thin — lead their coven into the temple. Mother-daughter they are, daughter-mother, neither will reveal who is what. Yet both are the same, weathered age. Laugh at that mystery, and your tongue will turn black, swell until you choke. Your cows' teats will run dry; your crops shall wither. Laugh at the Mistresses, and they'll hear for sure. Rats spy for them, spiders, crows. Best to say nothing at all.

Seth peers at the shadowy women in their thick white robes. The owner of the petulant tone, bloated as a toad. He lowers his eyes hurriedly. She's the quickest to punish. Her fellow daughter-mother, Thin Mistress, fouler of tongue, too lazy to do her worst — mostly.

'I will go down to the altars in Hell!' proclaims Fat Mistress.

'To Satan, giver of life!' shrieks her companion.

In they come, the Lord of Ennerdale hanging back as the Mistresses process his wife to the altar. Seven times anti-clockwise, they lead her around it, serenaded by the dancing flute. Gently they disrobe her, anoint her sagging breasts with dabs of petunia oil from a plastic bottle, given to them by the she-demon Laurel. Then they help her up stone steps to lie flat on her back across the grave slabs, her pregnant belly a mound pointing up.

No longer does she clutch her stomach in pain. Her eyes dilated by poppy juice; her fears softened. Three bairns lost to her before this one: two malformed and exposed on Wasdale Head, the third a perfect boy, snatched early by sickness. Now, her lord is impatient for strong heirs. This mass *her* idea, not his.

Fat Mistress busies herself, forming a pentagram on the barn floor with powdered chalk. The coven chants while she works: 'Respect neither pity, nor weakness! The disease which makes sick the strong!'

Thin Mistress shrieks encouragement, urging on the coven, waving a black book she produces from Laurel's box as proof of power, the origin of their litany puzzled out word-by-word, its meanings revealed in dreams sent by Satan himself.

Seth cowers deeper, afraid Maister Gil will spy him. The flogger paces the circumference of the pentagram, beating his own naked back with a leather scourge.

The coven chants: 'All that is great is built upon sorrow. All that is great is built upon sorrow.' The Mistresses emit moans and inarticulate cries. Frenzy builds; magical energies crackle.

'I will go down to the altars in Hell!'

'To Satan, giver of life!'

With the pentagram fully charged, it is time for the Lord of Ennerdale's part. His eyes, too, are glazed, his open robe revealing naked desires stimulated by the Mistresses' concoctions and his own excited hand. The girl that Seth saw perched on the cart is led forth.

So young! It surprises him. She, too, wears nothing beneath her dark-dyed robe, her skin pale in the candlelight.

'Blessed are the proud, for they shall breed gods!' urges the chant, each repetition emphasised with a thwack of Gil's whip.

Now flute and drum are trilling and beating in ecstasy, no harmony, no pattern.

'Agios ischyros Baphomet!'

'To Satan, giver of life!'

Seth squeezes his eyes. Dares not look. *Will* not look! *To bear witness and not act is to condone.* Uncle Michael used to say that.

Seth knows the rite, how the girl will be forced face down in the pentagram while the Coveners hold her fast, one on each arm, one on each leg. None will heed her cries and pleas, muffled by the dirt into which her face is pressed.

He will not look. Will *not* condone. If he could only close his ears as well.

The Coveners take up their triumphant chant: *Breed gods! Breed gods!* The Lord of Ennerdale grunts loudly as he labours. The ululations of the Mistresses urge fruition in the womb of the pregnant woman stretched out on the altar. Thwack of Gil's whip. Moans of fervour. The drum. The flute. The girl so young. Agios ischyros Baphomet. *Breed gods! Breed gods!* The girl struggles madly, sobbing and screaming into the earth. Whip. Drum. Flute. *To Satan, giver of life!*

A final bellow from the Lord, and it is done. Seth keeps his eyes pressed shut, sick to the root of his being. If he opens them, the memories will return. He forbids himself that. Because once the sacrifice forced face down in the chalk pentagram on the filthy, dirt floor of the barn wasn't a hapless girl. It was him.

TWO

Two drones waited by the reception desk outside Helen's living quarters. One, a security model, took up a defensive position in the lobby of the museum. Its companion was a type unfamiliar to her. Upon Blair's command, it rolled into her room.

'Look!' he said. 'Isn't she a beauty?'

The drone resembled an upright cuboid on spongy, globular wheels designed for broken terrain. Extendable arms and suction hoses extended from its sides. Behind it rolled a more rudimentary machine, a kind of mobile vat.

Blair commanded his screen, pointing at the pyramid of plastic tilth on the table. The cuboid rolled over. A panel on its front opened to expose an aperture like a gaping mouth. Suction arms reached out to the plastic on the table, swiftly feeding it into the hole.

'Naturally,' said Blair, 'I have designed variants with a far higher capacity.'

The machine vibrated and purred. Clear pipes emerged from the cuboid and connected to its partner, the storage device on wheels. Streams of different liquids and gases — some colourless, others a filthy yellow or black — flowed into its tanks.

Helen's face lit with comprehension. 'I think I see.'

'You see?'

'I think so.'

'All that plastic has been rendered back to its original elements: oxygen, nitrogen, sulphur, chlorine, hydrogen, even the dyes used to tint it. It might never have been plastic at all. That is why I call it an Eden machine.'

'Impressive. A remarkable invention. But I'm not sure I get—'

'Then, I shall explain.'

Once more, he sat at the table.

'Earlier, I spoke of history and must do so again.'

His story was familiar to Helen. How in the decades before the Great Dying, alarmed by global warming, mankind dispensed with combustion engines and found new uses for petrochemicals: duraplastic electric cars, layer upon layer of plastic packaging, furniture, clothes, novelty items, just about anything imaginable. A final flurry of oil extraction occurred in the Arctic and Antarctica, even as the polar ice caps and glaciers melted. The earth was cleared, probed, drilled, fracked, and split open, poisoning vast areas of America, Africa, Asia, and Oceania's heartlands. Unimaginable profits were realised by a tiny elite, a surprising number of whom now lived the Beautiful Life in the Five Cities.

A brooding expression settled on his face.

'Yes, we Beautifuls are responsible for what your beloved primitives call *tilth*. If pre-evolved humanity left one permanent legacy, it was the plastic residue. My research on the subject has been alarming and, may I say, dismissed as tedious do-goodery in the Five Cities. Yet fibres and micro-plastic remain ubiquitous: soil, oceans, atmosphere, drops of apparently pure water, the very flesh of living creatures.'

'My sister,' said Helen, 'believed the plagues were caused by tilth.'

Blair prepared to taste the cup of camomile tea she had set before him then thought better of it.

'She was not wrong,' he said.

They sat in silence.

TWO

'Sometimes, in dry, hot weather, tilth-clouds blow over the land and irritate one's throat for days,' Helen continued. 'Many people here wear masks.'

Blair's steady gaze met hers. 'Do you wear a mask on such days, Helen? I would advise you to do so.'

Helen nodded. 'So what is this new idea of yours?'

'To restore Arcadia. I call it Edenification.'

* * *

Helen had learned over ten decades it was unwise to deride Blair's genius. Though his visions were rarely kind, or anything but self-serving, they were seldom absurd.

'As I said earlier,' he continued, 'boredom lies at the heart of the dangerous mischief in the Five Cities. So it is my intention to give our idle, vain, and capricious Beautifuls — including myself — something useful to do.'

Helen stirred. Could tedium really lie behind the creation of new living beings? It seemed too simple. A more profound, perverted desire for God-like power lurked there, she was sure.

'I take it your wonderful new machine has a role in your scheme?'

'An *essential* role.' Blair's eyes narrowed as though scanning glorious uplands. 'I propose to keep the Five Cities busy for a hundred years. After that, the world will be pure and fresh again, the toxins bequeathed by the pre-evolved hominids rendered harmless.'

Helen pondered his words. Indeed, the machine represented Blair at his best: needful, functional, capable of marvellous adaptations. The kind of invention that gave the Five Cities complete dominance when the Great Dyings began.

'You would have to construct hundreds and thousands of your tilth-devourers to accomplish this,' she said. 'No, millions. Would that not require endless pillaging of the earth for resources and energy? Huge new cities of factories. I cannot imagine how many.'

He smiled immodestly. 'Naturally, I have calculated what would be required. Tilth-devourers, I like that name!'

'And?'

'Too great a price.'

'Then your idea fails before it has begun.'

Blair raised a playful finger. 'You underestimate me, my dear. There is another source of intelligent labour in this world.'

'I don't understand.'

'And yet, you dwell among them.'

Helen regarded him in surprise. A dreadful vision filled her imagination: ragged armies of people herded by pitiless drones into work gangs; explosives fitted around their wrists for detonation at the first sign of rebellion; a ceaseless toil of finding, digging, carrying, feeding toxic tilth into Blair's purifying machines. Oh, yes, he would allow them enough food and medicine and shelter to survive — enough to breed the next generation of slaves. Beyond that no more would be required. Was he not always rational about such things?

'Your... ' She tried to sound indifferent. 'Your vision alarms me. Would you really demote the remnants of mankind to bondage?'

For a moment, she feared he would grow angry. A hot glare did indeed appear behind his eyes. It soon faded, replaced by the tiredness of soul she had noticed earlier.

'You do me a great wrong,' he said.

'Do I?'

'You know better than anyone how I have argued for keeping the primitives alive, superfluous though they are. Culled when necessary, admittedly, but alive in considerable numbers.'

It was true: powerful voices in the Five Cities urged the extinction of Homo sapiens by Homo aeternum, just as Neanderthals became extinct by evolution. So far, Blair's moderating influence had proved decisive in those debates.

'Your vision is cruel,' Helen said. 'Why not let the poor, suffering creatures find their own salvation from plague and darkness?'

Blair laughed harshly. 'How little you understand the Five Cities these days, Helen. Even as we quibble over moral niceties, others are preparing a final solution for the primitive problem. Right now, I can reveal no more. But know this. I am the primitives' best friend.'

A grating, discordant alarm rang from the corridor, followed by a booming synthvoice.

Do not move. Do not move.

Blair was on his feet, sweeping up the large machine pistol from the table.

* * *

The temple emptied, but Seth did not leave his dark corner. A few tallow candles hissed as they guttered. He risked opening his eyes and saw the barn was deserted. He had been forgotten. That suited his purpose.

A wail of bagpipes and cheers arose from the old farmhouse occupied by the Mistresses and their men. The big barrel of strong ale brought by the Lord of Erringdale had been breached. That suited Seth even better.

Sounds of revelry filtered across starless hillsides: capering and singing to the strains of bagpipe, trilling flute, and hearty drum. Seth stealthily filled a small sack with potatoes, onions, a gristly hunk of lamb filched from the big ewe that had smouldered all evening above a fire pit.

Next, he snatched up a bottle of poppy juice used to quieten wild-tempered beasts. Easy to serve ale to his betters and empty the little bottle into the barrel. Not enough of the drug to stretch them out cold, but something.

'F-f-fuck yer, Pilgrim,' muttered Gil, holding out his favourite cracked, ancient china mug for a refill. It bore the fading red, white, and blue of the Union Jack along with a picture of an old crone wearing a crown.

Seth topped him to the brim. Smiled.

He found an axe in the Lord of Erringdale's cart, a hunting crossbow and quiver with a dozen quarrels. Then he hid. Bided, watched. Tapped at the ankle shackles with hammer and spiked chisel until the securing pins loosened. Joy filled his soul as he practised walking unchained.

Folk keeled as the night wore on, drained by drink and poppy-juice and hard travel over the hills, not least the drama of the mass. No one bothered to lock up the bonders with the horses. Let them run. Chasing the wretches down would make good sport.

Three hours after midnight. Two until daybreak.

Lighting a hooded lamp, Seth slipped away from his hiding place. Black as a cave the Mistresses' temple. He eased open the lamp's iron shutter, allowing a finger of illumination to reach the altar. Then he froze. A snore; a snuffle. A strange chuckle subsiding to a mutter.

Why are you doing this? Seth asked himself in agony. The answer echoed ironically: *Knowledge is power. And sweetest revenge.*

Slipping out of his clogs, Seth crept across the dark space. Again, the chuckle. He froze. Seth recognised the voice; his neck hairs stirred. His free hand dropped to the handle of the knife they had given him to butcher changelings in Sellafield.

'Yer f-f-fuck,' grumbled the voice. 'I'll learn yer.'

A contented sigh. Snuffling. Snoring.

Seth shivered with desire. The hated Maister of Floggers must have collapsed here in a drunken stupor. Hard to let a sleeping, helpless Gil slip through his fingers. Too many secret shames lay between them, too many wrongs. Yet he dared not risk it. Others might lie asleep in the temple-barn, ready to wake at a cry for help.

Seth advanced to the altar. There he found the prize. The Mistresses had been lax, for something so essential to their status and comfort in Lake Country.

He reached out and hefted the plastic box of sacred treasures. Seth's breath quickened to gasps. Words from the old flogger hymn echoed unbidden in his mind: *For thou art the power and glory. Forever and ever.* Now it belonged to him.

He crept to the temple door and peered out. Clouds were thickening. It would be a grey, overcast morrow. For a brief moment, Seth considered fleeing there and then. Hours would pass before they became aware of his absence, giving him the chance to put a dozen miles between him and his pursuers. But he could not. Harrowing memories of being forced down like the poor girl overcame his prudence. He would wait no longer for revenge, not he.

* * *

Lantern raised, heart hammering, Seth strode to the farmhouse. The dogs sniffed him as he scratched their heads. Strange how inevitable his next actions felt, rehearsed night after night in dark fantasies.

Long ago, all doors of the farmhouse had been removed, probably for firewood. When the Mistresses claimed Fell Grange, new doors were fashioned and hung, crude, thick, defensive affairs with one peculiarity: all opened outward, not inward.

Seth made his way to the back door. More than a dozen folk slept in the building: the Mistresses and those who served them, and tonight, the Lord of Erringdale, with his wife and servants, including the poor girl from the mass. Seth knew he must not consider her. She, too, was destined to become another guilt to defy – like Old Marley, Father,

Averil.

From his pocket, he produced sturdy wooden wedges and tapped them firmly into place. Now the backdoor could not open from the inside.

Seth padded around the long building, passing ground floor windows bricked up into arrow slits in case of attack. At a side door, he produced more wedges to tap home. That left the front entrance.

There, his luck ran out.

The dogs in the yard were slavering, cursed by a gruff voice. Their reaction indicated someone familiar. Seth pressed against the wall, lantern shuttered.

A long stream of piss hissed interminably followed by a satisfied grunt and stumbling footsteps. Would the man shut the door and bolt it from inside? If so, Seth's carefully prepared plan would fail. He heard the door creak shut on its leather hinges. No bolts banged home.

Peering around the corner, he merged with shadow. Still no one about.

He knew the exact layout of the farmhouse. Its wooden floors and joists and stairs, the rooms where the Mistresses stored bales of woollen cloth they received, among other valuables, as tribute for their magic.

Seth hesitated. The consequence of being caught, wedges in place, was unthinkable. He knew what his father would have thought of his plan, the name he would have given it. Uncle Michael, too, smug and implacable, always reluctant to take a life without a clear need. But Seth had a need: deep and dark as a well. He stepped through the front door, shuttered lantern in hand.

In the farmhouse, no light. Seth sensed drunken, poppy-juice fuddled sleepers all around. Easy to step on one and raise a cry. He crept to a side room down the corridor. It would be unlocked, having received the Lord of Erringdale's tribute. Tentatively, he lifted the crude wooden latch. Click. Seth stayed still, anticipating a hand on his shoulder, a punch to his head. Not much of a fighter, never had been, even when riding to the wars beside Big Jacko with every weapon available, armour on chest, helmet on head.

He breathed out. Deeply in. Hurry now, before he lost his nerve.

With a creak, the storeroom door opened, and he slipped inside. Here were bales of wool, bolts of cloth, hams, onion strings, sacks of spuds, and boxes of oats, the Mistresses careless when it came to locking away their booty.

Using the lantern, Seth let a little beam play over the room until he located a small cask of hemp oil used for the farmhouse lamps. His breath was ragged as he lifted it, splashing cloth and wool bales, the wooden floorboards.

Again he froze. A footstep? Maybe on the stairs.

No time to find out. Seth touched the lantern flame to the oil-soaked wool. Instantly acrid, curling smoke rose. With a whoosh, flames sputtered.

Already he was in motion, out into the hallway, out, out into the yard, closing the heavy front door behind him and ramming tight his last wedges.

The trap was shut. Seth Pilgrim raced to the weapons and bag he had hidden behind a wall then vanished into the darkness.

At the bottom of the hill, Seth halted, his chest heaving. Above him, Fell Grange was no longer silent. Shouts of alarm rose. A long wail pierced the night. Did he recognise that voice? The petulant, sly tones of Fat Mistress transformed by horror? A crashing noise indicated part of the roof had fallen in. Pale figures illuminated by the spreading fire ran to and fro. Red flames glowed through the rectangles of upper storey windows. A silhouette was framed by a window he recognised as belonging to the Mistresses' chamber. Then the dark shape was gone. Falling with flailing limbs to the stony farmyard below. Smoke and sparks billowed high.

'Hell is hot,' he whispered. Reaching into his sack, he waved the Mistresses' box of holy books. 'Knowledge is fucking power!'

He hurried towards Sellafield, where nobody sane would expect him to hide; sounds of alarm faded into night songs of woodland and stream.

* * *

Pistol raised, Blair took out his screen and accessed the security drone's sensors from where it stood guard in the vestibule of the museum. Data flashed. He lowered the large handgun.

'It seems we have an intruder,' he said. 'Of sorts. The scans show she is unarmed.'

'She?' asked Helen.

'Just a primitive. Perhaps it would be best if you investigated, my dear.' His smile was thin. 'After all, you are fond of such creatures.'

Helen glared at him. She could guess her visitor's identity and why the lofty Blair Gover would not lower himself to bother with her. She stepped outside into blinding searchlights. Just inside the front entrance knelt her assistant, Averil Pilgrim, beside the shell-riddled wreckage of the spydrone destroyed earlier by Blair. The hood of her thick woollen cloak was pulled low to hide her face.

Cold gusts blew through the museum's sliding doors. A second security drone kept aloft by four hissing propellers hovered outside. Helen shielded her eyes.

The security drone boomed: *Do not move. Do not move.*

Activated by the alarm, Blair's aircarrier landed with a whine of engines and steam in the former car park, armoured turrets of cannon, rockets, and flamethrowers sprouting from its roof.

Helen turned and shouted above the din: 'Is this really necessary?'

All of Baytown was waking in terror at the racket.

'Enough!' cried Blair, striding outside, pistol vanishing back into its holster. The drones went quiet.

He examined the young woman sobbing near the reception counter. She trembled convulsively, her face buried in her hands.

'Do not fear; it will not harm you,' said Helen. 'You are quite safe.' She shot an accusing glance at Blair.

'Come now, child,' he said, waving a hand at the young woman. 'Run along back to your own kind. Your mistress is busy.'

Helen stepped over to Averil. 'No one will harm you, I assure you. There's no need to be afraid.'

For the first time, the young woman truly noticed Blair Gover. Her mouth opened, her head lifting to see him better. She stared at the unnaturally perfect young man before her. Not a flaw or blemish on his face, his hair glossy, his teeth even and white. Not the faintest odour of stale sweat or bad breath, as was the case with everyone else she had ever known.

'This is Averil Pilgrim,' Helen said to Blair. 'She helps teach in the school I have established in the museum. Her uncle, Michael Pilgrim, is someone you should meet. Perhaps it would change your views of these people.'

A bleep sounded on Blair's screen. He glanced down at it.

'Fascinating as it would be to debate such matters, alas, I must be gone.'

A wistful expression touched his face as he examined his former lover.

'You are aging quickly now, Helen. The decay can only accelerate when the last trace of elixir leaves your cells. It's not too late to renounce your stubborn, foolish pride. Come back with me, on any terms you choose. Be young forever.'

She recalled his wonderful new Eden and grew afraid.

'My place is here. But Blair, reconsider the fate you intend for these good people. I beg you.'

He averted his eyes and nodded. 'I expect you will change your mind when hideous old age or painful sickness beset you. Remember my offer then. Let us hope it will not be too late.'

He strode out to his aircarrier from which a ramp descended.

'I will return in a few months.' He paused to wave. 'I will develop my plans in the meantime. Await me in the autumn. I shall find you.'

His drones followed him into the aircar. It rose, heading north, and vanished like a shooting star over the horizon.

'He is so beautiful,' murmured Averil.

The Baytown girl swung on Helen. 'He's more like a god than a man! And so *powerful*. He promised you could be young forever. Why didn't you go with him? Everything here is ugly, horrible, brutish. Why didn't you go?'

The implication hung plain. For choosing Baytown over the Beautiful Life, Averil Pilgrim considered Helen Devereux an utter fool.

THREE

Hob Hall was abustle. Harvest had that effect, as did its aftermath.

Michael Pilgrim walked across Hob Hall's wide, high-walled courtyard lined with buildings — rooms for farm labourers, stores, stables, a smithy, tack rooms, and the dairy. He greeted faces both familiar and strange, including a dozen wandering pickers he had hired that season who were still busy with the last of the late potato crop. Other residents of Hob Hall were securing the haystacks that would see the farm beasts through the winter or winnowing grain with a hand-cranked fan.

Beside Michael walked his friend and farm manager, Amar, the Syrian refugee he saved as a starving teen. He was now twenty-five and a fine man in Michael Pilgrim's estimation.

'You've worked your miracles again,' said Michael, the Master of Hob Hall and Mayor of Baytown. Branded on his right cheek was a less elevated title, though not necessarily inglorious. A deep, coin-sized mark: **F** for Felon Against the City.

Amar shrugged. His air of unhappy distraction confirmed Michael's suspicions.

'Let's celebrate your success with a drop of something warm in the library, shall we?' he said.

The long, oak-panelled room, Michael Pilgrim's study and bedchamber, contained fewer books than before. Many had been lent to the new library in the Baytown Museum, a crop of knowledge for all to glean freely.

'Sit yourself!' Michael said, tidying the long wooden settle by the fire.

Both produced pipes and tobacco. A sod of peat from the moors smouldered in the grate, warming their toddy.

'You're troubled,' said Michael.

'Yes, Sharif.'

'Is it Averil?'

'Yes.'

The men puffed, weighing their words.

'You mentioned she's with child again,' said Michael, 'only very early on.'

'Yes.'

It should have been a cause for joy. But Averil's short marriage to Amar had already bred sorrow: a very late miscarriage, then, a year later, a severely deformed boy. Baytown had suffered a rash of misbirths.

Averil had not forgiven the general consensus of family and midwife that the baby should be exposed on the beach at the turning of the tide, for its own and the community's sake. Harsh norms prevailed when hunger was often Baytown's fate: the child's withered, twig-like arms and legs offered small hope of a useful life. Yet Averil had not thought so. She regarded those who persuaded her with silent antipathy. There seemed no helping it.

'Sharif,' Amar whispered lest they were overheard. 'She is the sun and moon to me. Yet everything I do grates with her. Everything!'

Michael had little to say. His own experience with women offered scant reassurance.

'Trust to time, Amar. You're a good man, and she loves you dearly.

Averil has a pure heart. Be patient. She'll come back.'

Little enough, but it seemed to reassure his friend. They shared a steaming glass of toddy over speculations concerning the Council of the North, for a hard-won and prosperous peace had settled across Yorkshire with Pharaoh Jacko's fall.

After Amar left, there was a knock at the door. It opened to reveal the very object of their concern. Averil's expression was hard to read.

'Uncle, you have a visitor,' she said.

* * *

The visitor waiting in Hob Hall's grand, stone-flagged hallway cut short Michael's polite greeting with a raised hand.

'Something has happened,' said Helen. 'We must speak in private.'

A voice piped from the staircase in a Baytown accent thick as sugar beet treacle.

'I can see you, Daddy!'

A four-year-old lad peered down at them through carved bannisters. It was George, Michael Pilgrim's only child, the product of a chance coupling. In the casual manner of the times, his mother had returned to her native Hull to marry and start a new family, settling the boy at Hob Hall. His nursemaid, Fran, an orphan of fourteen who ruled the nursery like an empress, let go of the lad's little hand when they reached the ground floor.

'Daddy!' George cried as his father swung him up high. Fran stepped forward anxiously.

Michael made an awkward, clumsy father, his own model in that line having died of plague at a young age.

'We're off to the beach,' said the lad. 'Daddy should come too!'

Helen shook her head.

'Maybe later, George,' said Michael.

Handing the child back, he caught a dark look from Averil, mingled jealousy and bitterness. It inspired him to invite her to join his conference with Helen, so she would not feel neglected.

After Helen finished her story, Michael Pilgrim considered the matter.

'So this great man from the City wishes to speak with me? Me, of all the folk on earth. It seems scarcely credible.'

'Don't go, please,' said Helen.

'But you say he wishes to propose something of benefit to our folk?'

'It's surely a trick. I know him too well. I only agreed to pass on his message because he was so persistent.'

Averil stirred. 'When he visited you in the spring, he seemed kind. And ever so handsome.'

'You *must* trust me on this,' said Helen.

Michael Pilgrim recalled the last City-man with whom he'd had dealings, an outcast from that fabled place. The Modified Man had said before he died, *Remember their arrogance will destroy them in the end.*

'I'll go. If nothing else, it would be discourteous not to hear him out.' He added dryly, 'Besides, he might send a drone to pluck me up like an owl does a mouse.'

His eye fell on Averil. 'Perhaps you should come along to bear witness, Avi.'

The flush of gratification on his niece's face reassured him. They would bring her back from the tragedy of her exposed child. Through trust and love and responsibility, they would bring back his dead brother James's daughter. And yet, Pilgrim felt an old ache at the thought. Her wayward twin brother, Seth, had journeyed beyond help years before, perishing with his master, Big Jacko.

* * *

THREE

Baytown Museum boasted one exceptional treasure: the Baytown Jewel. Eight hundred years earlier, during the time of the last great plague, the Black Death inspired its making — a magic talisman to conquer death. Cast from pure Indian gold, a diamond-shaped locket with a mother and child engraved on its front in delicate, intricate relief. Set in the centre, a bright blue sapphire. Flip the jewel and another reality asserted itself: two engraved skeletons in a dance macabre. A *memento mori* that behind all love, hope, ideals, lurks death.

Blair paced before the jewel's reinforced glass display case as he waited for Helen to return. Had the security cameras once monitoring the jewel still worked, they would have recorded a strange sight. The man in City clothes stopped before the jewel, scanning it with his screen. Apparently satisfied, he produced a multi-use tool. This he applied to the lock of the display case. It opened with a click.

Blair reached inside. Lifting out the jewel, he frowned at the mocking skeletons on its rear. Guided by an image on his screen, he ran his finger down the locket's side. A tiny catch opened a secret, hollow interior. Long ago, prayers had been inscribed on parchment and hidden in there. Blair produced a microchip no bigger than a pill and hid it inside the jewel, gently closing the locket.

Again the multi-tool whirled, sealing the display case. One might think it had never been disturbed.

* * *

Uncle Michael led the way as he always did, and Averil was forced to follow. Low, grey clouds hinted at rain. Baytown would have welcomed a downpour. Summer's tale had been drought, then deluge, and then more drought. Still, enough crops had been harvested for winter, and that would have to suffice.

No one spoke as they took the dusty lane from Hob Hall to the

Baytown Museum. The grey, brooding sky framed the buildings they passed, many derelict, some in the process of repair from incomer families granted land and security. Averil noticed it all without pleasure. Nothing much gave her pleasure any more — nor did she care. Resentment clasped her soul. Against Amar for controlling her with doting, dog-like devotion. Against Uncle Michael for having assumed her dead father's position as head of the Pilgrim family. Even Father's old church was in the hands of the Nuagers. She was sure Uncle Michael had a hand in that, hastening Father's death from a broken heart. And maybe Seth wouldn't have turned bad without Uncle Michael's nagging disapproval; perhaps Seth might still be alive.

Averil conceded her thoughts were unfair. Why shouldn't they be? Nothing was fair. That some folks' sons were strong while she was forced to expose her own on the cold, stony beach until the tide took him. Tears pricked her eyes. If her boy had been half as strong as Uncle Michael's little George, she wouldn't neglect the bairn as he did. Nothing was fair. Baytown itself reeked of middens, backwardness, decay. Never mind her privileges as a Pilgrim, Averil had always felt she did not belong there.

She drew close to Helen as they entered the museum.

'So it will be the same young man?' she asked, smoothing her hair. 'As came in the spring?'

For a moment, Helen looked confused. 'Young?' A faint smile flickered. 'I should warn you, Averil, all that glitters is not gold.'

At the Jewel Gallery, Averil's chest tightened as she laid eyes on him. As before, the City-man's beauty astonished her. Perhaps all City-folk were perfect like that.

He was lolling in a chair. Averil curtsied as his grey eyes brushed past her and settled on Uncle Michael. Of course, he did not bow as he should. He just cocked his head and looked brazen.

'You are the one your fellow primitives call Protector of the North?'

THREE

said the City-gentleman. 'I see from the brand on your cheek you have had converse with the City before.'

The amusement in his tone shamed Averil. It was deserved, after all. What were any of them but primitives?

* * *

Much of what was said over the next half hour amazed Averil. Blair Gover spoke to Uncle Michael of tilth and machines and the poisoned earth. How the City might find a use for those he called savages.

A magical vision of the future projected from his screen as a holoshow. Wafted by heroic music, lines of happy primitives in clean clothes piled scraps of tilth onto hoppers, pushing their loads to waiting drones. Not nasty drones with pincers and cannons and flamethrowers. Nice drones that turned tilth into gas and oils — a miracle! — for everyone knew tilth was poison.

'In return, Pilgrim, we would grant you access to technology long forbidden to your kind. Sufficient to encourage literacy and even basic hospitals.'

At the mention of schools and hospitals, Averil felt a pinch of excitement. Could the dark days really be coming to an end? She waited for Uncle Michael to express his gratitude.

'Well,' he said, 'I don't see how all this requires me. If the City wishes these things to happen, then happen they will.'

The handsome youth nodded. 'That is correct. But I do have a mission for you alone, Pilgrim. Did you like serving the Five Cities in the Crusades?'

Strange emotions crossed Uncle Michael's face.

'No.'

'One can see why. You'll find my little task far more agreeable. Know this, I wish for you to come with me to the City of Albion and thence to a place far away. There I shall present you to a great conclave. You need not fear, just do as you are instructed.'

'Earlier, you spoke of a new Eden, a paradise,' replied Uncle Michael. 'I don't remember Adam and Eve being slaves in that old story. Yet it's what you want for us.'

The City-prince considered him. 'Slave is such a nasty word. Would you prefer corpse?'

Helen stepped forward.

'Blair! You promised not to threaten. You said it would be a free choice whether he went with you.'

The beautiful young man yawned. 'So I did, my dear. I might even remove that hideous brand from the brute's cheek. So that he makes a better impression before the Grand Autonomy.'

Michael's icy smile would have warned most folk to tread carefully.

'Perhaps Pilgrim should step outside to consider his options,' said the City-man.

With a nod, Uncle Michael withdrew. No one noticed Averil in her corner.

'I am very disappointed,' chided Helen, as soon as the door closed. 'I regret playing the slightest role in your scheme. Nor can I imagine it went down well with the Council.'

Their heated discussion soon confused Averil. How the leaders of the Five Cities narrowly rejected his motion; how Blair had called a meeting of the Grand Autonomy to settle the matter in a place called Mughalia. Words passed between them she did not recognise: progenitive, modification, terrible risks of gene infection. Others she knew: boredom, spoiled, folly. When the Grand Autonomy was mentioned, Averil detected unease in Blair's voice.

'Well, it's entirely up to Pilgrim,' he said, a little sulkily. 'He should fawn with gratitude, but these savages are seldom rational. This one looks far too full of himself.'

He grew aware Michael was listening from the doorway. 'Ah, there you are!'

'I've decided to come with you.' Michael turned to Helen, who was about to protest. 'If there is a chance to help my people, I must take it.'

Blair stretched. 'Good. I will depart soon, Helen. No one knows I am here this time. I left an avatar in my place.'

Then he noticed Averil and laughed. 'I see a little mouse has been listening in on our conversation. Now, Pilgrim, off you trot. Pack a few things that comfort you. Not many, mind. Your needs will be provided for. Shoo, now. And return quickly.'

Averil hurried after her uncle, leaving Helen to whisper at Blair: 'Harm him, and I will never forgive you.'

FOUR

Out on the sands, four miles from land, and strung in a line. The tide would turn soon, then they must retreat, "brisk 'n' steady" as Old Albert put it. For now, the score men and women knew no slacking. Between emptying his net on the sorting-sieve, Seth Pilgrim glimpsed the world's horizons and was struck with awe.

On all sides, compact sand and occasional ribbons of grey water from rivers feeding into the vast tidal bay. Mountains to the north and west, blue-capped in the dawn. Seabirds crying as they pecked, dipped, flocked. Cold wind and water pervasive as salt. Littered across the exposed bay, sea-tilth of every variety, tangled with weed and driftwood. Nearby lay the rusting hulk of a container ship on its side, half-buried by sand where it had ground to a halt a century earlier, its entire crew dead of plague.

Seth's fingers worked thoughtlessly, plucking out seaweed, crabs, jellyfish; sorting out the shrimps and sprats that teemed in the chilly waters. He added his voice to an ancient song as the line of shrimpers worked:

> There was a jolly miller once
> Lived on the River Dee.
> He worked and sang from morn till night,

FOUR

No lark more blithe than he.
And this the burden of his song
Forever used to be,
'I care for nobody, no, not I,
Since nobody cares for me.'

Seth knew how that felt. But he was happy — almost — at least happier than he'd been in years.

Six months earlier, Seth had travelled down the coast from Fell Grange, following old railway lines. A journey with one eye over his shoulder. If the Mistresses still lived, they would be desperate to recover their holy books. The lands he traversed were mainly deserted, such folk dwelling there easily bypassed. He saw no sign of pursuit.

Using his stolen crossbow, he had hunted for fowl to eke out the rations taken from Fell Grange. Even so, Seth was as hungry as a carthorse by the time he reached Morecambe, ten days' walk from his enemies.

The old holiday resort was reverting to piles of overgrown rubble. Despite this, a community had established itself there, constructing a crude trading fort by the beach. Four dozen hardy folk fed by sea and land. Their leader, Old Albert, coolly assessed Seth when he appeared at their gate begging for work.

'Do your share, and you'll get your share,' was his verdict.

So it proved. For six months, Seth worked the clan's fields and joined their forays out on the miles of bare sand at low tide.

* * *

On the very same morning that Michael Pilgrim met Blair Gover, a hundred miles to the west, his nephew was in conversation with another City-man — or, more precisely, a *former* City-man who went by the name Hurdy-Gurdy. He and Seth were boiling the dawn's catch of shrimp and sprats in a copper vat once used to boil toffee for holidaymakers. They dumped the cooked brown shrimp on a tray to cool before picking off their shells.

Seth watched curiously as Hurdy-Gurdy chuntered to an imaginary audience. Sometimes he sang or recited strange, impromptu rhymes. At other times he capered or danced. Perhaps, Seth speculated, the man's apparent lunacy explained why two years earlier, a drone had appeared over Morecambe Bay when the tide was out, and ejected him, stark naked, onto the sands.

'Do you know, Gurdy,' Seth said, as they pinched the crisp shells off the cooked shrimps, 'one day I shall go the City. How is it you came to leave there?'

The City-man generally answered such a question with streams of nonsense.

'Poor, poor Gurdy had a great fall,' he wailed. 'Poor, poor Hurdy had no friends at all. All the fine Be-a-u-ties in Cities one to five wouldn't let Gurdy stay forever alive. Ha! Ha!'

The madman's voice cracked. He brushed away tears with fishy fingers, leaving bits of shrimp stuck to his eyebrows and beard.

'What did you do to anger them?' Seth asked.

Hurdy-Gurdy drew back his shoulders like a proud king. 'Do? Do-o? I was a holotainer known to all, beloved by all. A doyen — and in my time doyenne — of the holocasts. The classics were my meat and drink.' His tone rose to a hysterical pitch. 'A plague on their houses, I say! Ninety years I laboured to perfect tricks for their pleasure. Watch this.'

To Seth's astonishment, the madman launched an astonishing display, juggling cooked shrimps in their shells, his hands, elbows, wrists, forearms, and even his knees a blur.

'If you were so damned good,' said Seth, 'why did they dump you stark bollock naked on the sands of Morecambe Bay?'

Hurdy-Gurdy froze. The shrimps fell to the floor. His haggard face contorted.

'Discordia, cruel Young Nuncle,' he said.

'What is this Discordia?'

But Hurdy-Gurdy had grown sullen. 'Poor, poor Gurdy had a great fall,' he growled. 'Poor, poor Hurdy had no friends at all.'

* * *

Seth strolled along the remnant of Morecambe's promenade beside the shore. Hurdy-Gurdy's garbled hints about the City played on his mind.

Waves rolled in fast. Soon it would be high tide, then just as surely low. On and on until world's end.

Picking up a flat pebble, he skimmed it across the waves. If he did not leave for the City soon it would be winter, a dangerous season to travel. Yet he felt safe among Old Albert's clan. Simple, hardworking folk who asked no questions. That helped the past fade a little — except in nightmares.

Seth glanced over his shoulder at the clan's compound, its walls constructed of old cars mortared together with stones from the beach and bricks scavenged from ruined houses. Old Albert traded in a salty shrimp and fish paste of his own recipe. Dolloped into winter stews, it provided protein and flavour, where otherwise shivering farmers relied on nuts or precious salt meat. Plenty to do, to be sure. But Seth felt restless. Hadn't he always wanted more? Even as a boy, Hob Hall and Baytown were never enough. Only the City offered escape. And if not now, when?

A flock of gulls formed a shifting pattern of dots against the sky, their cries all agitation and energy as they circled a small party of horsemen approaching with a wagon. Something about the strangers stirred a general warning. But Seth was too busy brooding to heed it.

Earlier he had posed a question to Hurdy-Gurdy: 'Is it weakness to show pity and kindness — what some people call *good*? You see, I once dwelt with folk who thought that way. They called good bad and evil good. See what I mean?'

The lunatic's bushy brows waggled. 'He who does no good does evil enough.'

'But that's the other thing. Is evil power? If so, why not want it?'

'No man better knows what good is than he who has endured evil.'

'You're useless, Gurdy. Why can't you talk plain?'

'Remember this, Young Nuncle. To see a man do a good deed is to forget all his faults.'

'Oh, bollocks.'

'Which come in pairs. Like turtle doves.'

* * *

As soon as Seth stepped into the trading fort, he realised why the merchants' cart was familiar. He last saw it at Fell Grange. It had carried the Lord of Erringdale and his pregnant wife plus a young lass ripe for the Mistresses' mass. Now it bore bales of wool among other tradeables. Of the Lord of Erringdale, there was no sign.

For a moment, Seth lingered in the gateway. Before negotiations, Old Albert would invite the merchants to partake of ale and bread in the former hotel the fisher-clan occupied. Sure enough, shadowy silhouettes could be seen on the ground floor.

Seth glanced round. Hide in the compound or ruined town until they left? Or gather his few possessions and scarper like a fox?

Seth dashed across the muddy yard to an old ice cream kiosk assigned as his quarters. Don't look back; walk naturally, he thought. Just

FOUR

because the cart belongs to the Lord of Erringdale doesn't mean someone will recognise you.

He entered the kiosk, grabbing stuff from the shelves. Knife in boot, clothes and blankets thrust in a sack, along with the pink plastic box containing the Coven's holy books. Seth's hand closed on his hunting crossbow just as a shadow filled the doorway.

'I'd put that down if I was you.'

Seth turned slowly. There stood a pockmarked young man he recognised from Fell Grange, one of the Lord of Erringdale's servants. In his hand, he held a flintlock pistol, its long barrel pointed squarely at Seth's chest.

'There's a price on yer head, mister,' said an older man, peering around his companion. He too held a gun, a short-barrelled, wide-bored musket.

'Which is coming my way, not yours, granddad,' said the first. 'I recognised him before you did.'

Neither took their eyes off the source of this bounty. It occurred to Seth he might be just as valuable dead as alive.

* * *

Seth knew that the instant he called for help, the gun would go off.

'Drop that bloody weapon,' ordered the young man, barrel wavering.

The crossbow clattered to the ground.

'Tie his hands, granddad,' he said. 'Fuck me, I'll blow his head clean off if he moves a muscle. Do you hear that, you bastard? I'll kill you!' The tremor in the young man's voice deepened.

His older companion gaped stupidly. 'What do I tie his hands with?'

'Get some fucking rope.'

In a moment, the older man was gone. Only pistol-boy remained.

'My lord will like to see you,' he said. 'His missus lost her baby from fear because of that fire you started. I was in there, too! Nearly choked, I did.'

Seth wondered if he could sneak closer, dig his knife into pistol-boy's gut. But he was too scared to move, let alone fight.

'They say you stole something from the Mistresses. Where is it?'

No mistaking what he wanted. The intensity of his question gave Seth an idea.

'If you let me go, I'll tell you where it's hid.'

'Oh, you'll tell me, will you?'

'I'll even show you.'

'Don't fucking move!' The pistol barrel quivered.

The older man returned with a small coil of rope.

'We'll have to be quick. Old Albert's people will be out soon, once they've supped their noggins with t'maister.'

Now Seth was truly afraid. Could Maister Gil be here as well? It seemed too unjust, too harsh. After all, many a man bore the title maister.

'All right,' said his young captor, 'out with yer then. We'll tie his hands in the cart. Move it!'

Seth shuffled out into the yard, covered by two guns. Neither of his captors noticed the crazed figure in rags with masses of filthy, matted hair lurking in the nearest corner. Or the ten-foot-wide shrimp net he carried.

High-pitched screams and squawks, the unmistakeable sound of a herring gull raising an alarm, poured forth from Hurdy-Gurdy. Seth's captors whirled. Just in time to feel the net envelop them.

Flashes of gunpowder, loud cracks. Seth's knife was out of his boot. He leapt at pistol-boy, sticking the tip in his Adam's apple.

'Move, and your throat's cut,' he cried. 'I'll do it! I fucking will!'

The gunshots brought out dozens of fisher-folk, many seizing weapons. Soon the merchants had been driven to their carts with

FOUR

curses and threats, surrounded by grim-faced clansmen and women. Firing guns in their home, with bairns about, was too grave a breach of hospitality to go unpunished. Old Albert insisted on a bale of woollen cloth as compensation before kicking them out.

'You'll get yours, Pilgrim!' shouted pistol-boy, stripped of his valuable weapon, his arse throbbing from a boot up the backside.

T'maister, a mere trader as it turned out and not the Maister of Floggers stalking Seth's nightmares, glared at Seth as they pulled away, as though memorising his face.

* * *

That same evening, Seth stood with packed bags and his newly-acquired musket. The stolen pistol poked from his belt.

'They'll be back before long, Albert,' he said to the old shrimper, who urged him to remain. 'It's best if I'm gone. If I stay, trouble will come your way. You've been too good to me for that. All of you.'

Old Albert nodded. 'I promised you, do your share and you'll get your share.'

He left Seth standing by a side-gate of the trading fort. Setting his eyes on the road, Seth prepared to depart when a sly voice called out, half-singing, half-chanting: 'Young Nuncle's a-going-o. Young Nuncle's a-splitting-o. Is it to Albion-o that Young Nuncle means to go?'

Seth peered at Hurdy-Gurdy, who sat crouched in a corner of shadow.

'You do talk shit sometimes, Gurdy. But yes, I'm going to try my luck in the City.'

'Albion, is it?'

'Aye. And thank you for saving me earlier. I owe you.'

'Then Hurdy will come, too,' the former City-man whined like a beaten bitch, squeezing out hot tears. 'Dying, Egypt, dying! Hurdy is dying. He must go back to save his soul, oh yes, and Young Nuncle will go too.'

Seth could hardly refuse. Besides, he was sick of travelling alone. Two dark shapes crept through the rubble-choked streets of Morecambe, heading east past collapsed novelty shops and amusement arcades, rotted fairground rides and open-topped buses.

FIVE

Michael Pilgrim knew better than to pack anything a scanning drone might identify as a weapon. Into a small satchel went decent spare clothes. He was determined the City would encounter a civilized man.

Accompanied by Tom Higginbottom, Helen, Averil, Mister Priest Man, Amar, among others, he walked through the dusk to the Baytown Museum. There, a long, sleek aircar had landed, having concealed itself in a nearby meadow all day.

No one spoke as Michael shook hands. When it came to Averil, he embraced her awkwardly. Finally, he turned to Tom Higginbottom, boyhood pal and comrade in the hateful Crusades.

'Remember those letters for the Council of the North,' he said. 'And patrols out on the borders for Reivers. Summer drought means winter hunger — they'll be garnering like squirrels this year.'

The wind-worn fisherman replied in a broad Baytown accent, 'You're a right bloody fool to do this, Michael.'

No denying that. Though they both knew no real choice had been given.

Fear and panic gripped Michael as a security drone escorted him up the aircar's ramp. His legs grew weak, his mind spinning with images from the Crusades, air transports laden with soul-sickened men, mounds of maggot-riddled bodies beneath an indifferent sun.

Tightening the broad strap of his leather satchel, Michael steadied himself. He caught a last glimpse of familiar trees and buildings silhouetted by twilight, then the bright interior of the aircar swallowed him whole.

* * *

'Sit!' commanded Blair Gover, pointing at a chair with manacles for armrests. 'I wish to question you, then you will be sent to a nice, comfortable pen.'

They were in a central cabin containing padded seats and burnished tables. A dainty drone waited to one side with refreshments. As Michael sat, the manacles whirred, pinning him to the chair. A security drone positioned itself by his elbow.

Gover took off his armoured vest of tools and weapons. The drone carried it into another cabin near the front of the aircar, returning with a silk overgown.

'Are these bonds necessary?' Michael asked. 'Remember, I'm here by choice. We're meant to be grateful, willing slaves in this Eden you envision, are we not?'

The City-man glanced up from a handheld screen projecting holo-images of data.

'Very well,' he said distractedly. 'Release him.'

The manacles clicked open. A moment later, they were airborne, engines rumbling. Michael's mouth tasted ashen. He watched Gover murmuring commands to his screen, manipulating holo-images with fluid fingers.

'Where are we going?' Michael asked.

Blair Gover deactivated the screen with a sigh. He summoned over the comfort drone, which offered him a fizzing goblet of ice-cold wine. Its scent tickled Michael's nostrils. No refreshment came his way.

FIVE

'I suppose it would be advisable to share some information,' Gover said, examining his passenger. 'You're a dangerous breed of primitive, Pilgrim. Unlike the majority of your tribe, you feel no awe for the Five Cities. I suspect you consider yourself morally superior. Still, your air of the noble savage lends you a certain innate credibility. It will be useful when I present you to the Grand Autonomy.'

The aircar rumbled.

'It makes you nervous having drones nearby, I see,' Gover said. 'Primitive psychology increasingly interests me. You do look nervous. Perhaps we should attach some monitoring feeds.'

Michael turned to the drone. It seemed very still. To defy Gover and confirm a suspicion, he tapped its plastisteel case. The drone did not react.

Gover smiled. 'I'm beginning to wonder if you will prove tiresome, Pilgrim.'

In response, Michael pinged the drone with his finger. 'It powered down a minute ago. That other one just stopped working, too.'

Blair Gover consulted his screen, at first with annoyance, then with naked alarm.

* * *

As his fingers played holo-keys, Gover muttered rapid codes and commands. Michael noticed the whites of the City-man's eyes for the first time. The aircar juddered over an air pocket.

'We're under attack,' Gover said, as though thinking aloud. 'The controls are being controlled externally. I have deciphered their primary intention. They plan to follow my planned flight path to Greenland then remotely trigger a self-destruct when we are over the sea. My death can be thus interpreted as an accident.'

Gover said no more. He battled to regain mastery of the aircraft through his screen. Nothing was compliant, doors, drones, even the lights in the cabin dimmed. Multi-coloured holo-data glowed as his fingers raced. Suddenly, shutters protecting the windows slid open to reveal a snow-capped mountain peak a hundred feet below.

Deep into Scotland now. Soon would come the sea then an explosion. Gover mumbled to himself and, even in that moment of terror, Michael sensed how often the City-man talked to himself. How he was virtually friendless in this world, save for his games and toys, always scheming to live forever.

'If you open the door and jump, it will warn them,' Blair muttered. 'Then they will send out drones. Not that then. But if you mask the door opening... Clever, clever, Blair! It *could* work.'

He worked the holocontrols of his screen. Stepping over to a lever marked ESCAPE, he pulled. Two metal drawers slid out, each containing a bulky body harness, thick with machinery and pipes. Gover wriggled into one, clicking magnetic buckles until the thing was secure.

Still, the aircar rumbled and shook. Were they gathering speed for the downward plunge?

Instinct drove Michael to lunge for the other harness. He shrugged it on as he'd seen Gover do, clicking its simple clasps in place over his small satchel. It was heavy, even for a strong man.

Gover typed a code into his screen with great care. Loud beeps sounded from the ordinarily silent device. 'Know this, whomever you are,' he spoke at the screen. 'Blair Gover alone decides the hour and means of his passing. So I assure you, your crime will be investigated. And you will be punished. Enjoy your brief triumph, fools!'

Gover applied a final tap to the screen, and a glowing pulse began to count down. Reluctantly, he placed the screen on a chair.

'What the fuck are you doing?' Michael cried.

Gover lurched to the escape hatch and activated a control. The door

FIVE

slid open. A buffet of cold night wind rushed in from the darkness. For an instant, the City-man hesitated at the edge of the hatch. Then he jumped.

* * *

Michael Pilgrim leapt from the aircar an instant behind the City-man, colliding with him as they tumbled downward. His strong hands grasped Gover's wrist as though his life depended on it.

Whirling, spinning, dark lands, cloud vapour, a blur of stars. The terror of absolute powerlessness. Down, like fallen angels, they twisted and turned. An incandescent flash in the distance as the air carrier exploded.

Wind bruising face and body — the sheer force of descent knocked the air from Michael's lungs. Amidst the din of wind, Gover screeched as he kicked and fought to free himself from the hands clamped on his arm.

Controlled by an irresistible, outside power, Michael gradually straightened, assuming a fixed, upright position. The harness whined and vibrated. They were slowing! For a brief moment, he glimpsed hillsides, the glitter of water below, the sea on one side, land on the other.

Slower, slower, still grasping Gover's wrist. Down, down through the darkness. The land rose up to meet them. The harness bleeped urgently. Seconds later, Michael felt himself lowered onto soft shingle. His feet found balance. He tottered, amazed to be alive.

Only then did he let go of Gover.

* * *

The hours of darkness passed slowly. Clouds concealed the stars.

Michael slumped with his back against a tree, shivering and in deep shock. Strange scents told tales of an unfamiliar land.

First light confirmed his instincts; they had landed beside a long lake between bleak mountains. A brisk wind from the west bore a faint sea-tang. Cloud layers scraped the hillsides. It must be cold here much of the year, despite the swirling midges. Jockland, he thought, what they called Scotland in the Before Days. Old maps from Hob Hall's library gave further clues. This must be the Highlands — hundreds of miles from home.

He watched Blair Gover huddling nearby. The City-man, usually so self-assured, clutched the empty pouch where his screen once hung, moaning to himself.

'It could have been worse,' Michael said. 'We might have landed in the middle of the lake.'

'You savage!' cried Gover. 'Do you not see my position? Without a screen I am powerless.' Again he groaned. 'I must check, I must... I have not been without a screen for a hundred years!'

'Why did you leave it behind then?'

Gover glared. 'Because it was blocking the information that I had jumped. Without that, the sky would be full of drones searching for me. As it is, my enemies believe I remained in the aircar, blowing it up to incriminate them. My screen did all that.' He shivered convulsively. 'I am lost without it!'

'Calm yourself.'

Gover shielded his eyes from the wilderness of mountains, grey water, and oppressive grey sky. 'Oh, God,' he whispered. 'I had forgotten the world.'

Michael thought it best to take charge. He discovered that the harnesses that saved their lives when they jumped carried small pods containing survival supplies. Not much, but enough to cheer him: ration bars; a multi-function tool with a razor-sharp three-inch blade;

a powerful torch; and a basic medikit. There was also a large ear-plug. Its use he could not fathom.

Gover observed sullenly, hugging his gaudy dressing gown for warmth. Michael made him don a top-layer of spare, homespun clothes from his satchel.

'You stand out like a rose in a pigsty in those fine City-garments,' Michael snorted.

'You're enjoying this, Pilgrim, aren't you?'

Michael sniffed the air. For all the danger of their situation, it did seem an exceptional country. Not too far to the west lay the sea. The coast was a line you could always follow, and if, as he prayed, they had landed on the east side of Jockland, they might trace it all the way down to Baytown. He carved a stout pine staff with the blade of the multi-tool.

'Good knife this, Gover.'

'I'm glad it pleases you.'

'It could save your life.'

Michael tossed the staff to Gover, taking up one he had prepared for himself while the latter sulked.

'I'm off,' he said, 'we can't stay here forever.'

Gover's eyes narrowed. 'Very well, I accept you as my follower — temporarily, and on the strictest probation. Henceforth, you shall address me as My Lord.'

He made a great show of extracting power cells from the harnesses, which he called *gravchutes*, explaining to Michael, as one might to a backward child, that such devices are powerful, dangerous, and best left to superiors.

* * *

Drizzle came down as they skirted the lochside. Michael was pleased to note Gover's trousers and shirt were made of tough City plasticloth, likewise his boots. As for his own kit, it would have to suffice. His socks were warm, his boots freshly re-soled. Upon such their survival might depend.

A land full of life yet empty of humanity. His senses tuned to the wind and rustle of young pines, the faint whisper of streams feeding the loch. As they waded through pungent waist-high ferns, he caught sight of deer on the brow of the hill. Then he stopped.

A black dot was heading their way over eastern peaks. Crow? Eagle? Too fast and big. Without a word, he hauled Gover into the cover of the ferns, wriggling to lie flat on his back, peering up through damp fronds. Peaty, acrid scents surrounded them.

'Stay still,' he whispered.

Moments later, an aircar streaked low over the glen. Not a large one. Not a drone either. The echo of its jet engines faded slowly.

'Are they looking for us?' Michael asked.

Gover struggled to his feet. 'I doubt it. I was far too clever for that. I told you, they believe I'm dead.'

'So you say.'

'Pilgrim?'

'Yes, Gover.'

'I instructed you to address me as My Lord.'

* * *

Towards noon, they stumbled on the remains of a tarmac highway running north-south beside a gravelly beach. Michael's heart leapt. The sea! Large, bare islands with cliffs circled by white birds. A few feral sheep scattered. He made a mental note to fashion a bow and arrows.

Now they faced a dilemma, whither to go. Michael was determined to follow an established road. Wandering in the wilderness could prove fatal; winter came sooner to such northern lands. They must hurry to avoid its fangs.

He struggled to recall maps of Scotland. The position of the rising sun indicated they were on the west side of the country.

'We shall go that way,' Gover said, pointing his staff south.

'No.'

'I say yes, Pilgrim.'

'No.'

Michael indicated a distant line of smoke rising behind a hill. 'We're going to ask yon folk where we are. Before that, rub this sheep shit over your clothes and hair. You look and smell unnatural. They might burn you as a witch.'

Hillsides of larch and ash rose from the coast, leaves golden with autumn. The road passed stray ruins of cottages, some were burnt shells, most simply abandoned to wind, rain and nettles. Crossing a headland, they arrived at the source of the smoke.

A fishing village lay above a strand of pebble and shingle. Most of the houses were overgrown, but half a dozen were occupied. Of boats, there was no sign, indicating men out at sea. The smoke rose from herring cured over wood fires.

'Let me do the talking, Gover.'

With that, Michael approached the line of cottages.

Their arrival caused alarm. Brawny women and girls gathered, along with a dozen bairns; Michael glimpsed a blunderbuss in a doorway beside an old man.

'Lay your staff on the ground,' he said to Gover.

They waited. The old man, his blunderbuss, and several women came over. All carried weapons, axes, spears, knives or threshing flails.

The old man spoke, and for a moment, incomprehension reigned.

Then Michael smiled with relief. Just as smells bring back memories, so voices...

When Michael was a lad, a traveller begged his grandfather for work one harsh winter and was set to minding the beasts. Solitary, surly, Aud Jacob was his name, and whatever deeds had forced him on the road he never disclosed.

Most folk in Hob Hall found Aud Jacob's dialect a meaningless babble. But for nigh on ten years, Michael became the canny Scottish beastman's friend — or as near as Jacob allowed — often helping him feed and tend the animals.

Jacob's manner of speech had been as Highland as heather. Now its cadences returned to Michael Pilgrim, and he replied in kind.

'Guid day to ye, sair,' he greeted the old man with the blunderbuss.

Waves broke and murmured on the pebble beach.

'An' ye,' replied the fisherman.

A stilted conversation followed, but satisfactory enough. Michael noticed Gover had placed the earplug from the gravchute's survival pods in his right ear. His face and outfit attracted wonder from the assembled villagers. One old woman hobbled forward to touch his cheek, exclaiming at its softness.

Time to be gone. As they left, Michael opened his mouth to explain what he had learned, but Gover raised a masterful hand. 'He said the road we are on is long and winding. But if we stay on it, it will lead us all the way through the mountains to Inverness, which lies on the east coast.'

Michael looked at him with new respect.

'Pilgrim, you will be relieved to hear my interests coincide with your own. There is something I left for safekeeping in Baytown. Something my enemies very much wish to find. So off we go. Chop! Chop!'

They set off inland through the drizzle, following the remains of the tarmac road.

SIX

A fat-bellied aircarrier angled towards the Yorkshire coast. As it roared over the cliffs of Baytown, Averil Pilgrim and Helen Devereux looked up instinctively.

'That's a high one,' remarked Averil, pulling her shawl close.

'Yes. It has no business with us.'

The two women were outside Baytown Museum. Averil had hurried there soon after breakfast for news concerning her uncle's decision to go to the City. Helen had the distinct impression the girl was envious of him.

'Folk have noticed a few big 'uns like that lately,' Averil said. 'They always come from the same direction across the sea, head inland, then fly back the same way an hour or two later. Tom Higginbottom is saying over his ale in the Puzzle Well Inn they remind him of troop transports in the Crusades. He says it cannot mean anything good.'

'They have no business with us,' repeated Helen.

Averil glanced aside nervously. 'Do you think your friend will come back soon to build a school and hospital? He seemed keen to help us with his marvellous machine.'

'Tom Higginbottom is right to be suspicious,' Helen responded. 'Never hope for good from the City, least of all from Blair Gover.'

Even as the faint rumble of the aircarrier's engines faded, others took their place. As the new rumbling intensified, Averil grabbed her slender companion's arm and searched the sky. Both knew that sound.

* * *

Two drone carriers appeared, painted in the gaudy colours of Albion, air and earth shaken by the roar of their unmuffled engines. No concealment intended, their aim was to strike terror.

'Quick!' cried Helen. 'Inside!'

Averil followed her into the heart of the museum, neglecting to bolt the door behind them. A long corridor led to a high-ceilinged gallery where the Baytown Jewel was displayed in its locked case.

Helen sat on a bench, squeezing her fingers. 'I'm sure they'll go away soon. We mean nothing to them. It is probably a big show to frighten the communities on the coast because the City hasn't been visible of late.' She secretly feared the drones were connected to Blair Gover's furtive schemes.

Concealed in the museum, Helen and Averil did not see the two drone carriers separate. One flew to the village green where it landed with a hiss, the other to the car park outside the museum, settling on the skeleton of a car with a crunch of rusty metal and crack of plastic.

Doors on the side of each carrier opened. Out flew a dozen aerial drones, powered by whirring propellers. None was larger than a small cask, nor needed to be. Their task was to seek rather than destroy. For that, other drones on caterpillar tracks waited in the carriers.

Off buzzed the scouts, scanning concentric circles, applying a scenting device programmed to detect a particular man's body odour. The aerial drones in the village sniffed for him in streets where people cowered. Those drones in the vicinity of the museum hovered and bleeped urgently. They swarmed around the exterior of the building to monitor all exits, stubby barrels pointed.

The largest aerial drone approached the front entrance. For a

SIX

moment, its cannon took aim. Then the machine, or someone directing it, altered its intention. A metal arm extended. With the delicate finesse of a brain surgeon, metal digits opened the double swing doors. Propellers thrumming, it edged inside the lobby, gathering scent traces until a clear trail was identified. The aerial drone advanced slowly down the corridor towards the Baytown Jewel.

* * *

Unconcerned about events in Baytown, the aircarrier that had passed over the Yorkshire coast continued inland, just as Averil predicted. It was not the first to go this way. Nor, until the programme was completed, would it be the last.

The aircraft banked towards Geordieland, seeking an ancient wall of limestone and granite running east to west, coast to coast, the half-forgotten border of a vanished empire. The surrounding country offered violent tests of a useful kind. They deposited their cargo, sparing little time in the process, before speeding off towards kinder landscapes.

* * *

She, it, they — each appropriate. She, the identity preferred by the strangeling herself. Through fogs in her brain, habitual shocks of pain, fear, sudden equanimity whenever the bracelet pricked, she dredged forth deep-buried seeds of self.

Hours earlier, they'd come for her in the cube that had been her world, the two-legged Gods and the others with round feet. They ordered her to pull a sack over her head that tightened suddenly, binding her arms. No question but obedience, flickers of electrical activity in her brain charted by the bracelet. Fleeting clouds.

Then a smooth upward slope beneath her bare feet and claws, a seat surrounded by close walls. The urge to run. The necessity of running free, to be what she was made for. Each time a pinprick of thought glowed too bright for the bracelet, mind vapours doused the flame.

* * *

Helen sensed the flying drone in the corridor before she heard its low hum. 'They are searching for something. Or someone.' She met Averil's wide blue eyes.

No difficulty guessing who. Nor was Helen vain enough to believe it was herself. Yet part of her did not fear Blair's enemies, so weary had she grown. That thought stirred a strange detachment that was easy to confuse with courage.

Averil trembled, and Helen drew her closer on the bench. She wondered how her poor dead sister Mhairi would have comforted the quaking, pregnant girl. As so often, she missed Mhairi's strength badly.

'Do not run or resist,' Helen said.

She made no attempt to whisper. If the drones wanted to find and kill, perform a dance, or dismember them limb-by-limb, they would. Even if they hid in the most inaccessible part of the museum, flamethrower, poison gas, cannonade, and rockets were all options. If one method failed, the next would be attempted. Drones were thorough that way, never tired or bored, resourceful within the parameters of their functions.

A moan of terror came from the girl; Helen squeezed her hand. She had suffered enough in her short life.

'Oh, God!' cried Averil.

The hum of the aerial drone vibrated the gallery's double doors. Smoothly, handles turned. The doors opened. There it hovered, a

SIX

grotesque giant wasp with four whirling circles for wings. The red cross of Albion adorned its glittering plastisteel armour. Two arms protruded ending in pincers. Where a wasp's proboscis would have hung, pointed a stubby cannon barrel. Sensors glittered over its bulletproof body.

Helen's mouth filled with bile. The thing was scanning every inch of their bodies. A slow, unusually thorough scan for weapons, she guessed, unless it sought something else. As before, an intelligence was exploring her through the machine — a very human and intent one.

'What is it you want?' she asked.

The propellers hissed as the drone hovered.

Then the back doors of the gallery swung open, and a second drone appeared. Glancing up, Helen saw a third scratching at the skylight with its extendable pincers.

'What do you want from me? Let the girl go! She is of no interest to you.'

Where was Blair, the protector, whose power she had relied on from the first moment she arrived in Albion so many decades ago? He had abandoned her.

Whoever looked and listened through the drones did not reply. The machines advanced, scanning the room.

'What are you looking for? We have nothing of value.'

When the drones reached the display case of the Baytown Jewel, Averil gasped. She closed her eyes and buried her head in Helen's chest.

One drone halted a few feet from the women, cannon trained. Wind from its propellers stirred their hair.

Another drew close to the jewel's display case. Sensors flashed as it dissected every atom of the steel case and plastiglass cover. A beam played over the golden locket and its pure blue sapphire.

Then both machines turned sharply, faced the exits and flew back the way they'd come. The sound and vibrations of their propellers slowly faded from the museum.

'What does it mean?' croaked Averil.

Helen stroked the girl's head, still pressing her to her breast.

'Peace, child, we're safe,' she murmured. 'For now...'

* * *

She, it, they — her bracelet favoured a plain numeric for her identity — shivered in the dark prison of the plastic hood. Faecal matter trickled down her leg. Her instinct to run was growing by the second towards an imperative. The fur covering her body bristled with tension. Her velvety, floppy ears tried to rise, swivel, detect danger, but were crushed by the hood, her clawed hands clenched.

So much of her was body — cells, ligament, muscles, and blood — but not all. The aircraft shuddered, and a cloud dispersed in her mind. The bracelet noticed but could not decipher the electrical impulses crisscrossing her brain. A memory? Connection? Another aircraft in a former life with someone alongside her, someone cherished. Then it had gone. Back to cloud. The bracelet pricked, and her mind swirled peaceably.

But not for long. With a start, she was suddenly aware of new sounds, voices, an inrush of scents. Something strong yet gentle had plucked her up from her seat, a god with wheels for feet, carrying her towards coolness, the source of many scents.

Then she was on her broad, splayed feet, the thick hood pulled from her body. The bracelet opened and dropped from her wrist. Instantly, she was buffeted by a sense of self, of will.

A moment of birth. She crouched on grass still thick from summer. Her nose understood it as food, along with insects crawling in its lush

SIX

forests, her gut adapted for small amounts of animal protein along with vegetation. The breeze told stories she had yet to relearn: leaf-smells peculiar to tree and season, water, resin, other tangs. Traces of wood smoke, there, and then gone. The decaying corpse of a hedgehog, its innards picked clean by crows.

She rose to a sprint position. Her eyes blinded by lights from the towering cliff of the aircarrier. Then she saw — as she smelt, as she sensed — others of her kind. Ten, at least.

Her drove of strangelings gathered and ran, leaping, gambolling, coursing into the night. And the aircar rose, banking over ancient ruins and a steep-sided wooded valley. At its lower end, interconnecting ponds glinted in the starlight. Then it had gone, turning east for a long journey home, over the North Sea and Germany and Mitteleuropa, over the toxified, radiated birch forests of Russia, onward with its cargo of data and secrets.

SEVEN

Seth and his impromptu companion avoided main roads east out of Lancaster for fear of the Mistresses. Instead, they climbed Clougha Pike, from where a panorama of sea and land opened. Blue-topped mountains ringed the distant waters of Morecambe Bay. Closer to the great hill's foot, old remnants of buildings and a motorway, its bridges still intact, trailing vegetation amidst scrubby trees.

Seth gazed while Hurdy-Gurdy practised walking on his hands, laughing, and chuntering odd rhymes. Turning inland, Seth saw young woodland colonising a hill country kept bare in the Before Times by nibbling sheep. An ancient map belonging to Old Albert's shrimping clan had called this vast country the Forest of Bowland. It seemed the trees were returning.

The two set off, neither really knowing their destination. In that way, they were like every traveller since the dawn of life.

Autumn had a trick to play. Or perhaps it was the lingering ghost of summer. As they walked, the sky softened to a poignant blue, hazy at the edges. Sunshine warmed their faces. Ash and oak leaves drifted down like dusty gold. When the old road east took them over valley or hillcrest where the trees thinned, they saw swallows and birds of all kinds gathering for long journeys south.

'Gurdy,' Seth said as they rested, chewing the last of the oat bread from Morecambe, 'my father used to say there were far fewer birds before the Dyings.'

Hurdy-Gurdy rolled pap from cheek to cheek as he chewed. 'Young Nuncle Seth shouldn't care about the past. Not if he wants to prosper in Albion. Beautifuls hate the past so they can last and last.' He blew a sustained raspberry, spraying out wet crumbs. 'But yes' —His voice became a smooth, sophisticated purr— 'Far fewer tweeters before the plagues. Hardly any bees or other insects. Trees sick. Fish sick. Everything natural dwindling, dwindling except for people. Your father was right.'

They carried on. Seth loaded the musket with buckshot and brought down a fat pheasant. Hurdy-Gurdy used the hunting crossbow stolen from the Lord of Erringdale to bag a quail.

The light stayed golden, and leaves fell slowly through the breathless air. A corresponding lightness settled on Seth's spirit. He felt free. With the feeling came that sweet sense of hope and anticipation natural to the young, but lost to him for so long. Bitter thoughts faded. He found himself humming along when Hurdy-Gurdy broke into song.

* * *

That night they camped by a river in a wooded valley bottom. The star-speckled night as balmy as the day just gone. Seth plucked the pheasant and quail while Hurdy-Gurdy scavenged a derelict cottage for a pan. Then they lolled with backs against trees while the meat stewed, flavoured with wild garlic, herbs, mushrooms, and apples gathered from the cottage garden.

Hurdy-Gurdy sang in a pure, delicate voice at odds with his stained clothes and mud-matted hair, a sad song concerning someone who 'got by' with a little help from his friends.

'Where did you learn to sing, Gurdy?' Seth asked, not without jealousy. 'You mentioned being a holotainer, and I thought of entertainers, you know, like in the pubs or at weddings and funerals.'

Hurdy-Gurdy raised his eyes. 'I was all those things, Young Nuncle, and far more. You see, I was famous long before the plagues rotted people's flesh.'

Seth frowned. 'Before?'

'Hurdy was a star on television and web and radio even before the holocasts came. But much, much more famous after. Millions loved Hurdy-Gurdy — though he used another name then, one given to him by his dear, dear Mummy.' A sob burst from the scarecrow. 'Mumsy-wumsy! Will you help your little Declan?'

'Why were you famous?'

'Talent, darling,' replied Gurdy in a womanish voice. 'If you've got it, flaunt it!'

'What was your talent?'

'What wasn't it?'

For a long while, they were silent. Seth tasted the stew. A mess of flavours but nourishing enough.

'I'm puzzled,' he said. 'You spoke of television. I've heard of it, naturally, and seen the leftover screens. My father and uncle taught us about electronic pictures, and likewise, the holocasts that replaced them. When exactly was you born, Hurdy?'

'A vulgar question,' growled his companion. 'Make sure you never ask it in the City. Never ask a Beautiful his or her age. It reminds them they might yet be mortal.'

'We're not in the City.'

'True.' Hurdy-Gurdy sniffed. 'What if I told Nuncle Seth I was already old when the plagues began?'

'I would say you was a liar.'

'Would you?'

'Aye.'

'Then I'll whisper the year I was born. Just so the trees don't blush at my lie.'

Gurdy whispered a date.

Seth barked a scornful laugh, rapidly calculating numbers. The date was in the late 20th century. He was growing tired of the madman's games. Yet he needed to know more.

'Tell me, Gurdy, because I really should learn about the City before we get there. What is this Discordia you mentioned?'

Hurdy-Gurdy stiffened. 'La-di-da-di-do!' he sang menacingly.

'Tell me.'

'Oh dear,' the madman sang in the same dark tone, 'what can the matter be? Dear, dear, what can the matter be? Gurdy's cast out in despair.' He paced and crooned by the gurgling river:

Oh, Gurdy did sing about people most frightening,
People he should have been very much flattering.
When the fine Beautifuls chortled and laughed at them.

The song stopped. Hurdy-Gurdy tugged at his long, filthy hair.

'Then what?' asked Seth.

'Discordia,' intoned the lunatic, abruptly calm. 'They banished me from the City because I mocked their perverse desires.'

'You offended powerful people?'

To Seth, it seemed the story of his own life.

'Yes, Young Nuncle. Very powerful people. And power hates to be laughed at. Why? Because it feeds on fear. Otherwise, there is no power.'

'Who did this to you?'

At first, Seth thought he would get no reply. The former holotainer stirred.

'A man and a woman. Gurdy worked for them long before the plagues. Why, I helped them grow rich, helped them grow powerful. Hurdy thought them his friends. Gurdy was not always a nice Hurdy. La-di-da-di-do!'

Though Seth asked more questions, none were answered. They ate their chewy quail and pheasant stew and slept in the warm darkness.

* * *

Clearing out created spaces, and some spirits refused to settle for civilization's stale crumbs. Seth was reminded of this as they approached Skipton between the Dales and West Riding, a market town long before machines dominated mankind, and afterwards, it would seem.

A dozen stalls in the old High Street were overseen by officials from a recently established town council affiliated to the Commonwealth of the North. To Seth, it was a bustling wonder of a place after four years spent at remote Fell Grange: two busy inns, a baker, butcher, cobbler, and draper, as well as two smithies forging guns and horseshoes.

At the sight of so many people gathered to buy, sell, or gawp, Hurdy-Gurdy cried out: 'An audience! Now, Little Nuncle Seth, I take it the word manager is familiar to you?'

'Aye.'

'They were mostly a species of parasite.'

'Like fleas?'

'Very good. Or tapeworms.'

'Not sure I'm with you, Gurdy.'

'You shall take off your hat while I do all the work. Yes, like so. Then, what we call punters will fill it with good things. You will purloin as much of these profits as you can. This is called business and free enterprise.'

Amidst a crowd of farmers, shepherds, and jacks-of-all-trades, Hurdy-Gurdy commenced a show. In the unnatural heat, he stripped to reveal a torso ribbed with muscle. First, he tumbled, walking on one hand, then he used volunteers from the audience as platforms to step nimbly from shoulder to shoulder. Next, he sang a series of ballads, borrowing a guitar from a busker, his skill humbling to behold.

As a finale, he performed a one-man play in which he acted many parts — king and murderer, and murderer's wicked wife, witches and good men who restored justice and order, a walking wood and a ghostly dagger. Seth recognised it as one of the dull plays Father and Uncle Michael forced him to read, Macbeth. Yet Hurdy made it interesting somehow. That set Seth to wonder if it might have been all along.

The folk of Skipton rewarded Gurdy with food and coins bearing the Council of the North's symbols, sufficient to purchase meat and ale in the Cock and Bottle. There, Hurdy-Gurdy earned more glory by calling for any musical instrument available. Trumpet, fiddle, recorder, tambourine. Seth marvelled at what he did with them. All produced some kind of song.

'Collect! Collect!' the madman urged Seth, dripping with sweat from his labours. 'I've had your kind of lazy agent before.'

They gathered a large pile of needful supplies at Skipton Market, not least a wheezing concertina, which the former holotainer set about to repair.

'How did you learn so much?' Seth marvelled during a break for refreshments. 'It seems there's nothing you cannot attempt.'

'In the City, much time needs much filling. Some use it well, perhaps out of guilt, while others allow their conscience to turn rancid and rot away.'

'Is that what you did in the City?'

'My, we *are* curious. Well then, let it be known, I did set myself a little mission to while away eternity. Forsooth, to keep alive the name of the eternal Bard. Aye, sirrah! I set up my own company, and as decent human actors were few and far between, I used drones to play many parts. That's what did it for me in the end.'

He leaned forward conspiratorially. Seth recoiled at his breath.

'I staged Titus Andronicus with the heads of certain important people projected on the drones. The pie I fed them in the role of Titus was filled with meat they would rather not have discussed in public. Alas, they did not find it amusing.'

Seth's expression went blank, and he shook his head. 'I don't get it.'

A mournful look crossed Hurdy-Gurdy's face. 'Discordia! That was the critics' verdict. Now fetch me some beer. Oh, and a large wedge of pie.'

* * *

As darkness fell, Seth settled in a corner of the inn, sleepy with meat and drink. Logs smouldered in the hearth. A few rechargeable power cells fuelled electric lamps. Hurdy-Gurdy had withdrawn to what he called 'the green room', a ruined shop at the back of the market where they intended to pass the night.

Before Seth could join him, a grating racket started up outside. Whispering and nervous glances through the window were followed by a rush of folk into the street. Draining his glass, Seth picked up his belongings and followed them out.

A strange sight; a strange smell, too. Sight, sound, and smell provoked one emotion in him and in many others — sheer, unashamed fear.

A motor car advanced slowly down the High Street. Its wheels from before the plagues, likewise much of its chassis, although a wooden frame of recent manufacture played some role in holding it together. None of that was forbidden by the City. Not so its means of locomotion.

A combustion engine had been devised from old car parts, spewing oily black clouds of smoke through a vertical pipe. A small barrel of liquid fuel brewed from plant oils fed the engine.

Its drivers perched on seats salvaged from a school bus guided the vehicle with a long tiller attached to a single wheel at the front. Both its operators were young and excited.

'See!' cried one, waving his hat. 'Freedom!'

'Fuck the City!' shouted his companion.

A ragged cheer rose. Seth sensed this was not the first time forbidden technology had been paraded in Skipton. He mastered a desire to run, staring into the darkness for an inevitable drone. Nothing glittered aloft save stars.

Then a commotion halted the ramshackle vehicle. A small group in old flogger robes stepped into its path, cursing and bellowing.

'You'll all burn for this!' cried their leader. 'The City'll make this town burn good!'

Angry voices replied, and fists shook. A brawl seemed likely, one that could not end well for the floggers.

'The City are devils,' shouted the driver of the vehicle. 'Mankind must rise again!'

Seth had heard enough. Best to find Hurdy-Gurdy and be gone. Did he not wish to serve the City, after all? As he turned, a hand gripped his arm. He wheeled.

The man, a former flogger if his robe was any guide, looked vaguely familiar. Since floggers were outlawed by the Commonwealth of the North, his kind had sought many ways to survive. This one and his companions traded in salvaged pots and valuables from the old times. Scavenger-tinkers, the lowest breed of merchant, forever on the road. And perfect spies.

'I know you,' the man said. 'Or who you was. Big Jacko's botty boy, that's who you was.' He laughed harshly, glancing over to his comrades for assistance. They were still arguing with the drivers of the motorcar.

Seth backed off, wishing his palms would stop sweating, that for once he could appear fierce. Drawing from his belt the pistol stolen in

Morecambe, he cocked and pointed it at the man's gut. 'Fuck off.'

Obligingly, the mangy flogger backed away. 'Seth Pilgrim's your name. I saw you back then, and I see you right plain now.'

With that, he joined his pals, currently surrounded by town constables with spiked clubs and firearms. They were being encouraged to gather their unsold goods and bugger off from Skipton.

As the flogger pointed at Seth, he and his companions muttered among themselves. Word of this sighting would fly as sure as migrating geese to Gil at Fell Grange – and that meant to the Mistresses. The mere thought of Maister Gil sent Seth hurrying off into the crowd.

EIGHT

One man bore a stout, freshly cut pine staff. The second cast his away as it was too heavy. One was tall, broad, steady in his pace; the other slender, unused to sustained walking. One looking around to read a new country; his companion staring down, frightened by vast horizons.

Low clouds flowed across the Highlands. To their left, miles of sea loch. When the clouds parted, ruffled water shone dull silver. Gulls hung in the wind.

The two men, Pilgrim and Gover, followed a pitted, tarmac highway invaded by tree roots, worn bare in places by streams tasting of peat and iron. An abundance of water and a mild autumn encouraged summer midges to linger. Gover complained bitterly about their deprivations.

Early in their journey, Michael realised that the City-man, for all his outward grace and beauty, lacked essential muscles for prolonged walking. In this wilderness, his superiority was challenged. Without toys, Gover became less than one's equal. Yet it gave Michael small pleasure.

'You know' —He watched his companion gulp the last energy tab from their medkits— 'I reckon you see half what I see. Did you spot yon hawk?' Gover sullenly followed his finger. 'Or that fox over there?'

'Your point, Pilgrim?'

'Imagine they were hairy Jocks who didn't care for us trespassing.'

Gover sniffed. 'What we see, as you term it, is merely an act of filtering. We choose to see what we consider important. Naturally, for a creature on your level, it is little more than flora and fauna.'

'No man is above the world, Gover. Or nature. Wasn't that the mistake our forebears made that led to the Dyings? Do try to step out, man. And open your eyes. For both our sakes.'

They camped in a house set back from the road. Michael looked up from the fire he had built using rotten floorboards. He was hardening the sharpened tip of his staff in the embers to make a crude spear. Gover huddled miserably, hugging his knees, reminding Michael of a child.

'Your whining is pissing me off, Gover. But I'm trying to make allowances.'

'Spare me your self-proclaimed virtues, please. Just count yourself lucky I chose to save you. Yet I suppose gratitude is out of the question.'

With a flourish of defiance, the City-man whipped out a ration bar from their dwindling stock.

'You'll miss that when your belly is hollow,' Michael said. 'Don't expect any of my share.'

Gover hesitated then replaced the protein bar in his pocket.

'We'll keep watch in turns,' Michael said. 'I noticed a flicker of light a few miles to the south. Best be careful.'

He knew Gover would fall asleep during his watch. There seemed no help for it.

Michael insisted they depart with first day-glimmer. Soon the sea lay behind, and the road climbed gradually past strips of crudely ploughed fields. A ditch and earthen wall surrounded a farmhouse from which smoke rose as they hurried past. Michael didn't like the look of the animal skulls on poles.

After that, the way steepened, and traces of humanity grew rare.

EIGHT

Shadows of clouds drifted across crag and mountain slope. Wind skirled through rock formations bearded with moss.

Towards mid-afternoon, footsore and weary, Michael noticed an aircraft hovering over a distant glen. He couldn't be sure it was the same one they had evaded by the loch. Gover was too exhausted to care; he slumped onto the wet ground.

Nearby spread a peat-stained pond and a wood of hazel and beech. The hulk of a rusty old truck offered some shelter.

'We'll stop early today and forage,' Michael said, indicating the wood. 'Plenty of nuts this time of year. Food will be scarce once we're deeper in the mountains.'

For two hours he loaded his satchel with beech and hazelnuts. Mushrooms he ignored for fear of poisonous varieties in a strange land. Crab apples, plantains, and wizened elderberries went into the bag.

When he returned, Michael found Gover asleep against a tree. Yet he had an odd sense the City-man had been up to something.

That night they sheltered in the cab of the truck and risked a small fire. Over berries and nuts roasted on a wheel hub, Michael asked, 'Who are your enemies, Gover? They went to a great deal of trouble to kill you. And in such a way as could be passed off as an accident. That suggests to me they are not entirely secure.'

The latter chewed moodily. 'You wouldn't understand.'

'Try me.'

Gover spat out a husk of beechnut in disgust. 'More important right now are my friends.' He poked the campfire with a stick, and sparks rose. 'Those fools who tried to murder me — yes, murder — a genius who has already changed the course of human history once. Those fools will find Blair Gover has powerful admirers and friends. Then they will squeal.'

Michael looked askance at his companion. 'Where exactly are these powerful pals? I don't see them.'

Gover's pale face caught a glimmer of firelight. 'Rely on it, Pilgrim, they will be working day and night on my behalf.'

A heavy shower started, dousing their only source of warmth. Michael lay down in the bare, seatless cab of the truck, bunking with beetles, cobwebs and old birds' nests. That night he heard a faint howl of feral dogs, or dreamt he had.

* * *

Soon mountains and peaks surrounded them. The road climbed a misty pass where hardy thorn trees, pine, and fern battled with heather for life. No longer cleared or burned, the heather grew three or four feet high, pierced through by saplings. Drizzle fell. White water tumbled over stony beds.

'Look!' murmured Michael, grasping Gover's arm and pointing. They had halted on a low stone bridge across a gurgling stream.

On the hillside was a herd of deer. Lording over its harem, a huge stag, antlers outspread like oaken branches, breath steaming. Michael remembered a framed oil painting back in Hob Hall, a favourite of his grandfather's, because it reminded the old man of walking holidays before the plagues forever ended holidays.

Old Reverend Pilgrim's voice echoed in his mind, explaining the magnificent, muscled creature depicted beneath layers of darkening varnish. Michael had worshipped his grandfather as a lad.

The Monarch of the Glen, Michael, the ghost-voice said. *That stag would lay down its life to preserve its kith and kind. So must all good men help one another, never forget that! Are we to be no better than beasts?*

The stag paced and tossed back its head. It snorted, sniffed, stared down at the two travellers on the bridge. Michael thought of the responsibilities thrust upon him by those eager for a leader: Protector of the North, an excellent title for a man struggling to protect even himself. How like this stag he was, strong enough to challenge wolf or bear and most likely perish doing so, but not to secure real safety for his people.

'We are wasting time here, Pilgrim. Chop! Chop!'

Michael ignored the peevish voice. Through wind, brook, trees stirring, he detected an entirely alien sound. 'Down!' he cried. 'Down!'

With that, he hauled Gover off the road. They cowered in the low dark aperture beneath the stone bridge, just in time.

An airbike swooped over the brow of the hill, a type he last saw in the Crusades, piloted then by Captain Eloise Du Guesclin. It was designed to resemble a flying horse, an air-steed, except that instead of wings, it bore two hissing, chuntering propellers in a protective mesh. Its pilot sat on the machine, one leg to each side, as a horseman occupies a saddle. On his head, a grey helmet capped with a pair of antlers trailing blood-red ribbons. A large wire basket occupied the rear of the machine.

The herd of deer scattered, flowing downhill towards the bridge where the two men hid. The airbike dove toward them, closing in on the bounding, leaping stag.

'Stay low!' Michael urged Gover.

Yet he peered out all the same, his attention drawn to something behind the pilot. Slung across the back seat was a human being of indeterminate gender, his or her hands and feet bound with manacles that Michael remembered from the Crusades. A prisoner then, trussed and strapped.

The pilot produced a crossbow with a vertical magazine of bolts. Revving his machine, he circled the stag, releasing dart after dart, the crossbow reloading itself. His aim was poor, yet so many missiles could hardly miss. One pierced the fleeing animal's back thigh, a deep wound. It rolled, staggering up to find the airbike above its head, the pilot fitting a new magazine into his crossbow. The relentless rain of bolts recommenced until a dozen protruded from the splendid beast's body and neck. It collapsed, bleeding, panting.

Further up the valley, the rest of the herd halted. Watched for a moment, tails ticking nervously. Then streamed into the trees beyond sight.

* * *

A scant hundred feet lay between the men under the bridge and the stricken stag higher up the hill. Still, the drizzle fell.

The pilot landed his air-steed a little way from the twitching deer. Propellers slowed then stopped. A stony silence settled on the glen.

From a canopy of acrid-smelling ferns, Michael watched. His sharp eyes took in the sword, hanging at the man's side. Like all City folk, he was smooth cheeked and apparently youthful. The helpless figure draped over the back seat of the machine was clearly visible now. A young woman in her prime, hair bedraggled by the drizzle, seemingly drugged. Then Michael understood why she had been taken, and his gut lurched. A reckless, grim resolve hardened.

The pilot fumbled for a flask. With awkward gloved fingers, he removed the stopper and gulped. Was he drunk? His use of the automatic crossbow had been erratic.

Michael drew out the razor-sharp, three-inch knife, part of the multi-tool from the gravchute's survival kit. He indicated to Gover to remain hidden in the culvert. Gover shook his head frantically. It occurred to Michael here was a golden opportunity for his reluctant companion to seek aid from a fellow Beautiful. What fear held him back? Perhaps the pilot was one of the enemies Gover claimed would squeal.

The man looked their way, searching the valley. In the deep shadow of the bridge, Michael froze. Was there a listening device in the City-man's helmet? Had it picked up their breathing? Heartbeats?

The stream splashed, muttered. Wind sighed through the thorn trees. Reassured, the pilot approached his kill.

Michael slid on his belly into dense bracken and ferns covering the slopes. No drone was present to save the lone City-man from being relieved of armour, weapons, sword, flying machine. No drone to prevent him from freeing the young hostage.

He crept forward. The pilot had drawn his sword — an officer's sword from the Crusades engineered to dice flesh. Michael had possessed such a sword once at the cost of half his happiness.

With a grunt, the pilot hacked the stag's neck, warm blood spurting on his green plastic clothes. Again Michael's eyes narrowed. The stag's head was not so heavy as to warrant the way the man's wobble and gasp upon lifting it. He crawled closer.

The City-man coughed, clutching his side. He's sick, realised Michael, and it puzzled him. A sick Beautiful? Could such a thing be? Alone out here instead of taking cures surely available in Albion.

Back at the air-steed with the stag's head, the hunter pressed a switch on the rear basket. It flipped open.

Later, Michael realised the basket saved the man's life. Or more probably his own. He'd been poised to leap up and charge the man, hopeful of getting the knife in before the pilot could draw his sword.

But the basket contained something unforeseen. A collection of shaggy-haired human heads — Jock heads ready for a taxidermist drone to clean, stuff, and mount for display. The pilot heaved in the magnificent stag's head to join them.

The man turned, suspicious again. His hand crept to a small pistol Michael had not noticed earlier. Even as he prepared to leap, knife in hand, panic flooded Michael's body with adrenalin. But the moment had passed for a successful ambush. He sank deep into the bracken and lay very still. His luck held.

The City-man stared in the wrong direction, hand on the butt of his gun. He struggled onto his airbike and its propellers whined to life. The machine rose and darted in the same direction as the fleeing herd, its chunter fading slowly.

Michael Pilgrim hung his head in despair. Yet again, he had failed. The young woman was lost. Tears of helpless rage filled his eyes.

* * *

Back at the culvert, Gover glared. 'What madness gripped you, Pilgrim? I fear the savage in you took over. The natural murderer in you.'

Michael met Blair Gover's eye. 'Yon City man is the murderer.'

'Nonsense,' Gover snorted.

'There was a basket of human heads on his flying machine. And he has abducted a young lass for purposes I don't care to consider.'

Gover dismissed the revelation with an impatient tut. 'We must be gone.'

'Not so quickly,' Michael said. 'Why didn't you ask for his help? Or warn him?'

'Those questions do not concern you.'

'They do.'

Gover glanced at the knife still in Michael's hand.

'Very well. It is useful for my enemies to think I am dead. Though they cannot be quite sure, of course, without my body. Happy now?'

'I don't understand.'

'Of course not. Now we must be gone.'

But Michael had other intentions. He tied the headless stag's legs and devised a lash-up sledge of branches. Meanwhile, he instructed Gover to collect every single crossbow bolt sprayed out by the pilot.

Together they dragged the carcase to a small quarry overgrown with ash trees beside a handy burn, half a mile back along the road. A spot secluded from aerial eyes.

Stripping off his shirt, Michael spent the afternoon butchering and roasting meat on skewers of crossbow bolts. Some of it they devoured, but much was wrapped in leaves then tied into parcels with stalks of thick grass.

As Michael's knife worked, the young hostage haunted him. Her long hair reminded him of Averil's. Surely the pilot had a base, he reasoned. If he could only find it...

'Why do you City-folk hunt your own kind?' he asked Gover. 'You're worse than cannibals. At least they seek sustenance to live.'

Gover glanced up from his meat. Fat glistened on his chin. 'That hunter was seeking sustenance.'

'How so?'

'Not all sustenance is of the body, Pilgrim, strange as that must seem to you. Some is required to maintain a noble spirit. For Beautifuls, this wilderness is a test of strength, ingenuity. One's skill and wit versus nature.'

'A very one-sided contest.'

'Perhaps so.' Gover's brittle manner softened. 'Remember, you are accustomed to constant danger. You have evolved without higher feelings unless you mimic them. Brutish nature is where you belong, along with all other lower forms of life.'

'So?'

'For a Beautiful the very opposite is true. Imagine if you seldom went into natural places without drones. Imagine the thrill of dabbling in a savage land. One can hardly blame someone for staving off boredom in such a noble manner.'

'Would this noble soul have a base up here?' Michael asked. 'A camp?'

'Probably, though please do not harbour any illusions of raiding it and setting that woman free. His camp could be anywhere. And it will be well defended.'

Michael pondered this information. 'From now on, we travel only at night,' he said after a moment. 'It's a clear enough road for that, even in the dark. I wouldn't wish to be captured by your trigger-happy pal.'

For once Blair Gover was in agreement.

Michael said no more, intent on preserving as much meat as possible. Then he stripped and bathed in the nearby stream until it ran red.

He returned to their camp, shivering as the cold wind dried his bare torso. Gover eyed his numerous scars.

'Have you ever gone hunting?' Michael asked him. 'Tested yourself in the way you praised?'

For a long moment, no reply.

'Oh no, Pilgrim.'

NINE

'Bye then, Esther! Go careful, Ryan!'

Averil Pilgrim closed the door of the Museum as the last child ran out into the overgrown car park, kicking piles of leaves, stooping for stray horse chestnuts to fatten the family pig. Her encouraging smile faded.

Smiling came easy before an adoring class. The little girls, in particular, loved Miss Pilgrim, patient and bright and kind even when screaming on the inside. That morning, she'd had another row with Amar. A terrible one, though Averil didn't understand precisely how it started.

'I don't love you no more!' she'd sobbed, her ultimate attack, the one releasing his own tears.

With her pupils gone, she asked herself if it was true. Did she really not love her husband anymore? It felt so. Often she would recall Seth saying his life was a prison and realise that she, too, longed for escape; that the urge to pluck up her roots had grown steadily ever since Father's death; that she would never be satisfied by Baytown, her life withering at the stem.

Meanwhile, the baby in her womb grew. At her bleakest, she didn't doubt it was crippled or deformed, too weak to live like all the others.

'There you are, Averil.'

She turned to find Helen holding a full teapot, one of the museum's artefacts. The corners of Averil's mouth rose obediently. Then she pointed behind Helen's back, drew a breath, and screamed.

* * *

A hologram was shaping, light expanding. Helen followed Averil's pointing finger and dropped the teapot. It broke into shards and a pool of steaming liquid.

Soon the hologram was complete — a vivid, life-size image. A man and woman on slender rattan chairs before an open window, framed by emerald-capped peaks and a flawless blue sky.

Averil shrank back. The couple were from the City — any fool could see that. The perfect regularity of their features, their room's shiny elegance, and the loveliness of the country where they dwelt. Bright clothes of many colours decorated with delicate, filigree jewellery. Unlike the other Beautifuls she had encountered, the couple were not young. Frost touched the man's smooth, distinguished hair. Likewise, the lady's coiled coiffure. Their maturity reassured Averil; also, the way they held one another's hand.

The man turned to the woman, surely his wife. 'I did warn you, darling, simply appearing like this would be rude and inconvenient for Helen. Look, she has dropped that teapot.'

Helen's mouth hung open.

'Perhaps you're right,' said his wife.

'Merle!' said Helen. 'Marvin. What on earth?'

'Do forgive the intrusion, darling,' Merle said. 'Shockingly bad manners, I know. But we're afraid something has happened to Blair.'

Averil felt a premonition of disaster. Fantasies featuring the handsome Dr Blair Gover were a favourite antidote to the pettiness of her life.

'He has vanished,' Marvin said, 'and at a most inconvenient time. I

NINE

take it he mentioned the upcoming Grand Autonomy?'

Helen hesitated for so long that Averil wondered what on earth could be the matter.

'Well, it's hardly a secret,' Marvin said. 'If his notion is to gain traction — and I do believe it to be sound, ambitious, but sound — he must work much harder with his friends to prepare the ground. He really cannot do this by himself. And we have only four weeks before the Autonomy.'

'It really is so typically Blair,' Merle complained. 'Drama! Intrigue! Never a dull moment. I suppose that's why we love him. Not that his opponents on the Council are pussycats, as you know very well, Helen. But Blair must involve his allies.'

'Hear, hear,' Marvin said.

'What do you want from me?' Helen asked.

Averil could tell she knew the couple well and respected them in her cautious, guarded way. Helen never pretended when it came to people.

'He told us he would visit you,' said Merle. 'After that, he went silent.'

'Then I know no more than you,' said Helen. 'Just that he flew off somewhere strange.'

'Greenland?' said Marvin with a chuckle. 'I understand he built himself a little cave up there.'

'Now, now,' Merle said. 'Discretion, darling!'

'Of course.'

Averil listened as Helen explained Blair Gover's strange, tilth-eating drones. How he flew off with Uncle Michael.

'The girl beside me is Michael Pilgrim's niece,' said Helen.

Averil crimsoned and curtsied.

Next Helen described the flying drones that scoured Baytown and the museum a few days earlier. This news made Marvin and Merle exchange troubled looks.

'That, I do not like,' Merle said. 'I shall make enquiries; indeed, I shall. Does Blair know of it?'

'It happened after he left,' Helen said.

'Of course, forgive me. Do let us know if he contacts you.'

'How? I have no screen.'

Merle laughed then realised Helen was serious. 'Goodness! How do you manage? Blair told me you were enjoying *la vie sauvage*, but there are limits.'

'You'd be surprised how well one can live without a screen,' replied Helen.

Averil understood the Beautiful-lady's disapproval. Why would one not wish to benefit from City marvels?

'Farewell, Helen, a means of reaching us shall be provided,' said Marvin. He coughed delicately. 'Not one of those unpleasant screens, naturally.'

'Farewell, my dear,' said Merle. 'Do tell Blair to be more considerate of his friends.'

The hologram shrank inward and vanished.

* * *

True to Marvin's word, a drone landed outside the museum in the late afternoon with a small box wrapped in scented tissue paper and pink ribbons. Averil was with Helen to avoid Amar and witnessed the former City-woman's amusement. The box contained a toy violin with a note: "Pluck each string once, and your friends will hear."

'Who are Marvin and Merle?' asked Averil.

They seemed so different from Uncle Michael's version of City folk: not a hint of cruelty or condescension.

Helen put down the toy. 'Marvin and Merle Brubacher are among the founders of the Five Cities.'

NINE

'They're nice!'

'Apparently.'

'They obviously like you.'

'Yes.' Helen hesitated, then added, 'Averil, I'm concerned you're quarrelling too often with Amar. He's a kind and good man. He has proven his loyalty to you and your family a hundred times over.'

'Are you suggesting I should be grateful he married me?'

'No, although one could consider gratitude a form of love.'

'I am not grateful to live with Amar in Baytown,' Averil said. 'My father hated it here, too, that's why he prayed and prayed all his life. To shut out this horrible world. He longed to go to heaven and join my mother. Why shouldn't I want more than Baytown? Or Amar?'

Helen's expression was grave.

'I'm not like my Uncle Michael, who you so admire. He would die for this place and its people.' Averil met Helen's eye. 'He longs to be like his grandfather. The hero everyone loves.'

Averil felt ashamed of her honesty. Glad, as well. 'May I stay here tonight?' she asked, her voice softening.

Helen sat beside her and patted her hand.

'Of course you may. Just remember your sunny nature, Averil. It's a wonderful part of you. Time will put recent misfortunes in perspective.'

Averil slept on a worn sofa. Her dreams dark and shifting. First the cliff at Ravenscar. Father and Uncle Michael, Amar there, too. The men were clinging with desperate fingertips to the cliff edge, begging for her help. Averil, safe on the brink, impassively watched them struggle. One by one, they lost their grip, tumbling down onto pitiless rocks. Waves rushed in. They were gone.

Then she dreamt of Hob Hall. The big, well-kept house, full of horse and cow manure, heaps in every room and corridor, its occupants squabbling about who should clean it up. A drone appeared, magically sucking away the dirt. Everyone praised Averil though she hated them for exposing her baby, every last Jack and Jill of them.

On the other side of the room, Helen snored softly in her bed.

Neither of the two women noticed the hologram opening until it was fully formed. Once again, Marvin sat on a rattan chair before the large window with its splendid view. This time his hair was tousled. His high cheek-boned face wore a look of alarm.

* * *

'Wake up! You must wake up!'

Averil opened her eyes, shrieked. She leapt out of bed, shook Helen from sleep.

Shielding her eyes, she peered into a glaring, three-dimensional image. Marvin Brubacher wore an ankle-length dressing-gown of dazzling silks. Although midnight was dark and cold in Baytown, a rosy dawn-glow spilt from his faraway room, along with the chatter of strange bird and animal cries. His amplified voice boomed.

'You must watch this urgently, Helen. I have this very moment received it.'

A second hologram opened up beside him, projected from his handheld screen. Fuzzy, wavering, it showed Blair Gover. There seemed to be a forest in the background, too blurred for Averil to be sure. 'My good friends,' Blair said, 'tell Helen she must join you at once. She must leave Baytown. It is no longer a safe place for her. Do not delay.' Then the indistinct holo-image faded.

'I have sent a transport to fetch you, my dear,' said Marvin. 'We enquired about the drones that came to your home. So far, it is impossible to trace who sent them, a fact of great suspicion. I fear it confirms Blair's warning. We may assume you had a lucky escape.'

Helen shook her head to clear it.

NINE

'This is so sudden, Marvin. What do I have to do with any of this?'

'We must heed Blair's warning. If anything happened to you, I would hold myself responsible. Where can an aircarrier land unseen? We must be discreet.'

Averil spoke up. 'I know, sir! Give us two hours. I can get Miss Devereux packed and to somewhere no one will notice her go.'

Helen listened as Averil outlined a route.

'Very well,' said Marvin, 'we will do as this girl suggests.'

Instantly the hologram contracted and closed.

* * *

Two women hurried through the darkness on this cloudy, moonless night, buffeted by a cold breeze blowing in from the sea. They wore thick woollen cloaks wrapped around their shoulders. The younger of the two bore a bag and a rechargeable torch to help them pick their way along the overgrown, disused railway line south of Baytown. The older one was nearly breathless, clutching a heavy, double-barrelled pistol, keeping a wary eye on the murky sky. She reached beneath her cloak to touch a solid gold locket bearing a single blue sapphire, a treasure taken at the very last moment: the Baytown Jewel.

They passed the burned-out shell of a hotel above the cliffs of Ravenscar, past houses with caved-in roofs. A fox barked as they crossed ground torn open by the sharp tusks of rooting wild boar.

'Nearly there!' said Averil. 'We'll be just in time.'

They reached a steep, furze-clad slope leading down to the stony beach. The tide was out, as Averil knew it would be.

'Last bit,' she urged.

A slow progress through brambles and thorns. At last, gasping for air, they scrambled down a ten-foot bank of friable, gritty soil exposed by last spring's high tides, their boots mired in shingle. It was then they became fully aware of the sea: its complex scents, the slow, repetitive roar of breakers coming in fast.

'Tide's a-turning,' said Averil. 'The torch? Shall I?'

Helen nodded. A glimmer blinked on and off from the beach. Any fisherman out at sea would have struggled to spot it.

'It's coming!' said Averil.

The two women clutched each other. Faint rumbling, engines muffled as a medium-sized aircarrier drifted low over the waves towards them. Shaped like a bird's beak with protruding wings, it sighed, hovering over the beach. Then it landed, still thrumming. A door opened to form a walkway.

'Thank you, dear Averil,' cried Helen. 'I will return as soon as I can. Keep the school open until then.' She hefted the bag and stepped boldly onto the ramp. At the top, there was a rush of light footsteps.

'Nay, I must see you settled! Then I'll go.' Averil pushed past Helen into the aircarrier.

'Go, Averil, you must go right now!' said Helen.

But it was too late. The ramp rose and clicked shut. A mild hiss joined the whine of revving engines. Moments later, both women sank unconscious to the floor.

TEN

The road was dark. Rain tumbled from thick layers of cloud. The travellers' only light came from torches set to a glimmer. Michael Pilgrim insisted on caution, and Gover, afraid of the vast gloom, stuck close to his heels.

Their road traced the shore of a loch. Tree shapes etched black lines across the darkness. Occasional night creatures cried or screeched, not least hunting owls.

Michael did not care for their situation, even when the rain ceased. Not only were they hemmed in by the loch to their left, but the City-hunter must have night vision facilities on his helmet. As for other watchers, natives of the Highlands, he chose not to speculate.

In the end, they walked right up to trouble. Faint in the darkness, a flickering fire. Michael sniffed: wood smoke, perhaps something else. Should they hide? Wait until morning? He sensed an opportunity.

'Let's see what's to see,' he said quietly. 'Keep your torch off and your knife handy. Remember what I told you. Always stab upward not down.'

Crude spear ready, Michael led the way, moving in light shuffles over the uneven ground. Turning a corner of spruce, a strange scene was lit by the guttering blaze of a bonfire alongside the lapping waters of the loch.

He crouched, stared.

Six or seven wild-haired men in skirts gathered around the scattered remains of the hunter's air bike. It must have hit the ground hard, wildly out of control, burying its nose in the mud. Its chassis had broken into several pieces; the propellers and their protective mesh were bent, twisted. Of its pilot, no trace.

Gover whispered excitedly in Michael's ear. 'We must drive them off, Pilgrim. I must have his screen.'

Michael watched the men. Spears thrust in the ground and what looked like quivers on their backs. So they were hunters then. The irony did not escape him.

'If those Jocks have his pistol and crossbow,' he murmured. 'We won't last long.'

'Neither device will work,' said Gover. 'They are coded to their user. But if I had his screen...'

He let possibilities dangle. Any magic was possible when Gover had a screen.

'Too many to fight,' whispered Michael. 'We need another way.'

'Leave these wretched scum to me.' Gover held out an impatient hand. 'Your torch.'

Michael warily handed it over. Gover produced the peculiar earpiece that came with his gravchute's survival kit and one of the power cells from the same source, which he connected to the earpiece with a thin cable.

'We need to be as close to them as possible,' Gover said.

Before Michael could restrain him, the City-man moved forward.

They flitted tree to tree. Gover paused only to stuff his ears with moss. By now the hunters' voices were audible, muttering over their booty. Several were bold enough to wear items of the pilot's clothes, including the antler-crested helmet. One waved a scavenged pistol, pulling the trigger uselessly.

Michael spotted a naked, maggot-white corpse by the bonfire. Then he guessed the purpose of the blaze. Burn the flying devil's body so he could not return from the underworld to haunt them.

Closer, closer until twenty yards from the crash. Now Gover rose, pointing the two torches. The searing incandescence of a searchlight poured from each torch, visible for miles. At the same time, a voice boomed from a loudspeaker in the earpiece, fuelled by the extra power cell.

Go! Go! Or die!

Michael reeled at the buffet of sound. The night's silence doubled its intensity.

Paralysed by the two burning, blinding eyes that bleached every inch of their bodies with light, the hunters fled into the darkness, pursued by Gover's voice, booming and echoing over loch and hillside.

Go! Go! Or die!

* * *

A whirlwind of fireflies danced behind Michael's eyes, his eardrums hissing and buzzing. He drew his knife and advanced. Now was the time, he thought, before the Jocks regrouped. Then the skies opened up.

Blinking back the rain, he scanned the ground for the crossbow in case it had been discarded. The expansive circle of debris from the crash suggested it could be anywhere. Picking through the wreckage, he came upon a second body and lowered his knife.

No longer strapped to the back of the airbike, the young woman lay twisted, arms and legs bound by plastisteel cuffs. Michael knelt beside her. Felt for signs of life. Her face was undamaged, but her body was a shattered mess. Beads of rain pooled on beautiful green eyes staring into the darkness. Michael passed his trembling hands over the woman's face and closed her eyes. Furious at the waste of the poor woman's life, Michael's own darkness swelled into a firm resolve: The Five Cities must not endure! If it cost his very life, they must not endure!

Gover frantically sifted through the shattered airbike, searching for the dead hunter's screen. His curses and low moans rose to a cry of despair. 'Those savages must have it! They stripped him of all his clothes, after all. I saw one wearing his coat, where the screen would be kept. Those animals!'

Michael stepped over human heads spilling from the trophy basket at the back of the airbike. Nearby lolled the head of the magnificent stag, antlers snapped by the violence of the crash. He stooped to pick up the empty scabbard of the City-man's sword. This pleased him least of all.

Assembling the clues of what had happened, Michael guessed the hunter must have been returning to his camp when something forced his machine to nose dive into the ground. But what brought him down? A missile? Not from the folk of the mountains, that was for sure. A terrible failure of the airbike? Unlikely. He recalled the City-man staggering and drinking from a flask. He had seemed very sick. Perhaps he fainted or died before crashing.

Michael approached the corpse by the bonfire.

'Bring over your light, Gover. Keep the beam low.'

Still cursing, the City-man handed Michael one of the torches. 'What infernal luck! Could those troglodytes not even leave me his screen? What is it to them, after all? To me, it is a doorway, a flying carpet, the keys to every library in the world. An oracle, a counsellor, wiser than any friend. It is—'

'Shut up. Look here.' Michael pointed the torch at the pale body in the mud. Not a handsome prospect, for all the care its owner had lavished on it to remain young forever. Stripped of all finery, quite bare, he appeared like any other man, though sleeker, fitter, comelier,

TEN

it was true.

Michael recalled lines of Shakespeare his grandfather sometimes quoted, upon discovering a particularly impressive nest of skeletons or when plagues revisited Baytown to render fresh victims. "Thou art the thing itself: unaccommodated man...a poor, bare, forked animal." He did not speak the words aloud as Grandfather would have done, taking comfort in their resonance and depth. Gover seemed immune to compassion and wisdom.

'What happened to him?' Michael asked, waving the torch at the body.

The state of the corpse could not be explained by the crash. One foot was shrivelled into a claw. The left ear was missing entirely, replaced by what looked like a nub of flesh. There were odd bumps on all over the body, denoting strange growths beneath the skin, perhaps misplaced organs, or grotesque tumours. No wonder the Jocks wanted to burn such a manifest devil.

Gover examined the dead man, inch by inch. When he looked up, Michael had never seen him so shaken.

'It has begun,' Gover stammered.

'What has?'

'I told them. The fools!'

'What has begun?'

Gover shivered. 'His own genes did this to him. I told them! It was always a possibility.'

'I don't—'

'Can't you see, Pilgrim? The treatment that kept him young by renewing his cells, the elixir that I and a few others perfected, has been corrupted. It is turning into its opposite.'

But Michael did not see. What he did see, however, launched a hope unanticipated in this cold, bleak land. As the beam of his torch swept the loch, he noticed something the Jocks would have surely found at daybreak. But Fate had other notions. The Lady of the Lake had left him a boon.

Michael waded out through the freezing shallows. In the mud was embedded the impossibly strong and sharp sword the hunter had used to decapitate the stag. Gasping with emotion, he pulled it free. He hefted the weapon and held it up, displaying it to the broken body of the young woman on the shore. Then he turned to the lapping, cold loch.

'Thank you,' he muttered. 'I shall use your gift well.'

* * *

Michael Pilgrim forced the pace. Neither he nor Gover spoke. Yet the sword comforted him. The Crusades had taught over and over the grim effectiveness of City weapons. Every so often, he drew the blade, practising a feint or a sweep, familiarising himself with its weight and balance, then slid it back into its scabbard.

Michael realised the hunter was the only Beautiful he had ever seen dead, despite witnessing bodies in every condition throughout his life. Corpses in mounds from plague, war, senseless slaughter, hundreds, thousands, he did not care to calculate. But never a Beautiful from the Five Cities. The Modified Man had predicted, "Remember, their arrogance will destroy them in the end." Perhaps the hunter's corpse was the beginning of that end.

Realising Gover had fallen some way behind, he waited impatiently for him. 'We must be undercover by daybreak. Every moment, I expect drones to appear. Your splash of light at the loch must surely have been seen.'

Gover sniffed. 'They would be here by now. Having examined the poor fellow back there, I see why he was skulking by himself in this hideous wilderness. He may have been here for some time, mortally

TEN

afraid.'

Michael leaned on his staff. Of course, Gover's sympathies did not include the abducted girl. 'Why's that then?'

To that, Gover had no reply.

As the sun rose, they entered woods dripping with rain. An abandoned bivouac constructed of duraplastic car bonnets offered some shelter, albeit a damp one. Michael dared not risk a fire.

* * *

If the two travellers had known the coast better, they could have avoided Inverness. Both relied on vague memories of maps and mistook the Cromarty Firth for just another loch. So they missed their chance.

Descending from the mountains, they entered a coastal strip where houses and villages were more frequent. Most were deserted save for clusters of crofts where ragged families scratched a living. Yet Michael judged the land fertile enough. Something else kept the people's numbers low: he suspected perpetual war.

'We need guns,' he announced to Gover. 'And I know what we could trade for some. First, you need sorting out.'

Gover arched an eyebrow. 'Morally, Pilgrim? Or something else?'

'You just look wrong. You look like what you are. It attracts attention, and it's dangerous.'

He contemplated knocking Gover about a bit: perhaps a black eye or a broken nose. Maybe rub some tar into the pores of his cheeks — soft as a maid's buttocks, like his manicured City hands. As for those perfect white teeth... Michael sighed and dug up a fistful of earth.

'I suppose this will have to do.'

Gover flinched as Michael smeared his face with peaty soil. It surprised Michael he submitted at all.

Autumn faded towards winter a little more each day. Michael knew they must keep moving. Find a boat capable of taking them around the long, wild, unfamiliar coast of Scotland. Then there were weapons and provisions and competent sailors to acquire. It felt hopeless.

They came upon a walled hamlet beside a crossroads of ancient highways. Plank tables suggested a regular market, though none was in progress. And markets suggested rules of trade other than naked robbery.

Loosening the sword in its scabbard, Michael led the way to the open gates of the village. The remains of red brick houses tottered on a sea of mud where half-naked children scampered among dogs, straw, dung, pecking hens. He sniffed coke burning, the smelting of iron. Good signs.

A watchman in a tartan skirt came over, bearing a well-made blunderbuss. Another good sign. Before Michael could speak, Gover pushed forward with his strange earpiece in place and his mouth concealed beneath a scarf.

'We want to trade valuable things for guns,' Gover said in a perfect, broad Highlands burr that appeared to issue from behind the scarf.

The watchman narrowed his eyes at Gover, then pointed at an old petrol station from which smoke curled.

Michael hissed in Gover's ear, 'Leave this to me. You'll get us both strung up.'

He led the negotiation with the blacksmith, a skilled craftsman with apprentices, clearly the basis of wealth and trade in the hamlet. A happy deal emerged: twenty precious plasti-steel crossbow bolts capable of slicing clean through the thickest armour and shield. The price? A brace of wide-bored pistols designed to double as vicious clubs, powder, shot, wadding, and a blunderbuss with a short barrel and gaping muzzle. Michael would have preferred something with a more extended range, but muskets weren't the smith's specialty.

TEN

Insisting on testing the weapons first, Michael found them to be surprisingly well-balanced and accurate. Meanwhile, the growing crowd of children and adults could not take their eyes off Gover, even with his face covered.

Michael reloaded the guns swiftly. 'Best be gone,' he muttered. His back itched uncomfortably until the hamlet lay far behind.

'The blacksmith told me Inverness is near,' he said after a space. 'He crossed himself after mentioning its name.'

'So I saw,' Gover said.

Michael did not mention that the man had also fingered a lucky charm and spat on the ground to avert evil.

* * *

That night they camped on the crest of a wooded hill overlooking the Beauly Firth. As dusk settled, Michael Pilgrim climbed an oak and looked out across the grey waters.

Below, a dual carriageway joined a four-lane arched bridge across the forth, nearly a mile long. Beyond that, Inverness itself. Jagged shapes in the drizzly gloaming. A few plumes of black smoke rose from the seashore north of the city. In the town, no evidence of life.

An irrational fear gripped him. Inverness could be no worse than other places, he told himself. But that night he dreamt of the deformed City-man and woke in distress.

* * *

Dawn rose fair, but Michael Pilgrim's disquiet lingered. Again, he climbed the oak and inspected the bridge. A barricade had been built across it to deter travellers — or tax them. He hoped for the latter.

In daylight, Inverness looked no more inviting than at dusk. Michael shared out the last of the tough deer meat, checked the weapons, then he and Gover joined the dual carriageway to the bridge, chewing as they walked.

To their left, the rusting hulk of a warship covered with mussels and clams poked up from the river. A pod of dolphins leapt and played as the pale sun pierced the clouds.

Walkways flanked either side of the twin carriageways of the road bridge; vines and creepers hung from the railings. Gulls cried out an eerie dawn chorus, perched on the suspension bridge's towers.

At the far end of the bridge stood a barricade of piled vehicles. A narrow way through had been allowed in the middle. Making no attempt to conceal himself, Michael scrambled onto the bonnet of a burned-out car and methodically surveyed the path ahead until Gover began to grow restless.

'It's obviously deserted, Pilgrim.'

'Shut up.'

Movement in a truck cab? Michael recalled using old vehicles as cover on several occasions. Now he was on the other side.

'Take this.' He passed the blunderbuss to Gover. 'Don't cock it unless I say. It has a sensitive trigger. If possible, take your time aiming, so several targets are within the fan of its blast.' He held Gover's gaze for a moment. 'And make sure I'm not in the way.'

As they approached the barricade, Michael's palms sweated, and his heart sped. Why had he not tried to make some armour? Cut up a car bonnet with his new sword? Too late for that. Twenty feet, ten feet. They halted. No one called out a challenge or demanded a toll. Using his left hand, Michael drew a heavy pistol from his belt. With his right, he took out his sword.

'Bugger this!' He dashed through the gap in the barricade. A second later he was blinking in surprise at what he encountered on the other side.

TEN

'My God!' cried Gover, having followed him at a run.

The bodies of a dozen or so men and women lay strewn on the path ahead, their stomachs and chests savagely sliced open. These were presumably the guards who had been charged with minding the bridge. A flock of crows hopped from corpse to corpse, tearing at the exposed flesh, having first gorged on open eyes. Rats crawled and scurried round the bodies. The sickly odour was sweet enough to suggest they had been there a few days. Michael had a sudden intuition the hearts had been removed.

'Somebody didn't like 'em,' he said. 'I've a feeling they might not like us either.'

More than a physical crossing, the bridge heralded a land of new rules.

* * *

The first rule was to move as unobtrusively as possible while maintaining a quick pace. Michael led Gover along an old waterfront that had reverted to shingle from a century's tides and storms. The houses were burned out, pock-marked by bullet holes, every window smashed. The town climbed a hill behind them, a ribcage of untrodden streets choked by trees and undergrowth. They passed a rusty battle tank with one of its tracks torn off, camouflaged by moss. A shrub grew from its caved-in turret. A brittle silence clung to the deserted town.

Michael sensed countless ghosts watching and paused to stare them down. It didn't do to display fear to the spirits that haunted the lost towns.

'What happened here?' he wondered aloud. 'A battle? Did anyone win?'

If he knew, Gover was not saying.

Past a football stadium they went, its pitch a young larch wood, walls riddled with holes for winds to fan. Twenty minutes later they touched the coastline overlooking the Firth of Moray and were heartened to see deer milling amidst the charred remains of warehouses.

Plumes of smoke rose from an out-of-town shopping centre beside the coastal highway. The same smoke he had glimpsed at dusk the previous evening, Michael assumed.

'We need information,' he said, calculating the danger. 'And a fair-sized boat as well.' He drew a deep breath. 'We'll need to take some risks.'

But as they neared the former palace of shops, he immediately reconsidered. At least thirty corpses dangled from gibbets outside the entrance to the complex of glass-fronted buildings, bellies and chests slit open, just like those on the bridge. Michael wondered just what sweetmeats the fires were cooking. He now understood why the blacksmith had touched an amulet when he mentioned Inverness.

'Stay low,' he said.

A large area of parked cars provided cover as they bypassed the cursed place and took a broad road east, with the sea to their left. Inverness fell behind and was lost in the hills.

'Do you have the slightest clue where we are?' asked Gover. 'You really are turning out to be a remarkable guide.'

The way ran beside a shingle beach, and Michael breathed more easily. The sea breathed with him, sharing odours, restless energy. He insisted on sitting for an hour to let his fears break like the waves.

* * *

The next morning, Gover announced he was too sick to go further. He looked pitifully wan, forehead hot and moist to the touch.

'You need to sweat it out,' said Michael. 'You've done well to get this far. We'll rest here. It's a good way from the road, so we should

TEN

be undisturbed. We've got those spuds I traded in the village, and I'll see if there's anything else to bag.'

Gover huddled miserably, jacket pulled tight, while Michael ventured out into the steady rain, both pistols loaded with buckshot. The blunderbuss stayed with Gover, in case of need.

When Michael paused to listen, the strip of woodland by the sea was alive with noise. Rain and its journeys, leaves stirred by the sea breeze. Wood pigeons cooed amidst pine and beech; wasps buzzed around rotten autumn fruit. It seemed to him the best hope for the world might be trees.

Exploration revealed the young wood enveloped a small, abandoned farm, with its ruined house at its centre. Michael found an ancient tractor clad in lichen amidst a tight stand of willows. Mostly he kept his eye on the canopy above, shooting a fat grouse as it roosted, followed by several quail. Then his attention turned to nuts and beds of comfrey, chickweed, moist fat hen leaves.

A deep peace descended on his spirit as he hiked the wood, smelling earth, bark, leaves and undergrowth, aware of the sea sighing nearby.

When he returned, he found Gover sleeping, or feigning sleep, for Michael had the distinct impression he was up to something again, just as he had felt during their rest day in the mountains. In truth, he welcomed the City-man's silence.

Plucking the birds to retain as much fat as possible, he slow-roasted them on sticks. Meanwhile, he baked a few spuds in the embers of the fire.

Coming back from washing his hands in a pond, he found Gover picking greedily at a quail and threatening to land all the birds in the fire.

'Leave it alone,' said Michael. 'You remind me of a tale we were told as children, of a busy hen doing all the work — that's me, by the way — while the other farm animals refused to help except for eating.'

'You are comparing me to an animal?' Gover snorted and sucked on a bone. 'This is delicious by the way.'

Evidently, the long sleep had done the City-man good, as did the meal, their heartiest since crashing in Scotland.

'Are not all men animals? Creatures allotted their hour on earth?' asked Michael, clearing his teeth with a twig. 'There's no disgrace in acknowledging a kindred. The true shame is in denying one's own nature. And that is a dappled thing. My Grandfather always taught, *Unto your own self be true.*'

'Ah, but you and your Grandfather erroneously assume all humankind is one species,' replied Gover. 'Evolution separates even as it connects. Thus, whilst you primitives are a mere step above the beasts, we Beautifuls have transcended biological decay with only the stars set above us. We are the pinnacle of evolution.'

'Why do you wish to return to Baytown?' Michael ventured after a spell of silence. 'It puzzles me. There must be easier ways of contacting the City.'

Gover hugged his full stomach. 'You would not begin to understand.'

'Try this then. You clearly have enemies. Are they still hunting you? Is that why you take so roundabout a route?'

Now the City-man sighed. 'I suppose you *have* been a good, hard-working hen. Even I must sing for my supper sometimes. Very well then, to your first question, I wish to retrieve something valuable from the Baytown Museum. Something of great importance, not just for your savage little world, Pilgrim, but for the civilized world. As for whether I am hunted, there are many possibilities. Perhaps my enemies, as you call them, believe that I am dead and seek my corpse as confirmation. Because I can assure you, they will desire confirmation. I am not a man to be trifled with, Pilgrim. And they know this very well.'

'Is that so?' Michael said. From where he sat, Gover didn't seem to be much of a threat.

'Another possibility, and perhaps more alarming,' added Gover, 'is that they have looked in the wrong places. Perhaps they are already heading this way.'

Michael waited for more. It was not forthcoming. 'You've never explained why they hate you so much.'

Gover shot him a look he found hard to read — scorn, fear, anger, a mixture of all three?

'It would give you bad dreams if I told you. Very bad dreams.'

* * *

Overcast skies cleared to a pale, soft blue. Inland, wooded hills led to mountain slopes capped by white clouds. Michael's heart found comfort in the beauty of the autumn-clad country.

'By sticking to the coast we'll strike a village for sure,' he told Gover, 'where we can trade City goods for a boat and passage.'

His hopes were dashed at the first fishing settlement. The folk there shook their heads and spoke of boats confiscated by the Prince O'Ness, forcing them to rely on their fields or starve. Michael learned the Prince was gathering seaworthy craft a dozen miles up the coast at the old defensive earthworks of Fort George, where he maintained his palace.

Many other words were spoken, and though Michael's fluency with Highland talk was rapidly improving, a good deal eluded him. Not so Gover, who listened in through his earpiece.

'It seems there will be a great autumn fair at Fort George in a few days,' Gover said. 'Merchants will travel there from all over the Highlands.'

'I imagine some will come by boat,' said Michael. 'I can guarantee them riches if they get us safely home.'

They joined an ancient coast road, encountering more farmsteads and hamlets. Yet the population was small and averse to armed foreigners — one a virtual strangeling, at that. Again, they were obliged to forage and shelter in a ruined house. Midway through the night, a downpour rattled what remained of the roof slates; melodies of drip and trickle to join the harmony of surf breaking on the beach.

* * *

Back on the road, they entered the deserted village of Ardesier and caught sight of Fort George on a spit of land projecting into the Moray Firth. Other travellers were headed the same way: traders and peddlers with wares on their backs; farmers from neighbouring districts, hoping to barter cloth woven by wives and daughters; a party of entertainers, bearing drum, fife, and a capacity to juggle and tumble. All converged on the earthen walls and tumbledown brick buildings of Fort George, as did grey clouds charged with rain.

A cold wind blew in from the Firth, ruffling Michael Pilgrim's hair as he counted ten sea-going boats beached around a small harbour on the east side of the fort. Here were the craft seized from the fisherfolk of Moray.

'A veritable armada,' observed Gover.

Michael's gaze rose to the silhouettes of Fort George framed by a slate-coloured sea crested with whitecaps.

'I don't like this place,' he said. 'Let's get within its walls before dark.'

It began to rain.

ELEVEN

Two hundred miles south, the unseasonably warm weather lifted. Chills settled hard. Hurdy-Gurdy had spoken to Seth of an old motorway, running south like a spine through the centre of England, that lead to the City of Albion, or near enough. All they need do was head east, and they were sure to find it.

A day of travel took them further north than either intended, though Hurdy-Gurdy seemed not to mind.

'Ring-a-ring o' roses,' he sang, 'Arms and legs and noses. A tishoo! A wishoo! All mown down.'

At least the road was clear and mostly safe, thanks to the Commonwealth of the North. They passed several villages recovering their populations, but when night fell, Seth was lost. A fact he acknowledged by pretending the opposite.

They resumed their journey the next morning into a thick, rolling fog.

By early afternoon, they arrived at an imposing gatehouse, the cold fog thinning to hazy mist. Trees old and young hemmed the road, hosting crows and rooks. The leaves on the ground were still dry enough to crunch underfoot.

The muddy track showed many hoof prints and well-established wheel ruts. It led past a church with a burned tower and empty windows. Cresting the hill, mist closed once more, distorting the sound of an axe chopping logs, so it might have come from near or far.

They pressed on through the woodland, reaching piles of rotten beams, slates, splintered glass, and concrete — once a large rectangle of buildings. When Seth asked Hurdy-Gurdy if he knew its purpose, the latter picked up a metal sign of an acorn and oak leaves.

'When no one feared the future, they visited the past,' said the madman. 'Hey ho, what a jolly day out. Now the only day out around here is filling your belly.' He rubbed his flat stomach and tossed the sign back into the rubble.

Minutes later, they glimpsed tall, ruined arches and walls, rising from a lake of mist in a steep-sided valley. Seth smelt wood fires. As the path descended, they reached a large hamlet of houses, pens, stables, and a barn, protected by a ditch and palisade. A faint lowing of cattle and the clank of bells suggested it was milking time.

Seth slung his musket and concealed his pistol after checking both were loaded and primed.

* * *

'Stay where you are, friends.'

The order came from a grizzled man with a shepherd's crook at the entrance to the palisade. His flock could be heard bleating in the mist.

'We're just passing through,' said Seth. 'If there's work in return for food, all the better.'

The shepherd examined them with undisguised scepticism.

'You look like yez bin dragged through a hedge,' he said.

Seth couldn't disagree. The man might have added a duck pond and dung heap as well.

'What's all this, then?' called a firm voice.

The question belonged to a lad around Seth's age, perhaps a bit older — a muscular young fellow with a warm, natural smile. Seth squinted

ELEVEN

up at him. The lad was taller than him by a good hand's length. By comparison, Seth felt skinny and hunched. A pleasant air clung to the lad, which, Seth knew, contrasted with his own effect on people.

'The name's Joseph Lyons,' said the young man. 'Folk here just call me Jojo; I'm happy enough with either. Take your pick.'

Something about the name stirred a long suppressed memory, as did Jojo's face — that distinctive nose, mouth, cast of eye. Then it came to him.

Seth edged backward and felt for his pistol. But Hurdy-Gurdy swept in and touched his arm. Seth took a breath and relaxed warily. No one was left alive on this earth to connect two and two — or so he hoped.

'Good afternoon, young master,' crowed Gurdy, bowing with great presence and grace. 'And to you other kind masters! Care for a song?'

He capered and warbled while accompanying himself on the squeeze-box. Jojo laughed, clapping the beat.

As me and my companions was setting off a snare,
'Twas then we spied the gamekeeper — for him we did not care,
For we can wrestle and fight, my boys, and jump o'er anywhere . . .
O-oh, 'tis my delight on a shining night, in the season of the year.

Gurdy executed a series of enormous leaps that earned cheers and whistles from the crowd. He twitched his nose to the beat of the song, just like a hare's — much to the merriment of young Jojo.

As me and my companions were setting four or five,
And taking on 'em up again, we caught a hare alive...
We took the hare alive, my boys, and through the woods did steer.
O-oh, 'tis my delight on a shining night, in the season of the year...

Gurdy concluded with a flourish and an exaggerated bow.

'That were good!' said Jojo, clapping his hands. 'We need a bit of fun round here. We'll have more later, if you please, in return for your supper.'

Seth felt slighted. Was he not the spokesman of this little company, rather than that crazy-haired loon?

'We're travellers,' he broke in. 'We'd be glad of some work in exchange for food.'

Jojo looked him over. Despite his light, pleasant smile, Seth knew the young man was assessing carefully what risks they posed.

'My dad is squire here,' he said. 'He's crippled by a horse kick, so I take his place for now. And make decisions on his behalf, for good or ill.'

'Oh, for good, Jojo,' said the shepherd. 'You do right. Most o' time.'

Other men and women of the hamlet who had gathered for Hurdy's song murmured their agreement.

'Though I care nowt for the look of this pair,' added the shepherd.

The young squire shrugged. 'Never judge a man by appearances, Stan. Especially if he's willing to clear out them ponds.'

Whereupon, they were offered 'hard work and mucky' in return for three hearty meals a day and a dry place to sleep at night. Hearing the terms, Seth felt an urge to tell this cocky, good-humoured young mister where to stick his job, for he, Seth Pilgrim, skivvied for no man. Except the opposite was true. Besides, they needed food and gunpowder badly, along with blankets and mended shoes, if they were to survive the long trek to the City. All must be either earned or stolen. Somehow he felt no desire to turn robber here.

'What's the name of this place?' he asked, still wary of the resemblance in Jojo's face to two girls he would rather forget.

'Why, Fountains. Fountains Abbey.'

Icy confusion lowered Seth's head. When he glanced up, Hurdy-Gurdy was watching him closely.

ELEVEN

* * *

The ancient ruins of the abbey and hamlet of Fountains lay at the head of a narrow valley clad with oak, ash, and beech. A small river, the Skell, fed a succession of ponds once used to rear carp by Jojo's grandfather. His father had neglected the trade, and now the ponds flooded each winter. It was Jojo's plan to clear the long-clogged culverts and sluice gates so the ponds could be restocked with fish.

Seth and Hurdy-Gurdy's lodging was an old summerhouse, a classically-columned mockery of a Greek temple, built to service a palatial home that had burnt down centuries before. This folly had survived, along with others scattered over the valley. It overlooked the principal pond

The culverts were blocked with rotting branches, leaves, mud, and plastic carried down by the river. Hard, cold work. Seth waded into the freezing pond clad in just a loincloth, his toes sinking in the slime, water up to his waist, dredging out debris that turned the water a muddy brown.

As for Hurdy-Gurdy, the ex City-man was next to useless, spending hours each day assembling fires that at least offered Seth a chance to thaw his bones. When Seth reproached him for doing all the easy work, Gurdy replied with outrageous versions of The Lincolnshire Poacher.

'You worked hard enough in Morecambe,' Seth grumbled, 'why not now?'

'Someone must keep watch on the watcher, Young Nuncle.'

Seth surveyed the deep woods surrounding the ponds. A breeze made half-bare boughs sigh. Nothing stirred save for falling leaves, birdsong, the whisper of thick undergrowth beneath the trees. He noticed Gurdy kept the wide-bored musket close.

'You're having me on,' Seth said. 'What frigging watcher?'

'It's interested in Young Nuncle Seth. Among others.' Gurdy

explained no further.

Twice a day, early and late, they walked the mile or so from their shelter to the hamlet, where generous meals were doled out to lines of folk at communal tables, with Jojo Lyons and his mother at the head.

Seth noticed two empty plates were always set by the pale woman and her son. When he asked the server about them, the girl whispered, 'Missus Lyons won't accept her two lasses — Abbie and Bella — won't never come home. Taken by slavers five years back, they was, and never heard from since. The poor woman. Cracked as plaster wi' grief.'

Seth took his portion and ate in the yard. Each time he saw Jojo, he was reminded of the girls whose trust he had betrayed in the service of Big Jacko. The lasses had been imprisoned at Fylingdales then carried in a huge flying machine to the City as "materials". What "materials" meant, he still didn't know; or even why the City needed young, healthy people in such numbers. Perhaps as bonders. Even Big Jacko hadn't known.

Loosened by a jug of strong ale one night, Seth told Hurdy-Gurdy about Big Jacko and Fylingdales and the trade in "materials" as they huddled by a well-fed fire, blankets around their shoulders. How he had promised to look out for Bella and Abbie Lyons. His shaky voice faltered.

'Stupid fuckers put too much faith in me.' He laughed in the harsh, knowing tone favoured by the Seth Pilgrim of Big Jacko days. 'Never trust nobody. Only a fool does that. What was I supposed to do?'

Gurdy listened then sang:

> *Pat-a-make, pat-a-make, maker man,*
> *Make me a strangeling fast as you can,*
> *Mix it and train it and let it run free.*
> *Make it alive as a baby for me-ee-ee!*

His voice rose into an operatic howl worthy of Madam Butterfly or Don Giovanni in their moments of final despair. The old summerhouse echoed.

Seth regarded him dourly. What had he expected? Sympathy? Reassurance? Now Hurdy-Gurdy knew his secret and might blurt it out any time. He dreaded the disdain and hate in Jojo's face if he learned of Seth's role in the disappearance of his little sisters.

'You won't tell no one, Gurdy, will you? Especially Jojo. I trusted you!'

'Oh no.' Gurdy licked his lips with comic slyness. 'Young Nuncle likes the young squire?'

'No. Young Nuncle don't like nobody.'

Seth rolled over and pretended to sleep. It occurred to him that Jojo's style of life should have been his own in Hob Hall. He should be lording it as the squire's son. He should be the young master all obeyed. Except, he would never have been so fair or generous. Everyone would have hated him. That was okay, he hated them all anyway.

Then Seth realised exactly who Jojo reminded him of — his Uncle Michael.

'Twat,' he muttered.

* * *

The next day brought wind-driven rain. The woods creaked and tossed. Sodden leaves fell in flurries to form mulchy drifts. Black skies promised a storm by late afternoon and did not lie. Work was impossible in such conditions. So they lingered in the old folly by the main pond to keep dry.

Hungover from last night's ale and revelations, Seth pulled out the pink lunchbox containing the Mistresses' treasures. With his finger, he traced the image of the plump, rearing pony on its lid. The

Mistresses had boasted the horse came to life at their command and that it could fly. If he learned the spell, perhaps he and Hurdy could ride to the City through the air like the drones. Across the front of the box, handwritten in a black marker pen by one of Satan's she-devils, a curse:

PRIVATE PROPERTY OF LAUREL ONLY
KEEP OUT OR .. ? ! !

Would Laurel come for him one night and drag him down to Hell?

How this gift from Satan came to the Mistresses was a legend in Fell Grange. Fat and Thin, scavenging an old house in Barrow one day, they'd found the box at the back of a cupboard, concealed beneath shoes designed for small, youthful feet. They spoke of demonic laughter, a long, satisfying hiss as the lid opened.

'Our familiars were released at that moment,' Fat would say, making her listeners uneasy. Everyone knew their familiars were invisible spirits who hid in the bodies of animals.

'Laurel was a witch who Satan blessed and turned into a demon,' revealed Thin. 'She has her own palace in Hell, and she sent the box so we'd find it.'

Inside the pink lunchbox, they'd found a net bag of many-coloured glass gems; a small plastic bottle of oil scented with petunias; and, most precious of all, the holy texts.

Seth warily opened the first book, the foundation of the Mistresses' rituals. Its black cover bore a red pentagram and the title: *Codex Saerus: The Black Book of Satan*. A circle of white paper glued to the front read: REDUCED £1.99.

Whenever he read the book, Seth felt afraid. Could the Mistresses sense his eyes on the sacred words? Laurel or Satan might even send directions in dreams where to find him. He knew the Mistresses must hunger for revenge — Maister Gil likewise, bad as either Fat or Thin.

In Morecambe, he had tried to act out half-comprehended rites in a suburban bungalow well away from Old Albert's trading fort. So dearly did he need power. But the chanted words brought neither comfort nor thrill. It occurred to him the bungalow made a poor temple, that really he should sacrifice something. Having been sacrificed himself — even partially — the prospect did not appeal much.

'Hey, Gurdy.' He pointed at the coloured glass. 'What are these for? Is that how the City powers its machines?'

Gurdy poked the bag with a long finger. It clinked. 'These are gullibility pills.'

'Ah! So are they powerful?'

'If you choose.'

Seth set aside the Black Book and took up the other holy text, *Witchcraft For Teens*. Its cover bore a picture of girls in short skirts, posed with hands on their hips, smug, knowing looks on their faces he recognised from teenage lasses back in Baytown. Expressions signifying they'd got one up on a rival. Beneath the image of the girls, it said: *Wicca for the Next Generation*.

Yet flicking through the book, he found spells without real power against a dangerous enemy. How to make boys notice you. How to hex your texts (whatever texts were). Scare away bad hair days. Glyphs of warding to protect your locker.

The patter of rain intensified on the roof. A roll of thunder. Lightning made the sky blink.

'What is a locker?' he asked Gurdy. 'I mean, what was one? Was it a kind of prison?'

The madman had cocooned himself in his blanket. 'Locker, you say? Let me see, Young Nuncle.'

'It's secret,' said Seth, hurriedly.

'Then Hurdy-poos can't help, can he?'

Reluctantly, Seth passed over *Witchcraft For Teens*.

Again, thunder. A flash in the dusk.

For long minutes Hurdy-Gurdy read, sighing frequently. When he glanced up, his eyes glittered with tears.

'You alright?' asked Seth.

'Ah, teens! How my generation betrayed the young. And their future. We sacrificed both for the convenience of our present. We knew, of course, what we were doing. Wasteful, cruel, greedy, tearing apart the whole world for trash. Yes! Raping beauty itself for trash. We knew; that's the point. Oh, we knew.'

'What's that to do with lockers?'

Gurdy waved a dismissive hand. 'If we adults would not allow a springtime, a pretty ring time, for our young folk — to be silly, to have crushes and passions, to get excited about parties and favourite clothes, to keep them safe and green and growing so they could play at casting silly spells on their innocent, stupid, fucking lockers — if not for that, what were we for?'

His question lingered, unanswerable. As the wind moaned, Hurdy-Gurdy sang in a voice of yearning sweetness:

> *It was a lover and his lass,*
> *With a hey, and a ho, and a hey nonino,*
> *That o'er the green cornfield did pass,*
> *In springtime, the only pretty ring time,*
> *When birds do sing, hey ding-a-ding ding:*
> *Sweet lovers love the spring.*

* * *

The storm blew north overnight. The next morning, Seth stared up at soft, billowing clouds, their white edges shiny beneath the autumn sun. How beautiful clouds are, he thought, remembering Hurdy's song about being young. It struck him with the force of a revelation.

He sighed, poking a culvert with a spade, up to his knees in cold, scummy water. Then the obstruction gave. Water flowed through to cascade into a runnel cleared of mud and moss that fed the next pond.

'You're doing good work.'

Seth turned and found Jojo Lyons standing behind him, holding a stoppered jug of steaming cider wrapped in cloth to keep it warm.

Jojo lifted the jug. 'I've brought you this. It must have been a rough night for you out here.'

The coarse cider warmed Seth's stomach as he dripped dry, watching the freed water drain through the culvert. As he drank, Jojo explained the history of the abbey, the valley's days as a former pleasure garden, and the numerous follies scattered in the thick woods.

'We've got an old book called *History of Fountains*,' Jojo said. 'Do you read?'

Seth pulled at the jug. 'Aye.'

'Fountains was built on the lives of generations,' said Jojo. 'Like each year's leaves building up the soil. One day I hope to add a bit to that history book.'

Seth put down the jug. He wondered what Jojo would make of the books stolen from the Mistresses.

'What of your history?' asked Jojo. 'Where are you from?'

Seth glanced at the clouds. Unless he was careful, folk would put two and two together about Big Jacko.

'No need to answer if you'd prefer not,' said Jojo.

Was that disappointment in his voice?

Seth said awkwardly, 'I'm from Scarborough way, on the coast, though I don't go there no more.' He struggled for something to add. 'Sometimes I think I'm happiest by the sea.'

Jojo grew thoughtful. 'I would love to see the ocean. Perhaps one day. What's it like?'

Seth handed back the empty jug and laughed. 'What's a forest like? Or the sky? Everything's the same in the end.'

Gentle wafts of the squeezebox broke into their talk: Hurdy-Gurdy, who'd been watching a particular corner of the wooded hillside while they talked, played the same tune he had sung the night before, accompanying it with a graceful dance of pirouetting dips and hops. The young men laughed.

Jojo stepped over to the next culvert due to be unblocked. 'That's a large task for one man. I notice your companion does little for his bread and meat other than prance, sing, and work the bellows of that squeezebox. So I'll lend a hand.'

With that, Jojo stripped to his small clothes and waded into the pond, cursing the cold. Seth felt pale and puny next to the strapping young squire of Fountains; ugly, too, his chest and back scarred by Maister Gil's whip. Yet the lads joked as they worked.

Hurdy-Gurdy fell back to examining the same corner of woodland as before, while piling stones dredged from the ponds into a mound like a grave marker.

TWELVE

Helen Devereux became aware of filtered air; the sterility of an atmosphere purged. The temperature-controlled sheet covering her body fit snug as a womb.

She opened her eyes. The room was almost entirely white: carpet, furniture, walls — apart from ebony carvings and some examples of a popular art form known as melange, utilising tasteful scraps from the Before Times in provocative juxtapositions. Here, a jewel-encrusted love heart hung on a stuffed rattlesnake, its fangs bared. There, an ancient automatic pistol capped with a condom that inflated and deflated. Right now it hung flaccid.

She sat up in bed. A second, smaller alcove contained Averil, also naked, snoring softly. Helen realised their bodies had been depilated and de-odorized. Her bag and clothes — sterilised then folded with exact precision by maid-drones — waited in shelved closets, along with dozens of outfits and shoes in the latest City styles. A dressing table and magnifying mirror filled one wall, stocked with cosmetics, creams, and seashells containing rings, brooches, tiaras.

Helen wondered which of the Five Cities encompassed this quiet, germless room. Unless they'd been taken to a satellite pleasure resort or production colonia, such a room might exist anywhere Beautiful: Albion, Mitopia, Mughalia, Neo Rio, Han City...

She pulled on a silk dressing gown, left on the bed, and stepped over to the wall window, currently set to opaque. She pressed a switch; the glass cleared. Sounds from outside were allowed to enter. A bright parakeet chattered on a nearby banyan tree, sprouting from lush, neat lawns that would never need cutting or watering. Like the tree, they were constructed of synthetic materials. Terraced hillsides covered with genuine tropical gardens rose above the tall boundary wall.

Helen recalled her joyful wonder upon first walking those green terraces, marvelling to be still alive amidst such exotic beauty. At the same time, the human world perished around her. She first came here with Blair Gover as he worked to construct and consolidate the Beautiful Life across the globe, all of them afraid to emerge from controlled perimeters and guarded communities. It had been a time when energies were focussed on making the new Cities function; an era of hope and astonishing productivity, of defiant scientific achievement before the Beautiful Life grew stale.

'Where are we?' asked a small voice behind her.

She turned. 'In Mughalia, Averil. They have taken us to the City of Mughalia.'

***

The door opened and a face topped with thick, silver-streaked black hair popped in. Beneath his craggy forehead, a rugged jaw and high cheekbones, so that he resembled an action hero from a holocast or other fantasy.

'Ah!' cried Marvin Brubacher. His accent was Australian, manner boisterous. 'If I'd known you were awake I'd have knocked. Can I come in?'

Helen pulled her robe tighter, conscious of coarse skin and spreading wrinkles.

Marvin spoke into his collar. 'They're awake, darling. Can you join us?'

He glanced briefly at Averil, who had pulled the bed sheet up to her neck, then turned his full attention to Helen. 'I owe you an apology for enforcing your little nap on the flight over. Merle was worried your servant would become hysterical. And —

please don't take it the wrong way, Helen — but she quite insisted on some very thorough scans for infections.' He cleared his throat apologetically. 'You know how Merle gets about that kind of thing.'

Helen's eyebrows rose. 'Were there infections?'

'A few. Nothing serious.'

'And so here we are.'

'Yes. And can I just state, our home is your home. At least until Blair decides to show up.'

'At which point I become his problem, not yours?'

Marvin's faintly puckish face broke into a wide grin.

Again the door opened. This time Merle hurried through, accompanied by a medi-drone, which rolled straight over to Helen for further scans and tests. Meanwhile, Merle hung back. A slight wrinkle across her forehead expressed a blend of surprise, wariness, and faintly patronising concern.

'Blair said you'd gone native all the way, my love,' Merle said. 'You've come back to civilization just in time.'

'By which you mean, I'm looking old and ugly,' replied Helen, 'or, what I prefer to call natural.'

'Now, now, ladies,' said Marvin. 'This situation is awkward for us all. I recommend we meet in an hour for a small business conference. Besides, I'm sure you would like to freshen up.' He coughed delicately. 'When in Rome, Helen, after all — or even Mughalia.'

As she dressed, Helen recalled what she knew of Marvin and Merle Brubacher. Despite encountering them on and off for nearly a century, it was surprisingly little. Although highly public figures in the Five

Cities, if not heroes to most Beautifuls, one rarely saw beyond their possessions or appearance. Once, when she remarked on it to Blair, he had said: 'It is known as distance, Helen. A policy Louis XVI and Marie Antoinette were fond of, too.'

Before the Dyings, the Brubachers had belonged everywhere and nowhere, owning a vast television then holotainment empire that made them among the wealthiest, most powerful people in the world — especially when they pioneered mass-produced virtual reality masks that kept a whole generation passive. Helen seemed to recall violent protests against that and notorious scandals. But all was eclipsed by the fact their fortune financed research into the science of cell renewal underpinning the Beautiful Life.

Blair had worked closely with the Brubachers and a few other enlightened mega-billionaires for many years before the plagues came, establishing the private, gated mini-towns and research communities destined to evolve into the Five Cities. For this reason, they staunchly supported his loyalty to the Founding Vision of the Beautiful Life. Like Blair, they were among the most influential of the Beautifuls — and, by repute, quite ruthless when necessary.

Of their characters, she knew little. All Beautifuls found it safer to live and mingle blandly, lest they risk the ultimate crime of Discordia. Nevertheless, rumours circulated of a small, very discreet island in the Indian Ocean. Such whispering probably grew from envy, the Brubachers, as Founders and leaders, received far greater access to credits and luxuries than ordinary Beautifuls.

For her own part, Helen admired their absolute devotion to one another and tactful instinct for working behind the scenes. It reassured her that Blair still had such allies. With their help, she could hope to return to Baytown all the sooner.

* * *

TWELVE

Obedient to the mantra "make every precious moment an aesthetic moment", business conferences in the Five Cities had evolved. Now information was relayed to an event organiser programme, which created holo-presentations in line with one's desired mood palette. So Helen was not surprised when a drone led her to a large, circular room, much like an amphitheatre. Marvin and Merle were there waiting, cocktails in hand. From their expressions, she suspected neither wished to be there.

'Grab yourself a drink, Helen, then let's get started,' said Marvin.

Stirring music set the conference's tone. In the central stage, a holo-display of Earth's evolution in snapshots, commencing with the Big Bang to indicate the cosmic scope of the discussion. An extended sequence followed — for Beautifuls possessed leisure in abundance — passing through the primal swamp, dinosaurs, upright apes on African plains, Ice Age Neanderthals, to Homo sapiens, destroying all they constructed — Babylon, Rome, the USA, and countless other fleeting historical landmarks — until the plagues seeded Cities serviced by armies of obedient drones. Here the music grew soft, joyful, benign.

As the display faded, Marvin activated an airborne holo-button.

Evolution, intoned a rumbling, sonorous synthvoice, *has brought humanity to perfection. Millennia of barbarism attain apotheosis. Praise to the Founding Vision for this miracle of nature. Praise to the Founders.*

Holograms of a dozen men and women walked across the amphitheatre, bowing to history and applauded by crowds of grateful Beautifuls, forever young and gay, replete with all Earth can offer. Prominent among the glorious Founders: Marvin and Merle Brubacher, then Dr Blair Gover, followed by his former close friend and associate — tragically killed in an unexplained accident at a private laboratory that also robbed Blair Gover of his sister, Dr Guy de Prie-Dieu, née plain Guy Price. Helen felt glad the Brubachers had no inkling of her own role in Guy de Prie-Dieu's untimely exit from immortality.

The music darkened, as did the lights. A deep, menacing vibration shook Helen's seat. *Now we come to it*, she thought.

Holo-icons formed then faded — bored, irritable faces quarrelling, deserted desks, creative enterprises and laboratories abandoned in favour of listless, drifting, chemical pleasures. Burning letters displayed a single word: DISCORDIA.

Again the deep, sonorous voice: *Amid the rose, a secret canker.*

A close up of maggots' mouths sucking and gulping.

'Really, Marv!' exclaimed Merle. 'Do you have to?'

'Bear with me, darling.'

A new form of Discordia arises, declared the voice. *One that threatens the Beautiful Life itself.*

Helen shrank back in her chair as holograms of monsters she had worked hard to forget appeared; creatures glimpsed years before when Mhairi led her to destroy Guy de Prie-Dieu's vile laboratory on the outskirts of Albion. Humanoid yet not human; flesh and brain nurtured from a frothy yeast of genes and animal cells. Angels, Guy de Prie-Dieu had called them.

One resembled a merman with gills for lungs and webbed feet and hands. Another, clearly bred to create perfect meat, half-pig, half-man, with the added advantage it could undertake simple manual labour while growing to edible maturity. Others pleasure-intended: sex toys, pets with strokable fur and winsome eyes, graceful sprites for dancing, or huge-chested dwarves with enormous mouths for singing hymns of praise to their life-making deities.

Discordia, rumbled the deep voice. *A secret growth-laboratory already uncovered.*

Cue holograms of drones blowing up and flame-throwing facilities equipped with computers and vats. Angels ablaze like living torches.

No one doubts that more illegal life forms lurk maggot-like in the rose. The Progenitors or Life-makers, as they call themselves, are suspected of

TWELVE

having powerful friends. So far, they have evaded capture.

A hologram appeared of a valley filled with Beautifuls, awaiting the verdict of the Ruling Council eagerly.

Soon, intoned the synthvoice, *the Council will decide whether Progeniting or Life-making should be permitted. Or whether the noble, glorious Founding Vision should prevail. Forever and ever.*

The same heroic music that started the display played it out. Fresh holograms of the Big Bang appeared.

Helen felt slighted and patronised. A ridiculously amateurish holo-presentation, lacking factual analysis, substance or meaning. Was this facile nonsense the level of debate for such crucial questions? She feared it might be so, at least, in public.

The lights in the amphitheatre rose.

'Right then folks,' said Marvin, 'that concludes our introduction. The question is: what's to do now?'

* * *

Merle was the first to speak.

'Do you think, Marvin, my love, the event organiser program got a little carried away with itself there?'

'What do you mean, my darling?' Marvin's tone bore faint strains of pique.

'I grant you, it was all very dramatic. But the Council is made up of sensible people like ourselves, who support the Founding Vision.'

'Blair is worried about it,' countered Merle. 'He must have his reasons.'

'Blair is always worried about something. If only he were here.'

Merle turned to Helen. 'Darling, do you really have not the slightest idea where he might be? Did he drop any hints of his plans when he visited you? Even just a teeny weeny hint?'

Helen shrugged helplessly. They all deserved better from Blair, who was being selfish, as usual. 'Nothing much. Just his scheme for conscripting the so-called primitives to clean up plastic waste. Oh, and he wanted to give Beautifuls something useful to do. Largely to keep them out of mischief, I think. But you know about that, I'm sure.'

'Yes. Talking of primitives,' said Marvin, 'what about this uncle of your servant that you mentioned? What was his name, Merle?'

The latter widened her eyes. Remembering a primitive's name was too eccentric a request to deserve a reply.

Helen narrowed her eyes. 'His name is Michael Pilgrim. He is a resourceful and principled leader of people struggling against every disadvantage. Human beings who the City has the power to help in numerous ways. People who really do not need to be viewed as a threat.'

'Hmm,' muttered Marvin, distracted by a vibration from his hand-held screen.

'And I believe,' ploughed on Helen, 'Blair hopes to show him to the Council as an example of what useful servants these so-called primitives might make— though *allies* would be a better word, in my view. Indeed, how pointless and wicked it would be to create new species. And dangerous in terms of gene infection.'

'Yes, yes,' said Merle.

'So you have no way of contacting him?' pressed Marvin.

'None.'

'Then we'll just have to wait for him to contact us. In the meantime, it would be wise if you were very visible. It would help Blair's cause immensely. In fact, I propose we take you on a flight round Mughalia's pleasures tonight. After that, a few excursions in the area. I'll arrange a chaperone.'

'See and be seen,' added Merle.

'I'm not sure,' said Helen.

Marvin raised a large hand. 'I insist.'

Helen knew she had no choice. They wanted to keep an inconvenient guest occupied. Yet it was also a kindness.

'Will I be safe?' she asked. 'After all, Blair sent that holo-message to say I was somehow at risk.'

'You will be very safe in Mughalia.' Marvin's lips spread into a grin, behind which lurked a dangerous edge. 'Trust me on that. Anyone foolish enough to cross me will regret it.'

* * *

They rode out when midnight cooled the streets and plazas.

Mughalia, the youngest of the Five Cities, had been founded twenty years after the establishment of Albion, Mitopia, Neo Rio and Han City. Spread across interconnected valleys in the Sri Lankan Highlands, complete with satellite resorts, its sole purpose was distraction. Beautifuls were drawn there as sugary water summons wasps — yet nothing much drowned, save for subtleties of soul.

The essential principle of Mughalia was Accordia: the coming together of free Beautifuls for joyful, ecstatic pleasure to fill long, empty days and nights.

The Brubachers' open-topped aircar could accommodate a dozen with room to spare. That evening it carried just four: Merle, Marvin, Helen, and Averil perched at the very back among the service drones. The vehicle blazed with light, flaunting its passengers via a giant hologram above their heads like a floating bubble, so all the world might witness their apparel, their laughter, and insouciance.

The hours that followed imprinted themselves on Averil's soul. Never had she imagined such light. Cascading colours. Fireworks rising continually over valleys lined with luxurious villas. Holoshows projected into the night. Crowds of gaily attired young people —

everyone was young aside from a few black-uniformed technicians — riding airbikes and charabancs, walking, dancing, drifting from attraction to attraction. Tens of thousands paraded and flirted, high on bespoke blends of stimulants, driven by fears of becoming nobody, of vanishing.

The Brubacher's aircar flew over districts dedicated to the Five Poisons of Buddhism, a pseudo-religion popular in Mughalia and Han City, where many Beautifuls believed they had attained Nirvana, transcending morality along with mortality.

For others, real pleasure required some transgression. For extra credits, live primitives or animals were to be had and disposed of as one chose. More sedate tastes acted out carefully staged recreations of the Before Times, of lost, beloved families expunged by plague. Borne upward by chemicals or implants, one could dote over a joy-drone parent, sibling, child, or long-lost friend.

Over collonaded halls and mock temples flew the aircar, artificial lakes scintillating diamonds of light. While Averil gazed in wonder, Helen sat impassive and numb. None of this was new to her. The lakes and fairyland gardens avenued by artificial trees, flowers, even moss. The very air was filtered to suck out irritating insects.

She well understood that the people in shimmering clothes, with their clumps of "friends", barely knew one another. Few aspired to lasting ties or bonds — for who did not tire of acquaintances known decade after decade and who lived out the same static life as one's self? Or tire of constant intoxication and enhanced orgasms? Few marriages survived such monotony, few loves. One craved novelty like oxygen.

She glanced back to check that Averil was safe. The Baytown girl stared with undisguised delight. Helen felt a stab of fear. She must take great care of Averil. It would not do for her to be swept away by Mughalia. Too many maggots fed off the rose.

THIRTEEN

The arrival of Pilgrim and Gover at Fort George was well-timed. A small crowd of traders and peddlers gathered around the entrance — not to mention gangs of bonders and overwhippers, returning home from a day of dreary toil on the Prince O'Ness's fields. The few guards charged with sifting out troublemakers slacked their duties in favour of the whisky jar.

Gulls cried on the firth, and there was a faint luminescence over the grey sea. Rain sleeted diagonally, darkening the early dusk at this northern latitude. Braziers burned, as did tar and pitch torches for light, not a single rechargeable power cell or glow lamp visible. That fact alone told Michael Pilgrim much about Fort George.

'Remember we're strangers here, Gover,' he whispered, as they queued in the jostling, cursing crowd. A reek of dried sweat and damp wool engulfed them. 'Say nothing if at all possible.'

Gover, his head covered by a broad scarf, obeyed the instruction.

Fort George had been constructed four hundred years earlier to thwart Jacobite rebels. Its earthen walls, jutting on a spit of land into the Moray Firth, had been seized by the Prince O'Ness's exiled court. This nobleman was son and heir to a more powerful ruler further down the coast, King Duncaine of Buchan. A tense, brittle love was said to exist between them. All knew the Prince O'Ness coveted his father's throne; that ambitious nobles, along with other desperadoes, had gathered to his cause. Hence his removal to Fort George.

Ditches and moats channelled the travellers through a stone-faced earthen bank, past a guardhouse without a roof. They followed a rickety wooden footbridge across a moat, marshy with seawater. At high tide, it flooded to a shallow depth. At the end of the footbridge lay a second, brick-lined tunnel through yet another rampart, wider than the first, collapsing in places, walls green with moss.

Here, more bored guards loitered, wearing leather armour and plaid cloaks. Michael's breath quickened. Amidst the caravan of peddlers, they shuffled into the tunnel over cobbles slippery with mud. The exit was framed by a dim day's fading. Then they were through. Fort George lay before them.

* * *

The gateway gave onto a large, rectangular field enclosed on three sides by thick ramparts. These earthworks were honeycombed with rooms built into the soil. Straight ahead, at the far side of a former parade ground, rose five and six-storied blocks of redbrick barracks and officer's quarters, sufficient for thousands of men in its heyday. That day was long gone. Most buildings were half-collapsed shells; a few had succumbed to gravity. More lay beyond the rectangle of barracks, but these Michael could only glimpse. He suspected they were former storehouses and workshops.

A terrible ammoniac reek lay on the parade ground of Fort George. The hooves of cattle, sheep, goats, and horses had churned the grass to a dung-impregnated mire, further loosened by barefoot wretches dwelling in the hovels beneath the ramparts. Fires had been built for cooking and comfort.

As dusk deepened, Michael detected three main classes in Fort George. Foremost, in terms of rank, were warriors bearing swords, spears and axes, but few firearms. These lorded it over a rabble of ill-clad, filthy, pinch-faced bonders and labourers. Nearby, a pair of wild harridans fought over some slight; meanwhile, their children watched or wrestled in imitation of their dams.

So much for civilization in Fort George, Michael thought.

A third class of humanity was also in evidence, pitching up stalls and booths near the ruined barracks. Here, merchants and mountebanks gathered in preparation for tomorrow's fair. Several pens contained livestock for sale. A drove of sheep entered through the tunnel, forcing Gover and Michael to squelch deeper into the square to avoid them.

In the middle, they came across a tall pile of greenwood, heather, and kindling stacked around an upright pole driven into the ground. Michael eyed it suspiciously.

A soldier had seized a slatternly girl — perhaps his regular quim, Michael could not say — busy taking her from behind, her face pressed into a mound of heather on the unlit bonfire. She panted in time to his grunting thrusts: he soon attained his end.

Michael realised Gover was retching from the complex stink. The City-man's fearful glance avoided the low, black clouds spitting rain.

'So vile,' spluttered Gover. 'So debased. What brought them so low?'

Michael's face hardened. 'You did.'

'I?'

'And you do still, by forbidding those brought low to rise. You made this place, Gover.'

He led the gagging City-man to the temporary village of merchants.

* * *

The merchants were a wary bunch, one eye on security, the other assessing those they hoped to fleece. Michael traded one of the City-hunter's unbreakable crossbow bolts for a handful of King Duncaine's bronze and silver pennies, the principal currency aside from barter in these parts.

Among the peddlers and their followers, Michael heard a familiar accent. A waterproof covering of ancient plastic sheets and carrier bags sewn together into a thick mat had been erected on poles; the rain clattered and clicked on its surface. Beneath, sat a short, wiry man with a low griddle on which he roasted honey-sweetened chestnuts, mulling wheat ale fortified with raw whisky. Choice delicacies intended for the Prince O'Ness's wealthy entourage. As was the private booth, where an attractive young woman slouched on a sturdy camp bed.

'Evening,' said Michael in his standard Yorkshire accent. Hitherto, he had attempted to speak Highlands.

'And to you, my good friend,' answered the comfort-peddler in a Scouse accent.

Michael did not care to suspect what had driven this man so far north. Yet he seemed to be prospering. Some folk always do.

It soon became clear the Scouser liked his own voice. He was also easily guided to topics of interest. Throughout, Gover slumped in misery on a crude stool.

'There are fewer people here than I expected,' began Michael. 'Less men, in particular.'

It was true: apart from male bonders, most of the 'frae folk' were women, children, or oldies.

The trader, who called himself Kenny, glanced around slyly.

'Not wrong there, mate. You know why, though? The Prince settled here five years ago, and he's been raiding the coast like a badger, collecting bonders and all sorts.' Again he glanced around. 'Fair play to him! Anyhow, this summer he quarrelled with his cousin, Dougie, across the firth in Cromarty. Took every boat he could find that didn't leak and sailed up there to burn him alive. So he swore.'

Michael sipped the mulled ale. Its fumes were giddy. 'What

happened?'

'A storm. Half the Prince's war-men drowned. Glug. Glug. But he swears he'll get revenge.'

'On the weather?'

'Nah. The Prince, he says it's witches what raised the storm and done it to him.'

Michael sighed. An old, old story.

Then Kenny told a more interesting tale. Six months earlier one of the Prince's raids netted a whole community of Nuager fisherfolk, already refugees from wars in Skye. Fine sailors, the very best. He had used them to guide his fleet on forays, ensuring their loyalty by hostaging their bairns. The Nuagers had warned him not to set sail before the storm, but he ignored their counsel. They were led by a woman, Mistress Priestess, she was called. Here Kenny paused significantly. 'Same again?'

Michael dutifully passed over another silver penny. 'Go on.'

'See that pile of wood?' Kenny pointed towards the bonfire in the deep darkness of the fort. 'The Prince O'Ness is going to burn this Mistress Priestess as a witch tomorrow. But there's more to it than that.'

'Oh, spare us,' groaned Gover, who could not help listening in disgust.

'Shut up,' said Michael.

The peddler licked his chapped lips significantly. He made a grinding, thrusting motion with his hips.

'The Prince wanted this Mistress Priestess?' suggested Michael.

'Got it, mate. Her name's Iona.'

'She answered nay?'

'Not for me to say.' Kenny eyed surrounding shadows. 'He should have taken a cruise with my Laura here.' He indicated the girl in the tent. 'The sort of storm she raises makes a man blithe. And for a very fair price.'

The girl on the camp bed stirred at the sound of her name.

'She's clean and tight where it counts,' continued Kenny. 'New to the game, if you understand me.'

Michael did.

'Not tonight, friend,' he said. He touched his hat to the girl.

* * *

They found an intact room in the old barracks with a wedgeable door and slept as best they could. Mice scurried, and beetles crawled over their faces and hands, waking Michael near dawn.

He lay for a while thinking of the Nuagers, a popular religion in the newly-established Commonwealth of the North. While ancient faiths — Christianity, Islam, along with nigh on all theories and verities — evaporated like puddles after the Great Dyings, the Nuagers somehow built bridges into terrified people's hearts.

Theirs was a message of pure hope. That if a community lived virtuously and in accordance with nature, they might be blessed. Cosmic ley lines to distant planets would whirl them from this poisoned, dunghill earth to begin anew.

The Nuagers thrived on visions and "sensings" of spirits lurking in tree, brook, or hill. They loved to dance, fornicate, and get intoxicated, for they believed altering dull patterns of the brain through mushroom, alcohol or herb was a holy endeavour, conducive to cosmic enlightenment. Michael had always found friends among the Nuagers. That their harmless creed had spread far north as Jockland heartened him.

Instead of the Mister Priestman followed by the Nuagers in Baytown, this lot had a Mistress Priestess. Iona. The doomed woman's musical name lingered in his head as he slumbered once more.

THIRTEEN

He dreamt of fishing boats escorted by dolphins arching through foam-crested waves beneath a starlit sky. A faint, mysterious circlet looked down: the pale moon.

* * *

With daylight, the fair commenced. Folk queued to enter Fort George with armfuls of homespun cloth, honeypots, leatherwork, beeswax candles. Others brought scavengings from the Before Times: bowls of ceramic and plastic, saucepans, knives repaired and whetted, every manner of object, including tattered books and magazines that few could read.

The sun banished last night's rain save for puddle and mire. All who queued were well-accustomed to mud sucking their toes.

The vast parade ground filled with buzz and hum. The tuning of fiddles brought a lump to Michael's throat. Ah, to be home with his own instrument. Acrobats tumbled, using the ramparts as elevated stages, or walked tightropes tied between stakes. Pipes and drums sparked a circle dance though evening would bring the real fun.

Every few yards a whisky-woman clutched a keg or jug of home-distilled spirits, calling her wares. At the food stalls, bread heaped beside cauldrons of broth simmering overnight. Sausages on sticks spat over fires, and big haunches of cattle boiled in briny water, fat, and scum skimmed off with wooden paddles.

Some peddlers sold exotic spices from the south: dried red chillies to make the dullest porridge burn, bags of lemons from sun-soaked Cornwall and Devon. Crabs sizzled in pans, washed down with strong ale. By late morning, more than a few stomachs unused to rich fare had emptied themselves into the already pungent mud.

Prostitutes' booths vibrated, canvas walls quivering to the rhythms of busy buttocks. A lively dog-baiting contest set champions against hopefuls, wild wagers cast as ears were torn off and the necks of fallen curs gaped open.

All in all, great success for the Prince O'Ness, proof he could bring prosperity as lord, not just disaster.

Not everyone was happy, though. A large group of folk in the motley-coloured outfits of the Nuagers, hats adorned with osprey feathers, sprigs of heather, seashells, prayed before the pile of wood and kindling in the centre of the fair. Half a dozen of the Prince's soldiers loitered nearby, guns, crossbows, and long swords ready.

Michael counted forty, fifty Nuager men and women, strong-boned and hale. No sign of the bairns kept hostage. Their tear-stained faces and cries for cosmic redemption were tempered by anxious glances at the guards. Michael approached their leader as soon as the prayer subsided.

'Sir,' Michael said.

'Aye.' The fisher-bonder was in his twenties, sturdy and long of limb. His eyes carried a glint of desperation.

'I know what's due to happen here,' said Michael quietly. 'This place is not safe for you and your people. I need a boat, several if you all join me.'

The man's red-rimmed eyes inspected him for falsehood. Finding none, he said: 'Aye, and nae doot ye'll help us to the moon as well. An' what of the Prince? Will he be letting us flee wi' ye like wild geese? And what of our bairns kept lockit away? What of them?'

Michael gripped his arm. Met his gaze. 'I speak of a land far to the south, beyond the Prince O'Ness's reach or revenge. I'm not saying it will be easy. But such a journey lies within your power. After this...' Once more, he nodded at the unlit bonfire. 'We shall talk, you and I, and then...'

A blare of bagpipes interrupted them. Folk fell silent as a procession of armed men entered the muddy field. At their head, two pipers blew a lusty, discordant anthem. Next came a large warrior in bear fur, bearing a sword at his side; on his brow, a crown of gold and silver jewellery melted and twisted together, studded with jewelled watch faces and strings of pearls.

His followers — Michael counted twenty — were also armed and dressed in dyed woollen plaids, furs, skirts. These must be his household men, though a few seemed little older than boys. A rough crew, not least the Prince. Their weapons drew Michael's attention: relatively few guns, a good sign. The Prince's sword was less encouraging. No blacksmith had forged such a fancy hilt. The Prince O'Ness wore a City-sword like the one hidden beneath Michael's cloak.

They swaggered over to the bonfire, the crowd gathering around. A few cheered; many were silent.

Michael noticed a slim, barefoot woman with bound hands among the entourage. She wore a white linen gown torn at the shoulder. Her skin was pale and in places bruised. Long, thick black hair hung from her shoulders. Her eyes were a deep green, alert and uncowed as she surveyed the crowd. A striking woman, her dignity softened by something fey, perhaps vulnerable. A young leader destined to never grow old.

Some of the raggedy frae folk, especially the women, called out hate. Yet the huddle of Nuagers wept openly to see their Mistress Priestess. Michael sensed a loyalty earned through kindness, not fear.

These impressions flitted across his conscious mind. And led him towards folly. Instead of distancing himself from the Nuagers, he stayed with them, even when Gover hissed. 'We need to be less conspicuous, you fool.'

* * *

The parade ground was large enough to drill whole regiments. The ragged circle of people surrounding the bonfire filled a relatively small area. In the hush, sheep and goats bleated; canvas flapping in the sea-breeze beat an irregular tattoo. Overhead, louring clouds drifted inland.

Into this quiet stepped a herald. A telescreen strapped to his arm like a shield denoted his station in the Prince's court, along with a wooden rattle he clacked and clattered. 'The Prince O'Ness!' he bellowed. 'Prince O'Justice! Aye, Prince O' Power! The witch must burn, says the Prince. And so she fuckin' shall!'

Calls of support from the crowd.

'Nae witch shall curse the Prince's ships wi' black de'il magic! Nae goodly men shall perish unvenged. The Prince O'Ness says: "Burn the witch!"'

Egged on by sergeants, the Prince's soldiers cheered. Michael assessed their dispositions: ten near the fort entrance, twenty or thirty round the bonfire, maybe another ten scattered around the parade ground perimeter. Maybe less.

'Savages,' muttered Gover beside him. Michael did not tell him to shut up.

As harsh hands bound Iona to the stake, Nuagers clutched each other for support. She stared out as though at infinity, oddly passive. Michael sensed deep struggles within her: how she wished to appear strong and proud to reassure her folk, how the longing for more life tormented her. Then the young woman looked down at her weeping followers and commenced a song. Her voice wavering and small at first:

> *Sing me a song of a soul that is gone,*
> *Say, could that soul be I?*
> *Merry of soul he sails on a day*
> *Over the sea to sky.*

THIRTEEN

One by one, the Nuagers took up the hymn. All knew that sky represented the Happy Planet true believers' spirits flew to after their brief lives on the poisoned earth. Iona had taught them so, as had the elders of their community before her.

> *Billow and breeze, islands and seas,*
> *Mountains of rain and sun,*
> *All that is good, all that is fair,*
> *All that is me is sun.*

The Prince O'Ness's guards shoved among them, dealing blows with fists and spear butts. Still, they sang, the defiant words swelling in volume, taken up by others in the crowd, secret believers.

Michael stepped aside to watch. Deep shame flooded his soul. A brave woman; a hideous, agonising death. No appeal, no court, no law. The caprice of a bully, deflecting blame for his failures — power's oldest story. He watched the angry Prince muttering into his herald's ear.

Then the herald shook his rattle, crying: 'If any man here dares fight the Prince O'Ness for the witch's life, let him stand for'ard now! Or are ye just women and bairns that can sing but nae fight!'

The Prince strode before the crowd, displaying his girth and sword, daring anyone to oppose him.

Michael's head lowered another notch.

'I'll fight! I'll fight!' called out a voice.

Michael looked up in surprise. It was the fisherman. Suddenly Michael understood: he must be the priestess's lover.

'No, James!' cried Iona as the young man shoved forward, desperate, afraid.

A roar arose from the Prince's retinue. Here was fun. Something for talk and jest at tonight's feast. A chance to confirm the man they followed was strong in a world punishing weakness.

'Chop his heed, laird!'

'Why aren't ye singin' now, witch?'

With great ceremony, the Prince removed his heavy bearskin cloak. Meanwhile, the Nuager had been given a sword and buckler. The Prince waved away his own right to a shield. 'I have to give the wee babby a chance,' he informed his men.

'You'll die, you bastard!' The fisherman rushed at the Prince through the mud.

The latter merely drew his sword — the City-sword that could slice an opponent down the middle like a razor splitting straw — effortlessly deflecting the hasty blow with the flat of his blade.

The crowd roared and a cruel game followed. A bold, confident swordsman, the Prince O'Ness soon had the fisherman slipping and sliding in the mire, panting with fear. Between feints, the Prince appealed for applause and was duly gratified. Others wept and prayed to the grey sky.

Michael's conscience writhed. Was this mankind? Gover called them savages. Grandfather would have done more than mourn so heartless a spectacle. He would have demanded justice.

At last, the Prince O'Ness yawned. 'I'm tired of this wee fuck,' he informed his men. Then with sudden violence, he struck the fishermen's sword, slicing it in two.

The exhausted Nuager fell to his knees, awaiting the end.

'Beg, and I might let him live,' the Prince taunted Iona.

'I beg you!' she shrieked. 'I beg!'

Casually, the Prince O'Ness grabbed the fisherman by his long hair, yanked up his head. With a single, jerky blow, he sliced it off. Blood gushed, bubbled.

Holding up the head, he tossed it to his followers. A wit among them used it as a football, kicking it to a pal, who returned the favour.

THIRTEEN

* * *

Michael Pilgrim's eyes were wide now. What he saw lay far from the reeking mud of Fort George. Far from the men preparing to light the bonfire on which Iona screamed. He was back in the Crusades, barely out of his teens. Where exactly? Syria. They used to call everywhere Syria, even when they knew it bore a different name. Somehow it didn't matter.

A city of concrete buildings turned to rubble and dust. The men under his command playing football with a human head, its eyes occasionally flashing white. Wearily, he had pushed into the scrum of players, shoving them away from the head. Boos, laughter.

'Spoilsport!' taunted Corporal Baxter, crazed by bong after bong of stuff. Almost the whole company off their heads. It was how you got through. 'Spoilsport, Lieutenant!'

Then Michael had laughed too. Did one more head make any difference? One among so many severed from life and love, eyes empty, mouth filled with dust?

Weary of responsibility, tormented by Grandfather's voice in his brain: *Remember the quality of mercy is not strained, Michael ... Remember, you must be better than others to remind themselves they may be better themselves ... Your duty to mankind is to help recover what is lost ... Justice, the rule of law ... Preserve, preserve, preserve...*

He had wept at his failures, his weakness, skulking in a ruined mosque, sucking oblivion from Baxter's bong.

The memory faded. Michael's eyes focused. He saw the woman tied to the pole. Saw men preparing torches to set the kindling ablaze. He saw the Prince O'Ness's men dribble the head from one to another. He remembered his shame as a Crusader, the heads taken by the Cityhunter on his airbike. He thought of the men and women his unit had flame-throwered in Syria, flesh and fat bubbling as it melted. And yet, for all his self-loathing, an icy sliver of mind sensed an opportunity.

Taking the pistols from his belt, he stuffed them into Gover's hands. 'Hold my coat and bag,' he commanded, squelching forward through the Nuagers.

'I forbid this!' came Gover's startled cry behind him. 'Idiot! I demand that you stop!'

FOURTEEN

Michael Pilgrim stood before the Prince O'Ness, who was busy toasting his success with deep gulps from a tarnished silver flask of whisky. He turned and addressed the crowd.

'I accept the Prince O'Ness's challenge!'

A long silence held as the crowd assessed him.

'I accept,' he repeated, 'on condition all here acknowledge one thing. You will not harm the woman if I win.'

The Prince listened with surprised amusement, the flask still raised.

'And,' added Michael, 'that you pledge to set her people, these Nuagers, free from bondership. Including their bairns. Oh, and that you return their boats to them.'

Amazement turned to mirth among the Prince's followers.

'Anything else you'll be wanting?' called one.

Michael considered. 'We shall also need provisions.'

'An' who the fuck are ye?' demanded the Prince. 'Wi' your stranger's talk an' rig?'

Before Michael could answer, a soldier pushed forward, pointing excitedly.

'I saw him, laird! I saw him in Tykeland. At Pickering Market where your twae cousins and uncle fell. He's a fucking Tyke, laird, a Yorksheer bastard. The Butcher o' Pickering he is. Aye, laird, he's kennit as

Pilgrim. Pilgrim!'

Michael faced the Prince. All was up now. 'Do you accept my challenge or are you a coward?'

That last word hung in the air. Perhaps it saved him from being dragged off for questioning by boot and fist. The Prince passed the whisky flask to his herald and touched the hilt of his sword.

'I've heard of ye, Pilgrim. There's honour in killing a cruel, heartless de'il like you. And they say twae heeds are better than one!'

His followers roared, clashing weapons together. This time the Prince O'Ness did not delay or play. He lunged forward and swung hard at Michael's freshly drawn sword. No doubt he expected to slice through the blade into his opponent's flesh. The hardest metal was no guard against a plasti-steel edge. But the swords bounced off each other with a reverberating hum.

'Yer fuck!' cried the Prince.

For the first time in his life, he faced a weapon equal to his own.

Circling. Swords pointed. Neither dared lunge. A pool of blackish-red spread from the fisherman's decapitated corpse. The Prince poised, trained to the blade from boyhood. Circling. With a shout, the Prince slashed. Plasti-steel whistled. A low hum after the swords clashed.

Michael retreated. He knew now the Prince was the superior swordsman. Knew his head would likely be taken. Fear had to be banished except as adrenalin, lest his limbs grow watery, his concentration fail.

The Prince attacked, pushing him back. Parry. Dodge. Again Michael scrambled to escape. Circling. Jeers erupted from the Prince's men.

Hum. Whip whistle. Dodge. Retreat.

Then Michael glimpsed hope. His opponent out-of-breath, red-faced, a fraction slower each time he attacked. In a flash, he saw the story: a long night of carousing and short sleep. A numbing hangover treated with more drink to cure it. The exertion of playing with the fisherman had tired an already tired man.

Michael stepped away, fleeter, unencumbered by armour, using the headless corpse as a barrier. The Prince mocking, breathless, called him a coward, forced to come after him. Michael pretended to attack so the Prince lunged, failed to connect, paused to whoop for air.

Circle. Swords whistled as they whipped. For the first time, Michael leapt recklessly forward.

His sword made it past the Prince's guard. Straight through armour, elbow, back out into the air. As though time itself had frozen, the lower half of the Prince's left arm dropped into the mud, followed by great welling gouts of blood.

Gaping shock as he gazed at his severed limb.

'Last chance!' cried Pilgrim. 'Surrender on the terms we agreed!'

Yet the Prince still had his right arm. His sword.

'Aaargh!' He rushed onto the point of Pilgrim's blade. As he wrenched it out, Michael sawed up and down. The Prince O'Ness collapsed in a heap, lumpy guts spilling grey and red from the gash in his armour.

No one in the crowd moved or spoke. Michael stood with sword raised to fend off invisible opponents, wild-eyed, heaving for air.

'Yer fucker!' bellowed the herald, drawing an ornate, long-barrelled pistol.

Boom. Gover's blunderbuss detonated at close range, smoke billowing. The warrior and two of his companions were caught in the blast. Then Gover pulled out a pistol and calmly shot another warrior in the face at point-blank range. The man's brains splattered over the crowd.

Chaos erupted. Bonders enslaved from all over the Highlands and even England during raids by sea and land, saw their chance, jumping guards, seizing improvised weapons. Among them, scores of Nuagers fighting for their very lives.

* * *

A short, cruel battle commenced in the enclosed parade ground of Fort George. People fled in all directions. Distinguishing friend from foe was no straightforward matter. The outcome, however, was hardly in doubt. The Prince's force comprised a rump of its former strength when the fair commenced. By the time it ended, half lay dead, wounded or dying in the filth. Most frae folk fled with the remnants of the soldiery, gathering outside the ramparts in a frightened, clamouring, leaderless mob. As for the merchants and peddlers, they grabbed what valuables they could and cowered behind barricades of overturned trestles, taking up hidden weapons to defend their possessions.

The field was left to a crowd of bonders and malcontents against the Prince's rule. Many fell straight to looting or besieging the thick-walled powder store and magazine of the ancient fortress, where the Prince's wives and bairns and last few loyal retainers defended his treasure house.

A group rushed to the old garrison chapel, where their children were kept hostage, discovering the guards had already fled.

Binding a slash across his arm with a strip torn from a dead soldier's cloak, Michael watched Gover squelch through the mud. During the battle, the City-man had taken possession of the Prince O'Ness's blood-stained sword. He had also taken sanctuary with the merchants. Yet Michael remembered the quick-witted blunderbuss shot that saved his life.

'I owe you,' Michael said.

'You do indeed,' mused Gover. 'May one assume that, by your own code, I am now your absolute master? Like Aladdin and his genie. At least, until you save my life?'

Michael resisted the temptation to tell him to shut up.

The Nuagers cheered and screeched hysterical thanks to the stars as

FOURTEEN

their leader was cut free from the unlit pyre.

* * *

Close up, Iona of Skye was younger than Michael had guessed. Dirt streaked her thin, delicate face. It was a hopeful face, unhardened by the world's many wrongs. Blue and purple bruises around her neck suggested the grasp of cruel fingers. Michael felt old in thought and deed compared to her, though less than ten years lay between them.

Iona knelt by the headless body of her lover until a burly, white-haired fisherman drew her away. For a long minute, she shivered while the fisherman placed a blanket around her shoulders. Finally, she spied Michael frisking corpses for weapons, ammunition, anything useful.

'I prayed and prayed the guid stars would send help,' she said in a voice edged with fear. Her accent of the Western Isles was light and musical.

Michael paused to meet her eye, tossing a vicious-looking dirk onto the pile of weapons he had gathered.

'Never before have the stars answered,' she said. 'Though our folk suffered terrible enough. I had begun to lose faith.' She laughed in disbelief. 'Then they sent you.'

Michael glanced awkwardly at the fort's entrance. Before long, the Prince's men and frae folk would come charging up that brick-lined tunnel, hungry for revenge. Numbers were on their side, as was the terrain.

'There's no time for that, priest woman,' he said, gruffly.

Gover glanced up, surprised by his tone.

'Assemble all your people.' Michael ticked off a list on his fingers. 'We need food. Water. Blankets. Whatever weapons and powder you can find in addition to this lot. Then we must take ship and escape.

Either that or perish!'

Iona listened distractedly. 'The bairns must be comforted first. They are frightened.' The young woman gestured at the bodies strewn across the parade ground. 'So much blood. Did it have to come to this?'

Before Michael could respond, a loud, deep voice interrupted: Gover, amplified through his translation device.

'You, Mistress Priestess, Iona of Skye! The stars did send us! Now is the time to commence your journey to the stars. Do as this man says. We are servants of the stars. Take us to your strongest, swiftest boats. Do it now.'

As the booming voice faded, many of the Nuagers fell to their knees, imploring arms upraised to the heavens, a ritual gesture of submission to a cosmic destiny. Still, Iona seemed uncertain.

A gunshot echoed outside the walls.

'Someone out there is restoring order and marshalling his troops,' said Michael. 'No more time for talk.' He turned to Gover. 'Boats. Food. Water. Weapons. Blankets. In that order.'

Snatching his pistols back from the City-man, Michael grabbed those Nuagers carrying arms, chivvying them into a rough line. 'Form up!' he shouted in his best drill voice. 'Stand firm. They'll not get in here if we stand firm. You, get that halberd!'

Another gunshot outside. To Michael's relief, Iona awoke to their danger.

'Do as they say!' she cried. 'Quickly!'

Michael loaded his pistols, commanding his small company to do the same with whatever firearms they knew how to use. Then he picked up a long-barrelled musket.

'Oh, and make sure you knock a breach in the hulls of any boats we aren't taking,' he called to her.

Desperate minutes followed; Michael couldn't be sure how long. He

FOURTEEN

gathered his force and led them to defend the entrance. Just in time. A small party of the Prince's soldiers were approaching to reconnoitre. A bullet hole in the shoulder of their leader from Michael's new musket persuaded them to withdraw in a panic-stricken clatter.

All Michael needed was to win time. Sooner than he had hoped, other enemies were sneaking along the shingle beach to enter the fort by entrances he did not know.

Gunfire erupted as the Jocks, never cowards or to be underestimated, formed a firing line to cover an assault of infantry. Lead balls bounced off the stonework. One of the Nuagers took an arrow in his arm. Michael counted a force of nearly a hundred, armed with clubs and spears, gathering to recapture the feeble defences of Fort George, spurred on by a wail of bagpipes.

'To the boats for our lives!' cried one of the older Nuagers, a leader among them, the white-haired fisherman who had comforted Iona earlier. The man's name was Dameron.

* * *

Michael followed Dameron through a collapsed sally port in the ramparts, down to the small harbour they had glimpsed when first approaching Fort George. Here, four wooden ships with high prows and sterns were being loaded with casks, boxes, bundles.

The vessels, known in that region as birlinn, resembled miniature Viking ships. Each carried eight pairs of oars and a large, square woollen sail. Modern touches had been added to this ancient design: a compass near the tiller; watertight storage boxes, and a water reservoir beneath a shell of thin planking over the keel and ribs; also hand-pumps to keep the bilges dry, as a well as a small, low cabin erected in the stern.

These same boats had already sailed east when the Nuagers fled the burning of their community on Skye, as well as surviving the storm that wrecked the rest of the Prince O'Ness's ill-fated fleet. Sturdy craft, capable of riding most storms if well-handled — and few sailors rivalled the Nuager fisherfolk.

Michael found Iona supervising the last loading. Gover already sat in a cabin, calling out over his voice amplifier: 'Hurry! Hurry! The stars are impatient. They want us to leave at once.'

'We are ready,' said Iona in her high, light brogue. 'There's a deal more food than water-laden, but streams run a-plenty along the coast. We are ready.'

Michael reloaded the musket, looking over the remaining seaworthy ships in the harbour.

'You haven't scuppered them,' he cried. 'We will be pursued.'

A stubborn, judicious look crossed Iona's fair, young face. 'It is a great sin to deliberately sink a boat without good reason.' She spoke with quiet assurance. 'There can be no passage to the Happy Planet for folk who needlessly destroy other folk's means of life.'

Michael listened in outrage. 'Gover!' he bellowed.

While the Nuagers climbed aboard and prepared to cast off from the harbour, he and the City-man ran from boat to boat, their plasti-steel swords carving large holes in the wooden planks of the craft. They had just finished when bullets whistled past. The Prince's men had re-occupied Fort George.

Michael and Gover scrambled into the last birlinn to leave — Iona's own — just as it was shoved off with long oars. Taking out his musket, Michael took careful aim at a lad waving an axe and jumping up and down. Then, wearied of killing, Michael Pilgim lowered the gun and uncocked it.

Into the Moray Firth rowed the four birlinns laden with folk and stores. A few bullets pursued them. Soon they were out of range, veiled by wave crests and spray. The walls of Fort George appeared squat and black against hill and mountain.

Iona steadied Michael's arm as he sank to the plank floor of the boat. His hands had begun to shake; sweat shone on his face. He had never felt so amazed to be alive.

'Where now?' she asked eagerly. 'Where is this land the stars promised? Your friend told me it is a place of peace and plenty. Is it far?'

Michael admitted to himself that he had no definite notion. One thing he did know — merciless, swift pursuit was inevitable.

'It's near enough,' he answered as the boat pitched and tossed. 'Trust us.'

Beside him, Gover snorted then vomited in the bilges.

FIFTEEN

The monorail carriage was not large — no need for many seats when passengers were few. Nor did it speed, though it could at need. Why hurry when today and tomorrow stretched ahead long and vacant? Besides, the view through the wall-high windows warranted more than a blurred glance.

Mughalia nestled in lush, tropical highlands cooled by winds from the ocean, an oasis compared to the irradiated, sun-scorched aridlands formerly known as India. Averil marvelled at peak and waterfall, sudden glimpses of vivid blue sky framed by waves of green valleys. She clutched the sides of her padded chair, unused to travelling faster than a horse-drawn cart.

Helen leaned forward with a smile. 'How do you feel? I heard you being sick this morning. A good sign, surely.'

Averil smiled. Marvellous as Helen's knowledge might be, she knew little of plain women's troubles. Averil envied her that, among all the other things.

'Are you ill?' asked their new companion, edging away on her seat.

That morning, Marvin and Merle Brubacher had introduced them to a dusky-complexioned woman so lovely — soft copper skin and hair like an angel's — that Averil felt an urge to cover her own face. Synetta, Marvin had explained, was to be their guide in Mughalia, for he and his wife had pressing business in the run-up to the Grand Autonomy.

Notably, he added, frowning at Helen as though it was somehow her fault, as Blair Gover was still hiding away. He had suggested a trip to the resort at Adam's Peak for a few days.

'Averil is not ill,' Helen told Synetta.

Averil could tell Helen didn't quite care for Synetta.

'It's just that I'm in a family way,' Averil said, as the monorail swept along the side of a steep valley, making her clutch the seat all the harder.

For a moment, it seemed Synetta did not understand. Then a look of astonishment, longing, and sorrow twisted her placid, doll-like face. She stared down at Averil's stomach.

'I won't show, as we call it, for months yet,' said Averil.

Synetta sighed. Bizarrely, she seemed almost envious.

Helen could have explained to her young friend why Synetta did not dare mourn aloud for the lost possibility of children. Sterility was an unavoidable by-product of cell renewal. Besides, to complain openly about any aspect of the Beautiful Life risked Discordia, and expulsion from the Five Cities. Safer to howl inside. So Averil remained none the wiser.

Later, Synetta produced a gift of a tight-fitting bracelet of gold and glittering stones. 'Wear this for as long as you are in Mughalia.' She was languid and self-contained once more. 'It will allow us to keep you safe here.'

Averil burst into tears at gaining such a generous new friend.

* * *

Discordia was much on Helen's mind as the monorail wove through the Sri Lankan highlands. While waiting to depart, she had overheard a conversation between a group of Beautifuls also bound for Adam's Peak. They were a mixture of Asian, Hispanic and Anglo — though outward appearances could seldom be trusted. Her high-backed chair beside Synetta allowed her to listen unseen.

'I believe we are being held back,' declared a proud voice. 'You cannot stop progress.'

'No wonder people are excited,' added another. 'Think about it. The first time in decades we've been offered anything that isn't the same old, same old. Not everyone is interested in science or whatnot. We can't all be gene-boffs or node-heads. This would allow all of us to run our own outfits, just like the old days. What is the point if you can never grow?'

Silence greeted that daring question. A woman with an Asian, singsong accent said, 'But is it wise to take risks? I've heard strange stories...'

What she had heard was clearly best unspoken.

On the journey, Helen wondered at such public carping. It cast light on Blair's predicament. In her years away from the Five Cities, it seemed divisions, always lurking, had erupted to the surface. Perhaps Blair was right to blame accumulated boredom. She also wondered who the men and women in the monorail carriage had been before the Great Dyings. Impossibly rich and spoiled, perhaps, to afford the Beautiful Life. Shareholders in the quest for immortality rather than positive contributors. Their minds ever more shielded and pampered from harsh realities as the decades unrolled, cocooned in fripperies and serenaded by strains of pleasure — until pleasure became the hardest thing to attain.

Many Beautifuls, like Marvin and Merle, had been super-tycoons, skilful at amassing wealth. Yet in the Five Cities, there was no commerce, no buying or selling. Most Beautifuls won credits through undemanding contributions to the smooth running of the system. Meanwhile, drones that designed drones — including drones that also built and maintained and repaired drones — did the rest. Here was an irony. The competitive instincts that had enabled many Beautifuls to buy their one-way ticket to longevity before the plagues began were not just redundant but banned as Discordia. It was a simple enough existence: accept the rules and your every need will be met, save one — contentment.

* * *

In the distance rose Adam's Peak, an isolated, conical mountain set apart by low hills. Red stone cliffs, clad with creepers, walled the mountainside, along with stands of jungle and dense undergrowth. Wispy cloudlets clung to the summit, dissolving in the morning sun. White birds rose in a flock from the trees and wheeled, their wings catching the sun like specks of light.

So much for nature. What drew Averil's eye was the work of man.

A fairy tale castle had been constructed on the flat table-top of the mountain. Towers with numerous balconies, walkways, pagodas, terraces, banqueting halls, and diversion facilities, lavish boudoirs for hundreds of visitors at a time. Windows glittered like jewels.

'I reckon this is what Heaven must look like!' she cried.

Synetta smiled indulgently, patting Averil's hand.

Helen's reaction had been ironic: 'When I was young there was a place called Disneyland. That looked like Heaven, too, to a child. It served pretty much the same function as Adam's Peak.'

A splinter of irritation entered Averil, though Disneyland meant nothing to her. Sometimes Helen reminded her of Uncle Michael, always denying her right to an opinion, always right.

'It's better than Baytown,' she replied doggedly.

'Better?' said Helen. 'Perhaps. In lots of ways. But it exists at the expense of so many people.'

Averil did not like such talk. Nor, she noticed, did Synetta, who began to nervously consult her screen.

After they disembarked and took a lift to the summit, Averil was nagged by remorse. Helen was so good to her! Yet the bustle of perfect folk and their servant drones soon drew her attention. She could never look at them enough. Aircars flew low over the valley, silver birds without wings. Holograms created light sculptures on the hillside lest travellers needed extra diversion on the way up. Averil knew she could never discover the end of the marvels here. She felt Helen's steady gaze upon her and blushed.

* * *

Averil Pilgrim's head whirled even as she slept. During the day, Helen insisted on trips into the hills and forests surrounding Adam's Peak, claiming the resort and crowds of Beautifuls gave her a headache. Averil stared at the strange insects and plants but felt happier when they returned to the safety of the pleasure complex.

Synetta accompanied them everywhere and soon began to call her Avi. This delighted and flattered the Baytown girl, who felt obliged to answer her new friend's frequent questions. Synetta possessed a respect verging on awe for Dr Blair Gover; she often enquired about his visit and mysterious disappearance.

Helen, too, was evidently impatient for him to contact her, though she said little. Yet Averil felt glad he kept away: his return meant her own to the cold and wet of a North Yorkshire winter.

After two days, Marv and Merle Brubacher flew over from the City of Mughalia, occupying a particularly lavish suite as befitted their status. Averil had already noticed how some of Adam's Peak's guests whispered and stared at Helen. Once the Brubachers arrived, elaborate bows and flattery were added to the attention their party attracted. That made Averil feel important, too, though she knew it had nothing to do with her. Back home, no one regarded her especially; here it felt like she was more than just a Pilgrim, Uncle Michael's niece.

For the first time in her life, there seemed too few hours in the day: holocasts you could watch forever; servitor drones quick to obey; stately dances in fabulous gowns; myriad delicacies she couldn't name, unlike the hearty but crude meals of home.

At dusk, she walked on the terraces and stared out across the jungle canopy, haunted by the knowledge all this must be taken from her, that Helen would decide everything.

Each day gifted fractions of growth to the baby in her womb. It seemed no harm or deformity could come to Baby here. Mughalia was a place without sickness.

Each day also lengthened her separation from Amar. Sometimes Averil felt guilty about how little she missed him, aware his face was fading in her mind. From the vantage of the high terraces of Adam's Peak, she wondered if her marriage had been decided by others. Everyone had expected her to melt with gratitude for Amar's help during Big Jacko's hideous reign — and she did feel grateful. Except gratitude felt less and less like love.

* * *

Averil's delight with Mughalia and her bouts of introspection did not go unnoticed. As days passed without further news of Blair, Helen passed through ever-darkening shades of anxiety.

One evening, she walked out to find her young companion staring west. A sunset of extravagant gold, crimson, grey and silver strands backlit the horizon of black mountain silhouettes.

Helen cleared her throat; Averil stirred from her reverie. She joined arms with the girl.

'Were you thinking of home?' Helen asked.

'Yes, I was.'

'Do not fear. I will make sure you get home safe and sound.'

'But I feel safe here! And more sound.'

Helen examined her carefully. 'Averil, you must be wary of this place. We know Blair's enemies are active and could be anyone we meet. People wear many masks in the Five Cities. It is how they survive. Besides, you must see that you cannot belong here. You are what these people call a primitive. At heart, they care about nothing deeply but themselves. Believe me, Averil, I know. You see, I once thought and lived like them.'

If the girl was swayed, she gave no sign.

'In the Five Cities appearances are almost always diversions,' continued Helen. 'This beauty, this plenty, is built upon deeper corruptions than you can imagine. Do not be seduced! You are far, far better than the Beautiful Life's false faces.'

Averil turned to her, trembling, though the day's warmth still lingered in the carved stonework of the terrace.

'That's easy for you to say. Oh, if you'd seen half of what I have! The dirt, the misery, the plague — oh yes — and you know full well what they made me do to my little boy, leaving him on the beach for the tide to wash away like sea-tilth. I hate them for that. And I always will. It's no wonder I prefer it here.'

'But you told me yourself your baby was malformed. He would not have survived. It was an impossible decision, meant as a mercy for the child.'

Even as she tried to justify a hungry community exposing babies, Helen shared Averil's disgust. Who they blamed for the tragedy, however, differed.

'Baytown folk need to be more like people here,' replied Averil. 'Civilization, that's Uncle Michael's favourite word. Only they don't deserve it. If Baytown were given a dollop of his precious civilization, they wouldn't know what to do with it.'

Helen took the girl's hand. 'The Five Cities are purposefully trapping your people in backwardness. They are to blame, Averil.'

The jut of the girl's jaw scorned such an idea.

'Let me show you something,' said Helen. 'We will use my screen to magnify what we see. Watch.'

She scanned a particular area at the foot of the mountain until she found what she wanted. 'I discovered this when I last stayed here. It ... it shocked me then, though I did nothing about it. Now it seems a fitting symbol of the foundations on which the Five Cities and all their wonders rest.'

The magnified hologram followed a winding flight of worn stone steps down the hillside. Helen explained it was once a pilgrim route to the summit when the mountain was topped by a Buddhist shrine instead of a resort. Then Helen focussed on rubbish heaped in a vast pit. Plain, functional drones were stolidly processing waste food and trash amidst dense clouds of black flies. This, in itself, was unremarkable. What made Helen point were the dozens of semi-naked, swarthy creatures crawling through the filth, seeking scraps of food or anything useful. Among them, two children fought over the remains of a chicken carcase. The sight made Helen recall Averil had dined on roast chicken the night before.

'Do you see?' Helen said. 'These are the local primitives. They could be you. Your family. Your neighbours. They are not allowed to practise agriculture in the Highlands, lest it spoils the view. So some of them have diminished in stature and skills to this. Averil, please do not allow your good nature to be blinded by what is false and selfish.'

Averil pulled away, tears starting. 'You don't understand! You'll never understand!'

With that, the girl ran heedlessly inside. She almost knocked over Synetta who bore an invitation for Helen to partake of synth-cocktails with the Brubachers.

* * *

Averil barely slept that night. There was a proverb in Baytown: 'A good friend's advice hurts; a bad friend's never.' Helen's words haunted a conscience finely tuned by her father's homilies, and the virtuous history of the Pilgrim family in Baytown.

Averil clutched her belly and wondered whether admiring the Five Cities was indeed to betray her own kind. Perhaps their marvels should be seen as the ultimate model to follow, orderly, secure, sanitary. She knew very well what Uncle Michael would say to that, let alone anyone who had ever been terrified by drones. And had she so soon forgotten her family's storehouses and animals, let alone poor Darren the herd boy, destroyed by City drones? No, the Five Cities were hardly friends of hers.

Perhaps Helen was right then; sympathising with these lovely gods and goddesses on their mountaintop was to deny her own good nature. She remembered the pilgrim path down the mountainside to the rubbish dump at its foot where primitives grovelled for food. Was she herself not a primitive and a Pilgrim?

Dawn rose over Adam's Peak; Averil went to the same terrace where Helen had shown her the rubbish tip. Steps descended the mountain, guarded by two squat security drones. Once, she would have fled at the mere sight of them; now she saw them as useful tools, well-trained, savage guard dogs. The drones scanned and ignored her as she passed, save for a single brief red flash.

She navigated the steep, crumbling stone stairs, slippery red soil. On either side, shrubs and trees grew tall, arching trunks and tufts of delicate leaves. Monkeys and birds chattered, shrieked, chuckled. Mist curled over moss-bearded boulders and crags. Butterflies flexed and unflexed brilliant red and blue wings to dry the dew.

Down, down Averil went, following the path's winding course, driven by a desire she could not articulate beyond a simple thought: I will find out the truth for myself. Sometimes she halted, afraid of animals or the debased people Helen's screen had revealed, glancing back for reassurance at the towering, mighty buildings on the mountaintop.

After an hour, she reached the rubbish processing area. It occupied a larger site than she had imagined. As Averil watched, hiccups of waste food and effluent spewed forth from pipes. Close up, the reek overwhelmed her: faecal, sweet, she gagged, and her stomach clenched. Beetles and flies fed in unimaginable numbers on the maggot-riddled filth, even as burly drones scooped it into machines for compression and processing. Rats scurried, afraid of snakes.

Averil cried out, her hand flying up to cover her mouth. People, or their approximates, tried to beat the drones to choice morsels, their skin stained many colours by the waste. Small and malnourished, eyes big and brown in skulls covered by gaunt, stretched skin. Savages. What other word applied?

Suddenly dizzy, Averil clutched her nauseous stomach. Baby would be infected by them! When she returned to Baytown, Baby would be exposed on the beach near Ravenscar. She must get away. Escape these diseased monsters. Protect herself; protect Baby.

Averil turned and shrieked. A small group of naked little people had gathered behind her. They fell to their knees, imploring in a language she could not understand.

Her head spun. The jungle, drones, savages, sky, rubbish mounds, all whirled. Each breath tainted her lungs, made her gag. She fainted.

* * *

Averil woke to light filtering through plasti-silk blinds. Dream-memories of diseased, filthy hands reaching out to devour her raw. Voices were conversing. Averil blinked at a gathering near the bedroom door: Helen, Synetta, Marvin and Merle Brubacher, and another man in the outfit of a doctor.

'Ah, here she is!' chuckled Marvin in his avuncular bass. 'No harm done. I told you ladies not to make a fuss.'

Merle rolled her eyes. 'My love, please consider, just for once, that not everyone is a roughty-toughty fellow like you. I really do not think Helen was fussing over her servant.'

Helen hurried over to the bed, smiling.

'What happened?' Averil asked, afraid they were angry with her for leaving the security of the resort.

'What happened, young lady,' said Marvin, 'was that you did a foolish thing. Especially given your condition, which Synetta has just mentioned to us.' He raised his hand. 'But never worry. I've sent a couple of drones to clean out the creatures down there. They won't be a nuisance again.'

'You really should have taken more care,' said Merle.

Helen perched on the bed.

'It's my fault, Averil. The shock of being in so strange a place ... I should have thought.'

Averil offered a weak smile. Whatever Marvin might say, it felt good to be fussed over. Flickers of childhood grief stirred. She remembered her dead mother feeding her broth in bed when she was ill as a small girl.

'I'm alright,' she said.

'It's bed rest for you, young lady,' insisted Merle.

Marvin nodded briskly. 'Now, Helen, concerning that business I mentioned...'

Averil watched them file out the door, Helen flapping an apologetic hand to show she had no choice but to follow the Brubachers.

FIFTEEN

Alone once more, Averil pulled the sheet close. She had gone down the path, looking for truth, and she'd found it. Yes, those pitiable, sad, and deformed creatures — what were they? — had taught her the truth. The existence of Beautifuls in this world counterbalanced a small measure of its dirt and danger. Helen was wrong to doubt that. Why shouldn't there be high and low? It was only natural.

She recalled Seth's dream of travelling to the City and winning a place there. Now she understood his desire. Besides, there was Baby to consider.

*　*　*

It was as though they read Averil's deepest wishes. The doctor showed her via his screen. Wonderful possibilities: holograms of her back as it had been, cured of the deep scars she'd received from Maister Gil's whip for defying Big Jacko — long ago, it seemed, in an unreal world. Next, holograms of her face improved, that was the word the doctor used, and when Averil saw herself with a straight nose and less pointy chin — a face more like Synetta's — she sobbed a single word, 'Please.' The doctor told her it was a small gift from Marvin and Merle Brubacher.

When Helen found out, she grew tearful as well. Not from happiness it soon became transparent. 'Do not do this,' she urged the young woman. 'Be yourself. Heal the scars, yes, but leave your lovely face as nature made it.'

Averil had grown angry. 'You're not as nature made you. You've been improved! Why shouldn't I?'

To that, Helen had no real answer. 'You will become someone else's image of perfection. Is that what you truly want?'

But it was. It was.

They operated that same afternoon. Why delay for such a simple matter? The supervising doctor explained the procedure and drones did the rest. Averil fell into a deep sleep. She did not sense — except perhaps at some deep, unconscious level gifted to expectant mothers — that more than just her nose and chin and scarred back were probed. Also her womb.

SIXTEEN

The four birlinns rose and sank in the swell, manoeuvred by oars to form a huddle of boats. Eighty men, women and children, the entire Nuager community liberated from Fort George. Food, scant possessions, nets, rope, tools, and weapons piled between the rowers' benches.

Exhilaration contended with exhaustion. On one craft, however, hurried counsels took place. A column of smoke rose in warning from Fort George.

'Word'll fly to the Prince O'Ness's daddy soon enough,' predicted Dameron, the white-haired fisherman. 'Then it'll be a muckle pot o' vengeance he'll be wanting.'

Michael Pilgrim held the side of the boat as it swayed. He'd never been fond of a choppy sea.

'They will expect you to head north,' he said. 'It's where you come from, after all. So that way is not safe. We should follow the coast eastwards until it turns south.'

'To the happy land predicted by the stars,' added Gover, his smile unctuous.

Dameron and Iona exchanged looks. They felt deeply uncomfortable around the City-man: Michael didn't blame them.

'We have nary a friend to the north,' Iona said, in her light way. 'But now's not the time for such a large decision. We need to staunch wounds and take on water. Dameron, can you find us a safe place along the coast for tonight? We'll think no further than that.'

The older man spat into the sea for luck. 'Ye'll find safe places rare as badger wings in the Kingdom of Buchan. King Duncaine is not a man to cross.'

Before the conference of vessels loosened into sailing formation, Iona stood and called out a loud ululating plea to sea, sky, and star for guidance. The Nuagers lowered their heads, repeating each of her phrases with one voice. Such unity made them powerful allies.

Blair Gover, his sea-sickness at bay, watched with a mixture of bilious amusement and contempt.

'Do you really believe that these things possess the capacity to carry me all the way to your home?' he asked, indicating both birlinns and their crews. 'A journey of hundreds of miles?'

'Further,' said Michael.

'You had better be right, Pilgrim. There is something I must collect from that ridiculous museum beloved of my former paramour.'

'What is so important?'

Gover seemed not to hear. Michael realised how very little he trusted his intentions. Safer all round to toss him overboard for the lobsters to nibble.

* * *

A slow crawl along the coast, waves and wind against them. Slowly the afternoon darkened. No boats pursued from Fort George, or none they spotted.

With dusk still a way off, the tired flotilla sighted a dense forest on the shore and Dameron indicated they should make for it. He had fished this coast since their capture by the Prince O'Ness, even as far as King Duncaine's capital at Peterhead, far to the east.

SIXTEEN

'There's a haven there,' he told Iona, leaning on the tiller. 'The forest's name is Culbin.'

To Michael and Gover, he spoke not at all.

They sailed through a narrow estuary into the mile-wide tidal lagoon of Findhorn, beaching at a tiny hamlet in the ruins of a larger village from the Before Times. A solitary community fed by foraging, fishing and hunting in the dark woodland overshadowing the lagoon.

'I'll ask yonder folk's permission to stay the night,' said Iona, hopping lightly from her boat.

Michael picked up his musket and sword. 'I should go with you.'

'Nay, put away that gun, Mister Star Man, if you please. We've seen enough killing for many a weary day.'

With that, she padded across the shellfish and plastic-littered strand.

'Perhaps you should go with her,' Michael said to Dameron.

The fisherman grunted. 'Ye have much to learn about that lassie. She does as she pleases, like her mother and grandma afore her.'

Soon enough Iona returned from the hamlet, beaming and bearing a clay pot trailing wisps of smoke.

'They bid us right welcome and said the Prince O'Ness is no friend of theirs. And the women gave us this fire-gift for our cooking and to warm the bairns.'

She looked closely at Michael. Dark strands of long, greasy hair fell across her cheeks from a centre parting; her thin face and nose were almost faery, so he thought. Mister Priest Man back in Baytown would take to her just fine. They could swap theories about cosmic ley lines while conversing with the local sprites.

'See, nay need for guns,' she said.

That night, the fugitives were too spent to celebrate their escape from Fort George, too weighted down by mourning. Large fires of driftwood blazed on the beach. Mothers fussed over children held hostage for months. Others wept quietly.

Michael chafed at the decision to spend the night just half a day's swift sailing from their enemies. But what cannot be changed must be accommodated. So he bathed the wound on his arm in stinging salt water, then rested as well as his restless fears allowed.

Gover stepped over to where he sat.

'Show me your wound,' he said. 'Yes, take that filthy bandage off.'

He applied to the gash an antibiotic coagulant salve from the gravchute's medikit. The cut prickled. Healing would follow swiftly.

'I thank you,' said Michael, surprised Gover should waste City-medicine on him.

The City-man examined him curiously. 'You're a brave fellow, Pilgrim, I'll give you that. I can see why you command respect among your people.'

'I'm flattered.'

'Don't be. In taking on that savage, you took a barely forgivable risk. My welfare should be your primary concern. And the odds were loaded against you.'

'I got lucky.'

'Yes.'

Again Gover frowned.

'I'm puzzled. Why did you risk your neck for the priestess?'

'As you often say to me, Gover, you would not understand.'

'And as you say, Pilgrim, try me.'

'It was a decision of the heart, not head. I pitied her. That is all. And my own guilt. And all humanity has become. For every soul in that midden of Fort George deserved pity. Maybe even you.'

Gover seemed about to reply. Then he withdrew, finding a bed beneath the awning of a birlinn, away from infectious bodies and the risk of facial scans by a passing spydrone.

While Michael sat by the fire, a woollen blanket around his shoulders,

Iona approached bearing basins of fish broth thickened with oats. She sat beside him, warmed by a plaid, homespun blanket of her own. It seemed his night for conversations.

'I have not thanked you, Mister Star Man,' she said, 'for fighting the Prince O'Ness. In truth, for saving my life. And not least for freeing my folk.'

He sniffed the soup. 'We're all gainers from it.'

'Not all.'

He could tell she was thinking of the young fisherman who had accepted the warlord's challenge and lost his head.

'You must make sure his sacrifice was not in vain,' Michael said.

Iona looked up sharply. 'You read my thought well. I was thinking of poor James. We were close since we were bairns.'

'He made his own choice and died with honour.'

'Aye, Mister Star Man.'

'My name is Michael Pilgrim.'

'It is a good name. Saint Michael was not afraid to battle with devils, so they say, and we are all on a pilgrimage.'

The whites of her sea green eyes shone brightly in the flickering light of the bonfire. Sparks blew high in the salted breeze.

'Tomorrow we must decide our future course,' she said. 'Whether north towards our old home in Skye or perhaps one of the other isles. Or east then south to the fair land you and your companion promise. You spoke of people following our own faith there. Is that true? Or just a way of bending us to your wishes?'

For one so soft-spoken, Iona's gaze was piercing. If Michael had been inclined to lie, it would have made him think twice.

'You will find kindred spirits among our people,' he said. 'I can promise you that. And many do follow your beliefs. There is enough empty land for all on our coast; too many fish in the sea to go hungry. We have no king but a commonwealth to protect us. We have no bonders, though all folk are expected to contribute to the community's defence and share food in times of hardship.' Remembering the corpses in Inverness dangling from gibbets, he added, 'There is no war between ourselves and our neighbours. We aim to live in peace with the world.'

He told her wistfully, for it put him in mind of his little son and family and friends, about the Nuagers of Hob Hole.

'Their leader is a good friend of mine. You could work together with him to bring better times for your people.'

She thought for a while then said, 'Where is this place?'

'I have no map...'

'Oh, but I have!'

Her high, innocent laugh surprised him.

'You can read?' he asked.

'Is that so strange?'

Then she told her own tale as Michael sipped scalding broth from the bowl. How her grandmother had been a naturalist on Skye when the Great Dyings began, a woman of science and vast knowledge, who sought to heal the earth's wounds, and how her mother, gifted with the cosmic magic newly loosened by the plagues, had gathered the community of Nuagers, fishing and crofting in peace, and how, upon her death, Iona had taken possession of her mother's nets and led their people to safety when pirates burned Skye, seeking slaves, animals, loot.

'Your grandmother taught you to read?'

It seemed uncannily like his own story. Now her face fell.

'Aye, and my Ma. But all our books are lost. Burned. Wasted. So much wisdom wasted forever. I have nothing but a map of lands that no longer exist. Countries taken from us by Mother Gaia as a warning and fitting punishment.'

'Let me see.'

SIXTEEN

She gingerly unfolded a plastic-coated map. Across it was written: QANTAS Fly Australia. He refolded the map and returned it.

'I have good news,' he said. 'I believe this Australia has not vanished beneath the waves. Its condition I cannot swear to.'

She smiled. 'That news makes me glad.'

'We have collected many, many books in my home. Some your grandmother will have known, I'm sure.'

Perhaps the books persuaded her. Iona's face relaxed. Like his own, it was dirt-streaked, bruised, cuffed by the world, with gaps in her teeth and deep scratches on her hands. Both stank of sweat, ingrained disappointment, and fear, but also dreams.

'I'll consider your proposition, Mister Pilgrim. Maybe you and your queer companion truly have been sent by the stars.' She smiled. 'Though Dameron calls you a pair of rogues and adventurers.'

When she had gone, Michael tried to sleep. He did not notice a drone passing high overhead amidst the stars and clouds. When Blair Gover heard it, he hid his face, just in case.

* * *

Before dawn, they were busy about the boats. When all was ready, Iona spoke long with her assembled people. Michael and Gover sat apart, awaiting the collective verdict, aware theirs might be a long, perilous journey on foot back to Yorkshire. Yet when the little fleet sailed, it was towards the rising sun.

The Nuagers had decided to heed the stars' summons and head east to Baytown. Nature seemed to confirm their choice as good. The sea turned from grey to shades of blue laced with foam. Hearts lifted. They raised sails and ran with the wind.

Michael was heartened by the innate co-operation among the Nuagers of all ages, whether rowing or managing the sails or moving as a kind of human ballast around the light wooden ship when it tilted. All done with good humour and promptness. Yet he suspected they would not fight so well.

Later that day, Spey's shoreline of long sandy beaches overlooked by forests and the remnants of houses changed. Towering granite cliffs framed the southern horizon with few coves in which stricken craft could shelter. Spirits sank a little at so forbidding a land, and the four birlinns fell into a tight diamond formation. Other sails were spotted by the lookouts, a distant scatter on the horizon.

'They'll hail from Fraserburgh,' said Dameron. 'Fishing boats, or so it's to be wished.' He pointed inland at the cliffs. 'These carry on many miles yet. We must use the wind while she blows, even in darkness.'

Another hour passed. Granite triangles towered. Giant shark fins rising from boiling white water to form a dangerous channel. Then a high, excited lassie's voice cried out a warning: they were being pursued.

Iona was on her feet, Michael beside her, musket instinctively in hand. An alarm sounded from the rear boat. *Muruchs! Muruchs!*

Iona pressed the gun barrel down. 'You will offend them, Mister Pilgrim! Nae need to point your weapon at a bonny, glad-heart of a muruch. Sea-singers we call them. The souls of good folk take their form upon death and dance in the waves.'

Michael watched a large pod of dolphins stitch the ocean, backs and fins arching. White-bellied, some leapt for sheer joy while others kept pace with the boats. A lilting hymn rose from among the folk watching from their oar-benches, the wind cracking sails embroidered with gaily-coloured whales and stars. Slightly ashamed, he stored his weapon.

He recalled his violin back in Hob Hall and felt a sudden urge to prove he could play better instruments than sword or musket.

Gover, too, seemed moved by the gambolling animals. 'Do you know,

Pilgrim,' he mused, 'the Beautiful Life has paid too little attention to the creatures around it. "Man is the measure of all things" has been too much my creed.'

He subsided, and the dolphins escorted them until dusk fell.

* * *

Luckily for the little fleet, the stars and crescent moon were not obscured by clouds. Dameron set a course around a curve of coast to head south. First, they slipped past the fishing port of Fraserburgh, a fortress loyal to King Duncaine of Buchan and much to be avoided. No one knew whether word of the events at Fort George had reached there yet. Hostile craft might already be out searching.

'We have been a-ship since afore dawn,' said Dameron. 'I'm nae keen to venture past King Duncaine's port of Peterhead until we rest and sup. From the smell of the wind, there may be plenty of oar-work on the morrow.' He added morosely, 'Aye, and far worse.'

Michael listened to the old fisherman's conference with Iona. 'Does this King Duncaine have ships he could use to pursue us?' he asked.

Dameron ignored him, addressing only Iona. Yet he answered Michael's question.

'The King of Buchan has many a ship, lassie, and fast ones. A great raider, he is, both by sea and land. We must pass Peterhead quiet as ghasties.'

'You've a safe place in mind where we could stop,' said Iona. 'I can tell.'

'Aye. If ye be not afraid of devils.'

Michael and Gover exchanged glances.

The City-man's lips drew back into a smile. 'Interesting. What devils exactly, my man? Or was it wee ghoulies?' He chuckled at his own wit.

Dameron's expression suggested demons very like the alien creature wearing City clothes beneath a camouflage of rags. 'Ye'll see,' he muttered. 'Ye'll see.'

'Whisht,' said Iona softly. 'You'll scare the bairns.'

'Then I'll save my breath,' Dameron responded, at which point he busied himself with the tiller.

Two weary hours south of Fraserburgh, strange silhouettes appeared against the moonlit sky. Shreds of cloud blew between glittering constellations. The wind had turned against them and they had been forced to take up oars.

Dameron guided them into a sandy bay overlooked by a dense, silent tangle of massive pipes and towering storage tanks.

'Is that where the ghoulies live?' Gover asked.

'Aye,' said the fishermen. 'If a man keeps to the beach, they no bother him.' He spat overboard for luck.

Near a small river estuary, they ran the birlinns ashore and dragged them up the strand. Driftwood was gathered; fires started. Wary of Dameron's warnings, Michael set up a guard rota after a brief muster and weapons check. He sensed Iona's disapproval as he attempted a short drill.

***

Michael stared at the complex of pipes, tanks, and buildings separated from the beach by a strip of dunes, while the Nuagers huddled over their fires. Gover joined him.

'What was that place in the Before Time?' Michael asked.

Gover shrugged. 'Some kind of gas terminal, by the look of it. There were many oil rigs off this coast. Gas was a secondary product. Did you really not know that?'

Michael checked his musket and pistols. 'I think we should look it over.'

'A-feared o' ghoulies, are ye?'

'You mock too casually.'

'Well, if you insist on taking a look at an abandoned industrial facility, I'll accompany you. We need a little private talk, Pilgrim. Oh, yes.'

They set off, using their City torches for a faint illumination.

Once the camp lay behind, Gover asked, 'Do you really trust these nautical primitives?'

'You mean our allies?'

'For now. A superstitious fool like Cap'n Dameron is scarcely to be relied on. Likewise their absurd leader, that wild-haired priestess of moonshine. Who knows when they might take it into their heads to sacrifice us to their Star Gods.'

'Unlikely,' said Michael. 'They are peaceable enough, too peaceful for my liking if we are attacked.'

'Still, I find them outlandish.'

'I'm sure the feeling is mutual.' Michael scratched his chin. 'Actually, Gover, I too have questions.' He halted a little way from a rusting storage tank twenty men high and broad. 'You mentioned leaving something valuable at the museum in Baytown. I ask you again, what was it?'

Gover sighed. 'You would not understand.'

'Try me.'

'It involves principles beyond your understanding. Leave our survival to me, Pilgrim. Remember that, and you shall do well.'

'Still, I would like to know.'

He could tell the City-man was weighing up his own self-interests. Any revelation depended solely on that.

'Very well, know this. It so happens my enemies are closing in on Homo sapiens even as we speak. The little surprise I have hidden in Baytown might just save you primitives. Otherwise, I predict you and your kind will join the orang-utan.'

'The what?'

'Precisely. No one knows or cares about that pitiful animal. It was a variety of ape, by the way, now extinct. Ponder its fate, Pilgrim.'

Michael leaned forward. 'For all your great superiority, right now, your life depends on us apes.'

A dangerous look settled on Gover's face. 'A temporary reversal only. Actually, I blame myself for my current predicament. I was too generous, too patient, too kind, it is a fault of mine.' He laughed. 'But after this jaunt with you savages, oh, what drawn-out, ingenious sufferings will come my enemies' way.'

'They seem to have the whip hand right now.'

'Do they?'

'Bluster isn't power.'

Gover dismissed his observation with a wave. 'Let me assure you, I am not as alone as I seem. On the other side of the world, my allies will be stirring and desperate for my leadership.'

Michael longed to get away from the City-man. So he missed the revelation on the tip of Gover's tongue.

'No more talk,' Michael muttered. 'Let's look at this gas terminal of yours.'

* * *

The two men trod warily around the perimeter fence. Pipes formed rusty heaps of metal. Plants had sprung up wherever bare earth or wind-blown soil allowed root-space. Michael detected evidence of fierce explosions and fires — scorched, twisted steel, craters of debris. No devils were evident, human or otherwise. Yet his torch picked out a surprising number of skeletons, some mottled with age: birds, rabbits, deer, possibly feral dogs. Nor was it obvious why anyone would dump

SIXTEEN

them there, unless the gas terminal was a shrine for sacrifices.

Michael's instincts prickled. 'I don't like it,' he whispered. 'Something's not right here. Let's go back.'

Gover's eyes glinted in the moonlight. 'Poo! Poo! A technologically advanced facility like this, hastily abandoned, might have some leftover devices I could use. Ah, there is the entrance, Pilgrim.'

Reluctantly, Michael unslung his musket.

The remnants of a road led into the terminal. Near it stood an office block, its windows broken. Few cars were parked around the building.

'As I expected,' said Gover, 'this place was hastily evacuated. Its safety systems would have failed when the electricity stopped. Although dying in a nice quick explosion does seem preferable to buboes spewing out vile fluids. But there's no accounting for taste.'

Michael Pilgrim halted. 'My parents died in the manner you describe.'

'I'm sure they did. Now, I have a feeling I might find a very rudimentary screen in that office.'

Gover strolled towards the building.

'Look!' Michael said, grabbing Gover's arm.

A large pool of dark, viscous liquid lay at the side of the building. Wraiths of chemical smoke or steam rose like spectres. Michael thought of Dameron's devils. Because the wind was gusting briskly from the sea, the gas-wraiths dispersed towards the landward side. Even so, Michael's nose sniffed something acrid and bitter.

Dozens of skeletons lay around the pool in varying stages of decay. No grass grew in the bare, gritty soil. Most bones belonged to animals, but among them were grinning human skulls, half-eaten by toxic fumes.

Michael dragged Gover back. Both held their breaths until their lungs burned. Only at the perimeter fence did they risk big draughts of clean night air.

Back at the boats, bowls of fish stew were going round. Nets had been thrown out as they sailed that day and there was plenty for everyone.

Michael sat alone to eat his supper, a blanket around his shoulders. Old doubts soured the meal. Even if mankind rose again, would they repeat the same greedy errors as their forebears, poisoning land and ocean, over and over, until they vanished like Gover's mythical orang-utan? On the road from Inverness, the City-man had mocked his faith in human decency and co-operation, claiming selfishness was coded in every living thing's genes, especially mankind. Poor, foolish, vicious humanity. He became aware Iona was watching from a warm circle round the fire but turned his back on her to brood alone.

SEVENTEEN

Water flowed between fishponds, draining into a large manmade lake and thence into the River Skell. Always, it sought a route to the same oceans Jojo Lyons longed to see.

Seth learned much of Jojo's hopes and dreams as they toiled to unblock culverts clogged with mud and vegetation. Truth was, the youthful squire of Fountains talked ten words to every one of Seth's, though Seth did sense that one word was listened to with attention. He had another sense as they worked: someone watching from the woods. Had the Mistresses found him? A fear, however unlikely, he could not entirely banish.

He said to Hurdy-Gurdy, 'Why don't you have a sneak around? See if it's just our imaginations.'

'Who-o-o-o!' went Gurdy, like an owl.

The loon-haired entertainer had recently gained new, deeper lines across his face. When he grinned, they grew more prominent still, until his smile resembled the centre of a mask.

One cold evening, wrapped in thick, coarse blankets, they debated who might lurk among the ponds and follies, the woods of larch, birch and oak.

'I'm thinking a runaway bonder,' said Seth. 'Why else keep so hidden?'

'Per-haps.'

'Or an outlaw, some kind of rule-breaker driven from his home.'

'Like you and I, hey ho?'

Seth laughed, for Hurdy-Gurdy had a point.

Yesterday Hurdy had mocked him for shaving off his beard and cutting his hair.

'Now who might we be prettifying ourselves for, I wonder. Shall Hurdy-Gurdy leave Young Nuncle all alone with his new friend? My! My! Three's a crowd, they say.'

Seth didn't know how to take that. Was Jojo Lyons even his friend? Besides, they must move on soon. The work on the ponds was almost done; they had earned food, gunpowder, blankets. No point lingering when the City and a glorious future beckoned. He hadn't any other future worth mentioning.

'Never mind Jojo fucking Lyons,' he said. 'Just see if you can spot our shy pal.'

'Perhaps Hurdy-Gurdy can do better than spotting.'

'What do you mean?'

With a lantern for illumination that cast strange, flickering shadows, the former holotainer tore electrical wiring from the plaster of the summerhouse.

'When me and my companions,' he sang, 'were setting out a snare...'

***

As the repairs neared an end, Jojo spoke of other work.

'We still need a smokehouse for the fish-harvest and lots of wood for seasoning.' He hesitated. 'You've worked damn hard.' Another pause. 'We thank you for it.'

Seth grew awkward. Had not Big Jacko then the Mistresses of Fell Grange also found him useful? In ways filling his head with dark fantasies of revenge. Yet Jojo Lyons seemed to value his company if their conversations were any guide.

Often the young man shared his desire to 'travel a bit' and 'see beyond Fountains, though I expect it'll always be home'. He talked of humanity's fall in mundane terms, without the air of sepulchral mourning favoured by Uncle Michael. Jojo believed theirs was a new, practical generation, concerned with the future, not the past, with finding ways of moving forward right under the City's nose.

Hurdy-Gurdy listened with his usual hangdog expression when not in what Jojo called 'an entertaining humour'. Seth knew he kept one eye on the woods. That the City-man was waiting for something to happen. Then it did.

'What the fuck?'

Squeals of pain and terror made Seth and Jojo drop the wood they were collecting. They ran back to the summerhouse where Hurdy-Gurdy was building a frame to smoke fish. Had it been necessary, Seth would have fought to defend his friend. But the battle was already won.

Gurdy stood at the side of the summerhouse, arms folded, a curious expression on his lined, sagging face. No trace of the clown about him now. He pointed at the screeching creature he had captured. 'Behold our spy, Little Nuncle!'

The creature's leg was trapped in a pitiless noose of wire fixed to the building. The more it struggled and screamed, the deeper the wire bit. It seemed almost human. A light pelt of golden hairs took the place of skin. Tiny, budding breasts and nipples, the sex between its legs, indicated a female. Its arms were short, curled; its fingers ended in strong, blunt claws as though for scratching soil. The creature's legs were heavily-muscled around the thigh, the powerful kickers of a hare or rabbit. Smallish, it was the size of a bony teenage girl. A rectangular lump beneath the skin of its shoulder suggested a hidden City device, melded into its flesh. Most horrible was its floppy, almost comical rabbit ears. Yet it possessed long, wavy chestnut hair that would not have shamed a comely girl, as well as other human features, especially the eyes and eyebrows.

The strangeling's face horrified Seth. In it, he detected the unmistakable likeness of someone he had kept prisoner at Big Jacko's behest. Far, far worse was the creature's likeness to the young man by his side. A likeness explaining why they had felt eyes upon them. Why this mishmash of human and animal haunted Fountains Abbey.

Jojo stared down at it — her — his voice shaking, 'Bella? Bella? Is that you? Why are you dressed up queer like that?'

The creature covered its eyes with a clawed hand, moaned, wept. She gazed up imploringly.

'Let her go!' he cried hysterically to Hurdy-Gurdy. 'It's Bella! You must let her go! It's my sister. You're hurting her!'

Hurdy-Gurdy, frightened now, sawed at the wire with his knife. The creature grew frantic, scratching out, screaming — a soul in torment. As the wire snapped, it landed a kick on Seth's chest. Winded, he fell. Launching into the air six feet high, it bounded into the woods, wire dragging behind its leg, gone in moments, save for a dwindling crash of vegetation.

* * *

As dusk deepened, Seth also fled. The night barely registered on his senses: scents of wintering earth, tang of plants, the murmur of wind stirring leafless branches, the cold glitter of stars. His consciousness turned inward, he stumbled through darkness.

Snatches of thought and fear ...Hurdy-Gurdy musing to himself, 'Ingenious, yes, and cruel as cats ... Created for hunting, perhaps, or even novelty footraces...' The madman's eyes opened wide. 'Or merely to prove a diabolical point.'

SEVENTEEN

Seth stumbled, his face whipped by leaves and branches, desperate to escape the valley where even now the creature might lurk. But Jojo's grief he could not escape. Why is Bella dressed like that, Seth? Why? How did she jump so high? Sobbing as the truth bit hard, she was no longer Bella, that more than a quaint hare costume transformed her ...A spell has been cast on her! That's it! What else could it be? Aye, wicked magic. But I could see Bella's face behind ...behind ...I know it is her!

Seth came to a wide stream gurgling down to feed the ponds in the valley below. Too weary to wade across, clenched with misery, disgust. Lost forever! He should take his pistol, blow out his brains. Images filled his mind: the long, sleek airliner landing at Fylingdales, his own rifle butt herding young prisoners aboard, overseen by drones and strange City-men. You promised, Seth Pilgrim, you promised. Yes, he had promised to help those two girls, Abbie and Bella Lyons. And he had betrayed that promise. Along with every other promise he had made, not least to the man he could have become. He now saw exactly why Big Jacko had been 'harvesting' young, fresh 'materials' for the City.

With a cry, he rose. On, on, through the darkness, until he came to an abandoned car behind a burned outhouse. Rain fell. Wrenching open the door, he was greeted by a stink of mould, dank as a grave. A soggy skeleton occupied the driver's seat, its head and shoulders covering the controls where it had collapsed forward.

Seth crawled onto the passenger seat and hugged himself, shivering and cursing. He was overwhelmed by fears of being locked in the dungeon beneath Flylingdales Radar Station by strange monsters with human bodies and animal heads. These fears gradually morphed into nightmarish dreams of Bella, and Abbie, and Jojo Lyons, in which they were guards and he was the prisoner. A dog-headed man slavered as it barked. Another with an owl's round face, razor-sharp beak, saucer eyes empty of pity. And Bella, the hare-girl, nose twitching, sniffing, assessing Seth. He knew she still possessed a soul and that, somehow, a sliver of her consciousness survived the horror visited on her flesh. Though she suffered constant torment, neither hare nor human nor hybrid, Little Bella Lyons, remained the beloved youngest child of a loving family.

To his waking dream came the speculation that if the soul remained, perhaps the body might be restored.

* * *

Seth awoke in the rotting car with the spongy skeleton beside him. He hurried through the dawn to find Jojo Lyons outside the summerhouse, talking excitedly to Hurdy-Gurdy. For a moment, Seth feared his role in Bella's transformation had been revealed. But the young man seemed pleased to see him.

'Did you find her? Hurdy-Gurdy told me you'd gone out looking for her.'

The lunatic holotainer chuckled disturbingly. 'Oh, I did, I did.'

Seth sat wearily. 'No, I did not find her.'

'Hurdy-Gurdy has been sharing his ideas with me,' said Jojo. 'He does not believe a spell has been cast on Bella at all. At least, not a magic one. No, and this will surprise you, Seth...' Jojo leaned forward as though a drone might overhear. 'He believes the City did this to her for its own secret reasons.'

Hurdy-Gurdy smirked, revealing teeth that were yellowing. 'Reasons without reason, they always have reasons.'

'You should know,' said Seth.

'Gurdy thinks Bella was dumped here as some kind of trial or experiment. Indeed, several folk hereabouts saw a large air-machine north of Ripon a month or so ago.'

SEVENTEEN

In his agitation, Jojo paced the ground. 'I am sure she recognises me. If I could win her trust, perhaps I could keep her safe. You see, I daren't tell people. If they discover her, they will kill her as a strangeling. They will not understand.'

Seth had to admit it seemed probable. From Bella's perspective, it might be a mercy, given his dream that she retained some knowledge of her former self.

'We must find her,' said Jojo. 'But how?'

A memory of when he served Big Jacko gave Seth a clue. After their father died, he had sought out his twin sister Averil in Baytown. Although then, as now, he had been an outcast likely to find himself thrown off the cliffs if caught. But he'd guessed she would visit their parents' graves very often, bearing a posy of wildflowers. With father being so soon under the sod, she had shown up just as he'd predicted. Folk only learned so many places and loyalties.

He said nothing. What were the Lyons family to him, after all? Then he looked up at Jojo's handsome face, and a strange feeling overcame Seth Pilgrim. One he despised even as it stirred his heart. He wanted to comfort Jojo, embrace him. The urge, strong and clean, made Seth look away in confusion.

'There may be a way,' he muttered. 'I promise nothing. But it is possible.'

Hurdy-Gurdy's smile grew toothy as he watched the two young men confer.

* * *

'You're sure this place was special to her?' asked Seth.

They were in woods above the ruined abbey, its magnificent arches obscured by bare trees.

Jojo nodded in reply. The sleek young man had aged in the last twenty-four hours.

Seth took hold of Jojo's arm to steady him. 'Do you think others know about her?' he asked.

'No one has spoken of her in the homestead,' mumbled Jojo.

'Good, good.'

Still, Seth held Jojo's arm. The reassurance he meant to give the other comforted himself. 'Why would she come here?' he asked.

The troubles lifted a little from Jojo's face. 'We came here all the time as kids. You'll laugh, but I always wanted to be more than a farmer. I used to drag Bella and Abbie behind my daydreams, I suppose.'

'Show me.'

Jojo led him to a small glade in the woods at the foot of a grassy bank. Grey stonework showed through the trees above their heads, built upon a sandstone outcrop. Below it, in the glade, was a tunnel entrance. Dark and discouraging it seemed to Seth.

'The tunnel leads up to the old tower,' said Jojo. 'That book about Fountains I told you of calls it the Octagon and says it was another folly for the rich folk who dwelt yonder, like the summerhouse where you sleep. We used to half live up here when we were kids.' He brightened further. 'You'll laugh, but we played that this tunnel was the entrance to Faery Land, where everything and everyone is magical. Just kids' stuff, like I say. Bella and Abbie would be faeries, and I'd be their wizard king. Together we'd cast spells to make the world back like it was before the plagues. Stupid kids' stuff, that's all. But I'm sure she'd come here.'

Seth felt nostalgia stir for his own sister, Averil. Funny, he'd almost forgotten there'd been fun as a child. As though what happened with Big Jacko cancelled his right to happy memories. Fuck it, he told himself, fuck 'em all.

They entered the arch-shaped tunnel. It climbed steadily, floor and curved walls lined with brick. Damp seeped, and cobwebs hung from the ceiling. The tunnel traced a gentle S-shape, and not a trace of light reached its centre.

'Don't worry,' said Jojo, his voice muffled by the walls, 'it's not dark for long.'

Yet the young men drew instinctively closer as they passed through the blackness. Seth struggled with a desire to hold Jojo's hand. The very urge to reach out made him afraid. His heart told him it was necessary, natural, but his head screamed caution.

Then the light reappeared, and his chance to pull Jojo close had passed. Yet, Seth felt short of breath as they emerged beside a grey stone tower with angled sides: the Octagon.

* * *

It was indeed a folly worthy of faeries and their wizard king. Stone steps led up to an ornate doorway on the ground floor. Arched windows offered views of the woods; above them, the tower rose to a circular pinnacle capped with stone spikes like a king's crown.

Ivy covered much of the stonework, and ferns besieged the ancient building. Many of the glass windows were intact, though streaked with pale green mould. A fresh trail wended through the greenery to the old stone steps. Raising a finger to his lips, Seth pointed it out to Jojo. The young men examined the mud: footprints, odd-shaped ones.

'Let's look inside,' said Seth.

The steps had cracked in places, so they trod warily. What remained of the door had been forced open and stood ajar.

They entered a high-ceilinged room with the same octagonal shape as the tower. Plaster lay in piles where it had cracked with damp and slid off the walls. At the back, a wooden staircase climbed through the ceiling to the top of the tower.

'Look!' whispered Jojo.

A corner of the room had been made homely from a certain perspective. A bed of ferns piled high. Around it, the remains of autumn fruit, nutshells, and the spiky skin of a dead hedgehog. An ammoniac tang of urine lingered. In one corner, there lay a fresh pile of spoors.

'She is not here!' cried Jojo. 'Perhaps she has gone away to die.' He brushed his eyes. 'I should have protected her, Seth. I failed her.'

In a stumbling voice, he told of the raid by a dozen riders when she and Abbie had been taken. How suddenly they appeared, capturing the two teenage girls at gunpoint and ordering the older women with them to lie down and cover their heads.

'They wore masks so we could not recognise them. Their accents were strange, Seth, not Yorkshire. I was just nineteen. We tried to follow, but they had a head start, and we lost their trail. I should have scoured the world for them, Seth.' He lowered his head in sorrow and shame.

They soon became aware they were not alone. Step by step, the strangeling, Bella, whatever she had become, limped down the staircase. The wire was off her leg, but a bloody welt remained. She shivered and cowered.

'Bella, it's me,' said Jojo. 'I've come to help you. To help you get better.'

The strangeling stared into Jojo's eyes, which were the same shade of brown as her own. Seth suppressed a tremble. Would she recognise him, too, and remember the wrong he had done her?

'Don't be afraid,' said Jojo. 'We'll find a way to bring you back. To make you what you once were. Won't we, Seth?'

Seth stepped back anxiously. He was saved from answering by Hurdy-Gurdy appearing in the doorway.

'Won't we, Seth?' echoed the madman with peculiar glee. 'Won't we, Seth? Won't we?'

EIGHTEEN

They rose in the hour before dawn. As the sun illuminated the eastern horizon, Michael Pilgrim sought out Dameron. Gloom wreathed the man's brow.

'I must ask what you know of Peterhead, sir,' said Michael. 'You gave the impression it is a place to be feared.'

Dameron's bloodshot eyes strayed to the sea. 'Aye.'

'It would help to know what dangers lie ahead.'

'Maybe.'

But Dameron did talk. It seemed he had sailed to Peterhead on the Prince O'Ness's business, transporting messengers to his father, King Duncaine.

'It's how I ken that coast,' he explained.

'What else did you learn?'

Michael heard how Peterhead harboured a fleet for fishing, whaling, and raiding, but that few folk were permitted to dwell in the town. A clan of merchant-pirates used the port as a base for activities up and down the coast. Their king took a plump tithe.

'What about inland?' asked Michael.

'Buchan is hame to trees and ghasties, nae many men. It is a deserted land, they say.'

Dameron reported the King had set up his court in a former prison with high surrounding walls, a grim, dark place of barred windows, cells and thick shadow. King Duncaine's raids had netted many slaves to work his fields. These were housed, along with his family and war men, in the ancient gaol.

'How many boats and soldiers does the King of Buchan command?' Michael asked.

Dameron's gloom deepened. 'Enough. A grim enough tribe.'

It occurred to Michael, the King of Buchan had achieved everything Big Jacko once schemed to win: lands, dominions, a small, walled fortress to defy his enemies, and vassals to pay homage — a tinpot empire now lacking an heir.

Iona, who had been listening, said quietly, lest others hear and grow alarmed, 'Such a mighty king will expect a high blood price for his son's life. Yet father and son quarrelled sore. The Prince O'Ness used to boast and brag of that when he ... when he forced his attentions upon me. There'll be guilt on the father's side. And anger.'

'Aye, guilt and wrath make for cruel revenges,' said Dameron. 'We're no out of the lobster pot, I tell ye.'

'Still, we must stay optimistic,' said Michael. 'Word may not have reached him of our presence on the coast. Even of his son's death. We might yet slip right on past before he hears. And then we'll show him our arses and laugh fit to burst.'

Dameron directed the Nuager flotilla away from the coast. The wind blew hard and cold in their faces. Even the most skilful sail work and tacking allowed scant progress; once more they took to the oars. The morning was well advanced, the swell high and loud, when he judged they were far enough away from land to turn due south and make a run for it past Peterhead.

'After that, I have nae more knowledge of this coast,' he shouted above the wave and wind-roar. 'So don't waste your time asking.'

'The stars will guide us,' replied Iona, her long hair blown into wild wet strands. 'Remember, Dameron, their will and favour flow from

EIGHTEEN

your heart to your hand on the tiller. I've always known it to be a stout heart.'

To Michael's surprise, the gloomy old salt relaxed. Such is faith, he thought, envying the comforts of religion. By the Nuagers' reckoning, the glorious King of Buchan was a mere pinprick in a benign universe where virtue might earn you safe passage to immortal heavens. Good luck with that one, he thought.

* * *

The wind forced them towards the shore. It took all the fishermen's combined efforts to maintain a zigzag course south. Michael borrowed binoculars to examine a dark smudge on the horizon: Peterhead, several miles to starboard. Behind it, shadowy mountains rose, the same range they had glimpsed following the coast from Inverness. All they had achieved was to sail around a rectangular corner of Scotland: long miles lay ahead before Baytown.

'Ship! Ship!' rose a cry.

A small fishing smack was heading swiftly inland from the south, the wind favouring its course. At the sight of the Nuager flotilla, it veered in their direction. Gover, who huddled in oilskins, leaned out of the birlinn's tiny rear cabin to assess the situation. A frown creased his smooth face.

The light fishing smack rode the waves at twice their speed. Michael realised they wanted a close view of these four strange crafts laden with folk and bearing images of whales and stars on their sails. Whatever they saw would be reported back to Peterhead within the hour. Gover came to the same conclusion.

'Tempt them near,' he cried, above the wind. 'Then kill them. Do you understand, Pilgrim? Kill them quickly.'

But no tempting would be necessary. The fishing smack had turned to intercept their course. Close up, they saw it possessed a crew of two: a young lad plus a bearded veteran of the tides, by looks his father. Five then four ship-lengths off, they swept past, staring at the women and children huddled around oar benches.

Michael's heart raced as he realised Gover was right. They must not report their presence. And yet, to murder father and son, no doubt leaving other children, and a wife without support...

'Kill them!' hissed Gover. 'Before they get away.'

And it could be done. Shoot the tillerman, pursue the boat if necessary. Michael reluctantly reached for his musket, the weapon wrapped in waterproof cloth, along with six or seven others, all loaded, sufficient for him to finish the job quickly.

'No!' Iona seized his arm. 'No, I say!'

'But ...'

'We'll not slaughter our brothers on the waves!'

Her green eyes paralysed him as they gazed into his blue. Moments passed.

'Shoot them, you idiot!' said Gover.

Then the fishing smack was slipping behind them, speeding towards Peterhead. Soon it was beyond range.

King Duncaine would chew over the presence of the Nuager ships with his breakfast, realised Michael. Probably at around the same time that he learned of the mutiny that cost his son's life. And what of the English stranger who took the Prince O'Ness's City-sword, most likely an heirloom of their family, after chopping off his son's arm and filleting his corpse? A stranger with a name in the North: Michael Pilgrim.

'Are the King of Buchan's ships swift?' Michael asked Dameron.

* * *

EIGHTEEN

After Peterhead, they drew closer to the coast. Long, sandy beaches gave way to sheer cliffs of granite, riddled with caves and ravines worn by boiling seas. Still, the wind blew west, and much tacking was required to make progress. Anyone watching the four distant sails from the shore, zigzagging in unison across a white-capped sea, would have marvelled at the disciplined formation. Always the Nuagers kept an eye behind them.

Great crowds of seabirds populated the cliffs. Numerous specks of white, circling, plunging, flocking: guillemots, gulls, terns, puffins and eider duck. Iona grew joyful at their cries; smiles dimpled her high cheek-boned face, the pure delight of a child. Michael contemplated his readiness to murder the fishermen while fearing the consequences of not doing so. He was doubtful, too, how she judged him, though that was plain enough. Iona considered him a man of ruthless, bloody violence. Given the evidence of his character she had witnessed so far, he did not blame her.

'You love the seabirds,' he said awkwardly.

Her dark eyes went to his face. 'Aye. Do not you?'

'I'm more a creature of earth than sea. I suppose that I prefer a swift or swallow or robin to a herring gull.'

She nodded in her calm way. 'The birds are nae so different from people. Each has its natural element. The gull casts its net out to sea, and the robin loves a tree. I'm always delighted to see many sea-fowl feeding. The old folk used to say the birds dwindled terribly before the plagues. Some disappeared altogether. Now they return where they belong.'

A shadow crossed her face. 'All things natural would be happy to see us vanish, I fear. Even Mother Gaia herself has turned her back on humanity.'

'Is that why you Nuagers wish to find a fresh planet, a way to the stars?'

'Aye. My grandmother called the plagues: *Earth's spring clean.*'

Michael pondered her beliefs. 'Only gods or spirits could fly to the stars without the aid of science. Is that your desire, to deny your material nature, to no longer be human, but like gods?'

She regarded him gravely. 'We can never be as gods.'

'Nonsense,' broke in Gover.

So intent on their conversation were they, his words startled them.

'You see, my dear,' he said, 'some of us have already acquired attributes you primitives, quite understandably, consider divine.'

Iona turned back to Michael. 'What do you say, Mister Pilgrim? Do you agree with your friend?'

'That he is a god?' Michael laughed harshly. 'More like a hollow idol.'

'Oh, come now,' said Gover, not in the least offended. It seemed nothing they could say or do shook his self-belief.

'But I have a question for you, Iona, and a serious one,' continued Michael. 'Should you Nuagers ever find a new planet, what is to stop you spoiling it, as we poisoned this one?' He nodded at Gover. 'I include *you* in that we, City-man, for all you hold yourself so far above us.'

'Faith in mankind's goodness must conquer folly,' replied Iona, sad reflections crossing her face. 'It is all we have left to trust.'

* * *

After twelve hours of hard sailing, they spied a city on the coast. Late afternoon was fading to a dark gloaming, and Dameron predicted rain.

Lines of buildings, streets and jagged tower blocks grew distinct. Wrecked ships filled the harbour, as though they had congregated there when the plagues began, their crews desperate for medical help or just to join their families. At the port entrance, an enormous container vessel lay at right angles, a mass of rust, barnacles and mussels.

Yet again they must decide whether to push on through the night along a strange coast or beach there. Although no sails had been spotted behind them, Dameron spoke sourly of pursuit. The wind blew strong and rain tumbled as they hove to outside the harbour entrance. Not a single light or sign of life was visible in the city.

'I suggest we rest on that beach, near the harbour mouth,' said Michael, stretching stiff, weary limbs. 'We could shelter in that line of houses over there, and keep an eye on our boats.'

'Ye may wake to regret it,' grumbled Dameron.

'That's true every morning of your life.'

'Aye,' sighed the fisherman, as though Michael was at last talking sense. 'Aye.'

They dragged the boats onto a strip of shingly beach by a collapsed sea wall. Musket and pistols primed, Michael scouted the area. Still not a glimmer in the town.

Light footsteps made him wheel, musket angled: just Iona. She stared around, rain dripping from her nose.

'Never have I seen so vast a city,' she said. 'It is a work of giants. Countless folk must have lived here, Mister Pilgrim. What did they all do?' She shivered. 'Gone forever, with their busy, heedless ways.'

He shrugged. 'They filled their time and never imagined it could end. My grandfather, a wise and good man, believed like you in progress and that nothing humanity did was therefore wasted. Me, I am not so sure. He saw himself as the exception that proved his own rules. And he thought his rules were better than the world's. There was a vanity about him, for all the great good he did and for all his admirable qualities. Perhaps that was his real strength.'

She hugged herself against the cold wind. It was the first time he had seen her thoroughly downcast. No doubt she felt obliged to wear a brave mask for her people's sake — a feeling he knew well.

'Your grandfather sounds a deal like my mother, strong and kind and a little frightening.'

'It can be hard to get close to such people for all their good nature,' Michael remarked.

Iona shot him a quick glance. 'Yes.' She sniffed and said, 'Somehow, I never live up to my mother's example as the leader of our folk. And now I have led them into greater danger than ever.'

For a minute, both were silent. There was much more Michael wished to say to her. It seemed hard to start.

'Let's build a fire,' he said.

In the row of houses overlooking the beach, they found exhausted folk already asleep on rotten floorboards, swaddled in blankets or clutching one another. Iona went from huddle to huddle with soft words of encouragement.

After arranging a guard rota, Michael lit a small fire on the concrete floor of a garage overlooking the boats. They sat silently, listening to rain and surf and thinking private thoughts as firelight flickered and shadows danced.

Sometimes he glanced at her face. The abandoned city had affected her deeply, he could tell. What she would make of his vile role in the Crusades he did not care to discover. Perhaps word of that genocide had never reached her isolated island home on Skye: he hoped it could be so.

* * *

From Aberdeen they passed bleak miles of grey cliffs interspersed with occasional villages clinging to small, steep coves, lifeless save for rare wisps of smoke.

Dameron regularly scanned the northern horizon through binoculars. He explained to Iona in a morose, cavilling tone that although

EIGHTEEN

the birlinns of Skye were nimbler on the water than the war galleys and merchant craft of King Duncaine, their heavy loads of people and possessions offset any advantage.

'No helping a storm, they say,' he concluded, 'nor a woman's fickleness.'

'Away with ye, Dameron Mackie!' Iona said. 'What would you know of women?'

Michael smiled at the exchange; it was clear the old salt would have leapt overboard in lead-lined boots for Iona's sake.

As darkness fell, the headwind shifted right round, allowing the light craft to skim over the waves. Clouds cleared and Dameron suggested they sail on beneath the half-moon. The fleet took a southeasterly course to avoid reefs and sandbanks. Tired rowers slept on their benches, heads and arms on knees while sails took the strain.

A few hours after midnight, the wind dropped entirely.

'We all need rest before sunrise,' said Iona, and Dameron agreed.

The boats were connected by long, light ropes to avoid drifting too far apart. As banks of cloud obscured star and moon, the four birlinn rose and fell like the breasts of the sleeping Nuagers, curled wherever a dryish patch of deck might be found. For the bairns, that meant their mother's laps.

* * *

Because of the darkness, no one noticed the sea-tilth gathering around their boats. As common as weeds along this coast: decayed bottles, lids, trays for long-digested meals and meat, fishing line, patches of net, endless varieties of plastic, large and small, half of every fisherman's catch if he trawled long enough.

At first, they thought nothing of the faint but persistent reek. A blend of rotten eggs, oil, seaweed. Still, no one raised an alarm. What harm could a scrape of plastic do to a well-clinkered hull? Dawn revealed how dense the sea-tilth was getting around the boats — and their actual predicament.

'Wake up!' urged the young lad on watch, shaking Dameron. Michael opened his eyes. At that moment, the clouds cleared.

'Fuck's sake,' he muttered.

They had drifted into the edge of a massive raft of sea-tilth, some of it nearly two centuries old. Miles of the stuff caught on the reefs surrounding a low rocky island capped by a towering lighthouse.

Several ships rusted on the reef. One, an enormous container vessel, had recently split apart, spilling barrels and vats of chemicals that floated or lay open, their contents clinging to the plastic.

Under normal circumstances, the lighthouse would have attracted Michael's awe. Yet it shrank to insignificance amidst so great a mass of sea-tilth. Each scrap of plastic haunted by ghostly hands that once found a use for it, outliving flesh and bone and blood, forlorn as photographs of people no one could name or remember.

The Nuagers cried out in surprise and horror. Trapped! They must escape this net of filth, the astonishing stench. Dawn began to unfurl flags of light.

'Whisht!' commanded Dameron. 'Beware yonder rock and reef most particular! Wait for the light to gather a little. Then we'll row out.'

Michael noticed Gover sniffing suspiciously. Leaning over the side, the City-man picked up a tar-black rope of seaweed and poked at it. The whites of his eyes were bright in the dim light. He reached out to grip Iona's arm in fierce warning. She jumped at the contact.

'Instruct your people to start no fires until I have investigated this. Do it now. Not a spark. Do you understand? Our lives may depend on it.'

She nodded, wriggling her arm free.

'No flames!' she called. 'Pass the word, nary a flame of any sort.'

EIGHTEEN

Gover and Michael stared at the bobbing island of toxic debris upon which their boat was stranded. Slow minutes fed the light of dawn.

NINETEEN

Helen Devereux glanced out of the air shuttle window at the ruins of a large city poking through tropical vegetation. Skyscrapers soared above lattices of green in the old business centre, while the low buildings of the suburbs were wholly obscured. Vines scaled the tallest office and apartment blocks, some of which had folded into mounds of glass and concrete tunnelled by roots.

Blair Gover was much on her mind. For the first time, she truly believed something terrible had happened and rebelled against the thought. To her, Blair seemed immortal, transfigured by the principles of the Beautiful Life. Ruthlessly clever, adaptable, beyond morality, and dynamic, he was also prone to sensual laziness, alone in a crowd — always, in the end, alone. A triumphant expression of the selfish gene.

North of ruined Colombo, the air shuttle slowed and approached Mughalia's main lifeline to its fellow Cities. A small, shiny port of plastisteel and concrete had been constructed beside the tidal lagoon of Negombo. Electric fences defined its perimeter, after which scrub and tropical woodlands marched into the depopulated central plains of Sri Lanka. Green and lush during the monsoon season, they were as arid as lost hope the rest of the year.

Large drone container ships entered and left the port, their manifests checked and unloaded by yet more drones. Goods produced in Mughalia's automated estates and factories were lifted by sentient cranes into capacious holds for distribution to Neo Rio, Albion, Han City, or Mitopia, each of those cities connected by seaports and rivers to form a global network.

As Helen's aircraft banked, a monorail train left Negombo with a dozen containers of goods for Mughalia up in the fresh, green highlands. Beside her, Averil gawped at these engineering marvels.

Averil was also much on Helen's mind. While she still bore some resemblance to the simple Baytown lass for whom she felt deep loyalty and affection, she now looked quite different. This was thanks to the 'improvements' to her face and body gifted by Marvin and Merle Brubacher. Helen could not avoid pangs of mourning each time she saw her young companion's altered features, however much they delighted their new owner.

She also noticed a subtle shift in the Brubachers' attitude to Averil. They had taken a shine to her. Perhaps her naïve enthusiasm for the wonders of the Beautiful Life cast a fresh gloss on things long tainted by ennui. This same gauche enthusiasm had persuaded Helen to share Mughalia's less savoury aspects.

The air shuttle descended with a whine of jets to an industrial zone beside the elevated monorail track. Buffets of damp heat washed over them as they disembarked, laden with scents of mud, dung, and vegetation. Beads of sweat appeared on Helen's forehead.

'You will find this interesting,' she promised Averil, 'and, I hope, instructive.'

* * *

Helen had brought Averil to a colonia, as production facilities outside a City's limits were called. All Five Cities maintained colonia dotted around the world. These were stark, functional places where raw materials were extracted, or select harvests gleaned. Diamonds from Africa; seafood delicacies from what remained of the Poles; rare earth minerals from desolate, irradiated America; drone-maintained farms for the rearing of exotic, climate-specific crops and meats. This particular colonia handled organic goods.

Roars and bellows startled Averil into clutching Helen's arm. 'Was that animals?'

'Yes,' answered Helen. 'Mammals, in fact, like me and you.'

Averil looked puzzled.

'Come,' Helen said, 'let's take a closer look.'

They were met by a Chinese woman in the drab, black uniform of an unBeautified technician, the small caste of servants who undertook jobs impossible for drones. Technicians were kept to a bare minimum. Each wore implants so they could be retired at the first sign of going feral.

The Chinese woman bowed low: 'The Supervisor welcomes you. Please follow.'

* * *

The supervisor of the colonia turned out to be a low-ranking Beautiful. As was customary for less important positions, he had been assigned this role at random. Not that he had much to do, he explained, with a fashionably long yawn. However, with the Grand Autonomy coming up, his work had taken on more importance.

'Perhaps you could explain to my young friend what your work entails,' said Helen.

'We provide all the animals for the sports,' he responded. 'All kinds. Tigers. Lions. Baboons were popular a while back, and we still keep a few. They make a nice comic match with primitives. Giraffes are in this season, though I can't see the attraction myself. Oh, and the other latest fad, duelling elephants.' He smiled. 'We have a surprise planned for the Autonomy crowds. That I shall keep under my hat.'

'May we see the primitives?' asked Helen.

'Of course. We've just had a fresh batch delivered.'

The supervisor led them from his air-conditioned office to a broad, glass-sided walkway around the circular, high-walled compound. The enclosed area was over a mile in diameter. At its centre, like the hub of a wheel, rose a six-storey operations block. Around it, more high walls with walkways to create discrete areas for the colonia's produce.

'Let's go for a ride, shall we?' said the supervisor.

He spoke into his screen, and a drone-buggy with seats rolled up. They circled the holding areas and pens below where caged lions lay in the shade. Drones fed tigers hunks of raw meat. The supervisor grumbled about the elephants refusing to fight one another unless goaded by implants. At the pens for humans, they climbed out of the buggy.

Wire cages lined the walls, stacked one on the other for maximum space-efficiency. Automated feeding systems provided nourishment and water; defecation and urination were catered for by a small steel bowl, streaked and stinking. Each cage contained a treadmill and a punching bag to keep its lone inmate active, as well as sufficient room to lie down. Open to the elements, the cages must be especially miserable during monsoons, thought Helen.

She turned to Averil with a look that said: Do you see now?

Averil was staring with undisguised surprise and disgust.

'They must have done something very wrong to be punished so,' she said awkwardly.

The supervisor yawned. 'Actually, they are the very worst species we have to manage. As you'd expect, I suppose. We make sure they don't band together or communicate, naturally, but getting them to perform is always hit and miss.'

'What do you do?' asked Helen.

'See the wrist bands?' he said. 'No point re-inventing the wheel, I always say. In the Crusades, bracelets worked marvels with my little unit of conscripts. A few good electric shocks and they couldn't be more eager to please. Let me show you.'

He commanded his screen to activate, and a holopad appeared. With this, fifty of the caged primitives were persuaded to perform a comical dance in reaction to neural targeting. Arms waving, legs high-kicking, leaping, hopping and yelping in pain – Averil stifled an uneasy, guilty laugh.

'We have a different colonia on the other side of the island for the pleasure primitives,' he said. 'These are purely for the contests.'

The specimens were young and healthy, of all races and colours. A few resembled folk Helen knew in Baytown. She raised her eyebrows significantly, 'Seen enough, Averil?'

The girl flushed but did not reply. For the rest of the tour, she was silent and self-absorbed.

On the way back to the exit, the supervisor pointed out some ingenious veterinary drones and a black-uniformed technician, who was consulting a screen.

'Nothing against drones and techs myself,' he mused, 'though you hear plenty suggesting their work would be better performed by those new organic machines. Totally new life forms apparently, very clever. Could revolutionise the entertainments we offer here. Not convinced myself. If it ain't broken, why fix it, is my motto.'

Helen shot him a puzzled look. 'I have overheard such conversations. Surely, to even propose such a thing borders on Discordia?'

The supervisor grew uncomfortable. He knew Helen as the former paramour of the great Blair Gover, after all. 'As I say, it is not my opinion.'

For the short distance it took to reach the exit, his chatter faded. He avoided Helen's eye as he bade farewell.

* * *

Every week Mughalia staged a grand gala evening for residents and visitors. A few miles from the centre, perched among hills, a small, oval valley had been shaped into a stadium. Flooded, with an island in the centre to serve as a stage, marble terraces upon sculptured hillsides, hanging pleasure gardens, pavilions, viewing platforms, perfect for strolling and refreshments, to see and be seen.

In a belvedere resting on a slender stem, like the top of a flat mushroom, the Brubacher party lolled. Ventilation systems cooled the party and removed irksome tropical bugs. Drones offered drinks and taste-wafers, subtly exquisite to the discerning palate.

Aside from Marvin and Merle, nearly forty Beautifuls were gathered, all of the highest castes. Several were permanent members of the Ruling Council like the Brubachers themselves, and Blair Gover, of course, although some spoke openly of appointing his replacement. His disappearance was an unexplained tragedy. Theories circulated that his aircar had suffered a catastrophic failure. A blackout of tracking systems increased the mystery. Some suggested he was in hiding until the Grand Autonomy, at which point he would make a dramatic entrance, thwarting those who wished to develop new, sentient life forms.

Helen listened to the gossip without contributing. Each day increased her longing to escape the Five Cities' intrigues and perfidies. Yet it was her duty to wait for Blair in Mughalia until the Autonomy concluded. She owed him that much.

'You know, they are calling these new lifeforms Angels,' said an influential, but dreary, Council-member, currently a nymph with a face far too knowing and cynical for the youthful body beneath.

'Mind you,' said another, 'it's nothing new. Even the primitives do it. They breed new dogs and horses all the time.'

'On one level it's just speeded up evolution,' droned the nymph. 'Humanity created religion in the hope of intelligent design. Now we are that divine intelligence.'

Another Beautiful chipped in. He stood seven feet tall, African heritage proudly displayed through glowing copper skin. Before the Dyings, he had thrived as a star of holo-horror snuff recreations. Except then he had been a dwarf, pale as a maggot.

'Intelligent design could sure be a kindness to these new creatures,' his deep, purring voice declared. 'They could be created perfect, no sickness, no defect. Obviously, getting there will involve a lot of waste materials. But, hey, you can't make a soufflé without breaking eggs.' He sniffed. 'I guess that's why some folks consider it a price worth paying.'

Further speculation was interrupted by the grand gala spectacle.

* * *

A blinding flash of multi-coloured beams emanated from the central island in the lake: all colours of the spectrum, illuminating one's skeleton-like an x-ray.

Averil screamed with frightened delight as she held her hand up to a beam, finger and knucklebones distinct. Most spectators carried on conversations in loud voices, glancing disinterestedly at the central island.

A series of tableaux followed. Each provoked exclamations from Averil, but Helen was less impressed. Was this the best that fabled Mughalia could offer as a prelude to the Grand Autonomy?

Large holograms of abstract shapes and images swirled in hypnotic patterns to a soundtrack scientifically proven to stimulate a range of emotions — or at the very least one's heartbeat and adrenalin glands. An art form popular twenty years earlier. Little wonder holocomments appeared like fireflies in the empty spaces of the stadium. Oh, not that again! Dull, dull, dull. The display carried on a full half-hour. Next, liquid sculptures formed from the waters of the lake. Towers of foam bent into impossibly intricate lattices tinted silver and gold by lasers. The music grew playful. Flower shapes, avenues of trees, a whole galleon complete with full sails and rigging. Same old, same old flashed up the holocomments. Averil clutched Helen's hand, tearful at such loveliness.

On it went. Programmed fish with electric motors and wings for aquatic and aerial displays. Drones overhead, spraying out vast clouds of scented pink and white blossom that on closer inspection turned out to be plastic. Numerous Beautifuls were obliged to brush blossom from hair and clothes, berating the inconvenience via their screens.

With yet another blinding flash, the displays ended. No one noticed. Much of the audience had entered that frustrating stage of intoxication known as peak, where getting higher by chemical means threatens to become its opposite — a moment of futility and melancholy learned through thousands of days, evenings, nights.

Then the ground trembled. An earthquake! If so, it was short-lived. An intense silence followed. Stunned Beautifuls were still drawing breath or reaching for their screens to protest when a voice boomed: 'For your entertainment and edification, behold!'

*　*　*

Next up, Helen thought, an animal fight. She prayed the people baking in their hot cages at the colonia would not be dumped on stage to spice up a dull evening. That the elephants would be spared, their peaceful natures distorted by brain implants, tusks capped with steel sheaths for maximum goring. She prayed, too, that Averil would fully understand the horrors lurking beneath wondrous sparkles, shapes, colours, phantoms. How these spoiled people she so admired — among the most vociferous, self-entitled complainers on the planet before the plagues came — would cavil and carp about the quality of her fellow primitives' grisly ends.

Yet Helen was to be proved wrong on all counts.

Walls rose around the central island to create an arena for a contest. Ramps angled up from storage areas underground. Out stepped a woman, face and body magnified a thousand times into a vast hologram. All recognised her as Mercedes Allure, a popular singer of saccharine melodies. Her face was flushed with excitement, eyes bright.

'What is the greatest thing you can lose if you live forever?' she asked.

Her question echoed. Tens of thousands of eyes watched in the stadium, and countless more via holocasts all over the world. Ennui receded a little.

'I ask, what is the greatest loss you can endure if you live forever?'

Music swelled; she sang. The tune was the anthem of the Five Cities, *My Precious Life*, celebrating the gifts bequeathed to Beautifuls in their eternal round of pleasure and joy: innocent gaiety, love, friendship ...

As the music faded, Mercedes Allure bowed to scatterings of applause.

'I have answered my own question,' she declared. 'The greatest thing we can lose is our lives.'

She let the scurrilous, indecent thought sink in. Discussing the possibility of a Beautiful's death was in the worst possible taste.

'That is why, dear friends, I am going to risk my precious life for your entertainment! Yes, and to show how our precious lives could be yet more precious still.' She beamed, looking around the stadium. 'Behold! My very own guardian angel!'

* * *

The stirring, mystical strains of a panpipe, harmonised by simulations of massed choirs humming the melody of *My Precious Life* filled the air. People rose from couches and chairs for a better view. Holocorders focussed on a circle of the arena floor that sank out of view. For long moments nothing happened. Slowly, the top of a bald head appeared, then horny-skinned shoulders and a muscled torso, long powerful arms and big hands, a tight waist followed by thick, enormously strong legs and large clawed feet. Its crotch was covered by a jutting, armoured codpiece; in its hand, a four foot metal staff, topped by a softly pulsating blue light.

What drew Helen's eye was its face. This was not the first time she had seen such a blank-featured, expressionless, snub-nosed face. The last time had been in Albion, a few minutes before her sister, Mhairi, was killed. For the Angel was no less than a new being, designed by science and spliced with a mixture of genes. A strangeling hitherto banned in the Five Cities for fear of gene infection.

Helen trembled. Tears filled her eyes. To stop this abomination against nature, Mhairi had sacrificed her life. Now Helen saw how lost Blair Gover's cause had grown. In essence, only a miracle and his immediate intervention in the Grand Autonomy might save him.

'Behold, my Angel!' cried Mercedes Allure.

Roars of approval and applause. Something entirely new! After a century of sameness, of drones and obedient technicians, the same old places and opportunities, here was a novelty. An invisible audience exploded all over the world. Holograms floated like a blizzard of white confetti: Bravo! My Angel! Hurrah!

Mercedes Allure stood erect, proud, powerful. Before her, the Angel fell to its knees, spread-eagled on the floor, worshipping her as its goddess.

'Oh, my!' sighed a woman nearby, rapt, ecstatic. Helen could tell she, too, longed for an Angel, a companion and protector entirely her own.

Suddenly, gasps of alarm. Another lift had risen through the floor of the arena. This carried not one creature, but ten.

Primitives, specially chosen for their strength. All were smeared with dried traces of their own excrement and blood from a previous meal, simple hygiene quite beyond them. All carried vicious clubs topped with spikes. Several slavered and made incoherent yipping noises as they blinked at the Beautiful singer in her splendid white gown.

'Behold, Homo sapiens,' intoned a deep voice. 'Even as we watch, their numbers spiral, threatening a resumption of barbarity.'

The Beautiful on the stage retreated as the primitives advanced upon her with ambling, ungainly steps. Drool from their mouths indicated hunger. It was plain they wished to devour her alive.

Silence settled on the stadium. Animal fights were one thing, this quite another.

'Angel,' commanded Mercedes Allure, her voice reverberating. 'Defend me. Defend Homo aeternum!'

The creature rose, interposing itself between the starving savages and its mistress. The primitives charged.

What happened next was a blur. The Angel's staff whipped left and right, sometimes stabbing like a spear, sometimes striking down to bludgeon. Spiked clubs bounced off its hide, leaving deep gashes that bled a dark blue ichor. One primitive, a giant of its kind, horribly strong, leapt upon the Angel's back, pinning its arms.

Groans from the audience, some of whom called out. Drones should be sent in! Mercedes Allure was in terrible danger.

Yet the Angel shrugged its mighty shoulders and hurled the primitive over its head to the floor. It stamped on the primitive, again and again, until blood and brains squirted.

Five savages remained. Two were quickly dispatched with the staff before the others fled, scattering around the arena, yelping like dogs. The audience realised the singer's danger had increased. If the Angel pursued its enemies individually, one might get a chance to rush Mercedes Allure, steal her precious life with a spiked club.

But her Angel was a guardian indeed. Seizing two clubs, he hurled them with astonishing force and accuracy.

Padding over to the last surviving savage, the Angel watched the man beg for his life. Its chiselled face was expressionless as moulded stone. Reaching down, it twisted the primitive's head, back and forth, until it came away. This gruesome gift was borne to the Angel's mistress, laid lovingly at her feet. The Angel assumed its former position, spread-eagled and facedown on the floor.

Wild shouting. Cheers. A fresh blizzard of holograms. Mercedes Allure once again performed *My Precious Life*, encouraging the audience to sing along. Some wept openly, applauding the magnificent Angel until their palms stung.

Helen bit her knuckles in horror. She was unable to tear her eyes from the creature. Averil clapped and clapped, complaining to Synetta that she needed a screen, too, to send holcomments of her own.

TWENTY

As dawn rose on the other side of the world, the Nuagers judged the full extent of the sea-tilth enclosing them. The long, flat rocks on which the lighthouse stood were almost entirely obscured by dense tangles of plastic, dead seaweed, driftwood, and larger manmade objects, including wrecked ships and cylindrical containers for transporting chemicals. Dead fish decayed into slime; sea snails and tiny crabs dined on the putrid vegetation. Gulls and other seabirds skimmed over the floating island. As the sea moved, so the raft rose and fell.

Dameron had his binoculars out again to search the horizon.

'Nae sign of them,' he muttered. 'Thank the good stars and planets. But see! There's a parcel of whales over there. I could tell 'em to seek better spots for their feeding.'

'Nay, it is a sign meant for us,' said Iona in her earnest way. 'Whales are our friends. They have gathered to encourage us. To show the honest path.'

Blair Gover rolled his eyes. He had covered his nose and mouth with cloth soaked in drinking water. 'We must be off. This place is exceptionally dangerous.'

With the help of oars and boathooks, they cleared a way through the plastic raft, until the four birlinns bobbed on a clear stretch of sea. Waves swelled as the wind blew north.

TWENTY

'We'll need muckle rowing to escape this mess,' said Dameron. 'Aye, sore hands and backs.'

The Nuagers followed the perimeter of the plastic until they could strike a clear route south, the blades of their oars pushing aside stray scraps. The pod of whales drew close. Their blowholes emitted gaseous spray; broad, dark grey backs bobbed and sank, short dorsal fins ringed with white poking from the sea.

'Minke,' said Iona. 'They are distressed…'

Then all saw why. A young minke was tangled in the raft of sea-tilth, twenty or so feet from the open sea. As it rolled and thrashed, strands of a large orange trawler net tightened. Its blowhole let out panicking blasts. Less than half a mile distant waited lighthouse and rocks: if the whale drifted onto the reef, there would be no hope for it.

'We must cut him free!' cried Iona.

Gover rose. 'No, no, you foolish woman. My patience with you is at an end. For all we know, we are being pursued right now. I forbid any more of your emotive folly.'

'Know your place,' Michael warned him.

Gover glared back.

'The minke is our clan's guardian spirit,' said Iona, her voice tight with resolve. 'If we allow it to perish, our good fortune will die with it. We cannot leave the poor whale-bairn to strangle itself.'

'Aye,' said Dameron.

Others spoke up, men and women, some with fists bunched as they stared down Gover.

'Mind your mouth!'

'Iona is right!'

'The whale must be saved right enough!'

The City-man sneered. 'I had no idea waterborne mammals determined anyone's luck.'

'There's much you dinnae ken,' taunted Iona. 'I fear you never will.'

* * *

Dameron took charge of the boats, sending three back into open water to wait and watch. The fourth birlinn, crewed by a dozen volunteers, edged back into the raft of sea-tilth. Agitated by fresh breezes, it shimmered and ruffled. So close, the reek of rotten eggs, tar-like oil and fetid vegetation made throats gag, eyes water.

Michael Pilgrim — who had insisted on joining the rescue party, even as Gover decamped sullenly to a safer boat — joined Iona at the prow. A fierce light shone in her dark green eyes as they neared the struggling minke calf.

'We must get a rope round him and drag the poor wee feller out.' She flapped her hands at the raft. 'Can ye swim to save a life, Mister Star Man? Or just shoot your gun to take one?'

Michael resisted a temptation to point out his skill with arms was the only reason her own hadn't burnt to sticks back at Fort George.

Iona stripped off in defiance of the chilly gusts. Her body was thin, pale, bruised in many places.

'You really mean to jump in there?' Michael asked.

'I do.'

A challenge implied. One he longed to ignore. The plastic was coated with raw oil, among other noxious things; an inadvertent mouthful might poison a man. The eyes of the Nuager fishermen were upon him.

Had his survival not depended on their goodwill, he certainly would have refused. But this trapped, frightened creature was the totem of their clan. He understood they were testing his fitness to belong — along with his courage. Should he ever need to lead them in battle, their respect would be essential.

'Alright,' he sighed.

Fumbling, he pulled off boots and coat and trousers. Naked, he felt oddly shy — an inhibition Iona seemed not to share.

Tying ropes around their waists, they jumped into the thick mat of sea-tilth and weed. Instantly, Michael panicked. The shock of the cold water seized him. He couldn't breathe. Couldn't move his legs, arms. He was drowning, drowning ...

His head sank beneath the waves even as he scrabbled and splashed. Kicking out, his right leg tangled in plastic. Then strong hands pulled him to the surface, where he gasped, staring wildly. His horizon reduced to bobbing waste. Iona's face was close to his own, streaked with oil, calling out: 'Stop fighting the water! I've got you. That's it. Let your body get used to the cold.'

She seemed as relaxed as a mermaid.

'Hold your head high,' she cautioned as his breath laboured. 'The air is tainted.'

It wasn't just the stench that made his lungs burn but something invisible: a film of dense gas across the water. Almost he panicked again until Iona forced him onto a plastic barrel. Using it as leverage, he lifted himself sufficiently to gasp clean air.

'I must swim under the laddie,' she said.

Without a word, she took a deep breath and sank into the oily sea. For long moments his panic returned. She would drown. Get tangled. Then who would save him? Was he expected to pull her free?

She pushed up through the debris on the other side of the tangled whale, drawing in lungfuls of stinking air. The big animal snorted its distress.

'Here!' She clung to the net draped around the beast. 'Take it! Take it!'

Michael Pilgrim reached over its back and seized the rope she offered. A loop had been formed over the young minke. Rather than swim beneath it again, she grabbed its dorsal and clambered nimbly over its back as it bucked and writhed and groaned.

'Dameron! Haul us in!' she cried.

Willing hands dragged safety lines until they were back aboard. Shivering but triumphant, Iona tied an expert noose and pulled it tight. Now the beast was firmly lassoed.

On cue, the Nuagers in the three waiting boats rowed hard; three stout lines attached to Dameron's birlinn went taut. Their craft and its cargo of young whale, along with a substantial quantity of net and trapped plastic, pulled free of the raft into the open sea.

A long cheer arose. Michael's teeth chattered as he rubbed himself with a rough woollen cloth. He retched up a lungful of phlegm.

'We're not done yet,' said Iona. 'The net must be cut off our poor, wee laddie. I fancy your sword might be just the ticket.'

* * *

It was quite certain Iona of Skye had never seen a ticket in her life. Or even understood the phrase learned from her mother. Yet it had always sounded clever to her, suggestive of better, kinder times. Before Michael could reply, a startled scream cut through the cheering around them.

It came from one of the sharp-eyed children who had shimmied up a mast to get a better view of the whale. 'Sails! Sails!'

The lad's finger pointed north.

Michael grabbed Dameron's binoculars, though it was difficult to focus while standing on an unstable deck. Sails all right. A dark cluster. Too far off to see the hulls beneath, but Michael did not doubt they were full of armed men. The King of Buchan had caught up with them.

Gover was the first to react. 'Flee!' His voice boomed through the amplification device he wore. 'For your very lives, flee! The stars wish you to flee!'

Mouths gaped, hands ducked fearfully. Michael grabbed Gover

before he could say more.

'Keep calm, man! You'll panic them.'

'I warned you of this, you fool!' Gover's finger jabbed at the approaching fleet.

Michael turned to Dameron. 'How long until they reach us?'

The old fisherman looked with the binoculars for a minute or so. The folk around him hushed. When he lowered the glasses, his gloomy face took on a grim cast.

'Cannae say for sure. But the wind's against them and so are the waves.'

'Have we time to free the poor laddie?' cried Iona. 'James's spirit is in him! I sense it! James has come back to test us after his sacrifice. To see if we are worthy. We must set him free.'

Much muttering bubbled up among the Nuagers. Suddenly, everything made sense. Gover twitched with disbelief.

'Who in the name of all that is rational is James?' he demanded.

Michael whispered. 'The lad who challenged the Prince O'Ness to save her — and lost his head for it. She is in deep grief, Gover, one she cannot show because of her leadership. I believe he was her lover.'

'That hapless hero?' said Gover, none too quietly. 'That noodle. Good lord, will this never end?'

No one answered, and no one was listening. The Nuagers were all babble and action. Michael hurriedly dressed while half a dozen young men stripped. He hadn't the slightest intention of getting back into the water. Gover slumped in the exaggerated despair of a thwarted child, massaging his milk-skinned forehead with long, pale fingers.

'I have the most abominable of headaches,' he complained. 'As for those aquatic mammals' —The pod of whales had drawn closer as the calf was dragged out into open water— 'Surely they are dangerous. Not to mention the toxic chemicals and gaseous matter emitted by that polymeric goulash.'

The rescue party readied itself, boats manoeuvring on either side of the netted beast. Plastic flippers from the Before Times were strapped onto their feet. Michael tried not to stare at the King of Buchan's fleet. What was the point? Looking would not slow them or change the fact they outnumbered the Nuagers several times over. Iona's eyes brightened with excitement. Here, he realised, was the kind of fight she relished. A battle for life.

'May I borrow your sword? It is very sharp, is it not?' she asked Michael.

'On one condition.'

'Aye?'

'Hold out your right hand.'

The City-sword had a wrist strap so its wielder could not drop it. This he pulled tight, adding extra twine as double security for his prized possession. He felt the warmth of her breath on his face as he fastened the knots.

'Be careful,' he said as he finished. 'It's sharper than you can imagine.'

'Then it's just the ticket!' she responded.

With a leap, Iona joined her companions in the sea, pulling and cutting away at the nets around the creature.

Dangerous work. The pod drew close, spouting and heaving, attracted by the young calf's appeals. Likewise, the King of Buchan's fleet drew nearer, hulls now clearly visible beneath the sails.

Soon enough, it was done: the ancient netting parted where it met razor-sharp fish knives and the even sharper City-sword. Brave swimmers attached to the birlinns by safety lines were pulled back, and the giant baby's fins splashed free. It lunged joyfully to join the pod of minke, diving so that its tail thwacked the water, inches from a prow. One by one, the rescuers were helped back on board.

Dameron turned his attention to the fleet approaching from the north.

'Row!' he bellowed. 'For our lives, row!'

A frantic grabbing of oars, settling of dripping, naked men on benches. No time for more than a shirt now. Twelve or more large war vessels were less than a quarter of an hour off by Dameron's estimation.

Again Gover's voice boomed over his amplifier, so loud folk covered their ears and winced. It was a voice of utter certainty.

'If you truly want to live,' he barked, 'you will do just as I say.'

* * *

The King of Buchan's fleet was near enough for men's silhouettes to be visible. Michael readied his weapons with forlorn hope. Gover, however, was busy gesticulating and browbeating Iona and Dameron in a mellifluous language translated through his communication device. This magic — and the proximity of capture by the Prince O'Ness's vengeful father — cowed them when nothing else would.

The City-man flounced back to his favourite position beneath the cabin awning.

'I am displeased,' he answered when Michael asked what that had been about.

Spurred on by Iona and Dameron, the Nuagers rowed to a rhythm called by each birlinn's tillerman. Round the great raft of sea-tilth they sped, aware their pursuers were changing course to cut them off. The island of waste was a rough rectangle centred on the rock and the lighthouse. One corner pointed north towards the enemy fleet. Round this point they headed southwest, along the border of the tilth-raft.

Michael was surprised they did not seek the open sea. Their course drew the King of Buchan's fleet back toward the floating plastic island while in no way hastening their escape. Worse, their oars inevitably snagged on floating plastic and weed.

A mile passed. Then another. They reached the rear of the plasti-raft's large rectangle. From here, open seas beckoned south. Still, the enemy ships were drawing closer, although an impassable mass of tangled weed, plastic and wood now formed a barrier between them.

Again, Gover barked through his communication device in the strange tongue. To Michael's surprise, Iona cringed. She had been silent since rescuing the minke calf — whether from deep emotion at freeing her former lover's soul or some other faith, he could not tell.

'What language is that?' he asked Iona.

She ducked her head. 'It is a secret not for you, Mister Star Man.'

At Gover's command, their birlinn halted while the remaining three carried on south, pausing only to raise sails. Their own boat creaked and rolled, the rowers gasping after their exertions.

'As close as you can now,' Gover ordered. 'Remember what I said. Ah, that patch looks perfect. There! Near the chemical barrels. No, not there! Follow my pointing finger. There, you fools.'

Gover clicked his fingers. 'Pilgrim, I need gunpowder. Oh, and that firepot. Chop! Chop!'

Michael passed over the requested items, and the City-man packed the pot with oil-soaked cloth and gunpowder. The container had a metal handle, which he hung from a boathook.

'What's your game, Gover?' he asked.

'Shoot oop!' snapped Gover, sarcastically imitating Michael's Yorkshire accent. Then turning to Dameron, he added: 'Now, sir, when I say row, I really do mean row. Understood?'

Dameron nodded warily. 'Aye.'

'Go-o-d.'

Licking his lips, Gover took up a flint-wheel lighter and sparked it. Touching the flame to the pot, he stepped back as it guttered and blazed. Then he extended the boat hook and lowered it onto a ridge of oil-blackened weed. His eyes closed, and he flinched as though in expectation of a blow. Nothing happened.

'I might yet survive this,' he grunted.

Leaning forward, Gover tilted the pot so that a tongue of flame licked the plastic raft's exposed surface. Instantly, a second blue flame appeared, spreading rapidly in a swift wave. A whoosh, a roar, then fire shot up in spurts. Gover jumped back.

'Row!' he bellowed.

Poised oars bit water. The birlinn shot out from the raft as a small explosion detonated. Smoke and choking gases rolled over the little ship. Still, the desperate crew pulled. Another explosion, bigger than the first, became a fireball ascending amidst plumes of smoke. The air swirled with heat.

Then they were free. Behind them, a gathering fog of black, oily smoke rose ever higher. Heatwaves wafted; the Nuagers moaned or prayed in terror. Still, they rowed, a reflex requiring no thought. The surface of the sea in their wake was obscured by a dense smokescreen punctuated by darting flames. No one spoke.

Gover settled heavily in his customary seat to mop his brow.

'Ha!' he declared.

* * *

'How the fuck did you do that?' asked Michael.

'Oh, just silly old science,' answered Gover. 'Not being nice or pretty or believing in sea fairies taking the shape of mammals. Not being sentimental or kind or having a gay, bonny smile for one and all. Ye ken.'

His smile grew cat-like.

'I realised as soon as we entered the concentration of polymeric substances that flammable gases lay low across the surface, denser than air gases, methane mostly, most likely the residues of a chemical spill. But without my screen, I could only theorise. In addition, the plastic raft had also drifted across a recent oil spill. Crude oil, as it happens, highly flammable. This coast is riddled with pipes that keep leaking oil, or perhaps a sunken tanker released its load. Either way, oil, methane, oxygen, driftwood, rotting vegetation, and other compounds as yet unidentified, let us call them Factor X. Et, voila! The perfect combustible soup.' He gestured at the hellish pall of fumes and fire behind them. 'I think we may safely assume it will slow down our barbarous pursuers, do you not think? There's an outside chance it might even asphyxiate them.'

'There's more to you than meets the eye,' said Michael.

'Quite.'

'What about that strange language you used with Dameron and Iona? It scared the daylights out of them.'

'Oh, that. I instructed the decoder to listen in while they muttered among themselves. It is a secret tongue the native Nuagers have devised for their most powerful discourses with the stars, rather as Christian priests once awed their followers with Latin. A mixture of Gaelic, Hibernian English and Spanish, would you believe, or so the decoder informed me.'

'It seemed to impress them.'

'Of course it did. The fact that I am apparently fluent in their divine gibberish lends me supernatural powers. A rather useful apotheosis.'

Michael had no idea what the latter word meant. He turned back to the northern horizon. The smoke was, if anything, denser.

Gover sighed with self-satisfaction. 'Science, Pilgrim,' he repeated. 'Your essential problem, you know, is what I term "rule-by-emotion". You positively revel in unreason. Consequently, you imbue nature with bogus moral qualities, whereas I understand it as merely a tool. A series of chemical and atomic reactions to serve my will. In short, I am nature's master.'

For a moment Gover's absurd arrogance exasperated Michael. Then he glimpsed the City-man's predicament: trapped among creatures he despised and yet, for all his bravado, must fear; exiled from the one haven in a perilous world he trusted. Was that not a feeling Michael had known when dragged off to serve the City as a conscript in the Crusades?

'You did well this time, Gover,' he said. 'Still, I have a nasty feeling it won't delay our pals back there long.'

TWENTY-ONE

Jojo Lyons' question haunted Seth Pilgrim. *Won't we, Seth?* Its implication plain: saving the freakish strangeling in her hideaway was somehow his responsibility.

Unspoken tensions gathered in the summerhouse by the ponds at the bottom of the valley. Hurdy-Gurdy understood, Seth was sure, the exiled City-man always saw more than he liked. His dilemma simple: whether to flee and continue south towards Albion or stay to help his new friend; not that Seth needed or wanted friends. Big Jacko had taught him a bellyful of loyalty.

Won't we, Seth?

Nobody on this poisoned crap-hole planet told Seth Pilgrim what to do. Not after the fists and pitiless whips of Maister Gil. Not after the cuffs and insults of the Mistresses of Fell Grange, those vile bitches he prayed had burned good and slow when he set their house ablaze. Seth owed nothing to nobody. Least of all some fuckwit ex-girl stupid enough to get herself taken by a loser like Big Jacko — a loser Seth had pinned his faith to like a shiny, unblemished star.

But when Jojo Lyons' came to the summerhouse where he and Gurdy huddled over their fire, Seth agreed instantly to what was asked of him. For once his madman companion declined to comment, busy stirring a pot of gruel and singing in a cracked, ironic falsetto:

TWENTY-ONE

My precious life, endless as oceans
Circling the Earth.
My precious life, a line unbroken
Birth to rebirth.
Oh, my precious life!
Oh, my precious life!
This whole world made just for me,
All I ever want to be.

Something about the way Gurdy sang gave Seth pause.

'You alright?' he asked.

The City-man's smile of reply was ghastly. 'I am dying, Egypt, dying. All the perfumes of Arabia will not sweeten this little hand.'

Jojo cleared his throat impatiently. 'She'll be waiting for us.'

They left Gurdy moaning to himself. Seth wondered which of his friends — and he possessed a grand total of two — needed his help most.

* * *

Through winter woods, chilly but not freezing, air moist with complex scents. Rooks cawed in anticipation of dusk. Outside the old Octagon Tower, Seth and Jojo halted.

'I've brought different kinds of food for her,' whispered Jojo. 'Blankets, as well.' His brown eyes swam with tears. 'I'm glad you're here, Seth! Even though she is Bella — I'm sure of that, no one will convince me otherwise — the worst thing is I'm afraid to see her. She… She disgusts me. My own sister! Isn't that shameful?'

It seemed fair enough to Seth. 'Perhaps it's best to get it over with then.'

The two young men climbed the ornate stone steps. The tower's one central room was murky with shadow.

She — it — lay in a bed of bracken and autumn leaves, shivering like one possessed by devils. All that disgusted Jojo on show: the golden pelt for skin and hare-like legs, floppy ears poking through the long hair of a normal girl, and her face, human yet crucially not. Especially her face.

In those altered features, Seth read more than he ever wanted to know about Bella Lyons. That she was weakened by hunger, desperately afraid, almost to the dark, swirling borderlands of insanity.

The last time Bella saw Seth, she appeared not to recognise him. Not so today. Hiding her face with clawed fingers, she struggled upright and lunged for the stairs leading to the top of the tower.

Jojo blocked her, wrapping his coat around her quaking shoulders; the creature hesitated, gazing up at him with big, pleading eyes.

'Don't be afraid, Bella,' whispered Jojo as he knelt by her. 'The City did this to you, didn't they?'

No sign of understanding, even recognition.

'We shall find a cure, I promise. Do you believe me, sister?' He pulled the coat tighter around her shoulders. 'You must trust me, Bella.'

At last, a nod, unless it was merely a twitch.

'Are you hungry?' he asked, encouraged. 'Look! Oatcakes. You always loved those. A pot of honey and some salt pork. And here is a blanket from your old room, the bed you shared with Abbie. Do you know where Abbie is? Can you tell me? No, don't get upset! I shouldn't have asked. Tell me when you are ready.'

He turned to Seth, struggling to appear strong. 'I shall return with more food. And yes, clothes, you must have clothes. Won't we, Seth?'

Again she shrank back.

'Don't be afraid,' said Jojo. 'Seth is a good man. You can trust him. Take heart, Bella, and wait for our return. We'll be back soon.'

TWENTY-ONE

* * *

Twilight was settling as the two young men left the ancient folly in the woods. Seth glanced back at the tower. Its windows singled him out like accusing eyes.

They followed the path through withered brown ferns and bracken to the tunnel, that dark, mossy way where Jojo and his sisters had imagined portals to magical lands, far from this world of plague and decay.

Jojo wept as he stumbled into the darkness. At the dog leg, where neither entrance nor exit was visible, a place untouched by light, Seth reached out for Jojo's hand. It was not planned. They stood silent for a long moment. Then Seth embraced Jojo — or perhaps it was the other way around — both meaning to comfort the other.

Seth became aware of a new tension. That even as he pulled Jojo close, he longed to seek his mouth with his own, to taste him. To touch his firm body and intimate places.

'Thank you, I feel a little better now,' mumbled Jojo, sniffing and wiping his eyes.

They stepped apart. Seth followed through the darkness until they left the tunnel, concealing tears of his own.

Later, Jojo sent a kitchen boy to the summerhouse with a message he would previously have carried himself. They would be wanted the next day to load and unload at the Salt Fair in Ripon.

* * *

They followed a long, winding track beside the River Skell, past low hillsides clad with oak and ash. Farms were infrequent but fattening on land fallow for a century.

Cold river mist swirled, and the packhorses left deep hoof marks in the mud. Half of Fountains hamlet was heading for the Salt Fair, a rare holiday. As befitted his status, Jojo rode at the head. The younger women and girls sang the old songs as they walked, songs with words barely understood, riddles from better times.

Mid-morning found them in deserted suburbs, passing through woodland and houses besieged by roots. Branches poked from windows and mould feasted on floorboards. Several warehouses by the Skell fared better, home to clans with extensive market gardens and skills as tanners. "Tough as Ripon leather" was a watchword in the region.

Outside the cathedral, dozens of booths, along with pens and folds, filled a former supermarket car park. Seth barely noticed the contrast between the lofty, ornate walls and spires of the cathedral and the bedlam of swine, sheep, and cattle. Most towns staged fairs to trade winter meat and the means to preserve it over the long cold months before spring grass sprouted. Ripon Salt Fair was also a hiring fair for labourers and maidservants seeking a year's bed and board, with fresh clothes and boots thrown in at the end of their bond.

Folk from near and far milled in the hoof-softened mud, yet Seth did not sense danger. Wandering off, he fell into gloomy thoughts.

Gurdy was right, the time had come to seek the City and a future worth living. But doing so meant leaving Jojo. His thoughts often drifted to his handsome new friend. Being with him lightened the drabbest day.

But Seth knew no one could be relied on. Sooner, later, the strangeling in the Octagon Tower above Fountains would be discovered. And he had a horrible feeling who would get the blame.

His feet took him into the ancient cathedral. Here swirled a complex stench of unwashed bodies, boiling vats of fatty meat, smoke from fires, and sweeter scents of griddle cakes, mulled cider, roasted corncobs.

TWENTY-ONE

Ripon Cathedral was hundreds of feet long and wide, a mighty building of outthrust stone walls, its lead-lined roof speckled with stars of daylight from tiny holes. Shadows lurked amidst pools of winter light spilling through tall stained-glass windows. It was cold in the ancient church, despite the scores of labourers gathered for hiring, the salt merchants weighing their wares into small sacks or barrels; despite the mountebanks' steaming food, the smoke and sizzle of fat.

He wandered further into the dark church, scarcely noticing the chanting from a walled-off chapel, where high altars once venerated the Christ-God. Fresh guilt touched Seth. He recalled his father's devotion to Christ, how cruelly he'd mocked the dying man's faith. Uncle Michael had warned he would rue hurting his father. Too late. Forever too late. Fuck it. Fuck them all.

On he pressed, drawn as though against his will by the droning voices. His heartbeat quickened. Seth passed beneath an archway, down a corridor lined with sarcophagi, and entered the ancient altar chapel of the cathedral through a low side door. He halted in disbelief.

* * *

A small crowd had gathered. Because the door was elevated above the area around the altar, Seth had a clear view. He shrank behind a burly farmer gawping down. The man's wet, pink mouth hung open.

Surrounded by a semicircle of folk, a rite was in progress: one he knew too well. Half a dozen gaunt men in stained robes held back the crowd, whips and scourges in their belts. Seth could name them all. The two Mistresses of Fell Grange, Fat and Thin, petulant and lazy, cruel and busy of taste. So-called mother-daughter, daughter-mother. And serving them, Maister Gil and the other floggers, one of whom Seth recognised as the scavenger-tinker he had encountered in Skipton a month earlier.

The reason for the Mistresses' presence in Ripon was apparent — and it wasn't to buy salt. More likely to rub it into whatever wounds they could inflict on him.

Right now, they were selling ceremonies to summon luck or fertility, curse an enemy or bring a lover to heel. Business as usual for the Mistresses, who had lived well off their mystery for decades.

Yet Fat Mistress's face hung slack, suggesting meals in short supply. She mumbled rather than intoned the magic words, stumbling over anything but basic invocations to Satan. Her partner, Thin, even more starkly diminished. Always gaunt as a crow, now her left hand dangled, twisted and burned, along with half her face, one blind eye surrounded by charred skin. Seth's farewell bonfire had left its mark. Though she shrieked and ululated at the climax of the rite, her frenzy was forced, even as she chopped the head off a dove, blood bubbling over the altar, wings beating frantically.

He became aware a man had stepped behind him. Adrenalin surged. Out of the corner of his eye, Seth recognised the Lord of Erringdale.

Much can pass through a human mind in the space of a second. Seth recalled all he knew about the Lord of Erringdale. His fame as a strongman with bullying, violent ways; his childish faith in the Mistresses; how he had raped his niece as she grovelled and wept in the Coven's temple; not least, that his wife had miscarried during the blaze Seth started.

So far, the Lord of Erringdale had not spotted him. Otherwise, he would have raised an alarm. Would he even recognise him? They had encountered each other in Fell Grange, but then he had been a field-bonder in filthy rags, unworthy of notice. Today he wore a freeman's clothes, his face recently shaven instead of smeared with mud; a broad-brimmed hat shadowed his features.

Seth's hand slipped to the knife in his belt. Indecision an agony, he lowered his head and tried to push past the big man filling the narrow

TWENTY-ONE

doorway.

'Hey!' grunted the Lord of Erringdale as Seth squeezed through the gap. There his luck ended. The wide brim that concealed him snagged on the wooden door frame and skewed to reveal half his face. A glimpse, but enough.

Seth half ran down the dark corridor at the side of the altar chapel.

'Hey!' called a gruff voice behind him.

He turned a corner and slipped into a short, narrow passageway. Behind, the open nave of the cathedral spread, crowded with hands to seize him. Out came his knife.

* * *

The low-ceilinged passageway extended five feet then ended in an arched door, dangling from a single hinge. Gloom beyond. Seth slipped through, stumbling up a steep spiral staircase, gritty with mouse and rat droppings. Sheathing his knife, he scurried on hands and knees, feeling a way. His breath came in jagged gasps. He prayed the Lord of Erringdale would blunder past and search for him in the main body of the cathedral.

A loud scrape echoed as the door below was forced open.

The spiral staircase ended in another half-open door, daylight showing beyond. Seth eased it wider, cringing as it creaked. Then he was through — to a place of little comfort.

He had emerged on a walkway fifty feet above the old car park, where the fair was being held. A low stone balustrade streaked with bird droppings separated him from a long fall. On the other side of the narrow walkway, a slate and lead-flashed roof rose steeply. At the end of the walkway, a good hundred feet off, another door, this one closed, an entrance into one of the cathedral's towers.

Behind came the unmistakable sound of footsteps on the stairs, the faint bluish glow of a flint lighter. The Lord of Erringdale's other hand would hold a weapon.

Seth longed for the pistol hidden at Fountains. Neglecting it was Jojo Lyons' fault for persuading him the world could be kind instead of a pit where every devil battled to save his own skin.

Seth stepped outside onto the walkway. What to do? Make a stand with his knife? But the Lord of Erringdale wore a thick leather coat and was skilled with arms. Run for it? Nowhere to go.

A flutter of wings made him wheel around, almost losing his balance on the strip of walkway. A pigeon flew up from the side of the doorway near the steep-angled roof. It had been perching in a large, hideous, grinning gargoyle that clung to the stonework beside the door, creating a place to hide beneath its jaws, a perch narrow enough for a man.

Seth pulled himself into this space and froze, knife in hand. Moments passed. Cautious footsteps on the staircase. The door opened slowly. Another pause. Unseen in the doorway, the Lord of Erringdale must be assessing dangers, as Seth had done. He dared hardly breathe lest his hiding place be revealed. He heard the familiar click of a pistol being cocked. The big man advanced, glancing from side to side. Had Seth not been hidden by the corner of stonework, he would have been spotted instantly. Had he been large of limb instead of a thin scarecrow, he would have been trapped.

As the Lord leaned over the edge of the balustrade to see if his enemy had climbed down to freedom, Seth lunged forward, shoving with all his strength. Hands lost their grip on stonework, scrabbled, dropped the pistol. Then the big man tumbled, flailing with feet and hands, one boot catching Seth in the chest, knocking him back onto the slate roof.

'Aaagh!'

A short cry. The pistol went off as it hit the ground, followed by a heavy crump. Seth struggled up, clutching his chest. Edging over to the balustrade, he peered down.

TWENTY-ONE

The Lord of Erringdale lay spread-eagled, blood pouring from his staved skull. People were rushing over, bending over the body. Among them, looking straight up into Seth's face, Jojo Lyons, Hurdy-Gurdy at his side.

*　*　*

He fled Ripon Cathedral, hurrying straight to the summerhouse near Fountains Abbey. Low clouds gathered. Stubborn leaves stirred on gnarled twigs. Images of legs and arms flailing as the Lord of Erringdale fell played in his mind. The bastard would have done the same to me, he told himself, far worse. Yet there was no triumph, just weariness. Jojo's incredulous face had looked up as Seth clung to the balustrade like a hideous gargoyle, fearful of a lynching. That much had been avoided, at least.

In the summerhouse, Seth packed his few possessions in a sack and tore out a blank page from one of the Mistresses' holy books. On this, he wrote, using charcoal from the fire as a crude pen:

Hurdy. Gone to the hare. Will wait til until morning.

He laid this cryptic note where Gurdy's could not fail to see it.

The Octagon Tower seemed his safest refuge. Even if Jojo turned against him as a murderer, he would never lead pursuers to his beloved sister — or what remained of her — and in Seth's opinion, that wasn't much.

He found himself high in the woods with musket primed. The strangeling might yet attack him and nor would he blame her. But when he opened the folly's door, it was deserted. Even the bedding of ferns piled in the corner smelt stale.

Seth built a small fire of ripped up floorboards in the old stone fireplace. Flames flickered, bringing little comfort. He chewed salt lamb for his supper and prepared for hungry days ahead.

When the knock came, it startled him. Readying his musket, he called: 'Who's there?'

'Poor Tom's a-cold, Little Nuncle!' cried a familiar voice.

Seth lowered the gun. Hurdy-Gurdy did not enter alone: Jojo Lyons, his shoulders covered by a cape, followed, heavy bag in hand. He looked around and frowned. 'Bella not here?'

'No.'

'Good,' said Gurdy. 'We shall talk better without her.' His smile recalled the gargoyle Seth had lurked beneath. 'It's time to decide not whether, but whither we should go.'

* * *

They sat around the fireplace with a bottle of raw spirits. For a while, no one spoke. Jojo stirred. His eyes met Seth's.

'Did you really push him off the roof?'

'Yes.'

He waited for Jojo's denunciation, however unfair. The young squire of Fountains took a long pull at the spirits, passed it on.

'Hurdy-Gurdy told me about … about everything. How you were a bonder and how you had to leave in a hurry. How those witches are after you. Why didn't you tell me? I'm your friend.'

He sounded genuinely hurt. For a moment, Seth felt misty. It must be the home-distilled gin.

'I don't know why. Because it's safer that way. Habit, maybe.'

'That's all very lovely, my dears,' purred Hurdy-Gurdy, arching his fingertips and tapping them together in rapid waves. 'But we have two dilemmas before us. The first concerns me. Oh, yes, me! It is this: Seth and I are bound for the fair City of Albion. It is time, I believe, to depart hence.'

'Agreed,' muttered Seth. 'Tomorrow at dawn.'

TWENTY-ONE

Jojo's look of uncertainty deepened.

'The second,' declaimed Hurdy-Gurdy, 'concerns you, Squire Jojo.' He pointed at the pile of ferns surrounded by husks of food and gnawed out hedgehog pelts.

Jojo cleared his throat nervously. 'The City did this thing to Bella. I intend to make them pay. I shall take her to Albion. Make them undo what they did to her.'

A fine chance, thought Seth. Yet he dared not take the thought too far. Doing so would expose the slim, impossible hope behind his own plan to reach the City.

'There's more to it than that,' continued Jojo. 'Do you remember the box hidden beneath the skin on her chest? How it sticks out? I believe her soul's trapped in there. I laid my hand on it when I last brought food. There was a pulse. Perhaps if we cut out the box, the curse on her would lift.'

'Interesting theory,' said Hurdy, his fingers still arched and busy. 'But I believe such an act would lead to a na-asty detonation. Boom!'

'Then let me come with you to the City,' pleaded Jojo. 'I could bring Bella.'

Hurdy cleared his throat. He caught Seth's eye and shook his head.

'I have a better plan,' Seth said. 'I heard the Council of the North will meet after Christmastide in York. Why don't we travel there with Jojo, Gurdy? They say a strangeling woman rules over York now the Modified Man is dead. One who never shows her face. Folk call her Lady Veil. They say she came from the City like you. That they did something wicked to her there, drove her out as they did you. Perhaps you even knew her. *She* might know what to do with Bella.'

Gurdy's drooping face grew furtive. 'Perhaps.'

Seth did not mention his own risks in travelling to York. If recognised as a leading follower of Big Jacko, a swift dangling would follow. But Jojo's guileless face in the firelight soothed his doubts. Inspired by a burning mouthful of spirits, he reached out and took Jojo's hand. It was not pulled away.

'You are a good friend to me,' said Jojo. 'The best imaginable. You must hide here for a couple of days while I arrange a horse and cart to York. Bella can hide in the back if need be. How clever you are to think of this Lady Veil, Seth.'

'Harrumph!' grumbled Gurdy.

The young men looked at him in surprise, their fingers still entwined. The leer was back on his face, but for once it was tinged with pity.

TWENTY-TWO

Beautifuls had it all. Except now they didn't. Those with a competitive tinge — the majority — hungered for their very own Angel as a bespoke accessory, pet, eternally loyal servant, protector, so superior to a mere drone.

If Helen expected a backlash from the Ruling Council for the rebellious display at the Grand Gala, she was disappointed. As were many tens of thousands who believed, along with Blair Gover, artificial gene sequences posed incalculable risks.

'We still have some days left before the Autonomy,' said Marvin Brubacher. 'Look, Helen, the ground's shifted, that's all. So it is no longer Discordia to speak out in favour of these Angels. It doesn't mean the Founding Vision won't prevail.'

'Of course not,' said Merle.

Helen sighed. 'I wish Blair were here. After the Autonomy, will you transport me home with Averil?'

'We'll take good care of you,' promised Merle. 'You can rely on that. Blair or no Blair.'

She soon learned something was expected in return.

Helen 'masked up', as it was known when a Beautiful concealed his or her face to enjoy the delights of Mughalia incognito. Holomasks were the usual method: she chose a facsimile of the Mona Lisa. Not that the disguise prevented the City from tracking her every movement.

Helen's concern was in being recognised as Blair Gover's former paramour by people she met.

'What do you think?' she asked Averil.

The young woman would have screamed in surprise ten days ago. Now she was blasé. Did not her own improved face wear a mask, albeit of a permanent kind?

'May I go with you?' Averil asked. 'I'd like to see the City proper. From the inside.' She shot Helen a reproachful look. 'Merle told me you want to take me back to dirty old Baytown soon as you can.'

'You wouldn't want to join me where I'm going,' said Helen. 'I've asked Marvin and Merle if you can accompany their entourage while I'm busy. Synetta will be with you. They'll keep an eye out for your safety.'

Averil's undisguised pleasure at this news grieved Helen, as had her reaction to the Angel's gladiatorial display in the stadium. 'How is it different from a drone?' the girl had asked. 'A drone would have done the same thing.'

'That creature was a living, sentient being, not a machine. As were its victims. What if it has what used to be called a soul?'

'Then it's lucky to have been given one! Anyway, those primitives were horrible. They deserved to die.'

Distaste for her own people had grown to ugly contempt since Averil's encounter with the scavengers at the foot of Adam's Peak. Fears for her unborn baby no doubt explained it. The sooner they returned to Baytown, the better, as far as Helen was concerned.

Helen wandered out into the chemical zones and stimulations of Mughalia. Yet she avoided the Five Poisons: some depravities require too deep a cleansing.

Why she was required as a spy, Helen could not guess. Marvin claimed she offered a fresh perspective, having been absent from the Five Cities for a few years. More likely they just wanted her out of their bouffant, matching hairdos.

On bar stools and in pleasure gardens where vacationing Beautifuls promenaded, danced, acted out the ritualistic inanities of Accordia, she learned much to report. One drugged young man from the City of Mitopia considered Angels-for-all a democratic revolution.

'Think of it,' he drawled, 'we could repopulate the entire earth with our creations. Then we would no longer be confined to the Five Cities.' He sighed happily, took another snort from his nasal applicator. 'We could establish huge estates around the Cities and reign like demi-gods. There's endless lebensraum, dammit. We would need drones, naturally, and plenty of them, to liquidate nuisances like primitives or other animals and do essential work. And we'd always need the Five Cities for fun and Beautification. But over time, we could phase out those boring old drones and replace the lot with Angels. In fact, I have a few design ideas myself!'

Weary work to listen and nod. Helen divined he had been a virtual reality game designer before the Great Dyings.

Another comfort room, another Beautiful. This woman wept ecstatically under the influence of a chemical cocktail. She sobbed how Angels would become all the children she could never have because of the Beautiful Life. Her own special family to love her and be loved in return. 'Think how much love Angels could bring into the world!' she exclaimed. 'It is impossible to be loved by a drone. I lost all my children in the plague. So, so much love!'

At a zero-gravity dining experience, Helen listened to a group of friends debating the Founding Vision, floating with the grace of formation swimmers, plucking titbit delicacies from the air. Not all Beautifuls were prone to intoxication. These were the sober variety.

'Angels offer astonishing possibilities,' said one, his long hair floating in a frizzled halo. 'I picture vast work gangs bred to clear up the mess Homo sapiens left behind. Cheaper than drones and far less wasteful in terms of raw materials. Replanting, deplasticking, clearing away the rubble of the old cities to create sculptured gardens. A happy, happy toil! One of renewal, not destruction, unless some pre-evolved hominids got in the way, *naturellement*. The most innocent of Earth's children setting right primitive humanity's errors. All under the benign guidance of the deities they have been designed to worship. Every Beautiful would be a god or goddess in the Angels' pantheon. Perfect!'

His friends concurred. The sooner traces of the primitives were expunged, the better.

Helen returned to the Brubachers' compound with a heavy heart, not least because when she got there, Averil seemed not to have noticed her absence, too intent on pleasing her new friends.

* * *

Days passed. Still, Marvin gave no indication when a flight would be arranged back to Baytown. Perhaps he and Merle had concluded Blair would never reveal himself, that Helen's usefulness was limited.

On a sticky, muggy afternoon, the Brubachers away on a jaunt with Averil and Synetta, Helen enquired of her screen what credits she still possessed. All Beautifuls were allowed a fixed stipend of credits, enough for a comfortable life if supplemented by a few hours undemanding work each week. She reasoned her old account must contain something.

Up popped a hologram displaying a healthy balance of credits. Not enough to purchase an aircar of her own — these were constructed to order, in any case — but more than sufficient for passage back to Albion and beyond for two people. She scanned the scheduled flights; all were booked up in the days following the Autonomy, as were individual aircars for chartering.

TWENTY-TWO

It occurred to Helen that anyone monitoring her screen would be alerted to her exact plans. This gave her an idea.

An hour later, Helen entered Mughalia's travel hub, sited where hills gave way to sun-bleached plains. A monorail connected it to the city.

The hub's designers sought to prevent the vulgarity of jostling bodies by way of vast, towering halls and wide corridors. These were negotiated on individual hover chairs designed to resemble gilded thrones. When Helen had previously travelled through the hub, it had been a temple of hushed voices, dull, eerie echoes, the faint hum of machinery, people ignoring one another as they floated by. So it came as a surprise to step into a world of noise-filled chaos.

Thousands of Beautifuls in party regalia milled, waiting for drones to service their luggage. The Grand Autonomy was attracting to Mughalia four-fifths of the combined populations of the Five Cities, such was the excitement around Angels and possible changes to the Founding Vision.

Helen soon realised the number of hover chairs was completely inadequate. Some Beautifuls were resorting to a weary trudge down long, bare tunnels in search of the monorail terminus. A few even carried their own hand luggage. Without sufficient drones, abandoned piles of suitcases were mounting.

What is happening to the Five Cities? she wondered as a crowd of Beautifuls argued shamelessly over who should take the next available hover chair. One burly fellow shoved over a slender hermaphrodite. Angry voices echoed round high plastiglass ceilings. All the while, indifferent to the distress of their makers, cleaning drones polished or vacuumed; maintenance drones trundled to undertake labours without thought of reward, and security drones scanned for intruders.

One special area was advertised by a revolving hologram of a golden honeycomb. Here crowds were densest and understandably tense. The Founding Vision decreed a single location on earth should be dedicated to Beautification. Because Albion had developed more rapidly than its sister cities, and perhaps because Blair Gover chose it as his principal home, this essential facility had been constructed within an easy travelling distance of that City.

Helen recalled Blair's excitement at the project, the final realisation of his life's work. He had confided this to her one night, recklessly high on chemicals to fuel gymnastic sex.

'I have designed it with bees as my inspiration. For that reason, it resembles a honeycomb. Thousands of hexagonal cells are connected by corridors, each awaiting its guest. Helen, it is I who shall lavish foreverness upon the most deserving remnant of humanity! My genius. My compassion. My inspiration. Every ten years, each chosen one shall spend a week secluded in his or her cell while the process of Beautification is renewed then re-emerge as a gorgeous butterfly!'

'Why not provide Beautification facilities in each of the Five Cities?' she'd asked. 'Surely that would be more convenient? Then no one would have to travel.'

'Control, my dear! Why else? The purity of the serum must be protected at all costs. Remember how mankind squandered antibiotics. Who knows it better than I?'

Despite his chemical high, he had grown morose. Helen knew well that Blair's first wife, the only person he had ever truly loved, died from an infection before the Plagues, in those decades when antibiotics ceased to work due to overuse.

Alone in the great halls of Mughalia's travel hub, Helen watched mobs of Beautifuls besiege drone-staffed service points, squabbling, shoving, eager to reach Albion and thence Honeycomb. Some looked pale and sick, in urgent need of Beautification. This, too, was new. The median gap between treatments that Blair once designated as ten years had shrunk inexorably to five.

Discordia everywhere! The Five Cities had been palaces of calm and order after the cannibalistic anarchy of the Great Dyings. Now she sensed panic beneath every façade. The reason simple: things meant to last forever were changing.

* * *

Helen walked to a tiny, isolated departure hall, far from the entrance. There she sighed with relief. No one around, just harmless drones.

It was still possible to make manual flight bookings on old-fashioned holo-keyboards. Bypassing the main enquiry system might just conceivably allow her to travel unnoticed. There were no passports or immigration controls between the cities, where a citizen of one was a citizen of all.

She approached an inverted pyramid on wheels and provided her screen for scanning.

'Provide manual entry point,' she commanded.

A virtual keyboard instantly projected. Awkwardly, for she was unused to typing, Helen entered: *Do not make a record of this transaction. I wish to acquire a one-way flight to Albion for two persons. Private cabin. Or, if possible, private aircar.*

The machine projected its reply: **None of the above will be possible.**

Why not?

I am not permitted to disclose why not.

Why are you not permitted to disclose that information?

I am not permitted to disclose why I am not permitted to disclose that information.

How may I gain permission for the flights?

Higher-level authorisation is necessary.

The machine's pleasant synthvoice sang out unexpectedly: 'Most, most sorry!'

Without Helen's permission, the virtual keyboard faded.

Reluctant to venture back through the seething travel hub, Helen rested in the small departure lounge. Electrified concrete walls were visible in the distance through a shimmering heat haze. A large aircarrier approached with a fresh cargo of people bound for the Grand Autonomy. This conclave was to be the biggest ever, four out of five Beautifuls crammed into Mughalia. It occurred to Helen no better way could be imagined of spreading subversive notions — and no idea was more revolutionary than creating new life forms.

The booking drone had warned higher level authorisation was necessary to escape this troubled place. She and Averil were trapped. Then Helen recalled Synetta expressing great fondness for Averil and that Synetta's screen had a very high level of authorisation indeed.

* * *

On the last day before the Grand Autonomy, Helen sought out Synetta's quarters. She lived in a bungalow bordering the grounds of the Brubacher's compound, shaded by bamboo and sweet-scented honeysuckle. Small, brightly coloured birds flitted and darted.

As Helen approached the bungalow door, a servitor-drone opened it wide.

'Is your mistress available?' asked Helen.

The drone, an all-purpose model with four legs doubling up as arms, bowed low. Its voice had been programmed to exactly mimic Synetta's.

'This way, please.'

Helen followed the machine down a corridor of parquet glow-tiles to a central living area dotted with low, comfortable furniture. Faded pennants crowded the walls, each decorated with symbols, lost phrases, echoes of a country abandoned to its own radiation and pollution: Dallas Cowboys. New England Patriots. Los Angeles Rams. Seattle Seahawks. Philadelphia Eagles. For a moment the names puzzled Helen. Then she recalled crowded football stadiums, padded young men in helmets with bright liveries. Strange to see such treasured relics in quiet, conventional Synetta's quarters. Doting upon the Before Times was viewed as the height of eccentricity. If taken too far, it might even constitute Discordia.

The determination required to gather so many rare antiques suggested a mind more independent than most. This gave Helen hope. Her request was for something also frowned upon: that Synetta would share the use of her screen.

The precious screen's owner sat on a sofa in the middle of the room, face buried in her hands.

'Am I intruding?' asked Helen.

Synetta lifted her head. Tears swam in her large brown eyes. 'Do not come near!'

'What has happened?'

A loud sob escaped her. 'I... I am not well.'

Helen hurried over. Sickness was never to be truly feared in the Five Cities unless it was of the mind. She had noticed hints of mental strain in the Brubachers' lovely companion, attributing it to that pervasive melancholy afflicting most Beautifuls, known as tristesse.

'Do not come near,' moaned Synetta again. 'You'll catch it.'

Helen sat beside her and patted her hand. 'Perhaps you should take a stimulant. Let me find you something to be gay again.'

The look she received in return was haggard. 'You really have no idea, have you? How could you, I suppose. No one tells you anything.'

'Idea of what?'

'*It*, of course.'

Still, Helen was confused. Synetta laughed mockingly.

'Perhaps it started after you went to live with your jolly primitives by the sea. If so, you are lucky, Helen, luckier than you know.'

'I really do not understand,' Helen said.

'I hope you never will!' Slow tears rolled down Synetta's lovely cheeks. 'It's not working properly. I should be fine! I went to Honeycomb as usual. Just a year ago. I did everything I should. I have always been a good girl, always. That was why the plagues did not get me because I was a good girl. I was a champion cheerleader, all the teams wanted me; everybody loved me. But now... Oh, God, look!'

Synetta opened her kimono; Helen gasped and recoiled. What should have been a pair of soft, full, balanced breasts, their nipples sculpted to the tastes of their owner, were no longer a perfect pair. One retained its beauty, true, but the other had shrivelled, its nipple bent and misshapen, its colour a strange, veiny blue. It gave off a faintly putrid smell like rotten meat.

'You must seek help,' urged Helen. 'This can be cured, I'm sure.'

Synetta attempted a smile showcasing her shiny white teeth. A dazzling smile learned long ago when her world was young. For a fleeting instant, the lost cheerleader revived. Then she lapsed to a weary, frightened woman, old, old beyond nature's limits.

'You see,' she whispered, 'I am not the first. I have heard rumours like everyone else. Anyone caught with the disease is sterilised.'

Helen squeezed Synetta's hand tighter. Sterilisation was the ultimate euphemism — and dread. 'What is this disease?' she asked.

'No one knows.' Again Synetta sobbed. 'Do not tell, or they will take me away!'

'I promise,' said Helen. 'Especially not Marvin and Merle. I will never tell anyone.'

'It's not working anymore,' whispered Synetta.

'What isn't?'

'Honeycomb. The elixir. The Beautiful Life.'

They stared into each other's eyes.

'How?' Helen asked.

'We have to go to Honeycomb more and more often. You feel

TWENTY-TWO

nauseous, listless, tired. Then wrinkles appear. You have to stay longer each time. Something's wrong!'

A deep suspicion bordering on certainty took hold of Helen. Oh Blair, she thought, you knew about this all along. Your visit to Baytown was because of this sickness. Yet again Dr Blair Gover was playing his games.

'I will keep your secret,' she assured Synetta. 'Just one person might understand this enough to help you. We must find him. We must! If he is still alive.'

TWENTY-THREE

From the burning raft of plastic and oil, they sailed due south across open seas. Blair Gover slumped beneath the awning as the birlinn rose and fell.

When Michael Pilgrim asked why he concealed his head beneath a shawl, the City-man replied: 'That much smoke will attract attention. Does facial recognition mean anything to you, Pilgrim?'

Michael pondered. 'That someone will recognise you by your face? I fear you have not the face you deserve.'

'Oh, spare me!'

With that, Gover subsided. Soon afterwards, a medium-sized surveillance drone came skimming from the south — the direction of the City of Albion — bound for the pillar of black smoke behind them. It changed direction to overfly the small fleet. All cowered at its roaring. Without slowing or circling, it continued north then was gone.

Gover lifted the shawl.

'That was closer than you can comprehend,' he said to Michael. 'You do realise I removed the power cells from the gravitational harnesses that allowed us to land safely in those hellish mountains?'

'Yes, and you made a grand old point of it.'

'With good reason. They store an astonishing amount of energy. So much so, a comprehensive scan would have detected them.'

TWENTY-THREE

He lapsed into brooding; Michael was too weary to care.

Under Dameron's direction, the small flotilla looped out into the open ocean then turned south again.

Food was short, clothes wet, freshwater rationed. A day passed miserably, the boats tossing and pitching through wind-whipped seas. Iona urged Dameron to steer west, back towards land, and reluctantly he did so, mindful always of their enemies.

As the wind slackened, they neared St Abb's Head, a rocky promontory jutting into white waters. Iona rose from the oar-bench and threw back her hood. Fierce joy found her tired, salt-streaked face.

'See! See! We are greeted!'

Seabirds dived or perched on sheer cliffs, ravines, jagged granite gulleys, the air raucous and urgent with the cries of shags, cormorants, and gulls. The heads of grey seals and their pups bobbed in the gently heaving sea.

'This is a good land,' she told her people. 'Or else the birds would shun it. I have a far-sight! All will end well for us!'

Michael had learned the Nuagers embraced their far-sights, or visions, with deep fervour. Small wonder they broke into a hymn.

The birlinns sailed on to a small village at the foot of the cliffs, where rising smoke indicated people.

'We must discover our location,' said Michael, examining the houses. The remnants of flaking stone and concrete breakwaters from the Before Times formed a small harbour. Masts were visible, along with nets laid out on the pebbly beach for repair.

He turned to Iona. 'Let me down in the surf, and I shall enquire in the village.'

'Then I shall go with you.'

'Not this time.'

A vexed look tightened her eyes. 'Are you my master now, Mister Star Man?'

'No, but your people need you. They are on the edge of losing heart.'

He returned half an hour later with the village headman and a few other curious folk. 'This good man has an interesting tale,' he said.

The headman's brogue was strong, but they got along fine. A sheep, along with sacks of oats and vegetables, was traded for jewels stripped from the Prince O' Ness's body as he lay in the mud of Fort George. Freshwater was taken on as ballast in the reservoirs beneath the birlinns' decks. Spirits lifted as folk huddled around driftwood fires. Meanwhile, the headman told his story.

First, he pointed north, the way they had come. A trading boat stopping by St Abbs had carried rumours of a fleet gathered at St Andrews in Fife. There King Duncaine of Buchan was joining forces with his brother-in-law, Adair, King of Fife.

'They mean for red vengeance, it's said,' the headman warned.

'How far off are they, do you ken?' asked Dameron.

The headman shook his head. 'Too near, however far.'

Then he pointed south and revealed there was a prosperous settlement of folk wearing the same bright-coloured clothes as the Nuagers, just thirty or so miles down the coast.

'Apparently, they live in a place called Lindisfarne, or Holy Island,' said Michael.

'Holy Island! That is a good name,' cried Iona.

Michael feared another far-sight coming on. 'Yes, and one I have heard before.'

He explained how the community of Nuagers in Baytown, led by Mister Priest Man, had links with Lindisfarne, exchanging news, pieties and trade once a year. 'They share your faith, and are potential allies. Nor are the Northumbrians weak-kneed folk. I suspect the Kings of Buchan and Fife might find a warmer welcome than they expect.'

Late morning, the wind favourable for a change. After a short rest,

TWENTY-THREE

Dameron ordered the folk to clamber once more into their boats.

'At Holy Island, we shall rest,' Iona promised, as she went among her people. Word had spread of fellow Nuagers ready to welcome them with open arms. Michael hoped it was true.

* * *

They arrived as the afternoon waned. Holy Island seemed flat and unprepossessing, with grassy sand dunes at its northern end. To the south, well laid-out fields for crops and pasture. Its castle, remarkably well-preserved, formed a silhouette on a stone outcrop near a modest village beside a small harbour. Dozens of smoke-ribbons rising from the village spoke of an unusually well-populated place.

The tide ran high as they rowed into the harbour. Bells clanged in the castle and village, the latter protected by an earthen ditch. Michael watched dozens of armed men and women hurrying to the beach where boats of all sizes had been hauled up onto the strand. One was large and flat-bottomed, a coastal trader. Something about it made Michael look twice: he had seen that boat before.

'Well, it's woo or woe,' he said, citing Baytown wisdom about the necessity for allies in an unfriendly world.

'Then let us woo,' said Iona, meeting his eye with a faint smile.

'These are English folk. Perhaps best if I introduce you first.'

'Perhaps.'

As their birlinn approached the shore, Iona dressed in a bright, multi-coloured ceremonial robe of yellow, green, red, and blue, embroidered with fish, and shooting stars, and birds, and trees. Around her neck hung a necklace of sharks teeth and whale chitin. On her head, a hat bearing feathers and shells that reminded Michael of Mister Priest Man's headgear back home. He hesitated before stowing his guns from sight.

Taking her hand, he helped her step into the surf, and they plodded over shifting pebbles up the beach. Nearly a hundred folk waited, armed men and women in the main, although older folk and children were also arriving, drawn by the Skye Nuagers' decorated sails. They wore the same garish outfits as their fellow believers from the Highlands, hair braided and beribboned. Quiet fell at the sight of Iona in her priestess's garb, crunching towards them. The sea's constant murmur filled the silence.

'We've come to Holy Island for sanctuary,' called out Michael. He could not readily identify their leader, so he addressed the crowd:

'Behold, yon boats contain folk who share your faith. Nuagers from the Western Isles, persecuted, enslaved, fleeing so they may practice their beliefs in freedom and safety. Even now we fear a large force of their oppressors are a-ship and in pursuit. They mean yon innocent folk terrible harm!'

At this news, the Nuagers muttered among themselves. Raids were common on this coast in both directions, though the star-worshippers eschewed marauding lest it made them unfit for the Happy Planets. Fellow believers or not, no one welcomed a large fleet. Easier by far to deny the strangers a landing and send them on their way. It might have gone badly for the fugitives had not two voices spoken up.

The first belonged to Iona. In her priestess's raiment, she raised her hands to constellations starting to appear with the dusk over Holy Island. Her clear, melodious voice sang out a hymn shared by all Nuagers:

> *Swing low, sweet universe,*
> *Coming for to carry us home.*
> *Swing low, sweet sun and stars,*
> *Coming for to carry us home.*

TWENTY-THREE

'May we find the Happy Planet together, good folk all, brothers and sisters, hand in hand!'

Stillness as her voice faded. Eyes stared less hard, melted by her appeal. It might not have been enough to persuade the folk of Lindisfarne to accept the risk of taking them in, except a coarser voice called from the crowd.

Michael Pilgrim had known its blunt nuances all his life, through boyhood, teenage years, the horrors of the Crusades, struggles to the death against Big Jacko. A voice he had learned to depend on, to trust with his very life. Its accent his own, as Baytown as cliff and sea and soil.

'What the bugger are you doing here, Michael Pilgrim? We thought you was away with them City-bastards.'

Tom Higginbottom stepped from the crowd, flanked by his eldest son, Ben, and other familiar faces from Baytown. For the first time since crash-landing in Scotland, Michael's smile contained no trace of shadow.

'What the bugger took you so long to find me, Tom Higginbottom?' he demanded.

* * *

By midnight, driftwood fires blazed on the beach beneath scatterings of stars. A half-moon travelled the sky, serenaded by songs and chatter from such folk as had not already found a bed. The fugitives from Skye were exhausted. They collapsed wherever their hosts in the village or castle bade them lie. Watchers were sent out on horses to the northern end of the island to warn of enemies should they be foolhardy enough to risk travelling by night.

Though he longed for nothing more than sleep, Michael sat over ale with Tom Higginbottom to hear his news. Both men had spent the evening on separate business, gathering weapons and assessing their forces in preparation for a muster early the next day. Ten other Baytown folk sat around them, some from the community of Nuagers led by Mister Priest Man.

'You look like shit,' said Tom.

'Thanks,' responded Michael. 'So how come you're here, Tom? I could have wept for joy at the sight of you.'

'Do you remember how Priest Man did a parcel of mining, burning the rock and soaking what was left? We all thought his brain had travelled to his favourite planet.'

'Aye,' said Michael, with a chuckle. 'He wouldn't explain what it was about.'

'Well, it seemed he wasn't so cracked after all,' continued Tom. 'He were making crystals for dyes that stay true in cloth. Alum, it's called. Priest Man found out they produced it near Ravenscar hundreds of years ago. Your pal Amar's helping him.'

'How does that bring you here? Fishing's your trade.'

'So is sailing. We've shipped a load of alum up here, and we're getting all kinds of stuff in return.'

Michael had noticed the Lindisfarne Nuagers' clothes were especially colourful. Perhaps alum explained it.

'What if the City finds out?' he asked.

Bitter experience taught what happened when 'primitives' attempted to establish industries, however basic. Drones proved their final customer.

'No sign of the fuckers. It's right strange,' said Tom. 'Something's happening. It's like they've lost interest in us.' He screwed up his forehead. 'But I have bad news.'

Michael listened with growing alarm as Tom related how Averil and Helen had disappeared a few days after he and Gover flew north.

'No one knows where they've gone. It's queer. Like they was spirited away.'

A voice broke in from the shadows beyond the firelight.

'What of the Baytown Jewel?' asked Gover. 'Has that gone, too?'

Michael turned. It seemed he couldn't escape the City-man for even an hour.

'Sod the jewel,' he said. 'It's my niece and friend that concern me.'

'Well?' demanded Gover, addressing Tom.

'I don't know, mister. Nor do I care.'

Fear tempered Tom's hostility towards the City-man.

A whinnying, almost hysterical laugh came from the darkness where Gover lurked. 'You *will* care. Oh, you will.'

* * *

The next day passed in preparations. Messengers were sent by boat and horse to allies in the region, warning of possible raiders and requesting what aid they could provide. For this was not the first time King Adair of Fife had troubled the Northumbrian coast.

It was decided those incapable of fighting would go straight to the castle on its stone outcrop should enemies appear. Defending the scattered houses of the village required many fighters. Yet, their full muster was barely sufficient, even swollen by the Skye Nuagers and visitors from Baytown.

It was also decided — after Tom Higginbottom pointed out his friend was the famed victor of Pickering — that Michael should be given command. His reputation as Protector of the North likewise preceded him.

First, he created platoons of ten and let them appoint their own officers. Each platoon mixed guns, bows, crossbows and archers with poleaxe and spearmen so that those with missile weapons might be defended while they loaded and fired. He reasoned this would work well for street fighting. Then he assigned a colour to each platoon, along with appropriate armbands. As he had anticipated, a friendly rivalry of taunts lent the new units a little identity.

While they drilled under Higginbottom's caustic eye, Michael rode out with the leader of the Lindisfarne Nuagers, a grizzled crofter born and bred to the island. His name was Allan. Too old to fight, he offered wisdom and memories of past incursions.

'They'll either land at the harbour,' he said, 'or where the dunes end and the causeway to the mainland begins. Them rocks and outcrops yonder make dangerous places for boats in winter. Over there, they can beach safely, unload men and stores, take their time.'

They rode to the northeast corner of the island, two miles from the village and harbour, a spit of grass-tussocked dunes known as Snook Point. Michael sat back in his saddle and looked around. It occurred to him any relief force crossing the mile-long causeway from the mainland to the island would get a chance to burn beached ships — assuming such a force even existed. It was a prospect Allan considered unlikely. Still, Michael tucked away the thought.

'We really don't want them to gain a foothold in the harbour,' he concluded. 'Let's return to the village. Perhaps we shall find a way to deter a landing there.'

Allan peered out to sea and spat on the sandy loam. 'You'll have to think fast, mister. Look!'

Michael followed his pointing finger. At first, he thought his eyes deceived him. Surely it was a trick of the horizon. One by one, he counted the sails: a large fleet was approaching, ten, twelve, fourteen vessels. Some were small and with a corresponding crew; others were large enough to carry dozens of armed men.

'Fuck,' he whispered, aware Allan was looking at him angrily.

'You did not say so many enemies were hungry for your head, Michael Pilgrim. I, for one, would not have welcomed you so readily

TWENTY-THREE

had I known.'

'Nor would I have blamed you, sir,' said Michael. 'Though I can assure you we've offered no deceit or tricks. When I last saw yon fleet, it contained not more than six sails.'

Allan regarded him suspiciously. Then his face relaxed. Life had taught him how to detect a liar, along with an acceptance of the inevitable.

'Six or fourteen, low tide must follow high,' he conceded.

With that, they galloped from Snook Point towards Lindisfarne Castle.

Cold gusts blew north as they rode through the flat island's well-tilled centre. This steady wind Michael also noted, even in his haste. He also pondered the high tide, a perfect time to launch a landing at the harbour.

* * *

Bells clanged in the village. Everywhere people hurried. Women and children laden with a few treasured possessions helped old dams and gimmers up the castle's steep steps. Younger men, along with the stronger women, strapped on crude armour and readied weapons.

Already afternoon showed the first hints of waning when Michael inspected his assembled army. Many looked fearful, barely soldiers at all. Enough among them could steady the rest, he hoped. Before each platoon he offered encouragement, commenting on the deadliness of their weapons, singling out anyone particularly tall, joking how the Jocks would need ladders to take a swing at him.

A mile out to sea, the combined fleets of Buchan and Fife were backing sails and heaving to, assessing the tide and time before darkness fell.

In his haste at Snook Point, Michael had miscounted the ships gathered to punish the Prince O' Ness's killers. Not fourteen, fifteen. Some were little bigger than fishing smacks. A few were flat-bottomed galleys driven by oar and sail, much like the Nuagers' birlinns, though broader in the beam to carry trade goods. Four were larger still.

'Do you think they'll risk it?' he asked Higginbottom.

The grizzled fisherman shrugged. 'They don't seem backward in coming forward.'

Any attack now would be bold. Allan had told him how rapidly tides came and went around Lindisfarne, exposing miles of mudflat and rocky outcrops twice a day. Michael hoped his force's muster on the beach would deter an attack. Even now, binoculars must be trained on them, judging their strength.

After inspecting the last squad, Michael turned to make an address. Out to sea, groups of men were scrambling from the larger ships to smaller galleys.

'Well, it's come to this, and I'm right sorry,' he said. 'We never asked for this trouble. Nor shall we run from it. Gathered here are three groups of folk with stout hearts and stronger arms. I mean, the Nuagers of Holy Island, whose generosity this day shall be repaid with my last drop of blood. Aye, and the eternal friendship of the Commonwealth of the North. That I pledge!'

Cheering met this promise. He hoped it carried across the water to the ships still transferring men.

'Next, folk who are just as grateful, I mean our friends from Skye who journey to find peace, prosperity and relief from slavery in good old Baytown.'

A waving of weapons by the Highlanders. Whoops from the younger Baytown lads at the mention of their home.

'I tell you this, folk of Skye. You shall have freedom and more. But only if you fight like the worst devils those bastards out there can imagine!'

Another cheer. He was doing well. He glanced at the fleet. Four crowded galleys were heading towards the harbour. Did they really hold their enemy in such contempt as to launch a direct landing without reconnaissance? Surely a bluff. Or a display of strength. His chest tightened with fear.

'Thirdly' —He indicated the Baytown contingent— 'That ugly crew over there, few in number perhaps, but men proven in a tussle. Men who will fight to the end for the sake of honour, justice and hearth. Am I right?'

Baytown! Baytown! Commonwealth o' the North! came back the cry.

Michael held up a single-shot rifle, a fine weapon, a breech-loader with a steel barrel made in the Before Times like his own back at Hob Hall. Allan had lent it to him, remarking dryly, 'You'll hit more with it in an hour, Mister Pilgrim, than I have in ten year.'

Speech over, his forces were still cheering, waving their weapons. One look out to sea told him they would need both courage and arms. The King of Buchan was sending forward four galleys full of men to attack Lindisfarne Harbour.

TWENTY-FOUR

Ripon to York was no great distance as the crow flapped, a long day's ride from dawn to dusk. The most direct way overgrown, a haunt of brigands, boggarts, and hungry ghosts. According to the wisdom of Ripon-folk, safest is longest.

The young squire of Fountains caused consternation when he announced a winter journey to York for its Yule market, St Nicholas Fair. Not that wishing to trade there was unusual, York excelled at metalwork and other intricate crafts, especially tools and weapons. No, it was choosing to travel with the two vagabonds, Seth Pilgrim and Hurdy-Gurdy. Moreover, Jojo steadfastly refused offers from reliable men to accompany him, though everyone knew safety on the road lay in numbers. Nor would he delay his journey by a single day, riding forth at dawn on his gelding, with a small cart containing wax, honey, and other homely goods for barter, along with the aforementioned brace of grim-faced tramps. Wise heads predicted Fountains would be lucky to see Jojo Lyons alive again.

* * *

Off they rattled, making slow progress on the muddy, rutted road. Farms soon grew scarce, replaced by young woodland where cow-cropped fields once stretched for miles. Here, the horses' breath

TWENTY-FOUR

steaming in the chill, they waited by the roofless remains of a large warehouse once dedicated to builders' supplies.

'I told her to meet us here,' said Jojo. 'She nodded when I named the place. When we were kids, we came here several times for tiles and bricks. Before Father's accident, before Bella and Abbie got taken.'

Seth coughed uneasily, glancing at Hurdy-Gurdy, who grinned.

The wait proved short. From behind a bramble-masked lorry, Bella half hopped, half scurried. Rooks cawed in alarm from dark thickets. Seth had a clear sense of hidden eyes, though barely a leaf stirred.

The strangeling's nose twitched like a hare's and the big floppy ears poking through her human hair rose a little. Then something happened that horrified Seth: the creature spoke or tried to.

'Jay . . . jay . . . jay,' it cheeped.

'Yes,' cried Jojo, jumping down from his horse to embrace her. 'It's me, Bella. We'll take you to the City and cure you. You'll see! Get in the cart, dear. That's it. You must stay out of sight. Hide beneath the tarpaulin.'

Jojo led the way with pride and assurance now, straight-backed on his big gelding. Seth watched from the corner of his eyes. So fine a figure on a horse, noble and confident as a knight of old, protected by a long suit of padded leather armour, sword and pistol, longbow by his side. Where Jojo's thighs were strong as they gripped the horse's flanks, Seth's were wiry shanks, his shoulders bony and narrow compared to Jojo's manly girth.

Inferiority of body was the least of it: Seth knew his soul as something stained, spoiled, whereas Jojo's was pure as polished glass.

So many fears. That this trip to the City was in vain. What possible use would those who owned the whole world find for a wretch like him? That he'd be caught in York and disgraced. Then Jojo was sure to learn who had imprisoned his sister in Fylingdales and despise him. Perhaps Gurdy would turn against him, too, ending all hope for an introduction to that place of light. But mostly he brooded upon Jojo.

The cart jolted beneath a grey sky, tiny birds flitting from hedgerows grown into wild strips of woodland. As a drizzle fell, Seth hummed softly to himself:

> *The water is wide, I cannot get o'er,*
> *Neither have I wings to fly.*
> *Give me a boat that can carry two*
> *And both shall row, my love and I...*

* * *

An hour later, they reached a motorway. It ran in a straight line north to south, four lanes wide on either side of a central strip colonised by briars and young blackthorn, crab apple, and elder. A circular bridge remained intact above the carriageways, where shrubs poked through crumbling tarmac. Cold wind played over car and vehicle hulks as far as the eye could see.

Gurdy shook his head at the sight. 'Here, our revels begin in earnest,' he said. 'Are we happy players on the stage bequeathed to us, Young Nuncles?'

'That depends if this road goes south,' said Seth. 'Will it take us to the City?'

'Aye,' said Jojo, 'I'm assured so. By and by.'

'Is it much used though? It seems a sad way.'

Jojo nodded. 'We call it the Old Ghost Road. But to answer your question, it is the safest route to York. More and more caravans choose these big old roads to trade. Some gather in York, though they usually avoid travel in winter. After St Nicholas Fair ends, we can join one heading south, perhaps.'

'It seems a good place for robbers,' said Seth.

Jojo could not disagree with that.

From a sloping road, they joined the motorway. A track had been cleared between old cars and lorries, presumably by trading caravans.

A grim, melancholy way in winter. Perhaps in summer, butterflies, birds, flowers, and bees softened travellers' hearts. That day a louring sky of slate-coloured clouds pressed upon them. Wind whistled through bare branches. Cars and trucks of many kinds lay in all conditions: askew, upside down, burnt out, constructed of rotting, rusting metal, or strangely intact. The most ancient, driven by combustion engines, had been obsolete even at the time of the Great Dyings. Far better preserved were the electric plasti-steel vehicles. A few contained skeletons in sealed cabs.

'We must be wary of ghosts tonight,' said Jojo. 'I have brought garlic and holly sprigs which they hate.'

'Young Nuncle is reassuring,' said Hurdy-Gurdy. 'Like plague doctors.'

A slow journey through sparsely populated country. Plumes of smoke marked a few steadings, all built well away from the motorway. Perhaps the ghosts deterred folk from settling there.

A couple of miles from a turn-off to Knaresborough and Harrogate, prosperous towns loyal to the Commonwealth of the North, the travellers grew alert. A long wolf-like howl broke the silence.

Jojo wheeled his horse and started north, the direction of the call.

'I've heard talk of a big pack out this way.'

For the first time, Bella poked her head from the tarpaulin, sniffing the wind. She beat her big feet on the wooden bed of the cart in warning. Seth looked around, troubled by a sense she was communicating to someone — or something — other than themselves.

'We should keep going,' said Jojo. 'We can be sure they smell us. Let's just hope they're not hungry.'

***

They hadn't gone far when the first dogs appeared.

The horses snorted and bucked. Seth rose in the wagon for a better look. Mongrels of many breeds, ragged coats and ears set back, sniffing for scents of weakness. Five, six, eight, another appeared, soon there were dozens. A big pack used to bringing down big prey. The horses alone must seem a feast to them.

'Tie your horse to the cart!' Seth called to Jojo, who was struggling to calm the nervous gelding.

Checking musket and pistol, Seth turned to find Hurdy-Gurdy readying his crossbow. What had Uncle Michael told him about dog packs? Kill the leaders to scare them off. Stay as high as possible: they want you on the ground.

More and more of the shaggy, mangy creatures were appearing — ill-fed, doubly dangerous. They flowed around the wagon, yelping, sniffing, their dark, expressionless eyes fixed on horse and man — four-legged, two-legged, all the same.

'Climb onto the wagon,' Seth called. 'Quick!'

But Jojo held his ground by the terrified horse, comforting it with one hand, the other gripping his sword tight.

Slowly the top dogs advanced, canines slavering. Seth raised his musket. Aimed. *Bang.* The shot missed. If he hoped it would scare off the pack, the opposite occurred. Forward rushed the first wave of alphas, even while Seth frantically reloaded. Hurdy-Gurdy's crossbow twanged, bringing down a cross between a Labrador and Doberman and several generations of mongrel in between.

Another bang as Jojo fired his pistol at point-blank range. A bitch rolled over and over, head blown open. Then he was bellowing, his sword swinging back and forth, the gelding kicking out iron-shod hooves at jaws eager for its leg.

TWENTY-FOUR

Seth turned to find yet more of the creatures rushing the carthorse tied to the shafts. He fired his musket and pistol in rapid succession. Another dog went down.

Suddenly a blurred figure leapt from the cart and landed beside Jojo, muscular legs back-kicking dogs with such force they flew in the air, scrabbling with screech and howl on the pitted tarmac. Evidently, Bella's creators had not neglected self-defence in her design.

'Young Nuncle! The horse!'

A dog had its jaws around one of the carthorse's front legs. Then Seth, too, was out of the safety of the cart, smashing the musket butt onto the animal's head, once, twice, until it folded. Rushing at another, he swung the improvised club, bellowing curses. Snarling, the dog backed away.

But the fight was over. By some signal known to its collective self, the big pack scattered and fled, leaving their dead or crippled so that finishing them was a mercy.

* * *

Little reason for celebration on the Old Ghost Road. No humans (or former humans) had taken a potentially gangrenous gnawing, yet the front leg of the carthorse was torn open and bleeding. Jojo almost took a kick from the beast as he knelt to bandage its wound. Replacing the injured animal in the cart shaft with his gelding took some coaxing.

The watery sun had long passed its zenith by the time they set off again. Even then, their pace was set by the limping horse, a creature too valuable for fattening up feral dogs. All the while, Bella sniffed until Seth guessed they were being followed. The dogs? Unlikely. Perhaps something, or someone, else? He thought instantly of the two Mistresses and Maister Gil with his band of floggers. Whoever it was, Bella's agitation grew until she leapt nimbly from the wagon and, with a long, imploring look at Jojo, scampered into nearby woodland and disappeared.

More time wasted calling for her. It was dusk when they approached another large junction on the motorway, where Jojo assured them they would turn off to York as he recalled from a previous journey.

'Had all gone well, we'd be near the outskirts now,' he said, ruefully looking back for Bella the way they had come. 'Instead, another twenty miles lie ahead. Be that as it may, let's camp here tonight. It will rest the horses and give my sister a chance to catch up with us.'

'What is this place?' asked Seth.

Hurdy-Gurdy pointed at a sign covered with mould. Just discernible were the words *Junction 44*.

* * *

A dozen roads converged in long curves to form a central circle for vehicles to ebb and flow. To the west, grey as rotten teeth in the twilight, tower and office blocks rose.

Dense rows of cars, lorries, buses, tankers, vans, every kind of multi-wheeled transport in vogue at the time of the first Great Dying, formed a cataclysmic traffic jam stretching for miles in all directions. An unusual number of drivers were still behind the wheel, felled by plague even as they fled. Some cars had clearly tried to break out across fields and were half-consumed by scrub. The bones of those people who preferred to die in the open littered the wayside.

Jojo led the cart through a path used by trading caravans to a site dotted with black rings of ash from campfires.

'We stopped here when I last went to York,' he said. 'The caravan master told me the ghosts here gather round at night and watch, longing for the warmth of a fire. But I did not feel that.'

Seth turned to Hurdy-Gurdy, who was looking into a large car, its doors and windows still sealed. Vague shapes on its front and rear seats were just visible through a shroud of mould masking the windows.

'What happened here, Gurdy?' Seth asked. 'Do you remember?'

For once, the crazed holo-entertainer dropped his role as a clown.

'Imagine the panic and sweat and cursing,' he replied. 'Horns blaring, herds of doomed cattle in a queue for the butcher. Imagine the prayers and tears to gods abandoned and recollected, like frightened children trying to appease their parents, all so that lovely Mummy and Daddy will keep them safe.'

The young men looked at him uncomprehendingly.

'Do you really wish to learn what happened?' Gurdy asked.

'Yes,' they said in unison.

'Then I'll show you.'

He plucked Seth's pistol from his belt and fired it at the lock of the car. The dull report echoed over miles of overgrown road.

'That was foolish,' said Jojo.

Gurdy's mask of meekness slipped. 'Foolish?' he hissed. '*This* is foolish.'

With that, he yanked open the car door, revealing five skeletons on its seats, two fully grown ones in the front, those in the back tiny and strapped into odd chairs like scooped-out shells — toddlers and an infant. The interior of the vehicle reeked of bitter decay. Objects lay piled behind the backseat: a folded pram, bags of rotting clothes, electrical devices — a holoprojector, handscreens.

'Look!' he cried, brandishing the screens and tossing them onto the pitted tarmac. 'Foolish! Oh, how we worshipped the babble from those things. Trusted it. Thought its voices eternal. Put our faith in toys. Foolish.'

Craziness took hold of him. Wrenching off the skulls of the adults, he put on a hideous puppet show, making the skulls address one another in a mad colloquy:

'Oh, Daddy!' he called out in a feminine voice, shaking one of the skulls. 'Mummy does feel icky. What is that strange swelling thing in my armpit? And in my knickers. It is horrid.'

'Don't scratch, dear,' replied gruff, bass-voiced Daddy-skull. 'It might burst. Oh, look what you've done! Pooh! Now I'll have to get the upholstery cleaned, dear, and you know how much that costs. You've made a nasty pong everywhere.'

'Sorry, Daddy.'

'You *should* be, Mummy. All those fluids and blood and slime you're leaking. It smells worse than Junior's nappy.'

'Oh, yes, Daddy. Oops, there pops another naughty bubo! Silly old me.'

Gurdy snatched up one of the children's tiny skulls and whined, 'Are we nearly there yet, Daddy? Are we nearly at the shopping centre? I want more toys! More toys! More! More! Burn the planet, so I can go shopping, Daddy! Kill everything so I can go shopping! Are we nearly there yet, Mummy?'

'We certainly are,' said the deep-voiced Daddy-skull. 'We're nearly dead-a-doodle-doo!'

'Funny Daddy!' giggled the toddler-skull. 'I'm going to laugh and laugh when my own armpit goes pop...'

'Stop it! Stop it! I beg you.' Jojo quivered with horrified rage. 'How can you do this? How can you laugh? Have you no pity?'

Coarse mirth died in Seth's throat. He felt ashamed. Gurdy hurled the skulls back into the car, humming a tuneless melody.

'Gurdy was just joshing,' said Seth. 'It helps somehow, you know. If you don't laugh, if you think about it too much, it sends you crazy.'

Jojo was not to be appeased. 'We will build a fire,' he said stiffly. 'In case the dogs come back. And to lift our spirits in this terrible place. Then Bella will see where we are. Yes, that's what we shall do.'

Seth shrugged and went in search of firewood, musket slung on his shoulder. Gurdy kept up a wordless, keening moan as he helped unload the cart; meanwhile, Jojo tended the horses.

* * *

Since he first learned to walk, Seth Pilgrim's footsteps had trodden upon bones, invisible or visible, ghostly or crunchy. Relics of the Before Times formed his greatest education, his consciousness. Like most of his generation, he was hardened to the pathos of previous lives, and also, by degrees, to the lives around him, including his own. Yet as dusk gathered on the old motorway, deep melancholy settled.

So many, so many — the cars and lorries, buses and tradesmen's vans, travellers halted in long, patient lines. Most vehicles had been looted by scavengers long before Seth's birth, drivers and passengers and looters consumed by hungry bacteria or animals.

As he gathered firewood, Seth felt a vast weight of inconsequence. Yet Jojo always seemed on his mind. What use was it, after all, to love? Let alone to love someone so far above him — a novel kind of heartache. He had cared for no one properly since Mother died when he was a child and dared not risk such pain again. Yet Seth knew he wanted Jojo more than with just his heart, but his body; it felt too natural and right for shame.

Best to forget the hope, however fugitive, that his feelings might one day find their echo. For when Jojo finally discovered who he was — who he had been — their friendship would cease. For Seth Pilgrim knew himself as soiled, utterly filthy — to the last coin on the scales.

Memories lit dark beacons across his mind. How Big Jacko had used him once — just once — to prove a point, for his tastes did not lie that way. Maister Gil in his cups, brutal with his whip, did far worse. Not least the Mistresses, Fat and Thin, and the mass when he'd played the same role as the Lord of Erringdale's poor niece.

Yet where was the Lord of Erringdale now? Dead. Buried. Killed by his hand.

Seth felt a flash of power at the thought, then gloom reasserted itself, even as night advanced across the Old Ghost Road. Jojo would never love him. Tears stung his eyes. Seeing he couldn't love himself, why the fuck should anyone else?

For a bleak half-hour, he surrendered to despair, perched on the dented bonnet of a sports car with doors wide open like wings. Muttered curses and sighs joined the murmur of trees and saplings. At last, he regained mastery of himself.

Seth considered his likely fate when they reached York. Better to perish alone than face the final humiliation of being hanged as a traitor. He would leave Jojo and Hurdy-Gurdy at the outskirts of the city and head south. Where else was there left to go?

He glanced back the way he'd come. The campfire glinted on the motorway bridge as he retraced his steps, musket slung on his shoulder, firewood tied in a bundle.

A gunshot rang out. Jojo's pistol! He recognised its bark. Ululations and triumphant whoops followed, cruel, gloating cries. His gut contorted.

Dropping the firewood, Seth cocked his musket and crept forward. On the outskirts of the camp, he halted. All was as he had left it: horses, cart, fire, and cooking pot. Jojo and Gurdy, too, though now on their knees. What had changed was their visitors. Old friends had come to call.

TWENTY-FIVE

The castle's lone cannon, constructed from a thick, steel waste pipe, belched out smoke, flame and noise. Whether anything dangerous flew near the Jock fleet was doubtful.

'To your positions!' cried Michael Pilgrim. 'Tom, get them in place.'

Platoons jogged up and down the shingle beach, armour and weapons rattling. One group caught Michael by surprise.

'What's she doing here?' he cried.

Iona bore a pathetic looking hatchet and a slingshot probably last used for hunting rabbits. The effect of her death on the Skye Nuagers' fragile morale might sink them all. Already he could see the first galley entering the harbour, armed men ready at the prow.

He stepped towards Iona. 'I beg you, get back to the castle. We agreed you are more use there.'

To his relief, she hesitated and headed back, glancing over her shoulder as she went.

'Every platoon to its ground!' he bellowed. Earlier, they had divided the beach into zones marked out by coloured rags tied to stakes, so the inexperienced men didn't huddle for security, leaving areas unguarded. He was also hoping to establish a crossfire and the possibility of outflanking.

'Tom, get your lads ready. You know what to do!'

The galleys were closing in on the surf.

'Barrels up! Aim! Take your time. Fire!'

Acrid smoke from the volley rolled back in their faces, thick and white, sulphurous steam with a hint of piss. Then they were loading, firing at will. Already Jocks on the boats were down, more wounded. One wearing a heavy breastplate and helmet toppled overboard, vanishing at once, too laden to swim.

As he aimed, Michael estimated more than twenty men to a boat, a good ninety in total, nearly as large a force as his own and damnably more used to war. Despair touched his heart. Untested troops versus veterans of countless raids did not bode well. Then they got lucky.

Channelled by harbour defences of tree trunks and the hulks of sunken motor yachts and pleasure cruisers, three of the Jock galleys veered towards the same spot of beach. They were forced to slow and form a logjam. Oarsmen and rudder men cursed one another; warriors shouted warnings to let them through first. Now the Lindisfarners' crossfire grew brisk, aided by flights of arrows.

A single galley evaded the tangle, aiming for a patch of shingle near where Tom's special platoon crouched, flaming torches stuck in the ground beside them.

'Do it!' shouted Michael, though he need not have bothered. Old Crusaders like Tom Higginbottom knew how to kill and maim. Who better?

Four Baytown men rushed forward, each bearing a torch and swinging a wooden bucket in which something stayed hidden. Twice their number formed a shield around them.

'Let 'em have it!' shouted Tom.

Crashes and bangs as muskets and pistols were discharged into the galley at close range. Just as the prow ground onto the shingle, the four Baytown lads rushed forward to greet it. At that moment, two things happened.

First, the Jock warriors prepared to leap into the surf. A brawny, fearless crew, among Fife's best, each worth two or more Nuagers hand-to-hand.

The second consisted of carefully rehearsed actions: Touch the burning torch to a short fuse on the clay pot in the flimsy bucket, which itself contained broken glass, sharp flints and stones; swing back your arm; toss the lot into the open galley, right among oarsmen seizing weapons of their own; hurl yourself onto the beach . . . and pray.

Four loud booms in rapid succession rolled over the harbour as the canisters exploded, spraying coarse shrapnel into eyes, hands, arms, faces, legs.

The hapless galley, full of stunned men, was surrounded by two platoons, firing at close range. Worse, its wooden hull had been split, so that it was slowly sinking.

Meanwhile, the three galleys still out in the harbour, watched aghast as their comrades were slaughtered beyond help or reach. Cautious now, the first Jock galley moved towards the double lines of men awaiting them on the beach.

How it would have gone had they landed, who could say. But trumpets called urgently from the bulk of the Scots fleet out at sea. The galley captains shouted commands; oars were put into hasty reverse, halting their advance. Soon they were retreating, peppered by gunfire until they rejoined their fellows out in the bay.

Desperate men fight desperately. Most warriors in the Jock galley trapped on the beach were dead or wounded. Still, they struggled to escape the boat and reach their foes. Suddenly a Highland voice rose in appeal: 'Quarter! Quarter!' The disease spread. Weapons were cast aside. Arms raised in surrender.

One by one, they were dragged from the smouldering ship and forced to kneel on the hard shingle of Lindisfarne Harbour. Michael surveyed the captives with distaste. Prisoners were a damned nuisance, and now he had six, most of them severely wounded.

'I want those men searched to their very arseholes then trussed up so tight they can hardly breathe. Take their boots. Any attempt to escape, shoot them.'

He paced before the kneeling Jocks. A wild-looking lot, but some seemed less used to war than others. He selected a quivering young man in a fancy cloak and chainmail shirt, his outfit marking him out as nobility.

'We'll question this one.'

Armoured bodies fallen into the harbour were revealed on the beach as the tide retreated. The Nuagers dragged them ashore to take their weapons.

A costly attack, a flourish of arrogance and bravado. No more attempts at a landing were possible for at least twelve hours. Michael turned to look at his ragtag army. Scarcely a casualty among them, yet he detected little sense of triumph. Perhaps they realised the Jocks would never make it so easy again.

***

Michael assessed the lad's age: sixteen, seventeen. They had dragged him to a large barn near the harbour between castle and village. Here they had set up their headquarters, amidst piles of nets and tools for ship repairs.

Perched on a barrel, Michael drank ale from a clay beaker and chewed a large hunk of gritty oat bread. It seemed he could not eat enough. The boy's eyes found the bread and stared defiantly at the wall. So he was hungry as well as scared.

'What's your name, lad?'

No reply.

Michael sighed. 'Look, there are two ways to do this. Answer a few

TWENTY-FIVE

simple questions and you get food. If you force us to break your fingers, one by one, you'll still answer. Only then you won't get fed. Which is it to be?'

Michael waited. Time was short, but he must not appear impatient. Except that he longed to be anywhere but here with this miserable boy. Oh, he knew full well how it would end. Still, the lad did not speak.

'Start with a little finger,' said Michael wearily. How disgusted his grandfather, the unflinching Reverend Oliver Pilgrim would be to see his grandson turned torturer. Never mind that Michael had done far worse in the Crusades, and for the worst of possible causes. And he did not doubt that if the Jocks had prevailed, their slaughter and rape of Lindisfarne would just be starting.

Tom Higginbottom walked over to the boy, who cowered, bound hands held before him.

'It doesn't have to be this way, lad, you know that,' said out the fisherman.

Ten minutes later the lad was kneeling, sobbing, tears streaking his cheeks, a finger bent at an unnatural angle. His face bore open cuts, and his nose was broken.

'So your name's Colm. Tell us all about it.'

And he did, the truth teased out with patient questions. This is what Michael Pilgrim and Tom Higginbottom learned.

Colm was the sixth son of King Adair of Fife, who happened to be King Duncaine of Buchan's brother-in-law, married to Duncaine's younger sister, Goneril. A few days earlier, Uncle Duncaine had sailed into St Andrew's Harbour with a force of six ships and well over a hundred fighting men.

Colm, the youngest of Goneril's children, was close to his mother and picked up more than was public knowledge. All knew King Duncaine had sworn bloody revenge for the death of his firstborn son at Fort George. Likewise, that the Prince O'Ness had been stripped of a precious heirloom, a magical City-sword, passed from father to eldest son by the line of Buchan, ever since Duncaine's grandfather established the kingdom.

That much was obvious. Through his mother, Colm heard darker tales. That the Nuagers were followers of a devil-wizard, who made the sea burn, driving back Buchan's fleet. Survivors from the slaughter at Fort George had reported a faery-faced, smooth-cheeked man with odd powers, clearly the warlock in question. Other rumours spoke of the Nuager witch; that she was using evil spirits to cloak herself and evade pursuit. Finally, that a demonic Tyke, no less than the Butcher of Pickering, led them in battle. King Duncaine had sworn to burn both warlock and witch at the stake, thereby restoring the natural order and defying Hell.

Colm had also overheard his uncle, when drunk and morose, regretting quarrels with his firstborn and heir, sharing fears he would lose great face with his followers if the murderers went unpunished.

So much for the King of Buchan. After more encouragement, and a second dangling finger, Colm revealed his own father, King Adair of Fife, had sensed an opportunity along the coast for a profitable raid for loot and slaves. Adair was a fine one for raids but generally assigned the conduct of them to his sons. This time, however, he had left his palace at St Andrews, certain no one could stand against so strong a combined force.

'Which brings us to the final point,' Michael had said. 'What is your total strength?' They had asked over and over to catch out deceit. Both fleets together, separately: numbers, compositions, warriors, sailors, bonders.

This Colm had refused to disclose, loath to betray friends and kin. Ten minutes later, a figure was forced out of him, though it sounded ridiculously high.

TWENTY-FIVE

* * *

When Colm had been dragged out, Michael fell to brooding and chewing more bread. It tasted sticky, sour. Whale oil lamps provided orbs of light: mostly the barn was in deep shadow. The number of Jock war men eclipsed everything they could throw against them: weapons, experience, troops. The wisest course would be to take flight into the night over the causeway to the mainland while the tide was out. Or sailing off as soon as it was in. Doing so would abandon the Nuagers of Lindisfarne to their fate, but perhaps that fate was sealed anyway. The oil lamps flickered as the barn door opened. Iona entered, her arms folded across her chest.

'I saw what ye did to that laddie,' she said quietly. 'He seems scarce alive.'

Shame joined his anxieties. 'I am not proud of it, Iona. None of it. But this is war. I learned from him that they mean to burn you alive if you are captured. And Gover, too. Better to shoot yourself than to be taken, that's my advice. As for everyone else on Holy Island, who knows what they have in mind beyond slavery and ruin.'

Iona seemed not to hear. 'I trusted in you, Michael Pilgrim, that you were of the right not the wrong.' She shivered, pulling her cloak tight. 'And now I learn it is common talk you were in the Crusades, a monster serving the City, and likewise yon man, your bosom friend.' Her accusing glare turned on Tom Higginbottom. 'Monsters, both!'

Michael sighed. So word of the genocidal Crusades had even reached isolated Skye, borne by traders no doubt, a rumour of the City's ruthless cruelty. Good. Some infamies deserved to be remembered forever.

'Neither of us had much of a choice,' he said. 'Apart from suicide. Perhaps, if we'd been braver, we'd have taken that path.'

Her voice took on an edge of hysteria. 'There is always a choice! No wonder you are so close to the City wizard with his dark powers. A fitting companion he is to you. No wonder you bear a mark on your cheek!'

'Iona . . .'

'No, Mister Star Man. We have a name for the kind of stars your kind would lead us to, where goodness is swallowed never to be seen again. A black hole, we call it, where black souls go when they die.'

She turned with a swish of her cloak; Michael started up as the door banged behind her.

'Perhaps I should follow her,' he said.

'No good closing the barn door after the mare has bolted,' pointed out Tom Higginbottom. 'She's strong of will, that one.'

'Aye,' Michael said. 'Well then, let's to the castle for a talk with our hosts.'

* * *

After they failed to storm the harbour, the Scots fleet sailed back the way it had come, beaching just where Allan predicted, at Snook Point. Michael stood with the old Lindisfarner on the battlements of the castle, watching fires twinkle in the distance. The wind whistled, obscuring and framing a bone-pale moon with clouds.

Gover appeared, wrapped from head to toe in a black cloak like a vampire.

'Where have you been?' asked Michael.

'Exploring this end of the island for a means of escape. I'm disappointed in you, Pilgrim. You should never have brought me here. Until high tide, at least, I am trapped.' He turned to Allan. 'What of that second, smaller island a hundred yards from the village, behind the remains of an ancient monastery? Is there a way from there to the mainland?'

TWENTY-FIVE

'It is called St Cuthbert's Isle,' said Allan. 'At low tide, you can wade out to it. But from there to the mainland is a perilous way.'

'Hmmph.'

'We must gather for urgent and private debate,' broke in Michael. 'A great deal needs to be decided.'

Lindisfarne Castle was a tall, broad keep atop granite outcrops. Although it contained many rooms, most were occupied with men, women, and children, their stores, bedding, bundles, weapons. Some of the Lindisfarne Nuagers muttered at the sight of Iona. Not all were as philosophical as their Priest Man, Allan, when it came to dangers inflicted on them by their Skye brethren.

The conference that night consisted of Michael, Iona, Gover, Allan, and Tom Higginbottom. Iona studiously ignored the two Baytown men. Like all of them, her mood was grim, especially after the enemy's number was compared to their own. One wild Highland charge in the open would overwhelm them like a wave collapsing a sandcastle.

'We must consider our options,' said Michael.

Gover stirred. 'I have a suspicion you intend to set them out, tediously and at length.'

'I do.'

'Very well. If you must.'

The first was obvious. Gather everyone into the small castle and hole up. The Scots could lay on a siege, sit it out by ravaging the area for food and booty, and even send ships back to Fife for extra provisions and reinforcements, using the village as a snug winter shelter. All they need do then was wait for hunger and bickering to flush them out.

Allan considered help unlikely this side of New Year, given the size of the raiders' force. Gathering an army to drive them off would take much diplomacy and, more importantly, time. He predicted most of the local rulers would prefer to wait and see.

'There is another point,' said Michael. 'We came here unbidden. Nor do we seek to bring ruin upon you. If less folk were in the castle, it would be easier to defend.'

'Aye,' agreed Allan, 'it's always served us in the past.'

'I would say, let us load up the birlinns and make a dash for it,' said Michael, 'except that would still leave hundreds of angry Jocks on your doorstep. It would be a cowardly act, I fear.'

'There is another way, sirs,' Iona said. 'If I surrendered, perhaps the King of Buchan would be satisfied.'

All looked at her in surprise. Gover leaned forward confidentially. 'There is more chance of flapping with your arms through space, my dear, all the way to your Happy Planet.' He imitated the action to help her understand. 'No, those savages are unlikely to be appeased. We should flee to Baytown in the boats. Nothing else is to be done. Bad luck for the local natives here, of course, but c'est la vie.'

Everyone ignored the City-man.

'This is what I suggest,' said Michael. 'It is a desperate plan, some would say. And you will see that everything depends on the tides. It is nearly low now, but will begin to turn again a couple of hours before dawn.'

For a while, he outlined his proposals. Yet they were simple enough, and desperate indeed.

***

Each member of the council scattered to prepare. Michael withdrew to his temporary headquarters, making cartridge after cartridge for Allan's shotgun. His thoughts fluttered between past, present, and future.

What must grow from the morrow lay beyond anyone's control. Had it not always been thus? Every action connected to consequences seldom foreseen. Thence to the next decision, the next improvised response to fate, the next bud breaking from the branches of a man's life, the next season of leaves. All his Grandfather's treasured books revealed there had been no making sense of life before the plagues; nor could there be now.

His nimble fingers made cartridges while speculations grasped only air. He was glad to sleep in a bed of folded woollen sails, exhausted but determined to strive at dawn.

Iona, too, was busy: her preparations took the form of soothing words to frightened folk she had known since she was a girl, and to new acquaintances among the Lindisfarne Nuagers, especially those whose anxieties made them harsh towards the newcomers. Allan accompanied her to explain their plans for the morrow.

A sizable number of his flock approved that the brunt of tomorrow's fighting should fall on the Skye Nuagers and their Baytown allies, but far from all. Bitter memories of the last occasion King Adair of Fife came a-raiding for slaves made some eager for revenge. The younger men and women were especially tired of living in fear of sails on the horizon. It would have heartened Michael Pilgrim's uneasy dreams to hear them.

In one small, secluded room Iona came upon Blair Gover working at a table. The room was unnaturally bright for her eyes, lit by his torch. Before him, lay solid rectangular blocks, fusion-charged power cells from the gravchutes. He was fiddling with scavenged wires and other oddments, including components from antique screens.

Earlier, he had found some children playing a game they called *old days* with a pile of monitors, handheld screens, and other technology beyond living memory.

'I'll fly and fly!' one had cried, using two tablet-sized screens as magical wings, his pals chasing him with roars and drone noises. 'Drone, drone go away, come again another day!'

A look, deep and lonely, remarkably like sorrow, touched Gover as he watched their antics. Then he grew purposeful, confiscating from the children the best-preserved of their relics. They cowered, surrendering their treasures without resistance. The City-man didn't smell right, and his intense gaze frightened them.

'What are you doing?' Iona asked, shyly. She, too, found his presence disturbing. He repelled and fascinated her in equal measure.

'Trying to save everyone's life, as usual,' he answered. 'Especially my own. Do run along, there's a good girl.'

Iona lingered. 'I am no child.'

He put down one of his toys, looking her over carefully, as though noticing her for the first time. She pulled her cloak tighter around her.

'True,' he conceded. 'To answer your question, during my little wanderings today I noticed much inter-connected standing water in the village — ditches, moats, ponds. Not to mention the sea. I conceived of a faint possibility, just a notion, but a deliciously inventive one.'

With that, he resumed his work, absorbed entirely. After a moment, Iona crept away.

Like condemned prisoners fearful of the dawn, they slept or talked or lay awake dreading the morrow, each after their fashion. The sea breathed in and out regardless.

TWENTY-SIX

Once more, Helen Devereux found herself in the flooded valley transformed into a vast, open-air stadium on the outskirts of Mughalia. No entertainments were scheduled, unless one considered high politics a spectator sport.

She stood beside Averil Pilgrim on the Brubachers' private viewing platform. The mushroom-shaped edifice of plastiglass rose above milling crowds below. Holocasts proclaimed excitedly that four-fifths of the Five Cities' combined populations, four hundred thousand Beautifuls, had journeyed to attend this Grand Autonomy. Like no other, it might change the course of human evolution forever.

'Aren't they all amazing,' said Averil.

Her multi-coloured dress shimmered. For once, no Synetta accompanied them, and Averil complained her bosom friend had vanished without warning. For the absent woman's sake, Helen did not reveal why. Given Merle's obsessive phobia for minor infections, she was certain Synetta's disease would be cured by swift, permanent sterilisation.

Holo-images of the crowd swelled into immense bubbles over the flooded floor of the stadium before dissolving in waterfalls of sparks. Chattering, laughing voices created a tumult like the buzzing of innumerable wasps.

Helen's individuality felt besieged. Everywhere she looked, Beautifuls surgically and chemically improved until they resembled one another, clones of the same assumptions of perfection. The Five Cities practised ruthless conformity, those dependent on the Beautiful Life policing themselves, censoring thought and emotion to avoid Discordia. Every aspect of their repetitive days hemmed in by invisible walls.

She understood, looking out across the multitudes in their gaudy costumes, how like children not allowed to grow up they had become. To live without death or change was to sacrifice free will. And now —so intoxicating!— this Grand Autonomy offered a chance to break free, to revive ambitions suppressed for nigh on a century.

Helen dreaded the monstrosities such freedoms must produce.

Then it began. Four hundred thousand voices roared as a circular air-platform held aloft by dozens of whirling propellers flew over the stadium, hovering a hundred feet in the air. On the platform, twenty empty thrones faced one another in a circle, the twenty seats of the Ruling Council.

Beams of all colours in the spectrum, infinite blends between, raked the sky. Excitement doubled in the massive crowd.

Behold, a deep voice urged above the cheering. *Our wise Ruling Council.*

Averil clapped as aircars angled in to deposit passengers upon the floating platform. Holocasts zoomed in on the faces of these worthies, introducing each by name. One by one, the members of the Ruling Council bowed.

'Look! Look!' shrieked Averil.

From the last aircar to land stepped a couple, hand in hand, Marvin and Merle Brubacher. Matching costumes of wafer-thin gold flashed in the glare of the lights as they performed a perfectly choreographed bow.

Helen stared at their strange, flawless faces. Terrible doubts stirred.

TWENTY-SIX

Nothing was as it seemed here. Nothing and no one. How could she have forgotten that?

* * *

Once the Ruling Council had taken their seats, save for Blair Gover's, walls rose from the rim of the hovering platform, hiding whatever business they chose to conduct. Those watching from below were permitted to know no more than the Autonomy's central proposition: that the Founding Vision should be discarded, permitting the creation of sentient servitor-creatures to replace the Five Cities' reliance on drones. From that core decision, a thousand others must logically flow.

For a while, people chattered and circulated in the stadium. Holograms flashed of soundless debates within the council chamber. No more would be revealed until the Ruling Council's decree had been made absolute. Terraces slowly emptied as Beautifuls drifted back towards the pleasure districts of Mughalia, not least the Five Poisons, where a little deviance might spice up the wait for the Autonomy's verdict.

As Averil prepared to leave, Helen took her arm, chiding more angrily than she intended: 'I fear for you, Averil. Your newfound loyalties are increasingly dangerous. It really is time for a frank talk.'

* * *

As Helen gripped her arm, Averil's long-suppressed anger broke free. Lately, her old friend had become a source of irritation, even embarrassment, rather than the model of learning and grace she once seemed in Baytown. Averil knew better now. It was she herself, not Helen, who had changed, and in ways too numerous to count except as blessings. Besides, this 'frank talk' was certain to end in a sermon, just like poor Father from his pulpit, or Uncle Michael with his calm superiority and carping sense of duty.

'You must be aware of how dangerous it is here, Averil. If nothing else, we have a responsibility to warn your people what must occur should the Ruling Council agree this horrible proposition. If only Blair was with us! I'd forgive him everything. But I'm certain he is dead. We must find our own way home now.'

Averil shook free of her. 'Well, I don't see what's wrong with Angels.'

Helen gaped. 'Surely, you must. This is not just about simple modifying, as has happened to your face. Have you really not understood the scale of the proposal? Progeniting means new species on a massive scale. For all we know, gene infection is already widespread. I am beginning to suspect these so-called Angels have been in secret production for decades.'

'I think they're wonderful,' said Averil. 'In fact, I'd like a few of my own.'

There, it was said. A weight dropped from her shoulders. Why should she pretend to always agree with Helen? Marvin and Merle Brubacher didn't respect the old curator, that was plain. And nobody referred to Averil as a mere servant any longer. She had been elevated to the status of companion.

As though reading her thoughts, Helen broke in: 'You must be more careful around these new friends of yours, none of whom are what they seem. Marvin and Merle are especially dangerous.' She laughed bitterly. 'If you knew what I know, Averil! In fact, I do wonder at their interest in you.' She fell silent, frowned. 'Could it be the child you carry? Remember, all who take the elixir for the Beautiful Life become sterile, unable to breed even viable clones. Their genes are altered permanently. They, nay *we*, become deficient forever in that regard.'

Averil shook her head. None of this meant anything. It was just a way to confuse her. Had not the Brubachers treated her as special, and kept them both safe?

Defiantly, she reached into her reticule and produced an intoxicant spray, a special gift from Merle, and discharged it into her mouth. Tingling became a ripple of gladness.

'Please listen,' urged Helen. 'Our lives may depend on the next few hours.'

Now the drug came in waves. Yet Averil felt shadows behind her gayness. It was Helen doing this, spoiling anything she could not control, anything that belonged to her alone.

'I am not your little toy no more,' she muttered. 'I shall do as I please.'

Even as she inhaled a second spray, odd memories filtered through the haze. Of Seth at the family dinner table in Hob Hall, telling Father he would never return, that he was Big Jacko's man now. She realised how like him she sounded. But why not? Marvin and Merle Brubacher were not feeble primitives like the former Mayor of Baytown. All Seth had ever wanted was a better life. Even as a kid, he dreamt of the City, of becoming someone. Though poor Seth was dead, she could yet make those dreams come true. For Baby, most of all.

Averil stepped away from Helen, laughing exultantly as fresh waves swept over her. 'Goodbye,' she said. 'I'm off to find Synetta for a bit of fun. I might even go to the Five Poisons. Yes, why not?'

'No! Do not corrupt yourself in that terrible place.'

Averil's smile was triumphant. 'Merle says there's no harm in the Five Poisons. But then, she isn't afraid of living, unlike like some folk.'

With that, Averil stepped quickly towards a travel tube. And did not look back.

* * *

All Helen could do was follow her young friend. Yet she allowed a good distance between them, wary of deepening Averil's resentment.

Progress slowed to a series of jostles and shuffles. Walkways and boulevards overflowed with Beautifuls, many silent, even tense, as they awaited the Ruling Council's verdict. To be seen advocating one side or another was to risk future Discordia. Change brooded like an oppressive fog.

Hard to match Averil's pace, keep sight of her. It amazed Helen how quickly the girl had adapted to life here. As they neared the tunnel entrance to the Five Poisons, Helen panicked. Countless bodies blocked further progress. She saw Averil climb the wide stone steps into the dark tunnel and disappear. Whether back to the Brubachers or towards the Five Poisons, she could not say.

Helen headed for Marvin and Merle's mansion. With the usual transport amenities besieged by crowds, she chose to walk, despite stifling, tropical heat and a dusty wind. Even in the quieter residential areas of Mughalia, knots of Beautifuls lingered near public holovision displays. Helen prayed for an anti-climax to their feverish waiting. Surely, Founding Visioners like the Brubachers and their powerful friends would assert their authority, if necessary, by expelling large numbers of Progenitors from the safety of the Five Cities.

Helen reached a small, stony gorge carved from the hillside by a busy stream that revolved an ornate waterwheel. Since joining the Brubacher household, she had spent many secluded hours there, shaded by tall fern trees and banyans on a bench carved from living rock.

Leaving the road, Helen entered the shadowy gorge. Earth scents and water scents perfumed the air. She craned her neck to watch birds flit through the dappled light of the canopy. Plant and bird and countless more creatures she could not detect had evolved over aeons. They were evolving now, embracing temporary places in nature like this gorge, destinies beyond human comprehension. Nothing could stop that process, nothing. Even if mankind devastated the world, life would survive in some form, however primitive, and slowly, slowly reassert itself.

 Helen realised twilight was coming fast, as it did in this tropical latitude. Her screen bleeped an urgent warning. Eagerly, she took it from its pouch. Stared. Read. Read and stared again. As she dimmed the holo-message, tears trickled down her tired face. Beside her, the waterwheel kept turning. The stream murmured.

* * *

Messages beamed between satellites and transmitters ringing the earth. Codes buried deep within codes activated, mastering screens small and large, holocasts and projections, from Albion to Neo Rio, Han City to Mitopia. Those brave enough to think for themselves realised someone, or something, now controlled the central systems connecting the Five Cities, an unimaginable power. For the first time ever, it was being exercised brazenly.

 Crowds awaiting the Grand Autonomy's decree stirred. Faces lifted to hear or read messages meant as commands. A million holograms displayed the double helix, symbol of the Five Cities.

 A soft, avuncular, priest-like voice intoned.

 Dear, dear friends. What a miraculous journey we have undertaken since plague destroyed the old world! A journey taken together. And now the Grand Autonomy has decided upon a new journey, flowing from the past as a small stream joins a greater river, a brand new voyage to seek out yet greater seas.

 Insect-twitted dusk in Mughalia. Fiery dawn in Han City. In Albion, a grey winter's afternoon, while in Mitopia, shadowed by the Swiss Alps, a cloudy twilight gathered. Yet whatever the time or weather,

Beautifuls listened, some alone, some in public places, others hiding like Synetta, tormented by a disease that consumed them cell by cell.

Yes, dear friends, the Ruling Council has decided for us all. Deep, deep their deliberations. Little wonder evolution placed them in positions of lofty sagacity, a perfect conclave!

The suave, soothing voice paused. Half a million hearts beat a little faster. It was coming, the verdict.

Dear friends, the Beautiful Life is over. It served us well for a time. A hundred years! Such a short time to our kind, destined to live forever. Yes, we must praise the Beautiful Life, just as one praises the sunrise for commencing a bright new day. But now the stream of time joins a larger river. Friends, dear friends... The voice rose proudly. *Behold the Life Perfected!*

A million holograms of slowly rotating double helixes dissolved into images of Beautifuls surrounded by adoring creatures. Angels! Their blank, expressionless faces yet to be written upon by humanity, to be shaped by mankind's desires and whims and greed and madness and cruelties and ruthless intelligence. Empty faces born to obey until the sun itself expired. Few cared to notice, however, the glimmers of will, flickering behind apparently vacant pupils.

Life Perfected! Consider it carefully, dear friends. Endless opportunity!

After a pause, the voice took on a subtle menace.

But where there is natural perfection, so must imperfection exist. New Discordias to be hunted down wherever they arise.

A longer pause let the implications sink in. Everyone knew the price paid for Discordia.

Dear, dear friends, what could be more fitting? Anyone opposing perfection is flawed. Only the Perfected can be free. The Ruling Council have set Homo aeternum free forever. Rejoice! Rejoice!

The voice quivered with joy and enthusiasm.

Prove it now, good people, dear friends, under the watchful eyes of the

Ruling Council. Prove it to those beside you! Prove yourself among the Perfected!

With this stern injunction, the holocast faded. For awkward moments, people examined neighbours and screens that were certainly spying upon them, possibly applying codes to read their innermost thoughts from facial expressions. Then the first person called out, followed by a second, third, thousands upon thousands shouting:

'We are free! Perfect, at last! Praise the Ruling Council! Free! Free for eternity!'

Newly-anointed Perfects embraced, eager for their instant loyalty to be monitored. That way, they might be among the first rewarded with personal Angels.

'We are free! Free! Perfect and free!'

In Neo Rio, Mughalia, Albion, Mitopia, Han City, explosions of light and lasers poured into the sky. From this time forth, new armies of slaves would make anything possible. Replant vast rainforests destroyed before the plagues? Why not? Recolonise blighted North America and its irradiated cities? Why ever not? Set right, indeed, all nature's silly errors? Why not?

Yet in every City, thousands did not rejoice. Those tainted by sickness like Synetta, awaiting discovery. The technicians in their drab, ugly costumes, were aware the explosive implants in their cortexes would be activated as soon as Angels replaced them.

Many Beautiful wept for the Beautiful Life that had kept them flourishing and green when nearly all mankind withered like leaves in autumn. Even a few on the Ruling Council protested, and were thrown into punishment cages, their authority revoked without appeal.

As for Helen, she watched in horror and disgust. She must escape the Five Cities together with Averil. Without hesitating, Helen hurried towards that odious zone of Mughalia where she last saw her young friend: the Five Poisons.

TWENTY-SEVEN

Glimmers of dawn. The tide still high, though on the turn. Michael ordered a parade of armed men and women on the beach of Lindisfarne Harbour. His agreement with Allan and the Lindisfarne Nuagers stipulated that the children and old folk from Skye should shelter in the castle. The rest capable of bearing arms, including Iona and the other young women, would take up such weapons they knew how to use. As for the Lindisfarne Nuagers, disciplined from childhood by a warlike border region, no one knew who among them would join the muster or defend the castle.

So it came as a joyful surprise when they heard feet crunching on shingle and saw scores of well-armed Lindisfarne Nuagers, marching out to join them. Cheers broke the pre-dawn stillness, the whispers of surf.

Michael hurried to meet Allan. The older man introduced a burly fisher-farmer who would lead the Lindisfarners into battle, Cuthbert, by name, in honour of the Holy Isle's patron saint from long ago. As Cuthbert explained to Michael, his parents had dabbled in the discredited faith of Christianity, though less credulous folk knew better now. Hence, he and his fellow Nuagers would assist their brothers and sisters to escape bondage, in the hope of smoother passage to the Happy Planet when their flight time came.

This declaration gave Michael a notion of how to inject some spine into the motley, inexperienced little army.

'It is clear to me,' he declared so all could hear, 'destiny is working through our assembly. Look above!' Necks bent obligingly. 'Can you not see the stars glinting bright? Look, there is the Plough; there the Great Bear! They are watching us, assessing who is worthy and who is not. Could my idea be far-fetched?'

'Nay!' 'No, feller!' 'I believe that!' came various cries.

'Well then, who will risk their lives alongside me and stand firm? Who will understand we have nowhere to flee? Who will hold their positions and obey orders? Who, I say, will drive these enemies of the bright stars and all that offers hope for mankind's recovery, aye, and our very redemption, back into the sea!'

Cheering. Weapons waving. Earnest nods and raised fists. Yes, religion was a fine way to breed killers from peaceable folk. As was any cause rendering one's enemy less than human. A hot memory of the Crusades stirred Michael Pilgrim's guardian demons: self-loathing and doubt.

But surely this cause, at least, possessed justice? Was not the freedom to live in peace a justification to kill? Yet half the men and boys opposing them were conscripts, as once he and Tom Higginbottom had been for the City. Defying power took a strength of will few possessed, especially when, as for these Scots peasants and war men, your bread depended on obedience.

Fuck it, he told himself, and not for the first time in his life. If he must make killers of fishermen, let them at least kill to win.

'I'm asking for a dirty, bloody fight in those streets.' He indicated the village. 'Some of us may not make it. But keep knocking them down, one by one, and they'll get the message. Holy Island will not be polluted or robbed. Remember your loved ones as you strike. None of us will submit to become miserable bonders!'

A voice called out. Michael recognised it as Dameron's. Perhaps he recalled the cruelties his folk had endured at the hands of the Prince O' Ness.

'To the stars! To the stars!'

The cry was taken up. Soon the gathering of believers was singing their master-hymn:

> *Swing low, sweet universe,*
> *Coming for to carry us home.*
> *Swing low, sweet sun and stars,*
> *Coming for to carry us home.*

The hymn had a surprisingly large number of verses. Michael took Tom to one side.

'Well, that fired up the Starboys,' he said, quietly. 'Are the Baytown lads ready?'

'Aye.'

'With the stuff we agreed?'

'Ready in the boat.'

'Go careful, Tom, if you don't pull it off there's little hope here. The numbers are against us.'

'I know.'

'I keep wondering whether we should have just made a run for it.'

'Course we should've, Michael.'

'But we didn't.'

'We never do. That's our problem.'

'Watch for the signals,' said Michael.

The friends shook hands, aware it might be for the last time.

Tom led a dozen hardy Baytown folk to a flat-bottomed trading boat, oars ready in their locks. Then Michael remembered another phrase of his Grandfather's, culled from the old man's beloved Shakespeare.

'Ripeness is all, Tom,' he called out. 'Remember, ripeness is all.'

TWENTY-SEVEN

* * *

There were fifteen horses and mules on Lindisfarne suitable for what Michael Pilgrim had in mind.

As light gathered and Cuthbert prepared a welcome in the village, they cantered along the ancient road hugging the western shore of Holy Island. At low tide, it overlooked miles of mud and sand a man could squelch across to reach the marshy shore of the mainland. Right now, the tide was high, though receding.

Flocks of white birds bobbed on the water, waiting for feeding grounds to be exposed. To the east, across the low lying fields and sheep-cropped grass of the island, a blurred orange and red orb, day's faithful herald, rose from the hazy grey horizon. The sun gave him hope.

'I might need to re-join you in a hurry,' Michael told the men and women clip-clopping beside him. 'If you start shooting, make damn sure it's not at me.'

As they neared the narrow neck of land connected to Snook Point, his escort halted, picketing their horses and taking up positions on high dunes. All carried muskets, single-shot rifles or longbows — the best shots on the island, according to Cuthbert. Michael hoped so; also that his hunch concerning the Scots' disdain for firearms was correct.

Attaching a white flag of truce to the barrel of his rifle, he raised it high. Then he trotted towards a knot of men on the road running parallel to the beached fleet. Ten, twenty warriors. Behind the line of grass-covered dunes, masts poked up from the ships.

At the edge of shouting range, Michael halted. He wore a breastplate made from a plasti-steel car bonnet he'd found in a garage, carving it into shape with his City-sword. Whether such protection would stop a bullet was questionable, it would certainly deflect an arrow or a sword.

His white flag fluttered in the sea breeze. Minutes passed. He sat with back straight, still as a statue. After a few minutes, a group of men in armour and fine cloaks strode from the encampment, led by two standard-bearers.

One flag was deep blue with three white stars: the banner of Buchan's King Duncaine. The second, that of Adair, King of Fife, bore a red lion rearing across two bands of yellow and sky blue.

Michael noted the flags with interest, how each of the royal standard-bearers hurried to gain a lead over his rival and take prominence. Like master like man, he speculated. He also noted they chose to respect his own flag of parlay rather than fire off a treacherous volley. In essence, it suggested some willingness to negotiate, at least for the time being.

* * *

The two kings debated with one another while Michael remained on his horse. Then Duncaine, the King of Buchan, advanced alone. His standard-bearer followed with the flag of dark blue and white stars. When he was close enough to see and hear properly, Duncaine halted.

He was tall, almost a giant, heavy of limb. His armour shone from burnishing. In his belt were fancy two-barrelled pistols; a long claymore hung from his back. His helmet was topped with a crown of gold and silver trinkets, scavenger spoils. Michael detected a strong resemblance to the Prince O'Ness in his ruddy face. They regarded one another. Michael lowered his gun so that it lay across his lap.

'King Duncaine?'

'Yes, laddie. Let it be known. And you?'

'Michael Pilgrim, Protector of the North.'

'I have heard that name. At least my son did not fall to a man wi'out a name.'

Both lapsed into cold scrutiny.

'Ye killed my ain son, my bonny lad. And you stole the sword he

TWENTY-SEVEN

carried, the Prince's Sword, an heirloom of my house. And you spoiled his body.'

'True.'

'So what d'ye wish to tell me, Protector of the North.'

There was no vehemence in King Duncaine's voice, which surprised Michael. Yet he sensed a strong, unwavering resolve.

'Your son issued a challenge to any who would take it. One man did, a fisherman, and had his head removed for sport. That seemed an unmanly game to me, for the fisherman was no fighter and little more than a lad. And your son bore a sword he could not match, a sword like my own.'

Michael displayed his weapon, a plain design retrieved from the dead hunter, yet recognisable as City work. He let it fall back into its scabbard.

'I accepted your son's challenge and beat him in a lawful fight. What is wrong with that?'

'A king is his own law,' replied Buchan.

'I disagree. No man is above the law.'

King Duncaine struck his chest. 'This is my law, the justice of my heart, the weeping of his mother, my honour. I'll have your guts before the tide comes in and allows ye a chance to escape, Protector of the North. And the witch who cast a glammer on my son, aye, and that devil warlock sent by Hell to aid her. All of you shall burn!'

His voice had risen now. Michael suspected it was for the benefit of his followers. Still, he tried: 'What if I were to return your son's sword, the heirloom of your family? Perhaps that would satisfy your honour?'

'No, it would not.'

Michael pointed at the flag of Fife and its master, prudently safe among the scores of listening Scots troops — a fact he also noted.

'What of King Adair of Fife's will?' he called. 'I have his youngest son, Colm, as my prisoner. A little bruised at the edges, I'll admit, but still alive. Will not Adair of Fife, his loving father, weigh his son in my offer? You get your heirloom and honour; he gets his son. Is that not fair?'

'What do ye get?' demanded the King of Buchan. His tone was dark now. Michael glanced nervously behind him. No one was sneaking up through the dunes so far as he could see.

Steadying his nerves, he called, 'I get peace. And not having to kill you.'

King Duncaine laughed with scant mirth.

'Many lives could be saved,' pointed out Michael quickly. But he saw it was no use. The King of Buchan was here precisely to take lives. Perhaps he had parlayed to demonstrate that he, not his brother-in-law, King Adair of Fife, made the decisions among the Scots.

Without further words, Michael wheeled his horse and galloped back towards the dunes, bending low and zigzagging in case bullets pursued him. No shots were fired. Glancing back, he saw the two royal standards returning to the ships and camp. There, they would gather their full army, ready for battle.

* * *

Michael raced back to the village, leaving his small band of horsemen and muleteers to keep watch on the road from Snook Point. His plan relied on separated groups playing scheduled parts. If one failed, all might fail. So it was a relief to find Cuthbert and the other Nuagers he had placed under his command, whether from Lindisfarne or Skye, working well together.

'How goes it?' he asked. His horse nickered and sweated, breath steaming in the cold air.

Cuthbert stood guard with thirty others at the entrance to the village,

TWENTY-SEVEN

a former car park ploughed to oat fields, exactly where Michael had hoped to find them.

'Remember,' Michael said, 'the danger is you get outflanked from that direction.' He pointed at a grassy area set aside for sheep. 'The moment you see them in that pasturage, head straight back to the first barricade in the village, and fast. With me?'

The Lindisfarner nodded. He had a cool, laconic turn of expression; Michael began to see why Allan had picked him to lead.

'Aye,' he said affably. 'Me and the lads have rumbled with those fellers before.'

'Good. Listen out for the sound of firing.'

Michael looked anxiously back towards Snook Point through his binoculars, a pair borrowed from Dameron. No sign of the Scots army leaving camp.

He galloped past a line of large houses into the village, where he found a score of others, including Iona. Her high cheek-boned face was flushed as they piled bricks and tiles round old cars to form barricades. The leather coat she wore for protection was several sizes too big for her. A slingshot and net of round beach pebbles hung from her belt.

'Mister Pilgrim!' she cried, her face lighting up. 'Just now, I led a wee prayer that the King of Buchan would see sense and avoid more killing. What were his words to us?'

He shifted uneasily. The last time they talked, she had despised him to his face.

'King Duncaine is all for war,' he said. 'So must we be. No other hope is available to us.'

He turned to the assembled Nuagers. 'Remember this. The only peace we'll get from those murdering, raping, slaving bastards will be written in their blood!'

The Nuagers muttered at this. He formed a silent prayer of his own, though he addressed it to no god: that when the test came, they held firm. With that, he cantered around the small village, checking that other barricades were going up.

No time left for more. Wheeling his horse, Michael raced back the way he had come, out of the village and back along the causeway road, the ancient pilgrim route to and from Holy Island's priory, now a pile of lichen-clad ruins between the village and sea.

* * *

He arrived back just in time. The Jock army was leaving its camp of beached boats on Snook Point, ready for battle. This was Michael's first chance to accurately count their numbers for himself through his binoculars. It turned out Colm's tearful revelations were broadly correct, assuming twenty or so had been left to guard the ships and camp. He prayed it was no more than twenty.

A grey sky covered Northumberland in that second hour after dawn. Low, pressing clouds threatened rain. The hidden sun could not gleam off the polished armour of the advancing men. Michael assessed them carefully; much could be learned from the way an army marches.

First, he noted their long, disorderly column — a sure sign of over-confidence as well as slack officering. The front half marched behind the banner of Buchan. Yes, there was King Duncaine, right in the van with his household war-kin. Well-armed and fed, this elite wore good armour and carried firearms suited for close work. Behind came the main body of Duncaine's troops: polearms, axes, swords. Doubtless a few bows and guns. An army designed to rush its enemies and overwhelm them hand-to-hand as soon as possible. No prolonged firefights for them.

The second half of the army straggled behind the King of Fife's yellow and blue banner. Adair and his bodyguard led the way, with a small company of archers, crossbowmen and musketeers. After that,

TWENTY-SEVEN

a hotchpotch of peasants bearing weapons, shields and crude armour.

What interested Michael was the fact King Adair permitted Duncaine of Buchan to lead the army. Subservience? Cowardice? Michael doubted that, although his son, Colm, had let slip Adair generally ordered his sons to do the raiding while he stayed snug as a flea in his palace. A cautious man then, a pragmatist, preferring certain victory to risk. Perhaps.

Looking at the size of the column, which far outnumbered the Nuagers, there seemed little doubt who would prevail. Yet still, Adair allowed his brother-in-law the honour of the van, as well as keeping physically apart from him. It crossed Michael's mind King Adair might only be there because he'd been nagged into it by his wife, King Duncaine's sister.

'Alright,' he told the small troop of cavalry. 'Ian, Calla, Marlin picket and hold the horses as we agreed. Remember, they are not accustomed to gunfire. If not tethered well, they may break free and bolt. Personally,' he added, 'I have no hankering to run back to the village with those hairy bastards on my heels. I'd sooner ride.'

His comrades' tense, pale faces revealed an urge to ride back now. An urge intensified by the discordant wail of bagpipes and the deep, repetitive boom of a marching drum.

'Let's kill a few,' said Michael. 'See how they take to it.'

They rode in a small column of their own towards the advancing Jocks, who were still two miles distant from the centre of the village. Four hundred yards off, Michael halted the troop, picketing the horses and mules, five beasts per groom.

Then the sharpshooters moved forward, musketeers apart from his breech-loading rifle, courtesy of Allan and two longbowmen with fat quivers.

'Shoot your arrows at the unarmoured men behind the van,' Michael said. 'Aim high. The rest of us'll trouble the front. Take your time.

Don't worry when they speed up. It will be their natural instinct under fire.'

It began. A single shared volley then each sharpshooter on his own. A simple routine: aim, fire, load. Hard to miss men packed in lines, but miss they did, for the range was necessarily long and their weapons crude. Yet enemies did fall with each salvo, enough to enrage their foes.

The skirmishing simplified Michael: aim, fire, load. When the Jocks drew too close — speeding into a stumbling walk, almost a jog, as he had predicted — they ran back to the horses then galloped a third of a mile back towards the village. Picket the horses. Fan out a line of musketeers. Repeat the same bloody business until the enemy again drew near.

The obvious thing for the Scots would have been to put out skirmishers of their own. Yet none of their commanders seemed to think of it. It also did not escape Michael's attention that King Adair's forces advanced more slowly than his brother-in-law's. Nor, he suspected, did the fact escape King Duncaine.

**

Half a mile from the village, Michael gathered his small band of cavalry. All were exhausted by the fear and tension of skirmishing. It was time to send up a sign.

'Ride back to the village,' he ordered. 'You've done well. Drink lots of water. Take up your positions with Cuthbert.'

As they cantered off, he extracted a three-foot tube of plastic drainpipe from his saddlebag. Taking out a signal rocket borrowed from Tom Higginbottom's boat, he used his flint-wheel lighter and touched flame to the fuse. Dropping the rocket into the tube, he stepped back. A fizzing sputter. No, he prayed, for fuck's sake, don't fail me... And it didn't. The powder caught. Up shot the rocket with a whooshing spark-trail, followed by a bang that echoed across the flat island. Moments later, a bell tolled mournfully in the castle.

As he remounted, Michael examined the advancing Scots. What happened in the next twenty minutes would determine whether his head stayed on his shoulders.

A sign from long ago hung askew by the roadside, its letters bleached by wind and rain:

DANG R
DO NOPROCE D
W EN WATER REAC ES CAUS WAY

After deciphering the letters, he looked across the two miles of grey water between Lindisfarne and the mainland. Hills rose to reveal young woods and a few ploughed fields. Turning south, he looked for Bamburgh, several miles down the coast, where a warlord friendly to the Nuagers was said to dwell in a mighty fortress of great antiquity. Would the people of the mainland aid their neighbours when the causeway was exposed by low tide? Michael Pilgrim frowned. Then he followed his troop of cavalry back towards the village.

TWENTY-EIGHT

Hours earlier, a hundred and sixty miles to the south, another Pilgrim had longed for help.

'Where is he?' shouted Maister Gil.

His question had been aimed at men forced onto their knees. Red flames from their campfire danced and flickered, glinting off crazed windscreens. Their horses nickered as if sensing what must come. Seth Pilgrim, peering around the corner of the truck cab that concealed him, knew what would happen.

'I said, pretty boy, where is he? And you, scarecrow!'

Neither Gurdy nor Jojo lifted their heads to reply. The flogger relished his role as interrogator. His hand reached by instinct for the scourge in his belt, its leather thongs terminating in jagged fragments of glass.

Despair made Seth's hands sweat and tremble. Not only did the two women carry long knives and pistols, but the men of their entourage pointed swords and guns at the prisoners.

'Who is this he you ask about?' demanded Jojo. 'There's just me and my servant here, bound for St Nicholas Fair in York. Steal what you need then leave us be. I warn you, we have powerful friends.'

His voice was firm and commanding. The two Mistresses exchanged narrow glances. Maister Gil, however, was having none of it.

'Hurt him,' he commanded. 'Before I do.'

TWENTY-EIGHT

A flogger stepped forward, smashing the back of Jojo's shoulder with the butt of his gun. The young man fell forward with a cry.

'Tha knows who we want, pretty boy,' said Gil. 'Seth Pilgrim. I'll learn yer not to treat us as fools.'

Hurdy-Gurdy jabbered in sheer terror.

'Over there! Over there!' he snivelled, pointing west towards the tower blocks Seth had glimpsed as they set up camp. Too dark to see Leeds or anywhere that might offer sanctuary now.

'What do you mean, over there?'

Gil readied his scourge. A miracle he had not used it already. Seth sensed darker plans for the captives, plans requiring them to be kept relatively unhurt for now.

'I reckon tha'd not like it if I tickled thee with this. Speak up!'

'The city yonder,' burbled Gurdy. 'He has gone there to meet his companions. Over there. We parted company, and he left us for good.'

'That right?'

Gil stepped over to Fat and Thin for a whispered conversation. Seth glimpsed a chance to escape. Run into the darkness now. Find a good place to hide and head south at dawn. What did he owe Hurdy-Gurdy, after all? The City-man was mad as mustard. As for Jojo, he'd never asked him to come along. Wouldn't they both do the same in his shoes? But he stayed in the shadows, squinting lest the firelight reflect off his eyes.

'Give me that, you idiot!' said Fat Mistress.

Always the crueller and more decisive of the pair, she snatched Gil's scourge. Thin watched to one side, the burnt half of her face exposed, along with her scorched, withered left hand.

'Are thee sure?' asked Gil, a little piqued. The whip was his personal prerogative and mystery.

Fat Mistress would not be bridled. She had suffered too much and ridden too far. She strode over to the prisoners.

'We want the books. Now!'

Jojo blanched at the sight of the big, black-robed woman, her pudgy face contorted with passion. Gurdy, however, smiled ingratiatingly. 'Books, Your Ladyship? What books?'

Thwack. Thwack. Soon blood was running from cuts on his cheeks and hands as he protected himself.

Seth comprehended what drove their fury. What brought them so far from Fell Grange. Not just a simple desire for revenge, but their precious holy books. The Mistresses craved Satan's power through their Master's chants and black masses and curses and spells. And would stop at nothing to win it back.

Thin Mistress let out a blood-curdling shriek ending in a wild ululation.

Encouraged, Fat Mistress turned on Jojo with the whip, her swollen belly and buttocks quivering from the exertion; she was aided by kicks and blows whenever the surrounding floggers got a chance to take a turn.

Seth watched in misery. His friends had one hope before being beaten to death. The sacred books lay hidden in his travelling satchel. It would not be long before they were discovered in the cart. Then he'd have nothing left to bargain with.

He concealed the cocked and primed musket by the truck cab door, stepping out into the firelight.

'Looking for someone?'

His question meant to sound casual, cool. It emerged as a squeak.

* * *

'Run, Seth! Run!'

The cry came from Jojo and earned him a boot to the stomach. Hands raised, Seth advanced into the camp. Gun barrels pointed at him like

TWENTY-EIGHT

pitiless black eyes. With a smile, as though to say, *You see*, Fat Mistress tossed the scourge back to Maister Gil.

Though the light was dim, there was no mistaking her surge of anticipation at the sight of him, or the sheer hatred twisting the unburnt half of Thin Mistress's face.

'Let my travelling companions go,' said Seth. 'They have done you no harm.'

He knew the Mistresses too well to expect mercy for himself. Mercy was a weakness they despised as impious. Nor did he expect an easy death. But, though he was half-paralysed with fear, this fate granted Seth an odd glimpse of relief. It offered a scraping of honour at the end.

Fat Mistress produced a long, thin-barrelled pistol from beneath her black, flowing robes and thick woollen travelling cloak.

'Where are the Holy Books?' she asked.

Seth realised the floggers had moved to surround him, just as the feral dogs had circled the wagon earlier that day.

'You'll not see them no more!' he threatened, looking around. 'I'm warning you. Unless you let my friends go.'

Fat Mistress pretended amazement. She turned to her fellow witch. 'Hear that, Richenda? Friends. He has friends now. That miserable, thieving, arsonist, rat-like bonder — aye, every man's plaything — that wretched little toy has friends. They must be desperate indeed, or knob-headed fools, to want a friend like ye, Seth Pilgrim.'

Thin Mistress's surviving eye blinked rapidly. Whether from amusement or darker emotion, he could not say.

'Which friend shall I shoot first?' wondered Fat Mistress aloud. 'The handsome young feller or the loon-faced beggar man? Which friend is it to be, Pilgrim?'

Her pistol wavered between Jojo and Hurdy-Gurdy, the latter curled up in a foetal position after his beating. Yet Seth caught a cold glitter of eyeball behind the hands shielding Gurdy's face.

'Do that, and you'll never get the books,' he stammered. 'I mean it!' With a click the flintlock pistol cocked.

Thin Mistress's mouth opened wetly as she stared at Seth. 'Do it,' she whispered. 'Just so I can see the expression on his face.'

'Patience, my love,' replied Fat Mistress. 'There is still the question of where to shoot his friends. In the groin perhaps?'

'There! There!' cried Thin Mistress, pointing at Jojo's gut, the most painful place for any bullet wound.

Seth's courage froze like a startled animal. She would do it alright! And savour it better than any sauce. What a fool he had been.

'In...in the cart!' he cried. 'Don't shoot him. In the cart! Beneath a pile of blankets. In a leather satchel.'

He wondered if Bella had returned to the camp while he was away collecting firewood. Even now, she might be hidden in the little wagon. But the flogger dispatched to search soon returned with the bag. The strangeling must be out in the night, running free.

'Give me that, you fool!' Fat Mistress unbuckled and rummaged. 'Ah. Aah! Aaaah.'

She pulled out the pink plastic lunchbox, fumbling it open: two books, Wicca For Teens and the one she craved, the book of power in a world of chaos, its imitation leather cover stamped with a red pentagram, the holy book leading straight down to the altars of Hell.

'The Black Book of our Master!' she cried, kissing it. 'Oh, Hell is hot tonight!'

Mother-daughter, daughter-mother whooped with blind fervour. Even Gil cracked his scourge to whip the road, transported with glee. Oh, they were back on top now. Blessed by a power as great as the City's, and more pitiless. All were distracted, and in a moment, Jojo was back on his feet, grabbing a dagger from a startled flogger's rope belt, stabbing the man before he could react. Hurdy-Gurdy, too, was wrestling with a pair of floggers.

'Do not kill them!' screeched Fat Mistress.

By now, Seth had run to retrieve his musket. Taking it up, in his haste, he touched the trigger of the cocked gun. The bullet whistled uselessly into a sapling.

Moments later they were disarmed, guns and sword-tips held to their bodies, prisoners once more. Gurdy lay unconscious, clubbed down by a musket butt. Seth and Jojo knelt side by side, the Squire of Fountains bleeding from a fresh cut on his arm. Their hands and feet were trussed with leather cords while their captors drew breath.

'Forgive me,' whispered Seth to Jojo. 'I brought this on your head. I...' Yes, he must say it. Tell Jojo how he felt for him. There was no other time left. But he could not speak. Did not deserve his own feelings. And so the three simple words stayed buried in his heart.

Then Fat Mistress's jowly face was between them, inches from their own. She held up the holy book.

'Why do you think we have not killed you?'

Seth struggled to loosen his hands.

'Why?' she leered, opening the book to a particular page.

He recognised the image of a man with staked out ankles and wrists, trapped in a pentagram. Oh, he knew why they had been spared. They wished to make amends to Satan, their Master, their Prince of Light. They wished to atone for their carelessness in losing the holy books granted to them by the demon Laurel. They wished to offer the Lord of Darkness a gift.

* * *

To every god its due. Jojo Lyons believed friendly spirits kept watch upon Fountains, dwelling in tree and stream, easily propitiated with small gifts of food or flowers. Hurdy-Gurdy's gods were unknown except to himself; certainly, he never spoke of them.

Seth Pilgrim? Oh, he had known a few gods in his time. His father, Reverend James Pilgrim, had tried to Jesus him, a lost cause as it turned out, for everyone in Baytown had abandoned the Christ-god as surely as Zeus or Thor. Then came Big Jacko's wife, queen, priestess, concubine, all rolled into one. She had tempted Seth with her Heron Goddess and cruel Old Gods until Seth understood sacrifice all too well, how swiftly blood-hysteria can wash a man away. Seth's dreams often reverted to the winter solstice night when Old Marley met his knife, all for the sake of power. And not just poor Old Marley, no, others without names. But those gifts of strength proved to be an illusion. Gifts of guilt, disgust, soul-weariness.

So it came as no surprise the same fate should come his way. He had earned it many times over. What grieved him most as he sat beside Jojo and Hurdy-Gurdy, trussed like fowl, was leading them to such an end.

'I should have realised,' he blurted, watching the Mistresses prepare the ceremony, 'they would never stop looking for their shitty books.'

Fat and Thin were as happy as he'd ever seen them, which said little. Unfolding and laying down a large black cloth painted with the pentagram on a section of cleared road. Chanting spells as they placed seven stones to seal the makeshift altar's magical energies. They even squabbled amicably about the correct placement of the old tin cans full of oil they lit instead of candles.

Jojo glanced into the darkness surrounding the camp. 'At least Bella escaped,' he whispered.

Hurdy-Gurdy was less philosophical. Writhing in constant distress, he sobbed, head and shoulders bent over his legs.

Seth made sure their guards were distracted with looting the wagon before murmuring, 'There is something I must tell you, Jojo. Before I die.'

TWENTY-EIGHT

It occurred to him his father had a word for what must follow, even a special rite, some magic Jesus spell involving forgiveness. Not that his father's crazy religion mattered now.

'Jojo, it is about Bella.' Seth squirmed inwardly. But he was on the hook, and there was only one way off. 'I know a lot more about her kidnapping, and that of your other sister, Abbie, than I have said.'

'Yes?'

Seth forced himself onward.

'You see, I was part of the group of men that stole your sisters both away. Don't get me wrong! I didn't raid Fountains. I was never there before me and Gurdy came. That was just chance, fate maybe. But I did help keep Bella and Abbie prisoner until, until...'

Jojo stiffened. His eyes bore into Seth's.

'Until what?' he croaked.

'An air-machine took them away to the City. There were drones, terrible fuckers. You couldn't have fought them. No one could. And a few City-men, all with guns. They loaded them up along with a load of other kids from the North and flew off. That's all I know.'

Jojo's stare did not waver or soften.

'I...I tried my best to help them!' said Seth. 'You know, they even mentioned you to me. I promised to help if I could. But I couldn't, Jojo. I did bad things in them days, bad, bad things. The man I followed — Big Jacko, you've heard of him, who hasn't? — would have killed me. I am sorry. So sorry.'

He sank back, exhausted. Neither spoke to one another again. No time in any case: the Mistresses were ready.

* * *

A curious spydrone on patrol that night would have detected patterns of fire on the old motorway littered with dead machines. Its vibration and infrared sensors would have identified human shapes, voices, plus a corresponding number of quadrupeds (Equus ferus caballus 99.8% probability). Intrigued, it might have switched to stealth and slowly descended. Now the gathering on the old motorway junction could reveal its purposes and complexion, though facial recognition was impossible from this angle.

Early overall assessment revealed two rival groups at interplay. One dominant: six adults comprising two females and four males, primitive weapons evident (no threat). The smaller group subservient: three males, unarmed, one of whom was expending unusual amounts of muscular energy while maintaining a static posture, the other hunched. This pair separate from the third male. He lay flat on his back, bound hands and legs pinned to the earth. Small flames in a geometric pattern, other symbols prominent. Most notable: pentagram associated with primitive fertility religion.

Conclusions: no threat — religious ceremony — primitives being primitive.

* * *

Seth watched it unfold in an agony of his own making.

'No!' he roared. 'You bitches! Do it to me, not him! I told you he had nothing to do with this. Any of it! He didn't even know about the books.'

Intent on their work, they simply leered.

Legs spread apart, wrists bound, stripped half-naked, Jojo lay in a helpless X on the rough black cloth. Maister Gil took his time driving home the hooped iron pegs normally used to tether horses.

'Be still, pretty boy,' he said when Jojo tried to struggle. 'Your immortal soul'll find out Hell is hot soon enough.'

'They want my soul,' moaned Jojo. 'They want to steal my soul!'

TWENTY-EIGHT

That seemed to him more terrible than losing a mere life.

Taking out a sharp knife, Gil cut away what remained of Jojo's clothes, especially his loincloth, slowly, lovingly, his hot breath and hands all over the young man's pale, muscular body. Seth seethed with hate. Then the sacrifice was ready, a cup of pure, unspoilt energy to be offered in adoration and fear.

Throughout these preparations the Mistresses stood aside, candles flickering in their hands. Fat rolled her eyes to the dark sky.

'Agios ischyros Bathomet!' she cried.

'To Satan, giver of life!' replied Thin.

Both turned to Seth before they began. Did Fat smile? Oh, yes. Certainly, Thin glowered.

'I tell you,' he pleaded, 'let me take his place! Isn't that what you want? I stole the books, not him. I burned your face and hand, you ugly bitch! Me! Make me suffer, not him. Fuck you!'

'Don't worry yourself,' said Gil, walking over to jab him in the stomach. 'We will, you little cunt. Doesn't tha see yet? We're going to carry you back to Fell Grange in a cage, so all o' Lake Country mark how you suffer. Your time'll come, mister. And it'll be slow as winter.'

Another hard jab. Seth snivelled on the churned tarmac and coarse grass of the road.

* * *

The Mistresses busied themselves. As though summoned by their energies, night wind picked up, making the naked flames dance and flicker. Overhead, indifferent banks of cloud drove northward. Stray stars peered through the darkness.

'We shall go down to the altars in Hell!' declared Thin Mistress with slow relish, kissing the Holy Book then passing it to her fellow priestess.

'Prince, giver of light, we summon you this night to ravish us!' urged Fat, also kissing the book. 'You who lead us to woe and struggle and to forbidden thoughts.'

'Prince of Darkness, come to us.'

'Come to us!'

'Bring us ecstasy.'

'Ecstasy!'

'Give us fire and reign over the world.'

'Satanas venire! Satanas venire!'

Seth struggled madly at the leather thongs. He could not let them do this. He would die first. Jojo's chest was heaving as he stared up in horror. Fat Mistress drew a short, sharp knife from her robes, holding it high for all to witness. Her piggy eyes glittered with sheer exultation.

Suddenly Hurdy-Gurdy whispered in Seth's ear. 'Stop wriggling, Little Nuncle. My hands and legs are free. Stop, you'll draw attention.'

Panting, Seth froze. He recollected the intense shivering Gurdy had appeared to suffer earlier — from terror, he'd thought — and remembered entertainers at fairs who escaped coils of rope by contracting their muscles. The long-lived holotainer's bizarre athleticism had never been in doubt, here was another of his many extraordinary skills.

'Free us with your joy, O Prince of Darkness, Fire-giver!'

'No guilt!' screeched Thin. 'No thought restrict! No meekness! No guilt!'

'Kill and delight. Delight in thy glory.'

'We shall go down to the altars in Hell.'

'Satanas venire!'

Hurdy-Gurdy pressed close to Seth as though huddling for comfort. A blade rasped against the cords binding his feet. All the floggers' attention was on the circle. They were beginning a slow, purposeful procession round and round the sacrifice. Jojo screamed for mercy.

'How did you...?' hissed Seth.

TWENTY-EIGHT

'Hid the knife in my boot,' replied Gurdy.

Then Seth's legs were free. All he needed were his hands.

The ritual was nearing its climax. No time for freeing his hands. No time for anything. Still, Gurdy's knife sawed at his bindings. The Floggers chanted and cracked their whips against the despised, dunghill earth in a rhythm led by Maister Gil.

Kindness is weakness. Mercy is weakness.

'Let the humble and feeble die in their misery!'

Kindness is weakness. Mercy is weakness.

'Satanas venire!'

Kindness is weakness. Mercy is weakness.

'Feast now, Prince! Feast from the cup!'

The knife raised high, ready to be thrust down into Jojo's heart. The strong blood would bubble up for Satan to drink. For the Mistresses to slurp avidly — oh, he had seen it, he had seen it! — fresh, young blood to be dripped into a cup and shared like elixir among the faithful.

Seth leapt to his feet. With hands still bound, he charged forward, head down, pushing through the circle of startled floggers, roaring defiance.

Suddenly Maister Gil was in his way, mouth open to cry out in rage or shock. Seth hesitated one moment then brought his head down with savage force, his forehead smashing into the flogger's nose, splintering it like matchwood in a leather sack, blood spurting. Gil fell away.

Simultaneously, dark shapes appeared. Leaping, bounding, part human, part hare. The knife hovered in its descent towards Jojo's heart. Headlong Seth launched himself. The knife rose and stabbed down once more. A corner of his consciousness registered a hare-like creature kicking a flogger in the face, so his neck snapped back. A gun banging. His long dive ended in a crump on Jojo's chest, face down, beating the knife tip by an instant as it arched.

The blade ripped into Seth's back: he screamed: it pierced deep, an inch or so from his spine. Lights danced. Flashed. Red. Gold. Cobalt blue. Two suns were beside his own: Jojo's wide, terrified eyes. Such pain! Such pain! He became nothing else.

Except, in a place beyond pain, odd joy touched him. He had saved Jojo, given his life for his friend, his love. Why hadn't he told him when there was still time? He saw clearly in a flash of knowledge. Love was the sharpest torture. Had not his mother's death taught that? And now he would never see Averil again. Half his life a desire to protect himself by hurting those he feared must either loathe or leave him. That fear had led him, step by blind step, to foulness. Not just in the eyes of the one he'd found to love, but family, friends, community. But it was all worked through. All finished. All his mistakes led to this sacrifice. He had saved Jojo. He had saved his friend.

In that last moment — summoned from weary, futile struggle — Seth Pilgrim glowed then went blank.

So he never saw how Fat Mistress rolled him off Jojo like a dead pig. Raised her knife again. And with her considerable weight behind the blow, stabbed down.

TWENTY-NINE

'How come it's always me as gets the worst jobs?' he complained. Complaining always made him feel better.

Tom Higginbottom had parted from Michael at dawn, rowing with a dozen men in his flat-bottomed coastal trader, a variant on the traditional Baytown coble. Pushing out of Lindisfarne Harbour, they sailed past the castle and round the island.

Close to the rocky shore, with a local fisherman as pilot, they had rowed to the north end of Lindisfarne, a voyage of a few miles. There they had pulled the boat aground in a quiet, secluded bay, concealing it and themselves behind jutting rocks that formed a natural gulley as the tide retreated.

'How far are we from the bastards?' he asked their Lindisfarner guide, an odd-looking chap by Tom Higginbottom's estimation. But then he found that true of most folk not from Baytown, especially closer to home in Whitby or Filey. You had to watch them buggers especially hard — the worst kind of stranger because they dressed and talked just like yourself. Still, the folk from Holy Island weren't too hard to understand, and Tom considered himself a tolerant man.

'They beached their ships about a mile west of here at Snook Point. Nigh where the island meets the causeway to the mainland,' explained the Lindisfarner. 'There's a stretch of high dunes we can use as cover if we stay low. Get right up close without 'em seeing us.'

'Aye?'

The Lindisfarner had nodded.

'That's your job, feller,' said Tom. 'We'll be happy to oblige with the rest.'

An hour or so later, as the kind of light Tom termed 'mucky' turned clear, tensions were building in the raiding party on the foreshore. For a while, they had heard gunshots coming from the direction of the village. Fusillades that stopped suddenly and resumed a few minutes later, only to stop then start again. This pattern repeated several times. No Jocks had wandered their way so far, nor were they likely to leave the safety of their camp.

What must follow set palms sweating among the Baytown men. Not for the first time, Tom regretted bringing his eldest son, Ben, a strapping lad of twenty-one. God alone knew what the boy's mam would say if she learned of the harm's way he had been placed in. At least, having him close meant Tom could keep an eye on his son. Small comfort in that.

'Now then,' he told his men, veterans of vicious battles with Big Jacko five years before, 'we don't know how many there'll be left to guard yon ships. I can't think it'll be many. Them that has been left aren't going to be big on fighting. The bastards sailed here for robbery, and the only loot at this end of the island is sand and sea-tilth. So the hardest among 'em will be with their kings, attacking the village. The twats.'

'What if there's too many of 'em for us to handle?' asked a fellow fisherman, a distant cousin of Tom's, though that could be said of most folk in Baytown.

'Why, John Ackroyd,' replied Higginbotton, scornfully, 'we do exactly as I've said. They won't know what's hit 'em if we're quiet.'

It all sounded easy enough when you put it that way. Tom suspected it might not work out so smooth.

TWENTY-NINE

'Dad! Dad! Look!' cried Ben.

A rocket had gone up to the south, the direction of Lindisfarne village. Its trail rose high and boomed into a flower of smoke. The low toll of a forlorn bell reached out from the castle.

'It's starting proper, I reckon,' muttered Tom, fingering his lucky charm of a shark's tooth. Even if it had gone a tinge of grey over the years, it had kept him safe through the horrors of the Crusades and many a sudden storm out to sea. In the next half hour, he would need all the luck he could get.

* * *

Near the village, the Scots halted, as Michael Pilgrim knew they would. He was getting a measure of King Duncaine's style by now. The King of Buchan wouldn't advance without a damned good look first.

Michael stood alongside Cuthbert by the old visitors' car park at the northern entrance to the village. Every so often, he glanced over to the northwest for signs of smoke. As he had told Tom, ripeness was all. If the smoke rose too early, the Jocks wouldn't be committed to their attack. Too late, it wouldn't matter anyway.

'What's this road called?' he asked Cuthbert.

'Chare Ends.'

'Get the men ready to use it at short notice.'

He had gathered his horsemen and thirty foot soldiers as a first barrier to the Scots. With luck, the Jocks would think this the best they'd got.

Bagpipes wailed, and drum tattoos started among the mass of unruly men half a mile off. He noticed from the progress of their banners that King Adair had joined his brother-in-law and that they appeared to be debating strategy. Focussing his binoculars, Michael didn't like the direction of King Duncaine's pointing arm. The bastard seemed to be urging King Adair to take his force around the western outskirts of the village. At the same time, Duncaine would attack the front, thus outflanking his defenders and trapping anyone lurking in the houses. Just the very thing Michael would have done in his place. Which was why it must be prevented fast.

He turned his binoculars northwest. Still, no smoke.

'Mount up!' he ordered his horsemen. 'And Cuthbert, you bring your men up behind us. March slow with drum beating. Make as much noise as you can.'

Cuthbert examined him sceptically. 'You sure?'

'Sure as oak.'

With that, Michael led his horsemen in a canter towards the dense mass of Scots, well over two hundred by his count.

'Aim only for the kings,' he told them, 'and the flag bearers. Picketers! You know what to do.'

Off their horses they slipped, the picketers looping reins in a steel rod driven into the ground. Gun barrels went up as they formed a line. He heard Cuthbert's men cheer as they had been instructed, slowly advancing up the causeway road, away from the car park. The Lindisfarne drummer, an enthusiastic lad, commenced a busy tattoo.

Michael could see the Jocks gawping and looking around for a trap. Forty or fifty attacking two hundred: surely here was some trick.

'Aim. Fire!'

An echoing volley rang out across the flat fields. At this range accuracy was possible. A bullet struck the King of Fife's standard-bearer. Down the flag tumbled.

'Load! One more! Fire!'

Another ragged volley. The Scots were agitated now, perhaps he had overplayed his hand. If they lost discipline and charged, his scheme might be trampled under their bare, horny feet.

A cry went up.

TWENTY-NINE

'Smoke! Smoke!'

He faced northwest as bullets and arrows whistled and skipped around them. One of his musketeers went down.

'That's enough!' he shouted. 'Mount! Back to Chare Ends!'

He checked his fallen comrade for signs of life then stripped him of gun and cartridge bag. Bullets whined as they cantered back toward the village, leading Cuthbert's panting men.

'What were all that for?' asked the fisherman.

'Bait,' shouted Michael.

Glancing back through his binoculars, he saw King Adair and King Duncaine in a passionate debate. Well done, Tom, he thought, now the bastards really have something to talk about.

* * *

Twenty minutes earlier, two heads had poked up an inch from the top of a sand dune. One belonged to Tom Higginbottom, the other to his Lindisfarne Nuager guide. Below lay an expanse of sand growing slowly as the tide retreated. On it were fifteen fat-bottomed boats, six of them large for the standards of that age, capable of a full hold of cargo or men. The rest were little bigger than the Nuager birlinns, light, frisky craft.

Gulls cried and dipped near the surf, a scene ancient as seasons. Before men brought their capacity for folly and love to Holy Island, the gulls had cried just so, melancholy calls lacing sea to sky. And would do so still when mankind had gone.

Tom's head withdrew. 'How many did you count?' he asked the Nuager.

'Four or five armed ones guarding the causeway by the old road,' whispered the other. Their voices blended with the murmur of surf and wind stirring the grass.

'Aye, me too.'

'Another fifteen or so round the ships.'

'Aye. Did you notice the fire they've got going to cook their fucking porridge? Pot's as big as a house.'

Despite their tension, both men grinned. Everyone knew all Jocks existed on a diet of oat porridge, whisky, and a creature like a hedgehog called haggis. It would have amazed Tom many Scots had theories of their own about what Yorkshire folk ate.

'That big fire will come in handy,' Tom said darkly.

'Looks like the only trouble they expect is from the direction of the causeway. Even then, they don't expect that,' responded the Nuager.

'I reckon they're not wrong. We'll get no help from that direction.'

Tom crawled on his belly down to a slack in the dunes and joined the men crouching there. All carried guns, swords, axes. And knew how to use them. On their backs were heavy rucksacks and slung bags.

'Game's on,' said Tom, using a favourite expression of his Dad's. 'I want all but them big bugger ships ablaze before the porridge-eating turds can fart. We mustn't burn 'em all. With me?'

Grunts of assent.

Nothing more need be said. Nor were excess words Tom Higginbottom's way. He led a crawl to the top of the last dune before the beach and waved everyone flat. Popping his head over, he surveyed the ships and their guardians. Nothing changed. The guards on the causeway were tough-looking customers; the rest seemed readier for a day's sailing or ship repair than a good ruck.

'Stay low,' he commanded.

With a swift wriggle, he was over the dune and moving in a crouch. A dozen men followed. Still no alarm. He could smell mutton simmering, wood smoke.

'Get 'em out!' he hissed.

Six bags were eased from shoulders. Flint wheel lighters prepared.

TWENTY-NINE

Wasting no time, Tom Higginbottom jogged towards the big fire beside the beached boats where the Jock sailors had congregated. He was halfway there when a young lad glanced their way.

'Fook!' screeched the lad.

'Give 'em a load!' ordered Tom.

Bang. Crack. Six muskets were discharged at close range. Almost as many men tumbled or clutched limbs.

Tom knew the value of surprise. Pulling out sabre and pistol, he led the way, shooting an old man in scale armour who dared to wave a sword at him, slashing another on the shoulder with his sabre so that the Jock lost his arm. Oaths. Screams of pain. Sulphurous scents of gunpowder. Stunned at this sudden reversal, the defenders of the Scots' camp fled.

'Reload! Reload!' he ordered.

Just in time, the guards on the causeway road ran to the dunes to attack. Twelve muskets and blunderbusses met their charge. Followed by pistol fire. All but one took a crippling bullet. Wounded, he skidded to a halt in the sand then followed the fleeing sailors.

'Burn the fuckers!' Tom bellowed, heading for the ships. 'Fast as you can.'

While six men guarded them from attack, jars of oily pitch were poured on boats and touched with burning sticks from the cooking fire. Bombs in clay pots were planted on hull planking and fuses lit. Sharp cracks followed, staving hulls and spraying splinters of wood. Black columns of smoke spewed upward. The men worked frantically to feed the fires with anything flammable, especially sails and tarred ropes.

Though tempted to destroy all the boats, Tom remembered Michael Pilgrim's plan. Three larger craft were spared along with a smaller. The last thing anyone wanted was to trap a large body of desperate men on this small island.

Nearly twenty Jocks were down with only a single Baytowner wounded — luckily not his son, Ben. He found the lad by a man with a terrible gash in his gut, blood pulsing in gouts every time he breathed.

'I did this, Father,' said Ben.

Tom reckoned his son looked just like his mother when troubled of mind. Twenty-one and he had just killed his first man. Higginbottom wished he could have said the same at his age.

'Get ready for the off, lad,' he said. 'I'm in high hopes we'll have to run faster than foxes.'

* * *

Wreaths of black smoke rose from Snook Point. Outside Lindisfarne village, the Scots army milled in confusion. Michael Pilgrim examined them through his binoculars. Now's the moment, he thought.

Somewhere among the Scots, the Kings of Fife and Buchan must be in urgent parlay. He prayed they were quarrelling. Given King Adair's caution when it came to putting his men in harm's way, the prospect of burning boats could hardly appeal.

Cuthbert watched, too, neither speaking. Go on, thought Michael, just do it. Then something in the milling mass of Scots changed. King Adair of Fife's banner was in motion. It was advancing at a very brisk pace indeed, except not towards the village, but away.

The diversion had worked better than he'd dreamed possible. Elation and hope flooded Michael Pilgrim. The King of Fife himself was scurrying like a spider with all legs working to save his means of escape, splitting his forces at the critical moment of attack. King Duncaine of Buchan, however, was staying put, determined to crush the puny force of fishermen and farmers set against him, to harvest a crop of revenge, honour, and blood.

TWENTY-NINE

Whatever cheer Michael might have felt soon faded.

'They're coming,' he muttered.

Still far outnumbering the Nuagers, better armed and trained than them, and a hundred times more experienced in the black arts of killing, they came on fast.

* * *

Lindisfarne had hosted comings, goings through years unimaginable: mammals long extinct when Ice Ages melted; spear-casting hunters before any thought of history; then warriors, farmers, churchmen and their servants, saints and sinners, so many, so many... Vikings burning, looting; sheep nibbling ashen remains of wooden houses shot through with young grass; more farmers; fishermen; then churchmen with gangs of masons, this time to throw up splendid stone walls... on, on until roof collapse and wall collapse, the modern village constructed of stolen stone, its pattern of streets and houses shadowed by the ruined priory, cars, visitors, families with buckets and spades... And now, another coming, going; uninvited guests, bearing sharp iron and gunpowder, as so often before...

In streets blocked with old cars and debris to create killing zones, small battles raged. King Duncaine's troops, maddened by skirmishers picking at them from a distance, surged into the village, all order lost.

At a barricade, peace-loving Nuagers discharged pistols and muskets at point-blank range, men hacked one another and fell, clambered and wrestled, screamed oaths or begged for mercy, stared in frantic hate and fear. Men cornered in a building were dragged out, foolish to surrender, a bludgeoning to death all their clemency. Screams pierced the steady crack of muskets, rifles, the occasional roar of a blunderbuss, barrels, and pans, flaring sparks, belching smoke. Clangs of swords, axes, bellows as a fisherman's net entangled an armoured laird, and he was surrounded, his face caved in by a sledgehammer.

Sudden charges cleared streets like waves rushing between rocks, then retreated, only to push forward again, each time a little deeper into the village, each time probing for its small central green before the ruined priory.

And Michael Pilgrim was everywhere, holding back the most disciplined of King Duncaine's men, loading, firing until nearly all his cartridges were gone. Resorting to the City-sword no armour could withstand, he sliced open a champion bearing shield, chainmail and axe, so the man's followers retreated in panic.

Friends' fates were beyond his power. Instead, the sickening realisation grew that even with King Adair of Fife's men diverted back to the boats, they were losing street by street, hemmed in from north and west into the old graveyard before the ivy-clad priory ruins.

Gathering thirty men in a lull, they charged. Then numbers told once more, back, back they were pushed. Finally, all that remained of his forces gathered in the graveyard; the rest were either dead or hiding in houses. Others kneeled before the King of Buchan and received the sole mercy of a swift death. Flushed by victory, blood-spattered, King Duncaine was beyond taking prisoners, too many of his closest allies and companions shot or mangled.

'Finish the bastards!' he ordered, and his men roared approval. Weapons clashed on shields. Guns were hastily loaded. The end of his battle for honour, for vengeance, for justice was at hand.

* * *

'Is this all we have left?' asked Gover.

A few dozen Nuagers, many wounded, all exhausted, stood ready to throw down their arms.

Gover repeated his question, shaking Michael Pilgrim's arm.

TWENTY-NINE

'I heard you the first time,' Michael said.

Blood flowed from a gash on the City-man's cheek. In his hand was the City-sword taken from the Prince O'Ness. Michael had seen him chop a man in two and shoot several others. There were good reasons why Gover had outlived the Great Dyings when nearly the entire human race perished. He possessed an instinct for survival without scruple.

Michael glanced down at a youth from Skye. The lad had taken a gunshot to the chest and was screaming in agony. Iona of Skye bent over him, offering water. Whether she had even fought, Michael did not know. For her sake, he hoped she would perish without blood weighing her spirit. Who knows, her soul might even fly up to her Happy Planet. Just as his own brother — poor James, so sorely-missed — once believed he would soar to Christ's Heaven on angel wings. Somehow it no longer mattered.

He pointed towards the village green. A few desultory gunshots rang out.

'They are gathering for a last charge that will wipe us out,' he told Gover. 'I have failed you all.'

Michael hung his head and sat heavily on a broken pillar from the old priory church. 'I was too confident in my own cunning,' he muttered. 'Too arrogant. We should not have fought so many.'

Gover inspected him as one might a curious piece of fauna. 'Goodness, Pilgrim, you are downhearted. The indomitable Pilgrim is defeated and wishes to surrender to despair? From a psychological perspective, you make an interesting case study. The man of pluck and virtue beholds his reflection in the pond, like Narcissus, and spies failure.'

'Shut up, Gover.'

'Protector of the North — did you think up that vainglorious title, by the way?'

'Shut the fuck up, Gover. No, I didn't.'

'Oh, that's more like it! A bit of temper. Shame it's directed at the wrong enemy. Our brawny Narcissus, our pocket St George, might even start quoting Shakespeare like his noble granddaddy, and think himself so cultured and wise.'

Michael Pilgrim found he was on his feet, fists clenched, ready to smack the smug expression from Gover's face. How he longed to do so! But he became aware Iona was nearby. People were watching, waiting for him to deliver a miracle. His weary brain struggled for a way.

'They are gathering a last charge,' he repeated. 'We have only a few minutes. As I see it, there are three options. Fight here and be overwhelmed. Make a run for the harbour then castle, but I think that's what they expect. The only way still open to us is to the south.' He pointed out a field of ploughed soil ending in a pebbly beach. Beyond that, separated from Holy Island by a narrow channel of sea, was another tiny islet Michael knew to be called St Cuthbert's Isle. The tide was receding steadily but not fast enough for his liking.

'The one course I can think of,' he said, 'is to wade across to yon little island, hold it for as long as it takes for the sea to retreat and expose the sands and channels between here and the mainland. Maybe we could squelch and wade across to yon shore. A few miles, I make it. Cuthbert, what do you think?'

The leader of the Lindisfarne Nuagers had survived the vicious street fighting unscathed. He followed Michael Pilgrim's pointing finger.

'Yes,' he mused, 'some of us might get across. But there are quicksands out there. It's a desperate way.'

'You mentioned three courses,' said Gover, examining St Cuthbert's Isle with brooding intensity. 'What is your third?'

'Surrender.'

Michael paused to let the idea sink in. As for him, he knew what fate he would choose. Maybe he deserved nothing less, considering the number of lives he had stolen and squandered at the behest of the City in the Crusades. His wheel of fortune had launched its final revolution.

Suddenly, he remembered his son, George, back in Baytown. How poor a father he had turned out, drawn away to help other people's children more often than his own. The lad no doubt viewed him as a stranger. Too late for aught else. Too late for bonds of love built by little moments, casual hours together, jokes, silliness, chasing one another across the beach where the tides came and went. How else was love ever built between father and child?

Disgust for the world washed over Michael, a scorn shared by most of his generation. Yet the more they struggled to set things right, the more savagery seemed to tighten its grip. Will we ever learn, he wondered, can we ever learn? Look at how his ancestors had poisoned the earth on which they relied.

He realised Gover was speaking.

'Perhaps there is a fourth course, Pilgrim. I did anticipate something like it last night, but I was only considering the flooded boundary ditch round the village — in the event that little plan proved impractical. Our foe was unobliging enough to avoid paddling across en masse. But I still have the device in my bag, Pilgrim. Here, right here! Why ever not?'

Michael nodded uncomprehendingly. 'I'm sure you're right.' He turned to Cuthbert. 'What do you think of the three options?'

But Gover was still talking.

'Ah, genius!' he declared. 'The more I consider it, the more obvious it seems. A delicious chemical reaction!'

'Speak plainly,' demanded Michael. 'We do not have long left.'

Gover could not stop chuckling.

'We must take shelter there,' said the City-man, pointing at St Cuthbert's Isle. 'And persuade them to wade over en masse and attack us. Do you know what? I believe those bloodthirsty brutes just might.'

Michael frowned at the tiny island capped by a ruined chapel. From movements in the village, he could tell King Duncaine had almost surrounded them. At least the island offered a faint possibility of escape across the exposed sands as the tide ebbed.

'Trust me, Pilgrim,' said Gover. 'Do you imagine I want to die?'

That question decided Michael. If anyone on this earth lived his whole life to never risk losing it, it was Blair Gover. Over on the village green, a skirl of bagpipes commenced a wail and drone. King Duncaine was ready for his last charge.

'To the island!' Michael cried. 'Quick as you can. For your lives!'

THIRTY

Helen spent a frantic hour pushing through drifting crowds. Tens of thousands filled Mughalia's enormous plazas, some jubilant and intoxicated, others strangely passive. Their faces like strangers in disturbing dreams. Some stripped, cleansing themselves for the future in one of the city's many ornamental ponds or lakes. Others danced in silent, sinister processions, sharing pills from ornate boxes to celebrate the birth of the Life Perfected. No one recognised her as Blair Gover's former mistress.

She arrived at a wide tunnel constructed entirely of human and other animal bones: skulls, tibias, clavicles and ribs, every type of bone imaginable from the Great Dyings. It marked the entrance to the Five Poisons.

How might one savour transgression when the only real sin was Discordia? Mughalia had the answer, for the requisite number of credits. Luxurious transgression did not come cheap. Its true cost lingered unseen in souls sipping the Five Poisons. There, what should have been shunned grew natural.

Just then, few Beautifuls entered or left the tunnel. Today was no occasion for furtive, compensatory pleasures. Today marked the restoration of freedom in countless minds, not least the official consciousness: it was much safer to be monitored as someone publicly rejoicing and praising the Ruling Council.

Helen entered the wide passageway, the echo of her footsteps on the marble floor dulled by walls and ceilings of bones. After a shadowy, twisting quarter mile, the path narrowed, terminating at an obsidian door. Shimmering golden drones stood guard. Helen presented her screen, and a sizable number of credits vanished. She wondered how Averil could afford entry here. Yet Marv and Merle had heaped clothes, jewellery, and a powerful screen on the naive girl. Perhaps the Five Poisons would be another gift to help corrupt her.

Helen projected Averil's image to the guardian drones.

'Did this person come here? Perhaps an hour ago?'

A hopeless question. The Five Poisons kept their secrets. The drones did not even reply.

A dishevelled Beautiful sat on a bench of bones, drugged, muttering streams of nonsense and cruel laughter.

'Pay for me to go in!' he cried. 'I will be your slave. Better than any Angel.'

Helen showed him Averil's holo-image.

'Do you recognise this girl?'

'Pay for me. Then I'll tell you.'

'Tell me first.'

'I recognise you,' he whined. 'Oh yes, Blair Gover's fiddle-playing paramour. Fa-la-la! I remember, you see.' He shivered, twitched. 'I remember everything.'

Despair contorted the man's face. 'I must go back in there! To undo what I have done.' A malicious giggle mastered his pain. 'Or do it right this time! Yes, nice and right.' Then he raged, 'Lying bitch! Bitch! Yes, go in after her, bitch. Frazzle your soul like me. You'll pay! You'll pay then.'

Helen hurried past the guardian drones into darkness.

* * *

THIRTY

The precept was simple, bring your own transgressions and run with them. For a sickened moment, Helen wondered what gloating sins had seized Averil when she donned the golden prayer-cap engineered to unleash one's darkest self — then she was negotiating delicious hells of her own brain's creation...

Drifting, drifting, not just in her mind, her body moving from chamber to chamber like a sleepwalker, cell to hexagonal cell, honeycombs blessed with stimuli to discover repressed sweetness, provoke pleasurable perversities, to magnify coyly vile fantasies lurking in the subconscious. Joyous pursuits innocent because entirely wrong; wrong because innocent. Here, the slow de-limbing of a favourite puppy or kitten could intrigue a whole hour, enjoyed *in flagrante* with a live animal, before tossing the carcase aside in search of fresh meat. Over in that cell, lingering, drawn-out transgressions, some milder than others. All involved power, one way or another, whether surrendered or inflicted on another living creature.

Living faces also floated around one in the Five Poisons, fellow seekers after sweet ugliness, features ghostly yet distinct enough to be recognisable. Though Helen searched, nowhere could she find innocent Averil Pilgrim among the shrieking, gasping spectres she encountered. After a prolonged episode with her little sister Mhairi when both were mere girls, she could bear no more.

Pressing a switch on her prayer-cap helmet, Helen was guided to the entrance. She awoke in an anteroom just off the tunnel of bones. The empty eye sockets of skulls leered and stared as she staggered past. Her heart still beat with dreadful intensity.

* * *

Helen found herself on an enormous boulevard flanked by tiers of marble steps to form low valleys, streambeds for crowds to gather and flow. Flow they did; a growing tension moved the jostling rivers of bodies.

Dazed by the Five Poisons, her mind still reeling from after-memories of vile indulgences, she drifted helplessly. Many of the Beautifuls hemming her were hysterical from hours of intoxicants, days in some cases. A growing number used personal narco-applicators to find refuge in that trance-like state known as *intermission*, where thought and emotion were shut down to avoid madness or despair. A necessary escape route for all Beautifuls, as the prospect of endless days stretching ahead could make reality unbearable.

Among the hundreds of thousands drawn to the Grand Autonomy were many unused to close, extended proximity with humans. By its nature, the Beautiful Life was solitary, as would be the Life Perfected, offering as it did a world where one might create casts of living toys to fill the emptiness: courtiers, slaves, flatterers, a chance to dispense with tedious fellow humans altogether.

Not all secluded themselves in fogs of chemical intermission. Those whose wits remained sharp understood the shuffling rivers of people had a destination. Vast holo-messages glowered in the sky:

PROCEED TO THE GRAND BOULEVARD!
BEHOLD THE LIFE PERFECTED!

Instrumental renditions of My Perfect Life boomed, drugged Beautifuls muttering the words like a charm as they shuffled forward.

Helen arrived at the Grand Boulevard. She stumbled on something soft, a body trampled by unheeding feet. A woman nearby fainted and folded onto the marble pavement. No one reached to save her. She vanished and was consumed by the mob.

Cries of pain and panic became more frequent in the massed ranks.

THIRTY

Helen feared a stampede, mindless, primitive. At that moment, drones flew low over the crowd, spraying out a fine, perfumed mist. Helen covered her nose and mouth, hiding her face beneath her hood. All around, frightened Beautifuls relaxed and sighed as they breathed in soothing joy-spray.

Suddenly synth-trumps blared out deafening fanfares. Collective excitement swelled as a long parade of aircars and carriers appeared at the far end of the Grand Boulevard.

How long has this been prepared, thought Helen? Someone must have arranged this spectacle long before today. Confirmation of her suspicion flew slowly overhead.

First, courtiers and counsellors of the Ruling Council in aircars, trailing gaudy bunting. These worthies cast out handfuls of gold-leaf petals to the people below. Next, flying cages projecting huge, close-up holograms of their inmates, cowering men and women found guilty of Discordia, their mouths working as they begged for mercies they had rarely allowed others.

Helen ducked fearfully. A few of the prisoners were known to her. Old friends and colleagues of Blair's, fellow Founding Visioners from the early days of the Beautiful Life.

Memories of school history lessons surfaced. In Ancient Rome there had been parades like this called triumphs, where conquerors displayed captives to cheering crowds, borne in a glorious chariot with a slave appointed to whisper in the god-like hero's ear:

Remember thou art mortal... Remember thou art mortal...

Last came a huge air carrier of unusual design. It resembled a glowing Mayan step-pyramid. At its apex, Marvin and Merle Brubacher lounged on gilded thrones, along with a handful of others Helen recognised as members of the Ruling Council.

Seeing their haughty, flushed faces, Helen, at last, comprehended the treachery and guile of the Brubachers. How had she been so blind?

Their one fear had been a man with sufficient authority to defend the Founding Vision: Blair Gover. No wonder they had lured her to Mughalia as a precaution. Now they acknowledged the crowd like emperor and empress, secure in their rule.

Lesser worthies surrounded them on the lower steps of the flying pyramid, confidantes and bureaucrats and leading progenitors, all waving to the crowd. At Marv and Merle's feet like a pet puppy, given a chair to denote special favour, perched Averil Pilgrim, her hands resting on a pregnant stomach padded out to make it more conspicuous and adorned with flashing lights.

Helen reached up, waving to catch the girl's attention. 'Averil! Averil!'

Her tiny voice was lost to the cheering crowd. Then the glowing pyramid flew on. She was left to mourn and weep alone among strangers.

* * *

Two hours later, back in Marvin and Merle Brubacher's mansion, Helen packed hastily. She had little enough. A few clothes and the modest screen she had been allowed. Most precious of all, though, was the Baytown Jewel, for it connected her to a saner world. As ever, its solidity comforted her. Untainted gold etched with a relief of mother and babe, decorated with a glinting sapphire, its blueness that of cloudless skies, summer oceans.

Helen's fingers brushed the jewel's golden clasp, and she was tempted to open it, for the jewel had a small, hidden cavity for prayers inscribed on parchment, to protect its wearer from the plague. But there was no time. Helen hung it around her neck, concealing the locket between her breasts, the gold cooling her skin.

She must go. If the Brubachers found her, she did not doubt a prompt

THIRTY

sterilisation would follow. Or maybe even a drawn-out one. It said much for her irrelevance that they let her roam free. Where could she go, after all? Her whereabouts were easily monitored via her screen and other surveillance systems, along with all the Five Cities' residents. Only the most favoured Beautifuls possessed invisibility codes.

Helen hurried through the Brubachers' silent compound until she reached the small bungalow where Synetta lived.

* * *

The doors were firmly closed, windowpanes dimmed to black. Helen activated the visitor sensor. She glanced around fearfully. Coming here was folly. Synetta would not answer, let alone freely offer what she needed. Perhaps she was dead already, or lay dying alone.

She was about to flee when the door slid open, releasing a faint, rotten scent.

'Synetta?'

No reply.

Gingerly, Helen entered the small bungalow, soon reaching its central living area. As before, Synetta lay on the sofa beneath a silk coverlet. Tired brown eyes met Helen's.

'Why have you come?' Synetta asked softly. Her breath came in light, painful gasps.

'To see how you are. Whether you are better.'

Helen took a seat beside the sick woman. Close up, the putrid smell was nauseating, reminiscent of the Great Dyings, the reek of buboes after they burst.

Synetta glanced away. 'That is not why you came.'

For a moment, Helen was tempted to protest. Or lie. One glance at the fading woman on the sofa argued otherwise.

'You are right,' she said. 'I hoped you would lend me the use of your screen, Synetta. So I could escape Mughalia. You know that if I am caught here, I will be killed. They have no reason to keep me alive now, do they?'

Synetta nodded.

'But enough of that. How are you?' Helen asked gently. 'Is it worse? The last time I came here, well, your breast...'

'It is worse,' breathed Synetta. She coughed, flecks of blood appearing on her lips. 'My organs are failing. How can that be?'

Tears swam in her eyes. Helen reached out for Synetta's hand.

'Perhaps it is your time. Just as mine approaches, I think. No magic can save either of us. We deluded ourselves otherwise for a while, that is all. What must be will be, always, sooner, later.'

Synetta squeezed Helen's hand back. 'Yes, of course, you are right. I am so glad you came.'

A sad smile touched her mouth. It was the mouth of a lovely young woman, a mouth meant for excited talk and kisses.

'Do you ever think about who you used to be, Helen? Before all this. You know, as I lay here, my mind went back to the time before. As if... As if, all that followed meant nothing. Do you know, I have lived a hundred years in fear, especially after Marvin found uses for me. Even now he makes me afraid. All those long years, Helen, the things I've seen and done. And for what? You see, I can remember just how it was before the plagues. How happy I was.'

Helen nodded. 'Why not tell me about it?'

She listened as Synetta spoke, hesitant to begin, then brittle and gay, forgetting Helen, consumed by memories...

'I was just a spoilt little girl, you know. Daddy was so very rich! He kept me safe behind electric fences and guards while America went crazy around us. But we were happy. I had two sweet dogs and a horse called Bilbao, because he was Spanish. And though I was lovely, a veritable Daddy's princess in a tower, I wasn't anyone special, really.

Then I discovered something to be good at... Pass me my screen, Helen. I will show you.'

The screen projected a holovideo into the air and, suddenly, there was Synetta at eighteen, gyrating in unison with seven other girls, haloes of hair floating as they danced, kicked high, thrust out hips and thighs, pompoms twirling provocatively towards the cheering crowd.

'I found this clip in the archives,' said Synetta. 'A miracle it survived. Look at me. Look at what I was meant to be, Helen!'

The slender body on the sofa almost mirrored that of the young cheerleader, dancing and smiling in the hologram. Except the heart could not be frozen in time or stay young forever, especially a heart wearied by loss.

'Why did we go so wrong?' asked Synetta. 'Daddy's main home and business were in Florida, you know, though he had a big place in Neo Rio, which was how I made it through. Marvin and Merle were our neighbours there. That's where Marvin first took a fancy to me, I guess. But why did it go so wrong, Helen? I didn't understand then. I still don't.'

Helen squeezed Synetta's hand tighter. 'Because we let it happen.'

'But the plagues? Why?'

'We were too passive, too obedient to those in control. And we still are. But don't think of it now. Look how lovely you were.'

For a while, they watched the clip of Synetta cheerleading. Then Helen rose.

'I must go. I have decided to walk into the jungle and vanish there. At least I shall be with nature at the end. And die on my own terms.' She laughed. 'I will leave my screen so no one can trace me. One up on Marvin and Merle, eh?'

Even when her body spasmed with a wave of pain, Synetta's big eyes did not waver from Helen's.

'I once dreamt of escaping them,' she said. 'They came to frighten me more than anything. I even made a plan so no one would know where I had gone. You see, I know too much about the Brubachers for them to ever let me be free.'

She gestured. Helen drew closer. 'Listen, and I will tell you.'

Helen listened while Synetta whispered her long-dreamt-of plan to escape. Then the sick woman sank back, exhausted. Taking up her screen a final time, she punched in a decisive code.

'Your eyes,' Synetta murmured, holding up the device. 'Quickly.'

The device logged Helen's retinas.

'Now your hands...'

Helen ran them over the screen's glossy surface.

'Your breath...'

Helen breathed her unique chemical vapour into the sensor.

Only then did Synetta pass the flat box to Helen.

'It's done,' she said. 'I have full clearance to deactivate facial recognition in Mughalia. Marv and Merle found it useful for me to wander unmonitored, so I could... Just keep the screen on you. Now you can cross the city unrecognised. And take this' —Synetta produced a small, short-barrelled handgun from beneath the coverlet— 'I kept it to kill myself if they came for me. But I'm too much of a coward.'

Helen took the weapon and looked curiously at the dying woman. 'But why?'

'Because you can escape from Marvin *for* me. I hate him! He, he made me call him Daddy; he wore a holomask of Daddy, whenever...'

'It's okay,' broke in Helen. 'Never mind him.'

'Plus, I want to help you. That way someone will still think fondly of me when I'm gone. But you must do one last thing for me, Helen. Don't hesitate, I have no cure. In fact, I know they will conduct horrible experiments on me to find out more about the sickness. I beg you!'

The lost cheerleader danced on and on in the hologram. The crowd cheered. Helen tried to persuade Synetta otherwise, but she would not be swayed. And though all must be alone at the end, as at the beginning, when eyes first open to seek love from an uncaring universe, Synetta did not close her eyes alone.

The small gun spoke once.

* * *

Night heavy on Mughalia, a tropical night, hot, humid and moth-haunted, scattered with bright stars. Except in the city, no stars were visible, drowned by light.

Exhausted crowds were thinning as Helen crossed central plazas and boulevards. Noble music accompanied vast holo-images dancing across the heavens: close-ups of the Ruling Council, magnificent Angels. Live broadcasts of Founding Visioners exiled en masse into the wilderness surrounding Mughalia, and likewise from all the other Cities. Long lists of names had been prepared for this moment. Naked men and women stumbled out into swamps and dark forests, suavity and power replaced by primal, primitive terror. The message was plain: Discordia against the Life Perfected would be ruthlessly punished wherever it existed.

Little wonder the streets were emptying. Safer to find a corner to sit out this coup and wait for calm to return.

As Helen walked, her face concealed behind a projection of the Mona Lisa and the codes in Synetta's screen, she tormented herself over Averil. Should she seek out her young friend, try to save her? True, the Brubachers had tempted the Baytown girl with a seat on their hideous pyramid during the triumphant parade. But it was Helen who had allowed sweet, innocent Averil to be corrupted.

At regular intervals, large aircarriers rose with a roar of engines into the night sky, bound for Albion or Mitopia, Han City, or Neo Rio. People packed in pressurised cabins risked sharing Synetta's gene infection, that is, if it could be transferred through airborne bacilli, like the plagues, breath-by-breath. No one seemed to care, or pretended not to. Anything to escape the stifling madhouse of Mughalia.

Towards midnight Helen reached an isolated monorail station on the outskirts of the city. Soon a sleek carriage shot into view, and she signalled for it to stop.

Climbing aboard, fear tightened her chest. Her hand crept to the stubby gun Synetta had given her.

A small group of Beautifuls muttered at the far end of the carriage. Among them, a man she recognised, the Supervisor of the colonia she'd visited with Averil — it seemed a lifetime ago — to witness human animals prepared for gladiatorial shows.

She sat with her back to them. The group fell silent, as if her presence made them wary. Suddenly she understood. Far from celebrating the new Life Perfected, these people were debating it. Clearly, some regretted the end of the Beautiful Life.

Concealed by her Mona Lisa holo-mask, Helen fell to brooding as the carriage sped from Mughalia towards the coast. Now and then, the Supervisor of the colonia glanced her way. His face shone with sweat, despite the air-conditioning. If he recognised Helen Devereux, he gave no sign.

* * *

When the monorail carriage reached Port Negombo, Helen Devereux was its only occupant. The others had alighted at a terminus halfway between the highlands and coast.

Night lay denser here than in Mughalia. A fetid stench of mangrove swamps blew in from the lagoon used as a safe haven for shipping. She left the terminus and walked briskly towards the dockside, little more than a mile off.

THIRTY

Synetta's voice lingered, describing a means of escaping Mughalia undetected. Aircars were always tracked, yet not all entry and exit points were monitored. Indeed, Negombo was deserted, without even a black-uniformed technician visible. No doubt they were in hiding.

Helen consulted the arrivals and departures on her new screen, marvelling at the access Synetta had been given to the Five Cities' central systems in her role as a spy for the Brubachers. Muttering a command, she watched numbers and words flash. There it was, precisely as Synetta had predicted; due to depart in an hour.

Guided by the screen, Helen passed a row of drone cargo vessels, loading and unloading containers. These were placed on conveyor belts and rolled off for transit, while others stacked themselves in ships' holds.

Helen came to a medium-sized drone ship and consulted her screen. It would do. It *must* do. She issued Synetta's pre-prepared override instructions to all surveillance systems on the vessel. Confirmation soon arrived. From now on, as far as the drone ship was concerned, Helen Devereux was invisible, even when making full use of its many facilities.

A ramp connected the ship to dockside, and she climbed warily. Yet nothing challenged her. Gun in one hand, screen held up as a bright torch in the other, Helen entered the dark hold and vanished.

Thirty minutes later, the ramp folded up into the vessel. Fusion engines powered. Without the need for a crew, the obedient drone ship left port for the open ocean. A small, frightened face peered through a plasti-glass porthole as the lights of Negombo dwindled then went dark.

* * *

A hundred miles away, up in lush, tropical hills surrounding the futuristic towers and plazas of Mughalia, a quite different departure commenced. In a pillared hall, a procession hundreds-strong approached wide double doors. At its head, aglow with finery, stepped what remained of the Ruling Council. Angels flanked these wise and puissant notables, along with more familiar drones.

Behind them, among a crowd of sycophants and place-seekers, came Averil Pilgrim, hands resting on her swollen stomach, glancing this way and that, feeling a mingling of awe, amazement, uncertain pride, and fear.

I shall become a Perfect forever and ever, she told herself. *I shall be Perfected forever.* The very thought trailed glory and wonder, though Averil could not help recollecting Helen's warning that the price for the Beautiful Life was perpetual sterility.

As she cradled the child in her womb, Averil dreaded its loss. But Marv and Merle would not allow such a calamity. It was typical of Helen to try to control her out of a sense of jealousy, yes, sheer jealousy. Somewhere in Mughalia her former mentor was hiding, afraid and abandoned, just as Averil herself had once cowered in pain when whipped by Maister Gil, tormented by Big Jacko's hideous queen. Just as she'd helplessly wept when they exposed her crippled child on the beach at Baytown, for the cold, heartless salt waves to carry him away…

Fantasises of power trumped those bitter memories. Helen would marvel how much influence Averil had with Marvin and Merle Brubacher, now Joint-Presidents of the Ruling Council no less. How she could persuade them to let Helen return freely to Baytown, as Curator, if that was what she wanted. And one day, years from now, perhaps, Averil would also return to the fishing village by the sea, except not as she had been, alone and neglected, but accompanied by Angels and drones. Of course, she would use her new power to rule the primitives benignly, accompanied by her child, the baby in her womb, forever and ever.

THIRTY

Marvin and Merle Brubacher passed through the high double doors. With an echoing clang, they closed. Averil was left outside among the flatterers and courtiers, to await their pleasure.

THIRTY-ONE

While Michael Pilgrim urged the remnants of his small army to wade across to St Cuthbert's Isle, Tom Higginbottom lay in the shelter of a grass-fringed sand dune, observing King Adair's tantrum.

There was nothing, in Tom's humble opinion, quite like a King in a rage. Half an hour earlier, Adair had split the Scots forces by dashing back to Snook Point as ribbons of black smoke ascended from his beached fleet. Although a vindication of Michael's strategy, it had not reassured Tom. The majority of the Jocks were still gathered to attack the village. He reckoned only seventy or eighty of the bastards had headed back to save their ships, leaving more than twice that number to be defeated by the Nuagers, which was a prospect Tom wouldn't bet an acorn on. Sure enough, not long after Adair dashed back towards Snook Point, Duncaine of Buchan advanced on the village, bagpipes and drums audible on the wind.

After that, all Tom could learn of the fighting in the village was gunshots. Not even houses burning. Whether his old pal prevailed was a mystery. Given the number of Jocks who had poured into the village, he feared the worse. Especially when silence descended on Lindisfarne save for the cries of gulls. Anything could be happening in there, but he knew full well that if the Scots had been bested, they would scarper back to their ships in dribs and drabs. No sign of that. Not a single straggler. Foreboding tightened into a clamp of pain.

It seemed impossible Michael Pilgrim might be dead or even captured, which amounted to the same thing. Losing his friend sat among the worst events he could imagine. All his life, Tom had valued and loved Michael as the stoutest of pals. Latterly, he had felt awe for the man who had been acclaimed Protector of the North, even an odd shyness in his presence. But that was all right. Tom detected no airs or graces in good old Michael, just leadership making him a tad colder, grimmer, broodier.

Meanwhile, King Adair fumed on the beach, mourning the burned and holed ships. Those still serviceable were searched carefully for hidden surprises. The surviving guards from Tom's raid knelt on the cold sand, awaiting punishment for their failure. So far, only one had lost his head as an example to the others.

Once more, Tom examined the village. The same silence as before.

Sliding backwards, he left the dune crest and padded with his head kept low to the boat, where it lay on the edge of the surf amidst weed-covered stone shelves. His own part of Michael's scheme had been entirely successful. What good it might serve if all went awry in Lindisfarne village was another matter.

'Well then, lads,' he said as they pushed the boat out into the waves and hopped aboard. 'We'll see what is happening in the harbour. If it looks hopeless, we'll make straight for Baytown and grieve as we go.'

The wide, flat-bottomed coastal trader was pushed out to sea, at which point Tom raised mast and sail. No one cared whether King Adair saw them now. Theirs was the only boat afloat.

* * *

It took little time for Michael to gather the remnants of his army. He suspected as many might be hiding in the village. If so, he wished them better luck than his own.

They waded across the channel to the islet, helping the wounded. Soon cold sea lapped above their waists; guns and powder were held high to avoid a soaking. Then they were stepping over stones onto St Cuthbert's Island, clothes and boots leaking. As usual, the wind whipped north, gusting steadily towards the village they had just abandoned. A few miles distant, Michael could see the mainland across a waste of mud, sand, and channels dotted with flocks of white birds. For them, there was no battle in the decaying village, only the daily struggle to feed and breed.

Michael looked back towards Lindisfarne. Warriors were running across the field at the rear of the priory to halt on the shingle beach they had just vacated. A handful at first, then more and more, along with the King of Buchan's midnight blue standard and Duncaine himself, claymore in hand.

Michael counted. At a rough one hundred, he stopped. Surely this horde wasn't made up of just Buchan's men. Many of the King of Fife's best warriors must have insisted on joining the battle. How else could they justify a share of the loot?

Schemes and stratagems and follies fell away like shackles from Michael Pilgrim. He sank to his knees, too tired to think, let alone command. Three cartridges remained in his satchel, but it hardly seemed worth reloading. The Scots spread out on the shore, taunting, bellowing insults, laughing at the hated Nuagers who had killed or maimed so many of their comrades, cousins, friends, brothers, neighbours. All they need do was wait, and the tide between Lindisfarne and St Cuthbert's Island would no longer be a barrier. As it was, less than a hundred feet of water lay between the two forces, much of that no more than knee-deep.

A hand shook Michael's shoulder. Gover pointed at the enemy.

'Persuade them to attack, Pilgrim. All of them! I need every one of them in a wide line attacking us like lemmings. Up, man! Chop! Chop!'

Michael stayed on his knees. It was restful there. And he made a smaller target.

'Why?' he said. 'The longer they delay, the more likely we can escape across the mud to the mainland. See how the tide is withdrawing. If we help each other, a few of us might make it across.'

'Get up, Pilgrim. On your feet, damn you!'

Slowly, reluctantly, Michael did as bid. The King of Buchan was conferring with his nobles, men in armour and fine cloaks.

'Do it, if you want to live, Pilgrim. I need all of them in the water, preferably in a nice little line.'

A line? A line? Anything else? How about singing pretty Highland songs and bearing gifts of haggis? But, why not? At the end of hope, why ever not?

'Everyone form a cordon on the shore,' Michael ordered, dragging Nuagers to their feet, who had collapsed as he had. Several had abandoned their weapons in the priory; Michael thrust stones into their hands.

'We need a line of our own facing theirs!'

When he came to Iona, she produced her sling and looked hard at him. He remembered an old story his grandfather had told of a shepherd boy with a sling and a giant called Goliath. Details were hazy, but he felt sure it ended well. Hope stirred.

'Can you use that thing?' he asked her.

A smudge of powder smoke on her cheek drew his eye. He resisted an urge to rub it clean. He was glad for her sake it was not blood, that stuff of life staining his own soul. So hard to wash clean. Yes, he was pleased for her.

'Watch me, Mister Star Man.' Her Highland lilt was defiant. 'I'll no more play the bonder in this life.'

'Where is Dameron?' Michael asked.

'Fallen. I... I saw him fall.'

What could he say? Nothing to the purpose.

'I'm sorry, Iona.' He shrugged helplessly. 'It seemed a good plan. And it almost worked. But they were too fierce for us. Too practised in war. I should have anticipated that.'

She met his eye. 'Still, we breathe.'

'Aye.'

Iona hesitated. 'Before the end, I wish to say sorry as well. You are no monster, Michael Pilgrim. I was wrong to name you as such. In times like this, the monster hiding in every heart is set free, whether we like it or no.'

'Thank you,' he said.

Cajoled and thrust into place, the line of Nuagers spread out at the water's edge. A few still had guns. And guts. Even in the short time it had taken to form up, the tide had withdrawn a little, shrinking the channel.

'Quickly!' urged Gover. 'Lure them into the water, you fool!'

Michael stared across at King Duncaine's retinue. They seemed in no great hurry to wade in. Taking up binoculars, he watched the big chief talking to a lad remarkably similar of features. Same jaw, nose; same dark hair. A son, perhaps? The resemblance warranted it. Close kin that was sure. Perhaps the new heir of Buchan, the new Prince O'Ness wanting his magical City-sword to seal the title.

Michael called out to the Nuagers. 'When I say drop your trousers, show those bastards your bare arses. And that is an order.'

A line of shocked faces.

'Just do it.'

Spotting a high point on the tiny island, Michael climbed to a ruined chapel and lay down on coarse grass still wet with dew, using the stonework as a gun rest. One by one, he laid out cartridges and percussion caps on his satchel. He loaded. Then he aimed slowly,

THIRTY-ONE

wind ruffling his hair. His mind emptied. Nothing mattered but the angle of the rifle, the point in space and time his bullet sought. He recollected a tiny leftward kick he'd noticed and adjusted the angle of the barrel minutely. His target bowed to his father then straightened to his full height, his chest square in Michael's sights. Michael aimed a fraction lower. Instinct squeezed his left index finger.

Bang! The rifle bucked against his shoulder. Smoke whipped away. He opened the breach, shook out the burnt paper cartridge, thrust home a second.

Michael shouldered the gun. The men in his sights were no longer stationary. The distance no greater than between two rival goalposts on a football pitch. Again, stillness in his mind. Emptiness.

Bang!

He snatched up the binoculars. Blinked to make sure.

'Show the bastards your arses!'

No triumph in his shout. While most of the Nuagers jeered and flashed white buttocks, he loaded his last cartridge and rejoined Gover. Across the shrinking water, the Scots roared. A few had already entered the seawater. From nowhere, bagpipes sounded their wailing summons. Drums beat a wild tattoo.

'What did you do?' asked Gover.

'Shot the King of Buchan's second son and heir' —Michael patted his stomach— 'Here, I think. In the gut. He'll be lucky to survive it. And, I reckon I winged one of his bigwig nobles, too' —He tapped his forehead— 'Right here. If they wanted vengeance before, now they want to eat our livers raw. It's your turn now, Gover. And it better be bloody good.'

* * *

Even so, the fury of the Scots' charge took Michael by surprise. They surged into the water, thrusting forward strong legs and bodies to be the first on St Cuthbert's Island. The few bullets that struck them had no effect, nor did Iona's slingshot, whatever miracle occurred in the Biblical tale.

Yet Gover seemed unfazed. He coolly produced two rectangular blocks attached to wires and controls taken from scavenged screens. When he activated a switch, a low humming commenced. Michael instantly felt uneasy. His nerves jangled, a tingle entered the marrow of his bones. The hairs on the back of his neck stirred.

Michael recognised the blocks as the power cells from the gravchutes, retrieved after they crash-landed in the Highlands. What use such batteries could possibly serve here baffled him. Even if Gover turned them into some kind of bomb, its blast would hit the Nuagers just as hard as the widely-spread horde in the water.

'I'm getting the fuck out of here, Gover!'

One by one, the Nuagers panicked, fleeing to the far side of the little island. From there, miles of sand and channels offered their last hope. Michael resolved to ditch all his equipment, boots and all, then take his chances with the quicksands.

'Stay away from the water!' warned the City-man.

Gover casually tossed the device into the channel where it sank. Michael's tingling sensation died away. He opened his mouth to protest. Was it for this he had killed yet another of King Duncaine's sons, guaranteeing horrible deaths for them all?

Then something started. The seawater where Gover had dropped the device bubbled, fizzed, popped. Michael sniffed an alien, metallic scent, foul yet caustic. His nostrils itched then stung. He coughed.

'It's working,' crowed Gover. 'I was certain it would. Well, fairly certain.'

His triumph seemed premature. The enraged Jocks were halfway across the channel. No stopping them now. Michael turned towards

THIRTY-ONE

the mainland and the miles of treacherous estuary.

'Retreat!' urged Gover.

With that, the City-man scurried and scrambled towards the shore of the little island furthest from Lindisfarne. For a horrifying moment, Michael and a few of the bolder Nuagers looked back. His eyes itched. Tears ran. He retched and coughed. Gasping, he followed Gover and grabbed the City-man's arm. Yet neither spoke.

Clouds of green gas rose from the channel between Lindisfarne and St Cuthbert's Island, blown towards the village by a steady north wind. The Scots had stopped bellowing war cries now. Screams, wheezes, whoops for clean air, wretched, hacking coughs were all their language. Michael stared in horror. The sea between the islet and Lindisfarne was boiling! Sickly green smoke billowed up, obscuring the Scots in venomous mist. Already men floated on the water, others desperately rubbed eyes blinded by chemical fire, throats scalded as if by acid. Their thrashing limbs raised yet more foam. With a crack, lightning played across the surface of the channel, blue, flickering tongues of raw, primal energy.

'Cover your mouths!' gasped Gover, stuffing a scarf into his nostrils.

For five endless minutes, chaos reigned in the strip of water between St Cuthbert's Isle and Lindisfarne. Then the last coughs and screams died away. Silence settled. Gover removed his face-covering.

'It is now safe to take a closer look,' he said. 'The power cells have fully discharged their store of energy.'

From the highest point of St Cuthbert's Island, they surveyed a massacre worthy of the Crusades. Piles of corpses in the water, some weighed down by armour, others floating. On the shore, the few survivors crawled, gagging and blinded, puking even as their clogged lungs drowned.

'You are the blackest of wizards,' breathed Iona. 'A black warlock! First, you set the sea aflame.' She stared with undisguised horror.

'Now this.'

Gover's attempt at a modest smile emerged as a smug leer. 'Blame science again, my dear, not me. Just silly old, unsentimental science. And, dare I say it, an exceptional knowledge of physical and chemical processes. Let me explain it to you in simple terms. Run sufficient electricity to power a small town through a narrow strip of seawater, et voila! You produce rather a lot of chlorine gas. Which is highly toxic. That means poison, my dear. Not to mention plain electrocution. Wet metal armour and weapons can be rather efficient conductors, as we have witnessed. As for fusion batteries...'

A gunshot rang out from the ruins of the priory. Gover jolted, staggered back. His eyes opened in amazement. This could not happen to him. To the rest of the world, yes, but not him. The grey sky span like a whirlpool. He folded with a crump onto the coarse grass.

* * *

It seemed to Michael consciousness was a vivid dream launched at birth, one you awoke from, at the last, to oblivion. A dream you sometimes steered, sometimes let drift like a boat on a fog-bound river. As he and Cuthbert wandered Lindisfarne village, gathering prisoners and putting the terminally wounded out of their misery, unreality stole over him. Sensations, the evidence of his senses, went vague, numbed by the aftershock.

In the channel between Lindisfarne and St Cuthbert's Island, so much litter left by the tide. Men on their front, side, back, bloodshot eyes staring sightlessly, limbs contorted. Some still clutched throats burned by the vile green gas clinging to their corpses. Long would folk mourn this day in Fife and Buchan, the cream of their manhood skimmed off and cast aside to rot.

In his head, Michael heard Cuthbert asking, 'Should we move them?'

THIRTY-ONE

Then his own reply, a stranger's voice, 'Let the next tide wash them away, along with the poison.'

More corpses in the village, more poison for the soul. Bodies in every condition, most of them still, emptied of spirit, some clinging to life, breath by breath, a few twitching. Cries of grief echoed as loved ones were recognised in the mud, their remains embraced.

A surprising number of Nuagers appeared from unlikely hiding places — attics, cellars, one from beneath a compost heap, his long hair draped with straw, potato peelings and a wriggling worm.

'What of Gover?' Michael asked Cuthbert, dully.

'I told you, man, taken to the castle. They don't give him long.'

That, too, meant nothing much.

He slumped on the beach of Lindisfarne Harbour, his trembling hands trying to light a pipe. The tangle of tobacco finally caught, and he puffed. His brain stirred from its protective stupor. Blinking, he watched a flat-bottomed coastal trader pick a cautious route through the shallow channels of low tide into the harbour.

When Tom Higginbottom crunched ashore, Michael rose.

'What the bugger are you doing here, Michael Pilgrim?' asked Tom.

'What took you so long to find me, Tom?'

His question was weary, small.

* * *

Mid-afternoon, the tide almost high. Again, Michael rode out with a white flag, this time accompanied by a sizable force and a flock of prisoners, many still retching up the contents of seared throats and lungs. His numbness had faded under the influence of raw gin and grilled lamb chops devoured eagerly, one after the other, along with fresh-baked oat bread still warm and steaming from the oven. A few hours' sleep did the rest.

By his side strode Iona of Skye and the strongest of her folk. He had offered her a mule, but she didn't know how to ride. Now was not the time to teach her.

The parlay had been arranged on the road between Stook Point and the village, a midpoint Iona deemed favourable after divining ley lines by casting osprey feathers into the wind. Michael Pilgrim made no comment. The levity in his spirit had taken a wound that needed much encouragement to heal.

Two groups of around fifty armed folks met one another. Reining up, Michael sat upright in the saddle, just as he had that early morn. Afternoon a very different world to dawn.

'Who will speak with me?' he called to the grim-faced Scots, far too close should they decide to seek revenge with their guns. Rather than treachery, however, a short man with florid cheeks and a bushy beard stepped forward. Stout as butter, he wore costly steel armour gaudy with numerous charms of gold and tinsel.

'I will talk wi' ye,' declared King Adair of Fife, his voice surprisingly reedy. 'But first, where is your warlock? We'll have nae speech if he be near. I'll nae have a glammer cast upon us!'

He clearly meant Gover. Word of the magic green cloud that snuffed out strongmen like candles had reached Adair via a handful of terrified survivors. Michael did not mention the City-man lay in a chamber of Lindisfarne Castle, unconscious and bleeding out his life.

'Be assured,' Michael replied, 'he'll not cast his spells unless you prove traitors to whatever we agree. But be warned! His reach is long. He who set the sea on fire can just as easily raise a storm to sink your ships. It is in his power to curse clan and family to the third generation.'

The King of Fife stroked his beard thoughtfully.

'What do ye want then?' he asked, in his high, mild voice. 'You have slain the flower of two kingdoms. Two sons have I lost, and I would

THIRTY-ONE

take home a third, who I see yonder, to his mother.'

Michael stayed impassive on his horse.

'We want a pledge of peace, King of Fife. Not just from you, but sworn on behalf of your children and their children, that you and your kin and allies will raid no further south than the Firth of Forth. And that if the need arises, you'll send your best warriors to help us.'

The demand was enforceable only by more ruthless war. Did King Adair recognise it as such? No doubt. Both sides simply wished the other far away by nightfall. Michael was well aware the Scots were playing for time until high tide allowed their ships to sail free from Snook Point.

'I can pledge that,' said Adair, stiffly. 'And ye'll nae find my word wanting. What do I get in return?'

'Your life. Your son's life. The lives of these prisoners.'

The miserable huddle stood under heavy guard. Among their number, Colm, the lad they had beaten to obtain information.

'Then let it be so,' said Adair. He hesitated. 'You have won a great victory, Michael Pilgrim, Protector of the North. And been muckle merciful in your terms. It will add to your fame and honour.'

Michael refrained from saying the victory did not belong to him. His strategy had led his small army to disaster. Only Gover's infernal science saved them. Without further words, he rode back to supervise the exchange of prisoners, for the Scots had taken a few Nuagers captive during the battle in the village.

The tide lifted the ships on Snook Point, and Michael watched them sail forth, a remnant of the fleet that first attacked Lindisfarne. Iona stood beside him, and Cuthbert, Allan, Tom Higginbottom, and scores of others, including men and women he was just beginning to know by name and nature. Shared adversity is a great teacher of character.

'Will this peace last?' Iona asked, the whites of her eyes vivid.

Michael almost uttered his honest thought. One look at her eager, hopeful face persuaded him otherwise.

'Yes, the sacrifices of Dameron and so many other good folk were not in vain. There will be peace on this coast for many years.'

She seemed reassured, and he was relieved to feel his own face soften into a slight smile. One smile led to another, after all, and maybe, by and by, even to laughter.

* * *

As dusk dimmed the edges of the afternoon, they found themselves separated from the straggling group of Nuagers heading back to the village and harbour. Both Iona and Michael Pilgrim were exhausted, in that state of high emotion between elation and grief when inhibitions are cast aside.

They paused between Snook Point and the village, by the weather-worn sign reading:

DANG R
DO NOPROCE D
W EN WATER REAC ES CAUS WAY

Both looked out across the channel to the mainland, two miles wide at this point. High tide had covered the causeway with grey, ribbed waves. Flocks of wintering birds bobbed. High tide was a time of rest for many of the birds before the mudflats and sand were exposed and feeding's eternal labour resumed.

Abruptly, a corner of the floating armada rose in panic. Wings beat loudly. The air filled with honked warnings. More of the birds followed suit, adding to the clamour as they wheeled en masse. Gazing up, Iona detected the silhouette of a lone eagle circling and pointed it out. Michael thought of drones.

'I called on Gover before we came out,' he said. 'I fear he will be dead by the time we return. Even if he makes it, he'll not be going anywhere for a while, that's for sure.'

Iona grew wary at his mention of the wizard's name. 'He scares me,' she said.

Michael nodded. 'I hate his conceit and contempt for just about everything. He is a heartless, dangerous man, not to be trusted. A masterpiece of selfishness. But twice, he saved our lives. He may yet prove useful to us. I hope to bring harm to the City through him if I can. Their terrible arrogance, like his, may yet be their downfall.'

They fell silent, watching the great murmuration wheel over their heads. Slowly, the combined flocks grew calm, the frantic cacophony of wing beat and goose-honk and gull-cry settling as a red twilight rimmed the eastern horizon. High streaks of cloud blushed the same tint.

'They'll soon settle,' he remarked, indicating the flocks, 'now that the eagle has given up. Maybe it will be that way for humanity, if we ever get the City off our backs. We'll start again, only better than before the plagues. Maybe it can be that way.'

Neither seemed in a hurry to return to the village. Iona looked at him sideways.

'Nae doubt you've heard that many of my folk, even my own kin, have asked the Holy Islanders for permission to occupy houses in the village and maybe even on the mainland.' She gestured across the shore. 'There's an empty village just over the causeway with rich, fallow soil and solid buildings from the Before Times. Good water and woodland and a strand for the fishing boats to beach.'

'I had heard it. Is that not good news?'

She looked askance. 'For you, it is. It makes your life simpler when you return home.'

Michael could not deny that. If the Nuagers of Skye never came to

Baytown, he need not find them land and homes and a place in his community.

'And for you?' he said. 'Does it make your life simpler?'

'I dinnae know.'

He patted the horse's head as he waited. It whinnied softly.

'This Holy Island is a haven for my folk,' she continued, 'but it changes everything. No longer will I be their sole priestess. Often I have longed to share that responsibility, now I am not so sure. My folk will mingle and marry with the Lindisfarners until two are one. As the years pass, they will forget Skye and all my grandmother and mother gave to them. And that is how it should be. But what then for me? Who will I become?'

'You will always be respected till the day you die.'

'Perhaps.'

He turned to look her in the face.

'You will always be more than respected by me.' Michael amazed himself with his frankness.

Iona glanced towards the village where her people waited.

'Let's go back to the castle,' she said, 'and be blithe for tonight, at least. I hear there'll be dancing amidst the mourning. And, look, the clouds are clearing. It promises to be a night when the stars themselves join us. They look down with blessings, for my people are safe. We have won through.'

Stars indeed twinkled in trails and ribbons as the clouds dispersed north. Michael led his horse by the bridle and walked beside her, Iona singing softly to herself as they went. The young woman's voice reminded him of her courage when almost burned alive at Fort George. Perhaps she sang for the souls of everyone who sacrifice themselves to bring a little good into the world. If so, it seemed to him, there were worse songs to sing.

THIRTY-ONE

Sing me a song of a soul that is gone,
Say, could that soul be I?
Merry of soul he sails on a day
Over the sea to sky.
Billow and breeze, islands and seas,
Mountains of rain and sun,
All that is good, all that is fair,
All that is me is sun.

Their eyes met again, his deep blue, hers sea green, exchanging a promise old and young as humanity.

'If there is dancing tonight,' he said, 'will you take a turn?'

He considered it a cunning question. Her eyes crinkled in a way he feared, somehow, for it fascinated him, and there lay the danger. His whole life warned him how love brings pain as much as joy.

'I believe I might dance, Mister Star Man. It would be expected of me as priestess. After all, it is the winter solstice tonight, though with so much war and madness we forgot it. It is our custom to dance this eve and thank the sun for its waxing.' She hesitated. 'Will you dance?'

'I am a clumsy dancer, I fear.'

What a bumbling fool he must look! But she smiled at his discomfort and raised her eyebrows.

'Perhaps you might tread a turn with me?' she ventured.

'Iona, I'd be honoured.'

'But would you be glad to? Honour is cold as stately old bones.'

'Very glad. If you are.'

'Then I will dance with you, Michael, so long as it pleases us both.'

He reached out his hand to enclose her fingers. They were not withdrawn. After a moment's hesitation, she squeezed back.

When the smoke and blood of battle was washed from their weary bodies and enough sleep, wine, and meat had been taken to renew strength, Iona of Skye and Michael Pilgrim did tread that turn together at midnight, risking the chances of a stranger's self — though most are strangers to themselves, let alone to others. They took the chance gladly until dawn signalled a new day. Even as they embraced, both knew they must return soon to cares menacing like a storm-black sky, and clasped one another all the tighter.

EPILOGUE: BLEAK MIDWINTER

The cart and its escort moved slowly along the decayed surface of the dual carriageway from Junction 44. Light, powdery snow blew almost horizontally. The sky was murky, faintly luminescent. It was the day after the winter solstice, the turning of another year.

Driving the cart was a lithe, wild-haired tramp of indeterminate age, singing an operatic aria as he flicked the reins. Beside him hunched a young man swathed in blankets. His shoulders and dazed eyes suggested deep defeat. Bruises covered his face, and each jolt of the cart made him gasp with pain. Sometimes he glanced back into the wagon bed and the burden it bore.

Next in the cavalcade, travellers entirely unique: a dozen creatures, half-human, half-hare, lolloping along, sniffing the grey lands for danger with damp, twitchy noses, their long silky ears erect. No reading the thoughts behind their modified faces: just as their makers had intended.

A third party stumbled amidst the monstrous, hopping creatures. These were the unhappiest of the travellers, terrified lest they be torn apart by claw or unnatural bucktooth. They walked with hands wired behind their backs, a fat woman in filthy black robes and a short, bony man wearing a faded flogger's cassock. They glanced around constantly for the slightest chance to escape. But the land was deserted, deadened by bleak midwinter.

In this manner, the procession reached the outskirts of York, the ancient city recognisable by the Minster's twin towers rising from the plain.

* * *

York reeked of damp and mould; many buildings were tenanted by root and branch. Yet much remained intact. Around the old castle, smithies were becoming small factories for metalwork traded throughout the region and beyond. St Nicholas Fair had brought hundreds to the ancient market on Parliament Street, loiterers, mountebanks, stallholders, folk daring to dream beyond a lifetime's oppression by the Five Cities. Times were changing, and all sensed it.

Perhaps that is why the guards at the city's medieval gates admitted the troop of strangelings. First, the soldiers sought permission from Lady Veil, who ordered the visitors to be escorted straight to the Minster, where she held court. Crowds gathered as word of half-human monsters spread, confirming rumours of their presence in the North. Some declared a new age of faery. Folk gaped, gasped, and pointed. A few shouted frightened curses and abuse. Hurdy-Gurdy took comfort that no stones were thrown — yet.

Having deposited his young passenger at a doctor's, the exiled City-man stood before Lady Veil's chair in the Minster. Like her predecessor, she chose to be framed by an enormous stained glass window depicting the Creation.

Whether she was old or young, even her intimates could not say. A thick scarf and hood covered her face, revealing large, plaintive brown eyes. Flanking her were guards and a young woman to serve as interpreter. Lady Veil never spoke, communicating only through writing or sign language.

EPILOGUE: BLEAK MIDWINTER

Hurdy-Gurdy waited. Stone carvings of saints stared down. The Minster was shadowy that winter's morning. A single large candle on a bronze stand green with age burned beside her chair. Gurdy remained standing, rocking back and forth compulsively.

'What a strange chance unites us here, my lovely,' he said, 'unless it is fate – but pooh! — who believes in that quaint illusion anymore? Science and chance are the world's fate now. Perhaps they ever were, world without end.'

Lady Veil's hands worked busily, and her interpreter spoke out.

'She says, "We have much to talk about, old friend. She is pleased to see you alive."'

'How kind,' said Gurdy, addressing the woman in the chair directly. 'I shall call you Lady Veil, and you shall know me as Hurdy-Gurdy. After all, a man in his life plays many parts. Eh, my dear? Perhaps our time to step back on stage has come.'

Then it was the prisoners' turn. Justice was soon delivered. The witch known as Fat Mistress and her flogger follower, Maister Gil, were questioned and found guilty of murderous banditry on the highway. The Commonwealth of the North enforced harsh punishments against those making travel or trade perilous. The malefactors were led off, Fat Mistress shrieking curses approved by Hell itself, Maister Gil silent. Perhaps he was simply glad to get away from the hare-headed creatures holding him prisoner.

Next, Hurdy-Gurdy ushered forward the crowd of strangelings. A vile sight they made, hatched by human caprice to serve depraved whims. Bundles of genes and improved flesh, each a living deformity with a unique spirit, unlovable except to themselves — and maybe not even then.

The woman on the throne stared at the assembly of freaks. Her hands grew busy again with words addressed to Hurdy-Gurdy.

'She says, "You are right. The time has indeed come. The arrival of these hybrids confirms a new phase. One we always predicted. I will help however I best can. We have received recent news of Albion and the Five Cities, which changes everything. We fear a war that will determine all mankind's future."'

Hurdy-Gurdy nodded. His voice echoed in the magnificent cathedral that had borne witness to generations of sin and penance. 'Then reveal yourself, my lovely! Show your people why this war must be to the death!'

Lady Veil's hands moved.

'She says, "Yes, it is time all was in the open. It's time my people saw who I have been made to become. For them to behold why we must help you. Why I will urge them to fight."'

The woman on the throne rose. She climbed the narrow stairs of a stone pulpit above the assembled people. Hundreds of her followers had gathered in the empty nave to gawp at the strangelings and discover what their presence might mean.

Slowly, she threw back her hood and unwound the scarf covering the lower half of her face. Then she lifted her chin defiantly.

Folk screamed in fear; a few fainted, others covered their eyes and moaned. For Lady Veil's lovely, deep brown eyes belied a transformation of hideous cruelty. Of all those present, only Hurdy-Gurdy understood its true meaning. A playful jeux d'esprit of modification, a warning, and punishment to anyone tempted to betray the Five Cities or the Beautiful Life.

Where once a nose and mouth had helped define her handsome face, an entirely new organ had been cultured. An organ grown from her living flesh. A remarkable feat of gene-engineering delivered faultlessly.

Every mammal must breathe, and two broad nostrils were provided for that purpose, inflamed and shiny with mucus. Every mammal must feed, and an opening to her throat and existing digestive system had been granted, through which liquid food might pass down, as well as oxygen to be inhaled or expelled. Gone were mouth, teeth, tongue. In their stead, a replica of a woman's pudenda, including the clitoris and labial folds. It glistened in the candlelight. All the perfumes in York could not mask its corrupted scent.

Hurdy-Gurdy stepped to the pulpit, where she stood firm and ascended its steps to join her. Amidst moans of terror and disgust among the assembled people, he took her hand and raised it high.

'If they wrong us, shall we not be avenged?' he cried, his actor's voice carrying to every corner of the vast building. 'Shall not humanity reveal our true selves and be avenged?'

***

Few attended the funeral. Who was he, after all?

They carried the body wrapped in an old tarpaulin to the Museum Gardens overlooking the patient River Ouse. Their route passed a gibbet attached to the side of the Minster. Two fresh corpses dangled: one a fat woman, the other a male, his back crisscrossed by scars. Whether it would have pleased the body on the cart that his murderers so soon followed him into darkness, none could know. He existed now only in memories. Emptiness had received back the life lent to him.

They stood around the grave without ceremony. The young man, wincing from a wound his labours threatened to reopen, shovelled earth and stones over the corpse in its sack. He was glad it hurt and wished it hurt more.

Through undergrowth, once ornamental shrubbery, nervous creatures appeared, noses twitching, comically long ears raised. They watched but did not weep. Whatever intelligence designed them had neglected tear ducts. Yet grief finds many gestures. They crowded around a short, young female among their number, touching her with lowered foreheads, wet noses. Then, one by one, they half-hopped, half-walked away. Still looking back, the last to go, she followed her kindred. The leaves of the bushes closed behind her.

Hurdy-Gurdy and Lady Veil waited to one side. As ever, her interpreter stood ready, though the ingenious old holotainer was already learning her sign language.

Was the body in the grave loved? The young man wept as he piled on soil like one planting a tree.

'He gave his life to save mine,' he sniffed.

For once, Gurdy made no cryptic or ironic reply.

Lady Veil gestured with swift hands.

'She says, "You must both stay here as her guests for the next few months. The Council of the North meets at the start of spring. Then important decisions will be made, including about the strangelings, whom she promises to protect. Messengers have been sent out to gather everyone with the power or wit to help our cause, especially the Protector of the North."'

Lady Veil stared down at the young man. Again she gestured.

"'As for you,"' the interpreter said, her voice hardening as her mistress's hands stiffened. "A trial will be held when the Protector of the North returns. Hurdy-Gurdy has said he will vouch for you. In the meantime, you may not leave York."'

Hurdy-Gurdy nodded. 'Earlier you spoke of City-news, my sweeting. What might it be?'

Whatever intimacy they had shared in times gone was ignored by Lady Veil. She was all business. Her hands moved, and the interpreter spoke.

'She says, "Something is happening in the Five Cities. Travellers report an unusual number of aircarriers arriving and peculiar lights in Albion. For a long while, she has noticed the absence of drones. Also, many Beautifuls are being expelled from the City into the countryside, as once they did to us both. It is said they are naked and soon fall prey to people or animals. Spies have been sent south to capture such fugitives, so we can learn more. One thing is clear: the Five Cities are divided, weakened. We must risk this opportunity to strike a blow to their heart. It may be the last chance we are allowed."'

Hurdy-Gurdy contemplated her words.

'Let us talk more of this,' he said.

With that, they withdrew to her private rooms. It seemed everyone except Seth Pilgrim had forgotten the man in his grave. He knelt on the wet grass after they had gone. Silent tears ran down his cheeks.

'Forgive me,' Seth murmured to the ghost of the dead young man. Crows and rooks cawed on bare branches awaiting leaves.

'I don't deserve it, but thank you,' he snivelled. 'If you can hear me, Jojo, thank you.'

For Jojo Lyons had restored to him the best of his own nature, qualities he had believed lost forever, and that hurt worse than the knife gash near his spine. Worse than any wound he had taken since his mother died. A good man's nature launches echoes of love. Echoes of impossible longing filled him. What bitter consolation — or none — that might have been to the young man already on the road to dust, there was no guessing.

'Forgive me,' he murmured again.

Then Seth arose and turned to face south, the direction of the City.

About the Author

Tim Murgatroyd was brought up in Yorkshire. He read English at Hertford College, Oxford University and now lives with his family in York. He is the author of several novels of historical fiction and a poetry series. Pilgrim Lost is the second book in his Pilgrim Trilogy.

Lightning Source UK Ltd.
Milton Keynes UK
UKHW010636251120
374072UK00002B/495